CATHERINE McGUINNESS

EMPERORS'
CLOTHES

D1452827

EMERALD
BOOK CO.

This book is a work of fiction. Names, characters, businesses, organizations, places, events, and incidents are either a product of the author's imagination or are used fictitiously. Any resemblance to actual persons, living or dead, events, or locales is entirely coincidental.

Published by Emerald Book Company
Austin, TX
www.emeraldbookcompany.com

Copyright ©2011 Catherine M. McGuinness

All rights reserved.

No part of this book may be reproduced, stored in a retrieval system, or transmitted by any means, electronic, mechanical, photocopying, recording, or otherwise, without written permission from the copyright holder.

Distributed by Emerald Book Company

For ordering information or special discounts for bulk purchases, please contact Emerald Book Company at PO Box 91869, Austin, TX 78709, 512.891.6100.

Design and composition by Greenleaf Book Group LLC
Cover design by Greenleaf Book Group LLC

Publisher's Cataloging-In-Publication Data
(Prepared by The Donohue Group, Inc.)
McGuinness, Catherine (Catherine Mary), 1961-
   Emperors' clothes / by Catherine McGuinness. — 1st ed.
   p. ; cm.
   ISBN: 978-1-937110-04-8
   1. Executives—Fiction. 2. Women executives—Fiction. 3. Office politics—Fiction. 4. Fathers and sons—Fiction. 5. Murder—Fiction. 6. Organized crime—Fiction. 7. Allegories. I. Title.
PS3613.C4896 E67 2011
813.6   2011927598

Part of the Tree Neutral® program, which offsets the number of trees consumed in the production and printing of this book by taking proactive steps, such as planting trees in direct proportion to the number of trees used: www.treeneutral.com

TreeNeutral

Printed in the United States of America on acid-free paper

11 12 13 14 15 16   10 9 8 7 6 5 4 3 2 1

First Edition

For Don and Maeve, for taking this journey with me.
And for Uncle Grandpa and Mima,
who told me I could fly . . .

PROLOGUE

S al Scruci twisted his silk handkerchief into a tight point and gingerly dusted the dirt off the tassel of his loafer. He gently blew over the shoe, carefully inspected it, and then opened the top drawer of his desk. He retrieved a well-used clip-point blade and expertly carved caked-on dirt off his shoe.

"That shoeshine kid oughta pay more attention to the details. These shoes are handmade in friggin' Italy, for Chrissake. Look at this dirt. He couldn't clean that up?" Sal picked up the second shoe for review.

Lenny "Knuckles" Chiasma examined the shoe.

"Talk about takin' the job home wit' you. That's not dirt, boss, it's bl—"

"Whateva." Sal's attention had shifted to locate the source of muffled shouting. His office was located in the back room of the Avenue B Social Club, which was sandwiched between a candy store and the best chow mein restaurant in New Jersey. Turned out the sounds were not the result of the dinner rush but were emanating from a television in the corner.

Sal allowed himself to be drawn into the news exposé about N.O. (Norman Olympus) Audette, the disgraced chief financial officer of VITE! Corporation. He watched as two burly officers led N.O. out of a packed courtroom and toward a heavily armed bus bound for USP Lewisburg, a maximum-security institution. Clad in a customary orange jumpsuit, handcuffs, and loafers (no socks), N.O.'s new uniform was a far cry from the hand-tailored suits and custom-made shoes to which he had grown accustomed as a senior executive of the now nearly insolvent financial services firm. Outraged at the misappropriation of their investment dollars on his watch, angry shareholders yelled profanities and threw red pens at the sobbing executive as he climbed into the bus.

A picture of N.O. and his estranged fiancée in better days flashed on the TV as a reporter detailed the accumulations of his storied career: pieds-à-terre and country homes; multiple Ferraris and a token DeLorean; various collections, including one of vintage tchotchkes; and his three-plus wives (the engagement having been in play at the time of his arraignment). Footage flashed on the screen of N.O. and his surgically advantaged betrothed surrounded by a large assortment of tambourines pre-owned by top rock 'n' roll bands. When asked why he had decided to collect tambourines rather than a more classic instrument, the fiancée chimed in and explained that the best guitar collections had already been purchased.

Lenny watched N.O.'s scantily clad fiancée drape herself across the heartier tambourines. "Wow. She's a fox. Reminds me of what's-her-name, Johnny Man's goomah. She was easy on the eyes. Never understood why he dumped her."

"It's not right having a girlfriend who's prettier than the boss's lady."

Lenny looked at Sal. "Ohhh."

Sal and Lenny grew uncomfortable as the reporter offered details about N.O.'s sentencing: twenty-five years for corporate malfeasance; three ten-year stints for fraud, money laundering, and conspiracy; and consecutive life terms for murdering the financial controller and secretary who had uncovered his scheme to defraud the company of $250 million. In total, N.O. had been convicted of more than twenty-five charges. "Oh, that really sucks," Lenny offered.

"I feel sorry for that prick," Sal agreed.

During the trial, the district attorney argued that the first time VITE! did not meet the growth and profitability targets that management had whispered to Wall Street, N.O. tweaked the company's earnings number to ensure that his bonus would cover the mortgages on his properties. When the following two quarters' results proved equally detrimental to his burgeoning real estate portfolio, N.O. did it again and again, each time with a heavier pen.

Testimony linked the killings to a failed sale of the company. The prospective buyers said it had been red ink, not red tape, that caused them to walk away from the transaction when VITE!'s controller presented corrected financial statements. The TV news had obtained photographs of N.O.'s secretary with a computer cord wrapped around her neck and a staple decleater pinching her nostrils shut. For some reason never fully explained during the trial, Wite-Out covered her lips. The coroner's report stated that the actual cause of death was the VITE! Corporation anniversary pen impaling her chest.

"Look at that lady. She was a grandmother of four. The guy had no choice but to make her go away on account of her big mouth, but she was just doin' her job." Lenny, who revered his own grandmother, was clearly conflicted.

Sal peered icily at Lenny.

"You'd never make a mistake like that?" Sal stuck his neck out in the direction of the TV.

Embarrassed by a mishap involving one of his less reliable cousins, a recently deceased business associate, a plunger, and Sal's car, Lenny slouched his 280-pound body into the couch.

On the TV screen, a chipper reporter discussed the case further with the station anchor.

"*To add insult to injury, it wasn't the secretary's pen.*" The reporter then deepened her voice to convey this somber news: "*She had only seven years with the company. Not enough to earn a pen.*" A clip flashed on the screen of another secretary, screaming as she identified her cherished pen as the murder weapon.

"Interesting. The pen." Sal looked at Lenny. "Good to remember, if you ever get in a jam."

The anchor pressed for more specifics about one of the murders.

"*And the nail gun used on the controller? Was that an inappropriate use of company resources?*"

"That tool was Audette's personal property. So other than inflicting lethal harm to another human being, there was no misappropriation of company resources."

Lenny whistled loudly.

"Gee, what a sin. Guy goes to work every day, does the books, and—talk about getting screwed by your boss—ends up wit' a two-inch-deep hole in his head from a nail gun."

"For what, I ask you? Fifty grand?" Less captivated with workers' struggles, Sal found the controller's motivation irritating. "Friggin' guy shouldn't have got out of line. If he'd partnered with the boss—like the boss asked—that controller would be chuggin' tequila with a bevy of broads in Veracruz right now instead of being crucified."

"Vera who?"

"Whateva. The guy took the wrong road, is all's I'm sayin'."

"The road to hell is paved wit' good intentions."

Sal thought better of correcting his number-two guy. Ever since his consigliere—his cousin-in-law once removed—went missing, the conversation around the social club left a lot to be desired. But Lenny was all muscle, and loyal like a dog, not like that S.O.B. relative. Sal's wife's cousin had been very smart, but it turned out his tongue was a little too loose for his own good. Although Sal missed the repartee, he thought that particular part of his cousin's anatomy would be better served with fennel, basil, and a little garlic, and buried heavily under gravy.

Yet, without a strong number two, other crews sensed weakness and were muscling in on Sal's business. Even the big boss said he might give the North Jersey numbers racket to a different gang. He told Sal straight up that he would have more confidence in the long-term health of the franchise if Sal had a solid leadership team behind him. Sal considered a few new candidates for consigliere, but he was still licking wounds from the last experience, having been betrayed by a relative, of all people.

Lenny flipped through the pages of the *New York Weekly Monitor*.

"Says here in the paper dis guy, N.O. Audette, had twenty-five years' experience wit' big-name companies. He was even getting ready to start a new job at a technology company, TMC Corporation, when he got caught."

"What's your friggin' point?"

"I think that company's gonna have a tough time finding another executive wit' dis much experience, what wit' him being in the slammer and all."

"Doesn't take a lot of talent to serve time. If he's so good, how come he got caught?" Sal said as he sliced the residue of work from his shoes, careful not to disfigure the imported leather loafers. The news segment reported another drop in the price of VITE! stock, and a background shot displayed hundreds of retirees protesting in front of the company's world headquarters, demanding an investigation into the decimation of their retirement funds. It was 1999 and, while seemingly every company's stock was going through the roof, VITE!'s share price had declined steeply as the full extent of N.O.'s skullduggery was revealed.

The main witness for the prosecution had been VITE!'s vice president of human resources, Piers Heartles. It was Piers who discovered the controller's contorted body affixed to the copy room floor, and Piers who led an internal investigation to determine which human resources regulations had been breached, allowing such a licentious environment to breed. A single sticky note, found inside the dead controller's tightly clenched fist, broke the case wide open and destroyed the defense counsel's assertions of a conspiracy implicating Piers, three prostitutes, several low-level Securities and Exchange Commission officials, and a canvas bag of cash. At trial, police testified that this crumpled communication, when held in a certain light, read, "N.O. stole the money." The TV reporter wiggled through the crowd surrounding Piers, who had just left the courtroom. She asked him about his testimony, the role he played at VITE!, and his thoughts on N.O.'s sentencing. She also congratulated Piers on his recent victory in securing a United States Senate seat representing New York.

With great enthusiasm, Piers discussed his love for human resources work (*"You've heard of a man's man? I am THE people's person"*) and specific initiatives he led (*"A golden parachute in every 401(k)"*). With dismay, he

discussed the current state of VITE! ("*No more afternoon lattes*"), the loss
of two respected colleagues ("*Do you have any idea how much it will cost to
backfill the controller in this hot job market?*"), and accusations that he had
been in cahoots with N.O. Audette ("*There is no truth to the rumor that my
Lamborghini is of recent vintage*").

Despite the role he played in Sal's operation, Lenny Knuckles had a
sensitive side. He sniffled as the news program built up the credibility of
the prosecution's star witness. Images of Piers shaking hands with VITE!
employees at a plant opening, dressed as a rodeo clown at the annual
Halloween Hoe-Down, and leading a building evacuation during fire and
safety week rolled across the monitor.

Sal looked at Lenny. "You better not be bawling! That rodeo clown rat-
ted out a big boss." Disgusted, Sal shook his knife at the sappy images on
the screen. "What kind of allegiance is that?"

Sal picked up the remote and clicked a few times to change the channel, but every news organization was reporting on this story. Even the local
weather station described the cloud cover over the courthouse as N.O.'s
sentencing was announced. Sal capitulated to the media. They had to make
a buck too. He flipped back to the initial coverage.

"Strikes me that guy Piers should have known something was going on.
That reporter said he was in charge of payroll and bonuses. Not for nothing,
that's the kind of inside job to have. You can build up a nice bank account if
you are willing to fly low, under the radar," Sal commented.

"But he looks like a good guy." The TV cameras zeroed in on Piers hugging the reporter.

Sal threw his freshly polished loafer at Lenny.

"OW!"

"How many times I gotta tell you, you wanna move up in this world,
you gotta get someone else to do the dirty work."

"Oh," Lenny said, massaging his head.

"And another thing, those senior citizens protesting the destruction of
their pensions can't be good for business. Who let that get on TV? Nothing
a little slap-down of a reporter wouldn't fix, mind you."

Across the country, at Oklahoma-based TMC Corporation, another executive was also feeling the heat. Stewart Narciss peered through a plate-glass window at a swarm of reporters buzzing with anticipation. The publicly traded stock of this communications technology upstart had run up almost ten points in the two weeks since its initial public offering. Though Stewart, as vice president of human resources, had the kind of inside job that Sal valued, some bloom had come off the rose when it was ascertained that TMC had tried to hire N.O. Audette away from VITE!. Although the deal had been taken off the table when N.O. was arrested, the media smelled scandal.

Stewart's public relations consultants had warned him that TMC would be in the media crosshairs, but he longed for an opportunity to gain national exposure. Setting aside the unpleasantries that had transpired at VITE!, Piers Heartles had emerged a hero. Stewart intended to hook his name to Piers's rising star and call attention to the influence that the human resources function could exert. After all, long before VITE! considered red ink any more ominous than a stain on a financial quarter, or Sal's operation was hampered by a dearth of sinister talent, Stewart had been meticulously massaging corporate images—first as an adviser with a global management consulting firm and now as vice president of human resources for TMC. He prayed his father was watching the TV news.

Stewart and Ted Barone, TMC's chief executive officer, pushed through the double doors of the corporate headquarters and were immediately assaulted by microphone-wielding fists in the parking lot. Hoping for a career-making quote, a phalanx of journalists lobbed questions at the TMC executives like fishermen tossing chum into the water.

"Mr. Barone, how do you explain the selection process that led TMC to offer an executive job to a convicted felon and murderer?"

"Are any TMC heads going to roll because of that decision?"

"TMC is a darling of Wall Street to some large degree because of your success in managing operating margins. Might the board have considered N.O.'s homicidal approach to workforce planning an innovative tool to influence profitability?"

Given the bizarre questions, the resourceful CEO thrust Stewart in front of the cameras.

"Stewart is responsible for our human resources function here at TMC. He can confirm our diligence in evaluating and selecting executives."

The reporters collectively turned their cameras on Stewart, who found the din created by an onslaught of questions confusing. Unable to hear himself think, Stewart's mind froze, blocking any connection to the talking points on which his highly paid PR team had carefully coached him. Stunned like prey the moment it realizes it is toast, Stewart smiled broadly and looked blankly at the reporters.

Unable to resist the pull of his own ego once the media attention shifted to his underling, Ted added, "But, before I turn things over to Stewart, you must understand that we did try to hire Piers, the VP who turned state's evidence against Audette."

Ted explained that once Piers announced his U. S. Senate run, TMC made the ultimate sacrifice and stepped out of the picture so that the broader citizenry might benefit from Piers's bold leadership as a member of Congress. A side benefit, as Ted noted, was that Stewart got to keep his job.

"Nothing personal, Stewart. It's just business," Ted said as he smiled for the cameras. "Would you like to tell these nice folks about our recruiting process?"

With that, Ted proffered his human sacrifice to the media.

Learning in so public a manner how close he had come to being sacked, Stewart opened his mouth but no words came out. His gaze circled the crowd, which ensured that all the cameras captured his wide, open-mouthed grin. He heard the familiar hum of an engine and watched as Ted drove his Lotus away.

Continuing to watch from the safety of the Avenue B Social Club back in New Jersey, Lenny linked the story to Sal's business advice.

"Ah ha. Dis guy, Stewart, does the dirty work for Barone." For someone who found it tough to follow Sal's shifting allegiances with union officials, Lenny was completely engaged with the evolving television storyline.

Sal looked up from his review of the prior week's take. He loved spring because basketball and horseracing overlapped, making for several profitable weekends.

"Yep," Sal responded. He located the business card of a clothing manufacturer in New York City's garment district. Sal had several rolls of Egyptian cotton left over from a job the previous fall, and he wanted a few new shirts before an anticipated shipment of Versace suits fell off a truck.

As the conversation with Stewart had not dripped with the sound bites that reporters had conditioned their audiences to expect, the TV news had returned to the courthouse, where Piers whispered au revoir to the journalist he had been hugging. Then, with clips from Piers's Senate campaign playing in the background, political pundits argued about the ramifications of N.O.'s conviction on Piers's nascent political career.

"I gotta say, boss, dis Piers guy's got a great smile," Lenny said.

Sal made an appointment with the garment district tailor and hung up the phone. "I don't know why you are so impressed with these corporate guys."

"Look what a sharp dresser he is! Got a hankie in the pocket of his jacket. I even like his socks. That N.O. guy and the executives from that technology company wear loafers wit' no socks. I don't trust a guy don't wear no socks."

"Remember my wife's snake of a cousin?" Sal poked Lenny.

"Yeah."

"Classy dresser. Great style. They used to say his smile could light up a room. Everybody loved his stories. That is, until his lying, backstabbing ways put a crimp in his storytelling, so to speak." Disappointed, Sal shook his head. "He had so much promise."

"Ohhhhh." Lenny rethought his argument.

Sal carefully wiped his clip-point blade and placed the knife back in the desk drawer. He walked toward the back door.

Persuasion not his strong suit, Lenny did not know when to leave well enough alone.

"Ya know, my ma always said I shoulda gone into business 'stead of bein' a street guy."

"What's wrong with our racket? We got loyalty, don't we?"

"Uh, yeah, boss." Lenny wished he had not mentioned his mother.

"Lot of these so-called businessmen got to learn to be invisible. That's how to get things done. That's how to hold on to power. What the frig's a tambourine collection anyways?"

"You got a point, boss."

"Our kind, we know what's what. After all, business is business. Nothing personal."

"So right, Sal. I have to say, this is why you're the boss."

Sal leaned against the open door leading to the back alley and cushioned the flame of his lighter from the afternoon wind. Taking a long drag on his Montecristo cigar, he motioned toward the TV: "That's NOT what I mean by laying low." On the TV screen, Stewart was shown shooing reporters from the parking lot as his assistant, wearing what he considered a third-rate suit, entered her secondhand car. Not the TMC image Stewart wanted investors to have.

"Those corporate types," Sal nodded at the image of Stewart pulling a microphone from a reporter trying to interview his assistant, "we could teach them a trick or two."

START-UP

I

The allure of increased productivity, driven by cheap, accessible technology, made investors giddy with anticipation in 1999. Companies that could transform an industry, create hundreds of new jobs, or streamline operations and reduce costs captured the attention of individual and institutional investors alike. Those organizations that could be positioned as tech plays, such as TMC Corporation, benefited from the high stock valuations made possible by Wall Street research analysts and investment bankers. The possibilities inherent in TMC's proprietary technology, and a huge opportunity longer-term in technology services, encouraged brokers to hype its stock so much that its initial success continued: The price quadrupled in the six weeks after its initial public offering.

Intrigued by the positive stock performance, local and national business press vied for interviews with TMC leadership. This particular morning, regional station Channel One was readying for an exclusive with Dandy Liege, TMC's vice president of procurement and fulfillment. Dandy's schemes for organizing the processes necessary to buy production materials as well as deliver finished goods differentiated TMC from its competitors. This secret sauce was highly coveted, and Channel One bet that its coverage of Dandy would be good journalism.

The live interview would take place in a makeshift studio set up in the company's boardroom. Not interested in a repeat of his own experience when Ted hurled him to the media wolves, Stewart, along with his assistant, Vera Konstanty, prepared their colleague for this experience. Beneath a set of car keys and a miniature, pink-felt teddy bear, Stewart discovered a powder compact in a random pocketbook. Reserving her comments for another time, Vera crossed her fingers, praying that the women setting up the interview would not notice Stewart rummaging through their bags.

"Here, use this one." Stewart threw the compact to Vera.

Only a month earlier, Vera had bragged about the improvement in TMC's employee benefits since Stewart assumed leadership of the HR team. She appreciated the positive impact to her personal circumstances and noted upbeat vibes around the company. What she did not tell her friends was that Stewart could be a real pill. Vera did not want to mar TMC's image. She quietly hoped his demanding, self-serving behavior would go away once the scrutiny surrounding the stock offering lifted.

"There's nothing wrong with the makeup I brought. I don't know why you are pinching things from other women's purses." Vera took the powder from Stewart and hurried over to Dandy. She knew that TMC's public relations firm had pushed for this interview, advising that a showcase of the executive who built TMC's formidable supply chain would erase lingering negative perceptions around the company's association with N.O. Audette.

Ted, desirous of propelling TMC's stock value higher still, encouraged the publicity. He thought the attention might even create a positive platform for Dandy.

"I want Dandy to feel special. Let him see himself on TV. Maybe a few magazine articles. Who knows? That kind of press could give a lift to his sorry personal life, too," Ted had told Stewart. "And throw more stock options at him. We don't want the attention to backfire and have another company lure him away. He should have no motivation to leave TMC. But whatever you do, make sure he steps up his appearance. His country bumpkin wardrobe won't play well nationally."

For his part, Stewart saw this interview as a chance to improve his position, personally and financially. While he had relished the opportunity to guide the strategic direction of a company through human resources initiatives such as workforce planning, corporate culture, and, certainly, executive compensation and benefits, the icing on the cake had been a seat at the movers-and-shakers table. As consigliere to TMC's CEO, a role he likened to campaign manager in Ted's business war room, Stewart intended to leverage his position to gain his father's respect. His father had not been impressed with Stewart's career choice, as HR was not an essential function when the elder Narciss was maneuvering the corporate ranks. His displeasure had been mildly appeased when Stewart explained that he would report to the chief executive officer.

"I guess if you don't have the wherewithal to be the top guy, you may as well be wiping his boots," Stewart's father responded to his son's detailed description of Ted's earlier military experiences. Examples of human resources executives referenced in prestigious business journals only drew more rancor from his father: "Don't mistake popularity for power."

Stewart's calculator offered a warmer response. Having watched consulting clients, and a few prep school classmates, accumulate private islands, residential palaces, and antique car collections, Stewart salivated as his financial analysis suggested that TMC equity could be a lucrative asset. Plus, his father believed in the self-made man. Lavish displays of conspicuous consumption—the kind that could influence people of influence, like his father—would have to be acquired directly. Stewart intended to witness the accumulation of his own wealth, via a spreadsheet displayed prominently on his computer, during Dandy's dialogue with Channel One.

The subject of the interview sat under three large, powerful television studio lights. Dandy held still and looked at Vera as she applied the soft, beige talcum powder from the pinched compact to his thick face and neck. Accustomed to playing the predator, Dandy appeared more lamb than lion today.

Powder clumped in wet spots on Dandy's perspiring face.

"Oh boy. This isn't going to work. Do you have a hankie?"

Without a tissue or handkerchief available and with the interview for the business segment about to begin, Vera wiped Dandy's face with the sleeve of her linen blouse.

"Thanks." Dandy managed a weak smile.

A robust man with a 6-feet-7-inch frame and pushing 400 pounds, Dandy had been a linebacker on his high school and college football teams. Normally abrupt and pushy, having grown up with eight similarly apportioned brothers around a sparse supper table, Dandy was overwhelmed by the attention that the recent public offering (plus the N.O. misadventure) rained on him and his colleagues. Channel One was the first in a series of media conversations that TMC's public relations firm had proactively organized to spin the company's tale.

As Dandy sat awaiting what he perceived as an interrogation, the heat of the lamps increased his discomfort. He pulled his slacks away from his skin as perspiration trickled down his legs. Nothing he experienced on the Arkansas football fields or around that Formica kitchen table had prepared him for the heightened interest in his every move.

Vera reapplied the powder after drying Dandy's face. She even applied powder to his wet hair.

"Stewart said if shareholders see you sweating like this on TV, they might think you have something to hide. That could affect the value of TMC shares." Vera evened out the patches of makeup clumping on Dandy's face.

"Stewart's linked his computer to an online financial network so he can watch the stock price movement during your interview. He'll wave at you from that corner if the stock starts to drop. If that happens, he wants you to smile brightly. Like this."

Vera demonstrated the smile.

Dandy reciprocated with a smile of his own, but somehow his expression more closely resembled that of a circus clown.

"Oh, I don't think that's what he meant."

Vera closed the compact and reminded Dandy that she had watched him build and then rebuild the supply chain function as TMC multiplied in size. Each time the company expanded, external naysayers said they would not be able to handle the new products or the larger size and scope of the organization. And each time they heard it, the employees took it as a personal challenge to prove the naysayers wrong. The workers were able to achieve increasingly more complex goals, build infrastructure, strengthen customer relationships, and swell the revenue coffers.

All the while, as a result of this teamwork, a strong corporate culture evolved. Vera asked Dandy to imagine the parking lot at seven-thirty in the morning (full), the employee pep rallies (burgeoning attendance), and the personal sacrifices of his own team (three divorces, one stint in the local rest home and, collectively, the highest blood pressure of any department).

"Dandy, the employees feel that we are doing something special at

TMC. We don't come here day after day, working crazy hours, simply for a paycheck. We feel we are part of something unique!"

Vera returned to the purses, and her boss whispered to her. She ran back to Dandy.

"One more thing. Stewart said if the reporter asks about N.O., to be sure to say that TMC rescinded the offer long before his arrest."

"Is that true?"

"You're kidding, right?" *Dandy picks now to have moral sensibilities*, Vera thought as Channel One's production assistant led her out of the filming area.

Candy Whittles, business reporter for bootstrap Channel One, sat on a box of equipment and laughed, a touch too enthusiastically, at the animated chatter emanating from the married-but-that-doesn't-stop-him cameraman. A recent addition to the Channel One staff, Candy was a graduate of the oceanography program at the landlocked NorthWest Regional College. She joined this community news station about the same time her dad, provost for the local university system, authorized a large donation to Channel One from the university's foundation.

Candy bounced up to her interviewee.

"Isn't this the bomb! I'm so excited! I hope you know what you want to talk about because I was up late last night—er, working." Candy blushed as the cameraman winked at her.

The cameraman focused Candy and Dandy with a five-point countdown, and then the live interview began. Stewart rocked back and forth in front of his portable computer and tracked the volatility of TMC shares in real time. He wrote $43.75 on his pad.

Stewart's stock options were currently in the money to the tune of several million dollars, but that value could go up or down, depending on market conditions, macroeconomics, and, certainly, the performance of TMC and its executive team. Plus, his employment contract stipulated that he needed to work at least three years before he could claim the lion's share of his TMC equity. Therefore, Stewart's single-minded focus was to energize that leadership team to drive the share price up. Hedging his bet, he also utilized his position as overseer of compensation programs to counsel the board of directors that additional stock grants should be awarded as incentive to the executive team each year. This longer-term compensation strategy would keep the leaders focused on driving positive results year over year, theoretically propelling the stock forward.

Stewart's paper riches did hold some near-term leverage. Given the perceived future value of his TMC stock holdings, Stewart's bank worked with him to secure a large mortgage to buy a vacation residence on the highly desirable Grand Lake. And a six-bedroom lake house needed the right furnishings and upkeep, so his wife, Mariellen, commissioned a dining room table from a North Carolina furniture master and imported rare Italian marble for the kitchen and bathrooms. With his TMC stock as collateral, the bank was happy to agree to a home equity loan as well.

Stewart checked the computer again. No movement in the $43.75 share price. Not great, but not bad either. He had an uneasy feeling about this interview, though Dandy had taken his advice and had worn a suit instead of his standard golf shirt and shorts. It was not a custom-made suit, but there was a world of difference between Dandy's rural Arkansas upbringing and Stewart's on Chicago's Lake Shore Drive—even though they were contemporaries.

The camera zeroed in on the bubbly and vivacious Candy. It did not hurt her airtime that the cameraman was repulsed by the perspiration cutting streams through Dandy's pancake makeup.

Candy initiated the interview with a description of TMC Corporation as a "way cool technology company that makes great stuff we need to make the planet a better place for all animals."

Then she asked Dandy what he liked about working for TMC.

Dandy momentarily forgot his discomfort and confusion over Candy's animal reference. He got straight to the point.

"I like being able to control things."

"Wow, Mr. Liege. Control is such an uncool word, especially for women."

Dandy did not like to be corrected. And, while subtlety was not recognized as a strength in his leadership profile, the good news was that the perceived slight took his mind further off the situation at hand.

"Well, control is crucial when you are running a complex business,

Candy. Some parts of our company operate on razor-thin margins. If we are going to deliver what our customers expect, our suppliers know they have to give us the best price. If they don't, we'll work with their competitors and force prices down. Occasionally, a vendor has to go out of business. Well, let's just say that kind of thing gets around. More than one company has learned how critical it is to do business the TMC way."

Candy flipped her stilettos in the air as she crisscrossed her legs.

"That's fascinating," she smiled, and slapped Dandy on the knee. Her teeth filled viewers' screens.

"Forty-three dollars and sixty cents," Vera whispered to her boss after peeking at his computer screen.

Stewart scoffed at her.

"I didn't tell Dandy to say that!"

Having replaced the last of the contents Stewart had pulled from the handbags, Vera closed them. "Hope I put these things back in the right bags." She glared at Stewart.

"Don't put those away. We may still need the makeup. He looks like he is in a sauna."

Stewart stood up and started waving wildly at Dandy. The camera technician, putting a finger to her lips, gave Stewart a silent, yet vehement, "Shhhhh!"

"Would it be too much to ask to turn down the lights?" Stewart whispered back at the technician, a middle finger perched on his own lips.

Perspiration racing down his neck, Dandy looked first at Stewart and then at Candy. Although he had begun to relax, Dandy got nervous again when Stewart started waving.

Candy asked another question.

"What is it you actually do at TMC, Mr. Liege?"

Dandy pointed to the lamps behind him.

"I'd feel more comfortable answering your questions if it wasn't so hot in here." He smiled weakly at Candy.

Vera wrote the latest stock price on a pad and slid it under Stewart's nose: $42.50.

"Does anyone have any water? Can't we give the guy water?" Stewart whispered gravely to Vera and the technician while waving again at Dandy.

The technician had a small fan going in the background, which she moved closer to Dandy. He smiled in gratitude. The market recorded a new trade in TMC stock: $42.75. "Smile more!" Stewart whispered loudly to Dandy, and the cameraman gave Stewart the slit-throat sign. Candy's smile froze as she thought about how she might explain Stewart's interruption, which viewers were sure to have heard.

With cool air blowing on the back of his head, Dandy described the supply chain function at this $1 billion technology company. He spelled out, step by step, the processes that he and his team used to purchase components to make the products, run the manufacturing lines, and deliver finished products to customers.

"Oh," Candy said through a yawn.

Eager to pick up the pace, the cameraman held up a whiteboard containing a list of questions he had coached Candy to ask. Long ago having realized the connection between a dramatic interview and the size of his annual bonus, he pointed to question number five, which Candy carefully read out loud.

"TMC almost hired N.O. Audette as chief financial officer. He'll be doing hard time for the rest of his life for what he did to VITE! Corporation and its employees, two of them lit-er-al-ly. Several thousand retires—er, retirees—are once again pounding the pavement looking for work since their VITE! pensions went bust, and there are four kids in Pennsylvania without a grandma since Audette did in his secretary."

She stopped a moment to catch her breath and read the next line to herself, then continued.

"How could TMC even . . . entertain . . ." She looked to the cameraman for confirmation that she got it right. He nodded.

Confidently, she continued, "How could you entertain hiring this scoundrel?"

Stewart shot a look at Dandy. This was the question they all feared.

But Dandy was not thinking about that fear. He had worked hard to build TMC, and he did not like the insinuation. In fact, the question angered him.

"According to his resume, N.O. had a very good record."

The cameraman scribbled furiously and held up a new question, which Candy read.

"Well, how do you—who made the decision, um, to offer him a job?"

Stewart stood in front of the cameraman and held up a notepad of his own. The cameraman pushed him out of the way. He stepped closer so Dandy could read his comments, which were intended to redirect the discussion. Dandy tried but could not make out Stewart's handwriting.

"N.O. had a friend on our board of directors who vouched for him, so we took a shot. We got lucky that he got locked up before he became our chief financial officer." Dandy broke the dead air with his response.

Vera flashed the TMC share price in front of Stewart: *$42.30 and dropping.*

Stewart collapsed in his chair.

Vera took over and held up a note reminding Dandy of her last piece of advice before the cameras started rolling. He could read Vera's handwriting.

"Oh, and we rescinded the offer before N.O. was arrested."

Now the cameraman was smiling. The additional viewers who would tune in to catch this revelation would surely mean a heavier stocking for him at the corporate Christmas party. Also, it did not hurt his chances with Candy that the segment would make her look good. She turned to him for the next question.

"So how do you define success, Mr. Liege?"

Candy batted long eyelashes at her guest and delicately crossed her legs again, her crimson red toenails accentuated by designer shoes.

Dandy smiled warmly. Candy returned his smile and, behaviorally trained, threw her chest out as far as gravity would allow. Dandy's gaze fell to her chest. Then he really smiled.

He had been working 100-hour weeks for a solid two years. The last time a woman batted her eyelashes at him was about three months earlier, when Dandy vigorously shook a container of salad dressing and accidentally squirted a seventy-something waitress in her eye. He had been so tired and lonely that night at the Down On Your Luck Diner that the waitress might have found herself with dinner plans for Saturday night if Dandy's cell phone had not vibrated. His transportation manager was calling about an urgent issue on the production floor. More often hostage to his phone, this particular evening the device had been his savior.

Dandy unconsciously took a deep breath as he experienced Candy's complete attention. Suffering from sleep deprivation, a side effect of preparing TMC for public ownership plus the more recent pressures from outside interests, and with Stewart waving like an idiot, Dandy felt himself floating away in the pools of the program host's iridescent green eyes.

Energized, Dandy answered the reporter. "There are a lot of ways to define success, Candy." He leaned in; Candy accommodated this new intimacy and leaned in herself. Vera whispered to Stewart that the stock was at $42.85.

"My personal financial gain since TMC went public is about $25 million."

Vera whispered that volatility in TMC shares was picking up. Stewart started writing a press release to obfuscate Dandy's reference to his compensation.

"Well, our viewers would really like to know how this town's most eligible bachelor intends to spend all that money. May I call you 'Dandy'?"

Candy's lashes fluttered feverishly. Dandy was quite taken with her. He carefully crossed his own legs and smiled again at Candy, encouraging her to call him anything she liked.

"Forty-three even," Vera sighed.

Smiling too, Stewart waved at Dandy. Dandy recalled the signal system, and his grin brightened. Candy also smiled, and then Dandy beamed as wide as he could. Confused over the smile power play, Candy looked to the cameraman for help. The cameraman indicated that the live filming continued, so Candy should keep interviewing and smiling. Candy's attention fueled Dandy's confidence. He threw one arm over the back of the studio chair.

The TMC team was grateful that Candy had been chosen to sub for the regular host of this local business news program. That reporter was a retired partner from a regional public accounting firm. Candy avoided the detailed financial questions that the former CPA surely would have posed. The repartee between Candy and her guest appeared to have encouraging repercussions for TMC shareholders as well.

"Thank God for little Candy-striper there," Stewart whispered to Vera. "Her teeth alone might help move our stock price up a few points today." Ever grateful for small favors, Vera smiled.

The Channel One interview wrapped up as Dandy proudly ticked off a list of charities and other organizations interested in an alliance with him and his bank account.

"Sounds like you could swing real influence in this town," Candy remarked.

Said that way, through those lips, Dandy readily agreed that this might be his opportunity to give back.

The discussion around Dandy's personal wealth was enough to convince several institutional investors that TMC was doing something right. The stock price rose again when he told Candy that he had a photographic mind for numbers. She wrote her phone number on her palm, which she danced seductively in front of Dandy during the concluding segment. As he bid the host adieu, his smile reached ear to ear and the stock hit $43.75, erasing any paper losses Stewart's portfolio experienced during the interview.

Feeling like he had survived something, Dandy unclipped the microphone from the lapel of his suit and wiped his brow with some napkins. Stewart opened a bottle of water and poured some of it into the palm of his hand. He hit his cheeks and tapped his forehead with the liquid and then ran his wet fingers through his hair.

"I can't go through this again," he told Vera between gulps of water. "Get me time with Dandy next week so I can coach him through this stuff. At the very least, he's got to get a proper suit before his next interview."

"What the heck's he doing now?" Vera asked as she watched a tug of war between Dandy and the camera technician.

The technician had picked up the Channel One coffee mug that Dandy had been provided during the show. Dandy grabbed an edge of the cup and pulled it toward him. Given Dandy's size and status as a guest on the show, the odds were stacked against the young lady retrieving the prop. Dandy walked away with it, insisting that it must be a gift for his participation in the program.

I I

S itting in the break room of a New Jersey office building overlooking the Hudson River and the west side of Manhattan, Carol Himmler watched a news clip from Dandy's interview. The wet, rumpled suit, coupled with the executive's dime-store edge, was not impressive to her. What was impressive, however, was the media exposure this company provided its executive.

I deserve to be at a company like that, Carol thought to herself. *I bet that guy has his own PR handler. My job is probably bigger than his, but instead of a profile on the business news, my recognition is an invitation to run the annual company picnic.*

Carol felt her grip tighten around the thin piece of paper advertising the upcoming team-building event. Catching herself, she relaxed her fingers, knocked on her boss's office door, and placed the flier on his desk.

"I agree that the picnic is a great opportunity to build morale, Ed, but—"

"Let me guess. You can't get out of another commitment."

Ed Simmons shook his head as he took in his director of operations. As leader of the production function at Chemix International, a multinational processor of raw materials, Ed took pride in his team's vigilant oversight of quality for the materials that went into pharmaceutical products and pet food around the world. He believed, strongly, that leadership success was part inspiration, part management, and 100 percent about teamwork. He expected his direct reports to follow this model.

Ed had hired Carol directly from graduate school, where her outstanding grades in chemistry and management boded well for a solid career at Chemix International. Had he asked about extracurricular activities or team-building projects, Ed might have assessed Carol differently. He considered what he had learned about her during the past five years. Brilliant: yes; bold: check, check; inspirational leadership: hardly; plays well with others: there were issues there, too.

Carol's five years at Chemix had been eventful. The growing business pressed leaders to assume increased responsibilities. Her early contributions, under the tutelage of renowned people manager Bob Smith, were extraordinary. With his support, Carol led a team that improved inventory controls while reducing raw materials costs, earning her a Manager of the Year award.

Bob also instructed Carol to evaluate the existing production systems to determine if equipment upgrades might be necessary. Carol bristled when Bob suggested that she work with the facilities department to install the new conveyor belts that her team recommended. The belts would be set up in tiers, one layer suspended above the next by cables, and Bob felt the end result would be better if the designer of the system were involved in its implementation. Carol rethought her objections when she learned that Ed had invited a local newspaper reporter to review the assembly of the new production lines. When bonus time came around, she proudly included in her self-assessment a newspaper photo that captured her standing on one belt as she affixed a cable to another using a soldering iron.

As the vice president in charge of manufacturing, Ed had been eager to promote a woman into the one executive position that had opened up in his department. It seemed a natural that Carol would receive the promotion because of her successful track record. And though they were not a job requirement, her attractive physical features initially drew people to Carol. This, Ed figured, was an asset that could help her build a good team.

Bob, her immediate supervisor, supported Carol but disagreed with Ed, his boss, about promoting her at that time. His recommendation was that she needed more hands-on experience as a manager of people before assuming this more substantial responsibility. Ed noted Bob's objection but promoted Carol anyway. Now, after a full twelve months in an executive role that reported directly to Ed, Carol was dismayed with the most recent review of her performance and what she viewed as the paltry salary increase that accompanied it. She had set up this meeting to give Ed a piece of her mind and try to change his, for the record.

"Look, Ed, isn't there something else on the table?"

Carol stiffened her spine and pulled back her shoulders. Her breathing was deep and purposeful, through flaring nostrils. Ed checked his clothes, subconsciously concerned he might be wearing red. He glanced at her feet to see if she was going to charge.

Pushing his chair away from his desk, Ed asked, "Like what, Carol?"

"Like Bob Smith. It's no secret that he wanted my role to report to him. And now that I am his peer and getting accolades, he's threatened!"

Carol was standing. Ed felt relieved he had created that extra space between them.

"Carol, Bob has been a great supporter of yours. And he is one of our most respected people managers. Managing others is a tricky business, particularly when you have an operations job, like the one you have, where people have to do the right thing every step of the way so that quality is not compromised. Bob's only motivation was to give you cover as you took on more leadership duties."

"Are you saying that I can't manage people well?"

Carol waved her arms wildly as she spoke. She clasped a crystal baseball paperweight that Ed had received as captain of Chemix's championship softball team. Ed glanced at the windows behind him and wondered what kind of arm Carol had. He hurriedly calculated the cost of a replacement window, as well as the embarrassment of having security guards walk his lead female executive out of the building.

"Carol, sit down. Relax. Take a load off. I know your job isn't an easy one."

"Damn right it's not! I get great results for this company. Seventeen percent reduction in cost of raw materials! State-of-the-art production facilities! What do I have to do around here to get noticed?"

"Yes, you and YOUR TEAM got those results. But Carol, c'mon. At what cost?"

Ed's voice rose as he reminded Carol that her team had so many people cycling on and off medical leave that the employees referred to it as the operations rotation program. He also informed her that the senior vice president of human resources had called to ask if a downsizing had been authorized in the operations function because so many workers on Carol's team were applying for job postings outside of her department. As he spoke, Ed recalled his assumption that Carol's alluring qualities would be an advantage to forming a team. Instead, her penchant for fashion trends with a decidedly masculine feel stood as a stark reminder of her no-holds-barred drive for results and, as such, had been off-putting to many workers.

What a shame. She could have been so appealing . . . but it's more like a cold beauty that turns everything around her to stone, Ed thought.

"Carol, the sales manager for our vendor R.A.W. Materials asked to be reassigned to another account because he couldn't take another browbeating from you!"

"Ed, that guy is a wimp."

"Carol, R.A.W. Mats is our best supplier!"

Carol sat down. Ed stood up.

"And you want more money? Last time I looked, Carol, you were in the business of ensuring the quality of chemicals for pharmaceutical companies, not making trouble for your boss."

Carol realized this battle was lost. She made the appropriate admissions and vowed to be a kinder, gentler manager.

"I'll make you proud, Ed. I will talk to Bob and learn what I can from him about motivating the troops. We'll have even better results next quarter."

"Carol, I'd be satisfied with the same results and fewer employees in the hospital, if you can manage that."

Carol smiled stiffly as Ed handed her the flier for the company picnic.

"Why don't you see what you can do about organizing a team for the egg toss?"

CAROL RETURNED TO her office. She viciously tore up the picnic flier and threw it in the trash. She looked out her office window that faced the end of the production line. Bob walked by with his arm around Erma Sinclair, who had recently transferred from Carol's quality team to a role within Bob's department.

"Urgh!" Carol exclaimed as she watched Bob walk away with a woman who had been one of her best employees. She remembered the one yoga class she attended years before and took in a deep breath. She never made it to the second class—yoga was too touchy-feely for her—but she remembered the breathing lesson. She especially liked the way it made her nostrils, which were larger than average, flair. Actually, she especially liked the way her flaring nostrils seemed to put men on edge. She felt it today in her meeting with Ed.

Her desk was covered with pink phone message slips for calls she had ignored the past few days because of her anger over her performance rating and negligible salary increase.

The message on the top of the pile was from Scott Landing, senior partner with King Neville & Associates, an executive search firm. Informally, but not always affectionately, referred to as headhunters, executive search consultants were hired by a specific company to find and recruit qualified executives to fill open positions. The message read: outstanding leadership role with up-and-coming academy company. Translation: former high-performing company is struggling and desperately needs someone to pull it out of the weeds. Curious, Carol dialed the number.

Who knows? It might be a big job that would better leverage my genius. I could kiss off this rinky-dink operation. That would teach Ed!

"Scott Landing here."

Why do executive search consultants have names that sound like they were pulled out of central casting?

"Scott, this is Carol Himmler of Chemix returning your call."

"Carol, how are you? I don't know if you recall, but we met at the last Quality-O-Rama conference in Hilton Head."

"I wasn't at that conference, Scott."

"Well, it must have been the conference before that. How the heck are you?"

Carol felt the insincerity of Scott's one-hundred-watt smile but decided to play along.

"Yes, it must have been that conference in Boca. I've been incredibly well here at Chemix. They take good care of me. Though, of course, I take very good care of our shareholders, so it is a quid pro quo. Ha-ha-ha."

Sensing a fish on the line, Scott turned up the charm.

"Yes, I've been hearing about your results, Carol." He flipped through his directory of Chemix employees to find her name and confirm her title: *Carol Himmler, Director of Operations and Quality. Extension 4576.*

"Ensuring proper quality for materials is vital," he went on. "You cannot lose the confidence of your customers." Scott referenced some companies whose image had been damaged because of product issues.

"Whatever," said Carol, nonplussed. "Didn't you call to talk about me?"

Quickly discerning what motivated Carol, and desiring to encourage an interest in the executive opening he was representing, Scott redirected his spotlight and appealed to Carol's ego.

"Carol, although we haven't known one another for long . . ." Scott started.

Not at all, Carol thought.

" . . . I can tell that you are smart, talented, determined and . . . and . . ."

Carol's boredom with Scott was edging toward annoyance. She wanted the punch line.

"Who's your client, Scott?"

"Carol, my client is a well-recognized leader in its field. My client has over forty-five years in . . ."

"Scott, what's the company and what's the job?"

He knew he would lose her now if he drew this out. He rolled the dice. "AmBeeance."

"That sleeper of a company? You want me to work for them? I thought you understood how good I am!"

"Ummm, Carol, we know AmBeeance has seen its share of tough times lately."

"Scott, the industry joke is that the AmBeeance execs are taking their sleep-aid product way too seriously."

"Carol, that is exactly why AmBeeance needs an executive like you—someone who can wake things up." He suspected that she would be interested only in a job of significance. "What is it that you want to get out of your career, Carol?"

"More, more, more, more! I want to be a CEO!"

Scott had not anticipated a declaration of such voracious ambition. But he appreciated, and could play to, her clear-cut style.

"AmBeeance is willing to pay whatever it takes to get the right leader on board. And they want a bold personality to rouse the management team."

Carol knew enough about AmBeeance, and executive recruiters, not to believe him. Scott tried another tactic. He knew, from what he had read, that Carol had an international background.

"I understand you have experience in Africa, Carol. AmBeeance has built a new R&D facility in Cape Town. You could really shake up the paradigm there—apply your keenly honed drive to win on an unsuspecting crew. This could be your opportunity to break away from the pack."

Scott had no way of knowing how closely he had skirted Carol's moral underpinnings. Carol's maternal grandfather, Wolfgang Himmler, had left Leipzig, Germany, with dreams of a better life wrought from the diamond mines around western Africa. He moved the family to a German colony town adjacent to the United Diamond Mines company facilities around present-day Namibia. When the reality of Wolfgang's dreams amounted to unsteady work in the deep and dangerous mines, his wife, Gretchen, took employment as a housekeeper for the local government magistrate. The magistrate was a family man with a handsome son the same age as Wolfgang and Gretchen's daughter Brunhilde.

Brunhilde had her father's ambition but was intellectually his superior. She realized that her own opportunities in this gem-infested region must be secured by marriage to the attractive, but dull, son of the magistrate. She created occasions to help her mother at the mansion, gaining face time with seventeen-year-old Karel. Attracted to the pretty and buxom blonde, Karel also invented projects around the house on days when Brunhilde would be around.

Jakob Kranx, the son of the magistrate's stable-keeper, had taken a liking to Brunhilde's fine feminine form as well. Jakob began following Karel and Brunhilde on their jaunts through the magistrate's property, challenging Karel at every opportunity. They wrestled and raced stallions, and climbed trees to pick fruit for Brunhilde's lunch. Jakob even scaled a thirty-foot cliff to pluck a rare African moon daisy from an outcropping. This last feat, and the uncommon bloom, captured Brunhilde's attention. Not to be outdone, Karel ascended the same cliff and proceeded to swan dive into a deep pond below. As luck would have it, a small family of crocodiles had sought refuge from the hot afternoon sun in the very same pond.

Soon thereafter, the magistrate fired Brunhilde's mother as one of his last official acts before returning to his ancestral homeland to recover from the untimely and grisly death of his much beloved son. Jakob eventually won the lady because a small town surrounded by a no-man's-land places limitations on a girl's prospects for marriage. Brunhilde sought revenge for her stable-scooping, trail-grooming life by reminding her husband every day of his part in the destruction of her dreams. With cool precision, she named her firstborn child Carol.

As Carol's dark hair and sharp facial features drew an uncanny resemblance to the magistrate's family, Jakob favored her younger brother. He rebuffed Carol's affection, and as time passed, she grew indifferent to him. Yet, she thrived under her mother's narcissistic tutelage. Brunhilde encouraged Carol to discover a way out of their confining existence. Given the uncertainties surrounding Namibian independence and general unrest in the region in the 1970s, Carol's mother promoted the dream of an American education.

Brunhilde anticipated that she would ride her daughter's academic coattails, so she packed a small bag, placed it by the door, and awaited results of Carol's applications to the top engineering schools in the United States. However, Carol had inherited more than her mother's strong intellect and fierce ambition. She had perfected Brunhilde's desire for self-determination. Calculating that her egotistical mother would be more a liability than an asset in her new life, Carol kept it to herself when notification arrived that she had received a full scholarship to the Massachusetts Institute of Technology. To escape her familial bonds, she secretly packed her own suitcase and slipped away, crossing desolate terrain, rich in diamonds but still harsh and forbidding, even in 1980. After walking all night, Carol reached the nearest town of any size early the next morning. Once there, she exchanged her surname for her grandfather's, purchased a one-way ticket to Massachusetts, and never looked back.

Her experience in Africa notwithstanding, Carol remained unimpressed and, worse for Scott, uninterested.

"Scott, my team held a best-practices session with AmBeeance earlier this year. We found their IT systems antiquated, the culture plodding, and the organizational structure top-heavy. After they took that supply chain–related charge in the last financial quarter, the balance sheet isn't so hot, either. Too bad, too, because the fat margins were the one thing they had going for them."

Scott's client was anticipating a progress report the following morning. He really needed Carol, whose name had been at the end of his call list, since he had struck out with all other prospective candidates.

"Carol, that's exactly right. AmBeeance needs someone who can motivate a tired workforce, straighten out the systems, and get the right processes in place to achieve great results. An inspirational leader like you."

A light bulb went on over Carol's head. Maybe Scott and his client could be useful to her after all.

"Now that you put it that way—you're right. There could be life in the old beast after all."

Scott gleefully kicked his feet under his desk.

"But of course, not for me."

Scott stopped kicking. His smile changed into a frown. She was going to require more work.

Carol watched through her office window as Bob Smith traded stories with Erma and a few other employees who had joined their conversation.

"I do have a colleague."

Scott's eyes brightened a bit as he listened for more.

"He is exactly the type of leader your client needs. Of course, I'd hate to see him leave Chemix. He's my mentor, after all. But our leadership doesn't appreciate him, and this sounds like such a good opportunity. On the QT, I understand he is none too happy with his last review and salary increase."

Carol's description of an underappreciated executive was characteristic of the circumstances presaging an executive move. People often made rash decisions coming out of a disappointing performance review. Scott, who was paid for his efforts when an executive was hired, wanted to be the vehicle through which Carol's colleague bandaged his bruised ego and made his next career move.

Saliva dripped from Scott's mouth. "What's your colleague's name?"

"Bob Smith."

Carol provided Bob's direct phone number and heard Scott scribble down his name.

"Please don't tell anyone that I recommended Bob. I wouldn't want my boss to think that I was involved with anyone poaching one of our top execs. Let's keep this conversation between us."

Eager to get off the phone with Carol so he could call Bob, Scott readily agreed with her terms.

"And don't forget to call me when you have a challenge worthy of my talents, Scott. You owe me now."

I I I

A week after the Channel One interview, Stewart met with Dandy in his office. The interest generated by that segment suggested there would be more media inquiries, and Stewart wanted Dandy to be prepared.

Considered a unique communications technology company, nevertheless TMC Corporation had had a bumpy history. Started as a private entity, TMC became a public company during a rising tech tide. Then, when the company had reached almost $1 billion in revenue, Ted Barone had persuaded a group of investors to provide the financial leverage needed to take TMC out of the public markets when the economy, and global stock markets, had languished a few years later.

From a strategic perspective, the corporation's leadership envisioned TMC becoming a multibillion-dollar, margin-rich, services-driven business. Significant capital would be required to build and execute this vision. However, TMC struggled with the debt it had accumulated to support its various incarnations. When the U.S. economy moved from recovery through resurgence at the end of the 1990s, Stewart, who had been a management consultant, was engaged by TMC's board of directors to recommend financial recapitalization options for the company. He suggested an employee stock ownership plan, an idea he had witnessed work successfully for a cash-strapped industrial client. Although TMC's board of directors noted the merits of Stewart's suggestion, mostly the fast, largely unencumbered, infusion of cash, Ted did not perceive this strategy as one that would add value to his portfolio. With the economy changing for the better, he encouraged the board to take advantage of soaring valuations in the public markets. Eager to reap the multiple benefits that a positive analyst's report could sow, the board voted overwhelmingly to take TMC public, again.

Yet, Stewart's guidance so impressed board member Rick Robertson that Rick sought his counsel on several other challenges that were tying up Rick's investments. Rick was particularly impressed with Stewart's design for surgically divesting his cookie-cutter marriage from his portfolio, a necessity thrust upon the capitalist when his wife discovered his betrayal of the free-enterprise system: Rick's affair with a fiery, redheaded, brick-house-chested Communist wannabe.

Ted was not similarly indebted. In fact, when encouraged by Rick—whose venture capital firm had provided financial muscle to TMC over the years—to find a home at TMC for the enterprising consultant, Ted had resisted. His leadership team was complete. Plus, he was not sold on Stewart. Much as he adored people hanging on his every word, the way Stewart did, it made Ted feel a little dirty. But Rick pressed him: "Stewart could manage human resources for you." When Ted inquired what human resources actually did, Rick explained the function, as he understood it: "When the company is growing, they'll hire the people you need to get the work done. If things go south, they'll fire the employees you don't need anymore. In between, I'm really not sure."

Urged on by his impressionable board, Ted had made Stewart an offer to lead the human resources function at the pre-IPO TMC. Making clear that he liked to run his own show, Ted had advised the former consultant that the best way he could help would be to take care of TMC executives:

"Make sure the executives get what they need when they want it. Make sure they have the right team to get the job done. And don't get in their way." To make sure his flank was covered, Ted had added, "If somebody screws up, get rid of them."

Stewart gleefully told Ted that he accepted this "unique opportunity to escort a blossoming corporation as it emerges from the safety of its cocoon into a powerful butterfly." Ted could have done without the insect images, but the board found Stewart's written acceptance of TMC's offer "inspired." Therefore, with a B.S. in strategic management and fifteen years of experience advising Fortune 1000 leaders around business miscues as well as personal foibles, the thirty-eight-year-old reinvented himself, securing a position of influence, and a substantial equity award, in an important, growing technology organization.

Certainly, in this first quarter, with stock volatility high and the share price moving up, the decision to take TMC public again appeared to have been a good one. However, since the board of directors and the executives were prohibited from selling any stock for six months per the agreement with the financial underwriters of TMC's stock offering, the business results of the first two financial quarters would be critical. The trick for the leadership team would be to keep the share price increasing until the trading lockups expired.

So, following through on Ted's directive and in support of his own equity stake, Stewart secured Dandy in his office, determined to teach him a few techniques to manage the spotlight. Stewart considered the makeover of Dandy his greatest human resources challenge.

Clad in a salmon-colored shirt and beige shorts with sneakers (no socks), Dandy, who was familiar with Stewart's credentials as consigliere to imposing people, ate up the advice. Before TMC's public stock offering, Dandy's experience with the media had been limited to the daily sports section and the weekend funny pages of his local paper. Now *Eligibility Magazine* wanted to do a feature on Dandy as Oklahoma's top bachelor. Moreover, innumerable civic and charitable organizations that relied upon the largesse of well-to-do patrons were eager to shape Dandy's altruistic choices. Moving in the right social circles could be valuable for TMC, so Stewart wanted Dandy to look and sound attractive.

A scholarship had been Dandy's ticket to engineering school. A succession of part-time jobs as well as bargains at the Third Time's a Charm thrift store enabled him to complete a graduate degree. Right out of school he landed a job as a test engineer for a memory technology company. Working double shifts, Dandy managed successively larger teams as the investor group that owned the company acquired other firms and merged them into the entity that would later become TMC Corporation.

Dandy's frugal personal lifestyle conditioned him to look for money-saving opportunities in the workplace. As senior management regularly swelled and then trimmed the workforce, Dandy encouraged his team to remain productive while resources were cut. His supply-chain improvements—some vendors called them hardball tactics—encouraged innovation and efficiency. These features also enabled TMC to gain a significant competitive advantage. An increase in operating margins captured the attention of the leadership team that promoted Dandy to higher levels and more responsible roles. Unfortunately, no one along the way considered getting a mentor for Dandy so that, when he arrived at the upper echelons of leadership, he would know how to dress and act the part.

Stewart did not underestimate the work involved in Dandy's overhaul. He blocked off the entire afternoon to coach him.

Dandy kicked off his sneakers and put his bare feet up on one end of Stewart's desk.

"You are now representing TMC, a publicly held company, Dandy. You have to think of that all the time." Carefully cajoling him to get a wardrobe fix, Stewart brushed Dandy's feet off of the desk.

"Buy a new suit? Are you serious? What's a good suit cost these days? Two hundred, maybe three hundred?" Dandy unwrapped a peppermint from the candy dish on Stewart's desk. He pocketed another three mints for later.

"More like one thousand to two thousand." The meeting was interrupted by a sharp whistle.

"What the—"

Dandy turned around to see Charlie Watkins, the senior human resources manager on Stewart's team. During the past three years, Charlie had helped Dandy staff the global procurement department, hiring four executives in Asia, one in Canada, and six in the U.S. He knew something about dressing for success; a wardrobe upgrade had been recommended to him, too, when he started recruiting. Luckily, a guide on his first trip to Asia had introduced him to a tailor and wholesaler, enabling Charlie to have a bespoke look at bargain-basement prices.

"Yep, unless you have connections in the garment industry," Charlie said, popping a peppermint into his mouth.

Annoyed at this disruption to his executive coaching session, Stewart made a face.

"Team, we are in the big leagues now. Dandy, you'll be asked for more interviews, to participate in community organizations, to donate to a variety of causes."

"Give away my money! I don't even have it yet. The executive officers can't access any gains for another four months. Anything can happen between now and then!" Dandy yelled.

Charlie sat on the other edge of Stewart's desk. He was eager to create a place for himself at this executive table.

"Dandy, you may want to talk to a financial planner who can help you get a handle on your new wealth. He can advise you on the best use of your charitable dollars." Charlie thought his advice might calm down Dandy.

"Whoa. Why are we talking about giving away my money anyway? I don't recall reading that requirement in the option agreements I got in lieu of cash during all those lean years."

Stewart viewed conversations such as this one as an opportunity to further ingratiate himself into TMC inner sanctums. Not a fan of competition, he felt Charlie's participation infringing on his influence.

"Dandy, you are entering an entirely new phase of life. You will be an obscenely wealthy man," Stewart offered.

"When the lockup period is over and my stock options vest I might be, Stewart. Right now, I don't have any more money than the next guy."

"Let me rephrase. This is an important juncture in your life as well as in the life and the future of TMC. You will no longer be seen as simply Dandy Liege but rather as the Dandy Liege who reinvented the supply chain, or Dandy Liege, senior leader of world-class TMC."

Stewart could see that Dandy reacted well to that. He nudged Charlie off his desk.

"Everything we do will be associated with TMC. How we look, what we say, who we associate with."

Stewart reminded Dandy of the specific charitable enterprises and civic organizations requesting his support. Newspaper reporters and government leaders seeking campaign contributions would also vie for his attention. He explained how these things might impact the viability and success of TMC: "We will be watched intently by institutional investors who can continue to take the stock up or run it down."

At the mention of shareholders and his financial future, Dandy refocused.

"Ahhh." Dandy nodded. "It's important to give back."

"Remember, 'From each according to his ability, to each according to his need,'" Stewart said.

"You're quoting Marx to support capitalism?" Charlie nearly choked on the peppermint.

"Hey, take what you need and leave the rest," Stewart said pointedly in Charlie's direction.

Although he looked up to his boss (Stewart was taller), Charlie's jury was still out on Stewart's leadership talents. Charlie allowed him leeway, assuming the management consulting experience provided Stewart, who was a good ten years his senior, with insights about business that Charlie had not yet experienced. Still, he could not shake the feeling that Stewart was not very deep.

"Let's practice some sound bites that you can take to that newspaper interview next week." Stewart erased the word Greed from his whiteboard. "Right concept, but it's so 1980s. We need something fresh."

Dandy continued nodding.

Feeling sidelined, Charlie sought an opportunity to re-engage. The son of a thirty-year lineman with a Pennsylvania utility company, Charlie anticipated a long career. Good thing he liked the work. Charlie's view was that, as a human resources manager, he could make a significant impact on a company through its workforce. This could be particularly true in a smaller enterprise with a risk-taking culture, which is largely why he decided on TMC as the place to build his career. The executive team relied on Charlie to get the human infrastructure in place as they built the business. The employees looked to him for guidance as the fast-moving company morphed regularly with even faster growth. Even the government counted on Charlie, as there were more forms to fill out and personnel data to track as TMC became a bigger employer.

All this he found intellectually stimulating, despite the eighty-hour workweeks. And, whenever his wife expressed displeasure that he had missed some family gathering because of a TMC issue, Charlie reminded her that, hedging his altruistic nature, he had successfully persuaded Stewart that the best way to align him with overall company performance was to include him in a very limited pool of nonexecutives to receive stock options. Their very own shot at wealth creation, or, as it was more commonly described, "F-you money," simply required time, and a little patience (Charlie's options were on a four-year vesting cycle).

"Maybe you should consider an executive coach, Dandy." Charlie interrupted Stewart's brainstorming of bon mots for use in future media interviews.

"A what?" Dandy asked.

"An executive coach is like your high school football coach but for the personal side of things. They provide counseling around how to handle the media or manage participation in outside organizations. They even advise on improvements to your personal life," Charlie explained.

"And what's wrong with my personal life that a high school football coach is going to fix?" Dandy was irritated again.

"Hold on, Dandy. That's a good idea."

Eager to shape TMC's leadership team, Rick Robertson, the TMC board member with whom Stewart had maintained a good rapport after helping him exit his messy marriage, recently had recommended just such a coach. Stewart saw an opportunity to work Rick's counsel into Dandy's lessons.

"Oneida Svenson is an executive coach who's worked with Rick's team at Critical Ventures," Stewart said. "She's spending time at Rick's Colorado ranch. Let's make a detour to our Boulder instrument facility after the executive team-building retreat at the Canyon Plateau Resort. You give your 'making history' speech, motivate the troops. Then we can finish the week together on Rick's ranch, focusing on the business without interruptions."

Dandy had been meaning to get to the instrument facility and kick butt anyway. He also thought he had earned a visit to the Colorado ranch of a TMC board member. Stewart made a mental note to call his realtor for a referral in the Denver area to show him après-ski properties. Charlie thought their trip might provide the right environment to test a project that he had been developing.

"Stewart, you might get the Boulder team's input on the *What's Your Forte?* initiative while you are out there," Charlie said.

"What's that?" Dandy was intrigued.

"Charlie has this notion that, after all the hard work over so many years, our loyal team will up and leave the company for a better opportunity," Stewart replied.

"I didn't say everyone would leave, but I do think we need to give employees reasons to stay, especially since the economy is so strong," Charlie responded. "This may be particularly true for the rank-and-file who aren't participating in the upside on the stock. The *What's Your Forte?* program would get people thinking about what they do best and how that contributes to the success of the company."

"What does this initiative cost? I mean, per head," Dandy asked.

"That's the beauty of it. Basically, the HR team creates program guidelines, the employees self-identify strengths, and managers help workers create development plans that apply those strengths to solve business problems. It's the power of positive thinking put to work for TMC. Rewards could be tangible, like trophies or team dinners. Or they might take the form of recognition in an e-mail."

"So it doesn't have to cost anything, but people might work harder because of it?" Dandy was interested.

"There are no guarantees, but research indicates that productivity often rises when employees feel better about their work environment."

Stewart was irritated that his vision of a trip to Colorado was hijacked by a discussion around employee morale.

"That's assuming we need a program like that," he said. "Charlie, we have an incredibly dedicated workforce. They believe that we are making a difference. We don't need to waste the employees' time with questions around what they do well. They know what they do well. And they do it very well. Look at our stock price."

Stewart winked at Dandy.

Charlie respectfully reminded the executives that what goes up can come down. If that happened, Charlie's research indicated that employees would stick with a company they believed in, even if it meant smaller bank accounts.

"It's best to keep employees focused on work, not some pie-in-the-sky idealism," Stewart said, ushering Charlie toward the door.

"Maybe we could meet on it again before you go," Charlie said. "I'm tightening up the specifics to give it more punch." Charlie waved to Dandy as Stewart closed the office door after him.

"Now, where were we on those talking points for the reporter?" Stewart said, then paused. He pulled a business card from his top desk drawer and handed it to Dandy.

"My personal shopper at Brooks Brothers," Stewart explained.

I V

The rich greens and blues of the Colorado mountains were a sharp contrast to TMC's exposed-wire, halogen-lit factory. Stewart, more comfortable with the mahogany offices of consulting firms, had not yet made peace with the stark technology environs where he worked. He felt rejuvenated as he exited the TMC facility in Boulder and took in the Rockies from the parking lot.

"What's an executive coach doing up here anyway?" Dandy wondered as he threw his duffel bag into the trunk.

"Apparently she has a thing for thoroughbreds," Stewart answered, laying his Hartmann leather garment bag carefully on the back seat.

"She races 'em?"

"From the way Rick describes it, she makes her money through executive coaching and life training, but her spiritual calling is caring for horses. She had been a talented fullback with the American Women's Soccer

League. Rick sponsored her team, the Nordic Nymphs. When the league fell apart and a series of other things didn't work out, like vet school and reality TV, Rick put her to work on his ranch. When she is not working with the horses, she uses her athletic training and TV experience as a framework for corporate team-building exercises."

Stewart recalled the first time he met Oneida. They had both been invited to speak during the Hired Gun Development conference sponsored by Critical Ventures. Joining them on the "Developing the Wholistic Executive" panel was a brilliant Stanford professor. The professor's elbow-patched sports jacket and inconsistent personal hygiene habits did little to endear him to Stewart. Fortunately for the TMC executive, on his right was Oneida, a sandy-haired, sweet-smelling vixen whose Amazonian physique straddled the line between the sexes.

Confused, Stewart found himself grappling with her football-player-sized biceps, squared shoulders and imposing 6-feet-2-inch stance. Still, he was drawn to her vivacious personality and open sexuality. So, he did what any self-respecting male would do. He turned off the left side of his brain, centering his attention on her ruby-red lips, blonde locks, and considerable upper torso. He applauded each comment and any observation she made. The Stanford professor took solace in a math equation with which he had been wrestling for weeks as Oneida led the discussion.

"She is really built," Stewart said to Dandy.

Dandy whistled a traditional catcall.

"Not like that. Or rather, not just like that. Oneida's, well . . . she's a big girl. Pretty, too—in a large sort of way. She's blonde, though, so it's all good."

Stewart started up the rented Hummer and moved from third to fourth gear as they headed onto the highway that would take them to Rick's mountaintop villa. He took a sip of his coffee.

"Damn. Wish that waitress had put more cream in this coffee."

"How many do you need?" Dandy asked, pulling a handful of little creamers from his jacket pocket.

"Did you knock off the diner's entire stock?" Stewart wondered if Dandy's actions might be considered a misdemeanor in Colorado.

"Who's going to miss it? But since you mention it, this is why I insist we need more security on our factory floors. You could steal a communications system in a week slipping parts out in your socks. I know. I've done it. Well, you need these socks to pull it off."

Dandy revealed knee-high white cotton tube socks under his jeans.

Stewart allowed Dandy to fill his coffee with the acquired cream as he answered his ringing cell phone.

"Hey, Charlie. How's it going at the old forge?"

Stewart glanced at Dandy, who was reading a text message on his electronic pager, but Charlie's news refocused him.

"What do you mean the controller's leaving the company? I read her e-mail on the 8K filing. She sent them at some ungodly hour. She's clearly very engaged. Has she forgotten that she can't access her stock until after the six-month mark?" Stewart referenced the constraint put upon executives that prevented them from benefiting too much too soon from the publicly traded stock.

Focused on Charlie, Stewart almost missed a right turn.

"Shit. What do you mean the controller doesn't have any equity in the company? What idiot didn't include her in the stock option grants?"

Stewart took his stewardship of the executive team seriously, maintaining direct control of leadership development activities, such as executive coaching, as well as rewards and incentive programs, including executive compensation and benefits. With regard to HR benefits for the balance of the workforce, Stewart's common practice amounted to a tacit approval of whatever the external consultants recommended. Charlie reminded Stewart that it had been his bright idea, as suggested by his former employer Evergreen Consultants, to eliminate stock grants below the executive suite to assuage the board's concerns about dilution. The directors wanted to maintain voting control, as well as prop up the value of their shares. Offering stock options to the entire workforce would have diminished their ownership percentage and reduced the initial stock-offering price.

"This is not the time for finger-pointing, Charlie!"

Stewart listened as Charlie explained how he strove to persuade the controller to stay, but she was not open to it. She offered a litany of complaints, including no line of sight to an executive-level promotion and the equity awards that would accompany it, despite 100-hour weeks preparing for a public stock offering and a consistent record of exceeding expectations. The insult of the CFO talking to her breasts when she presented financial information simply topped everything off. Then, when a critical question came up on that 8K filing—a report announcing a material event for the company, in this case a new executive compensation program—those familiar with the compensation scheme and its accounting treatment (Stewart, Ted, and the CFO, Iago Thomason) were on to the dessert wine and Cuban cigars segment of the executive retreat at Canyon Plateau Resort, where cell phones were verboten. The compensation program, also designed by Evergreen Consultants, included cash and stock awards that were noticeably hefty, particularly as the general workforce had been asked to wait for their stock options to be awarded at a later time. With the filing deadline approaching for the 10Q, another critical financial report, the controller had had a career epiphany. She traded her green eyeshades for rose-colored glasses and quit.

Why does everything fall to me to fix? Stewart thought.

"Well, it's not like we are losing an executive," he said aloud. "Doesn't Iago have a suggestion for someone to replace her? He's the dang CFO."

Charlie's attempts to contact Iago had been unsuccessful because a tropical storm prevented a clear connection to the investor junket that Stewart had arranged for Iago to headline following the executive retreat. Charlie did not think it wise to wait for Iago's return to take action.

"Charlie, TMC products are in great demand. Sales are growing. And thank God for our margins. How hard can it be to write down the numbers that the executives provide? Someone else in this company must know about accounting and external reporting! . . . No, I don't want to hire from outside. I don't want word to get out that our controller quit. Analysts will wonder what's up with our books. Find an internal replacement."

Dandy, with issues of his own, sent a message to his team. They were working on contingency plans in the event there should be a longshoremen's strike at the Long Beach, California, port. A strike could seriously disrupt availability of parts from Asia. Furthermore, a work stoppage could delay the delivery of finished product and, therefore, upset sales. On top of all this, the controller's latest internal financial reports indicated that TMC's operating margins had eroded somewhat, due in large measure to a preemptive move by suppliers to increase component costs in anticipation of a strike. The realization of a walkout by longshoremen could lead to even more margin pressure.

"Yes, Charlie, we can review your tweaks to the *What's Your Forte?* initiative when I return to the office, but one resignation does not mean everyone else will leave." Stewart hung up on his recruiting manager.

"Trouble?" Dandy asked.

"This is where Charlie falls short. He is overly concerned about employees losing confidence in TMC. Charlie needs to be raising awareness, not raising alarms."

They drove up an evergreen-canopied route without saying more. As the country road veered further north, the trees dropped off and the landscape opened up to reveal a large grassy knoll, at the center of which was a 5,000-square-foot stone and log cabin. A barn sat behind the house. To the right of the house was a fenced-in track. A tall, broad woman with a bouncing blonde ponytail walked a horse around the track.

"There's Oneida."

Stewart turned off the engine.

"Is she talking to that horse?" Dandy spied Oneida suspiciously.

"Kind of hard to tell from here."

"She sure is a big girl." Dandy said through a wide smile. "I always did like big girls."

He dashed out of the car. Stewart popped the trunk and handed Dandy his duffel bag.

"Couldn't take my advice and buy some good luggage, could you?" Stewart teased his colleague.

"Hey, this bag's been around the world as we built this company. By the way, your suit and tie look really natural in this mountaintop retreat." Dandy smirked as he closed the trunk.

"A classic look is never out of place." Stewart corrected Dandy.

Stewart was momentarily flustered when Dandy gave him a slap on the rear. He brushed off the gesture when he remembered that Dandy's employee profile indicated football as his high school activity.

But what about that wink?

"Naw," Stewart said out loud as they walked over to Oneida, who was engaged in animated discussion with a thoroughbred.

BACK AT TMC headquarters, Charlie advised Vera of his dilemma.

"I don't know what Stewart's thinking. Accounting and financial reporting are crucial functions that can help build credibility—or create real problems, if they're not done right." Charlie knew that the corporate controller, considered the number-two financial role within TMC, confirmed the integrity of the financial data upon which the credibility of the leadership team, and the strength of TMC stock, was built. "It's not like we have a bunch of controllers sitting on the bench who can take over."

Vera pulled the succession plan for future TMC leadership from her file cabinet. She pointed to three big empty boxes underneath the controller position, confirmation of a lack of internal successors for that job. She handed Charlie a copy of the outline, saying: "It's near impossible to get Stewart's attention on anything other than Caribbean real estate properties lately."

Travis Tweadle tumbled down the hallway. Wiping his wide brow with a handkerchief, he appeared all aflutter. The late-forties-ish executive assistant to the CEO was of medium build, with coiffed gray hair. Moving down from his profoundly round head, his physique got thicker around the waistline and thinned out only around his ankles. His habit of tucking his golf shirt into waist-high belted pants made him appear properly apportioned, if somewhat like a child's punching clown. His own assistant, Don Dombrowski, wiped his brow with a similar handkerchief as he walked behind his boss.

Ted's military service in Vietnam had provided a bird's-eye view into the organizational strengths of the armed forces. He was intrigued with the aide-de-camp position, especially how it enabled the successful function of a general's often complex life. When he assumed the reins at TMC, Ted created a similar role to mitigate the strife in his own complicated corporate existence. However, he decided upon a less militaristic, more benign, title when he chose the innocuous executive assistant label. Travis Tweadle was the very proud, and the very first, "EA" for TMC.

Travis received permission to hire his own assistant after he determined that the complexities of Ted's life created complications in his own. Don was of slightly smaller stature, but similar physique, to his boss. Ever eager to maximize his impact, the thirtysomething Don took to tucking in his golf shirts and belting his pants around the waist soon after he was hired. Don instinctively knew how to stay one step behind his boss at all times.

"Where's Stewart? Ted wants to see Stewart right away." Travis demanded of Vera.

Don handed Travis a clean, dry handkerchief and wrung out the first one in the plant in Vera's office.

"Hey," Vera reprimanded him.

"It's just water," Don said as he folded the damp, cotton square and put it in his pocket.

Word of the controller's departure had reached the boardroom. Ted and the board were worried. The controller's financial reports were critical tools they relied upon to make decisions, and they were not in any mood to entertain delaying the filing of the 10Q. This quarterly report detailing the financial state of the company was a necessary step before the trading restrictions would be lifted on the leadership's equity stake. Since Iago was being feted by the chairman of a Mexican investment bank on a megayacht about a mile off the coast of Baja, Ted wanted a geographically convenient neck to choke. The one belonging to the leader of the human resources department, Stewart, was the logical choice.

"Ted is concerned that a crisis may be upon us," Travis said. "We have our first 10Q filing coming up, and our controller has quit."

Sensing an opportunity to raise awareness about attrition, Charlie said, "The controller prefers to say she retired her TMC jersey."

"Charlie, is she currently an employee of TMC?"

"No."

"Will she be preparing the 10Q?"

"No."

"Then does it matter under what circumstances she left? Because SHE'S NOT HERE ANYMORE, IS SHE?"

"I see your point," Charlie acknowledged.

"YEAH! SHE ISN'T HERE ANYMORE, IS SHE?" Don felt the need to add value.

A testy discussion with Iago had left Travis agitated. Having bypassed the cell phone service issues by dialing shore-to-ship, he had had the ill-fated timing of reaching the finance executive as Iago was in the final throes of a forty-five-minute tussle with a sailfish. Never one to hold back his feelings, Iago let Travis know exactly how much he appreciated the interruption. He suggested that Stewart's HR team find the controller's replacement, given that he was entertaining someone whom he described as a future source of capital for TMC. Iago promised to return to HQ as soon as he landed this big investor. He thought it would take a week or two.

Knowing how critical investor interest was to TMC's success, and worked over by the CFO's tongue-lashing, Travis assumed Ted would give the CFO's prolonged absence a pass. Travis himself had no choice but to do so.

He turned to Vera, wiping his brow with the new hankie.

"You still haven't told me where Stewart is!"

Spraying the leaves of her plant with a homemade concoction of water and minerals, Vera pretended to spritz Don, who ducked, before she answered Travis.

"Stewart and Dandy are reviewing operations at the facility in Boulder."

"While we have this crisis?" Travis thundered.

"Yes, while we have this crisis?" Don echoed.

"Gentlemen, Stewart is on top of the situation. We were discussing the various solutions only an hour ago," Charlie offered.

"Are these actionable solutions?" Travis demanded.

"Yes, are they actionable?" Don seconded.

Vera and Charlie exchanged quick, questioning looks and made a unanimous executive decision.

"Very actionable." They answered in unison.

"Very good." Travis relaxed his frown.

"Yes, very good," repeated Don, who took the newer handkerchief from his boss. As he began to twist it, Vera took out her spray bottle and aimed it at him. He folded the moist material and put it in his pants pocket.

As they watched the two men waddle back to the boardroom, Vera turned to Charlie.

"You've got to tell me how much we pay Tweadle-Dee and Tweadle-Dom. I need to get me a job like that."

Charlie was amused by these nicknames. The EA roles were coveted because they provided access to real-time corporate strategy, bigwigs with deep pockets, and the personal connections that mattered. As Vera pointed out, the salary was not bad either. In exchange for visibility and long-term career benefits, Tweadle-Dee and Tweadle-Dom had to make sure everything was perfect, from the temperature of the coffee in the boardroom and the succinctness of the PowerPoint presentations to the timeliness, and personal habits, of the private pilots serving TMC's CEO and board of directors. Prerequisites for a career as an EA were an MBA, a father with the right golf buddies, Italian-leather loafers, and an all-star ability to kiss ass. Socks were optional.

"What are you doing?" Vera asked Charlie.

"Calling our executive search firm. We need them to find a controller quickly," Charlie answered her and pointed urgently to Vera's desk phone.

"Would you call Stewart and tell him that he's authorized an external candidate search for this key role so he has the party line in case Tweadle-Dee or Tweadle-Dom get to him before I do?"

V

E than Perrelle poured a cup of cold coffee from the dregs of the pot in the Chemix break room. He put the cup in the microwave and pressed the high button for a one-minute interval, during which time he yawned and stretched. Half-asleep, having gotten out of bed only thirty minutes earlier, he yawned again as he took a sip of the hot drink. The involuntary movement caused him to spill some on his shirt.

"Shit!" He hurriedly wiped it off and then threw the rest of the coffee out.

Ethan picked up his gear, which, for a Chemix quality engineer, consisted of a clipboard, a number two pencil, several forms, his Walkman, and protective eyewear. He set his CD player to Duran Duran's *Decade: Greatest Hits*, pulled the goggles over his glasses, and set off to examine the New Jersey plant for safety and environmental opportunities—plant jargon for problems that need fixing. "Hungry Like the Wolf" streamed through his headset as Ethan played air-guitar around the large expanse of the plant. Although he detested the *zing-zing-zing* of his alarm clock, he enjoyed the freedom of working when no one else was around.

The employees at this plant had worked together for a long time. Average tenure was close to eighteen years. The workers attended one another's Christmas parties and witnessed one another's weddings. Ethan rarely encountered issues at this plant. So, when Chemix's quality team was downsized to him, a peer, and his boss, he was unconcerned that he had not had the time to inspect this facility in several months. He peeked around corners of stacked boxes looking for telltale signs of spills, layers of dust, debris, or materials lying around, any of which would be a potential safety hazard. When Ethan heard the start to "All She Wants Is," visions of a lovely bridesmaid whom he met at his boss's wedding drifted across his mind. He turned up the sound to full volume and lost himself in the music and his fantasy.

As the song reached its crescendo, Ethan remembered her name.

"Audrey!"

He smiled, thinking that he would call this beauty and get his social life in order. Suddenly, a strong, unusual odor graced his nostrils. He sniffed up at the air in an effort to locate the offending material. His eyes became watery and his nostrils and throat burned as he took in a deep breath. He felt a little dizzy as he took a step forward. He lost his footing and fell into a hole in the floor.

"OWWWW! OWWWW! AHHHHH! HELP!! HELP!!!!"

Ethan jumped out of the hole and wiped his hands on his jeans. Through irritated, squinting eyes, he looked around for anything that could get this slimy gel off his body. The liquid dripped down his slacks and onto the floor, making for a slick surface. He fell again. Racing to get out of the muck, Ethan slipped and fell a third time. His skin was itchy and turning red with blotchy patches. It began to burn.

"I've got to get out of here!"

Ethan crawled across the floor, ripping off the headphones and disconnecting them from the CD player in the process. The "Planet Earth" track filled the empty warehouse as he reached for an emergency phone on the wall and hit speed dial for his boss, Johnny Egan.

The last thing Ethan remembered was throwing up on the floor of the emergency room of St. Alban's Hospital.

WHEN CAROL ARRIVED at her office that morning, she found a new mound of pink message slips on her desk.

Why can't that birdbrain of an assistant take care of these calls for me?

Most of the messages were from Johnny Egan, who, as the manager of Chemix's quality team, was a direct report to Carol.

That guy begged for time off for his wedding, and now he's calling me from his honeymoon. What an idiot.

The messages were marked urgent and referenced a chemical leak at one of the plants. The last one read: "CALL ME NOW!" In parentheses underneath this message, Carol's administrative assistant had written, "Johnny told me to write the message this way. Sorry."

As Carol picked up the phone to call Johnny, she noticed Bob Smith briskly approaching her office. Loyalty was a personal hallmark of Bob's, so he had not turned out to be the dispirited and underappreciated executive that Scott Landing had hoped to present to his AmBeeance client.

"Where have you been? Why didn't you reply to my messages? I've been calling you all morning!" Bob shouted as he ran into Carol's office. She kicked her expensive-looking heels off and under her desk, as the designer shoes would be a giveaway that she had had an interview that morning. Fed up with what she perceived as her boss's lack of appreciation for her talents, Carol had replied with gusto to Scott's next inquiry about a senior-level executive opening. Tomas Severe, chairman of the board of directors for StreamLINE Corporation, was keenly interested in fueling his personal investment in the financially solid but slower-moving freight and logistics company. He told Scott that he wanted to hire a vice president of operations who would not allow anything to get in the way of growing the business fast. Scott did not know how far the chairman was actually willing to go to get superior results, but he had a hunch that Carol Himmler would be the right one to push that envelope.

Bob noticed Carol's cell phone on the desk and picked it up.

"Carol, this isn't even turned on!"

Slipping her feet into flats, Carol grabbed the phone from him. She had turned it off before her interview with Tomas. After all, he was recruiting for a direct report to, and possible heir apparent for, the sixty-five-year-old chief executive officer of StreamLINE, a company with annual revenue of $2 billion. This was a leadership platform that Carol eagerly coveted. Phone calls would have been a distraction.

"Give me that. It's been on the fritz. I told Gayle to get it fixed. One more in a long line of reasons why I need a new assistant." She tossed the phone into the trash. "What's up?" Carol hoped to sound interested but not alarmed.

"Several chemical containers at the plant have been breached. Sounds like one was so bad it created a crater in the floor. Carol, how did this happen? Johnny and his quality team were supposed to be checking these containers each month! Now we have a crater in the middle of the production floor, employees concerned about their health, and a disposal issue to deal with. Wait until the Department of Environmental Protection gets a hold of this news!" Bob was furious.

"Were they called?"

"Not yet. I can't get a clear answer on what is going on at that plant. One of us has to go and assess the situation first. I was getting in my car when I saw you."

"I'll go."

"We can go together. I'll bring my car around out front."

"No. It's my responsibility. Let me assess the damage and I'll call you with a full report. Besides, someone should stay here to hold down the fort."

Carol grabbed her car keys, took her assistant's cell phone, and ran out before Bob could argue with her. If there was damage, she was determined to control the public relations impact.

She called Johnny from the road.

"What's going on, Johnny? I let you take a honeymoon and then all hell breaks loose!" Carol barked at her quality manager, frantic that news of a chemical leak could destroy her chances of getting that executive job at StreamLINE.

Worn out by the morning's discovery of the two-inch deep, eighteen-inch wide crater, Johnny was on his sixth cup of cold, black coffee. As he removed the mouthpiece he had been wearing, he thought about the damage the chemicals could do to the lungs of his preteen children from his first marriage, which had been abruptly interrupted when his bar-dancer girlfriend became pregnant.

Johnny had cut short his honeymoon with the dancer, at the local Motel Suites Deluxe, when he received the call from Ethan at four o'clock in the morning. Johnny had been with Chemix for twelve years, and he had worked on Carol's quality team for the past two. During those twenty-four months, his budget had been cut four times, and he had let two-thirds of his team go in successive rounds of layoffs.

While making plans for the first workforce reduction, Carol encouraged

Johnny to leverage the plant employees in Mexico and Malaysia to do their own quality work. Later in the year, before Christmas bonuses were distributed, Carol wanted to demonstrate more productivity and cost savings. She dismissed Johnny's concerns about cutting back further by pointing out that there had not been a blip in quality in the Mexico and Malaysia plants. Johnny grudgingly acquiesced when Carol suggested that if he did not downsize his team again, she would do it for him, and she was not so sure she would need a quality manager if she had to be the one making the tough calls.

Johnny reduced his team to himself and two engineers. Together, they were responsible for production quality globally, with ten plants in North and South America and Asia. Johnny's own quality of life deteriorated. He found himself on the road most weeks, inspecting plants outside the U.S. He left his two overworked quality engineers to tend to the domestic plants.

Exhausted, and astounded by Carol's tone, Johnny stammered a reply.

"We, we . . . we have a leak," was all he could offer. Then he added, "We have several leaks."

"Isn't it your job to make sure that toxic chemical containers don't get breached? How could you have let me down, Johnny?"

When Carol's directive around inventory controls affected the number of available containers, Johnny and his team sought to make lemonade, this time by combining elements within containers. Johnny now feared that this decision not only might have led to the breached containers but also might be highly detrimental to the area groundwater.

"And what's your plan to fix this mess?"

From the comfort of her air-conditioned car, Carol screamed at Johnny's suggestion that the state authorities be contacted. New Jersey's Department of Environmental Protection assessed stiff penalties and fines for environmental contamination. Infuriated with Johnny's lack of creativity, Carol crossed quickly out of berating mode and into insidious disdain. "Now, why would you call the DEP?"

It's just a lucky break that Johnny doesn't have the place swarming with police already, Carol considered.

"T-t-t-to assess and d-d-d, d-d-dispose of these c-c-c-containers," he stuttered.

With a lot at stake, Carol sped up.

"Imagine the community outrage over this leak, Johnny. Chemix's quality function would lose all credibility. I know that Chemix has asked your team to make huge sacrifices, but people outside this company won't know that. If news of this condition leaks, jobs could be lost and mouths could be left unfed," she suggested to the fifty-two-year-old father of two with a third child on the way.

"No, no," Carol continued. "We—you—should find an alternative to deal with this predicament, Johnny. We need to think constructively, not panic. Who do we know who can help with this problem? Think outside the box. I'll be there in thirty minutes."

Carol threw the phone on the seat beside her and floored the accelerator.

V I

A refreshing scent of mint lingered in Sal's office despite incessant cleaning. As Lenny sprayed Sal's desk with a disinfectant, his cell buzzed in his pants pocket.

"Hey! Tiny, how the frig are ya?" He greeted his cousin. "No friggin' kiddin'!" Lenny listened as Sal's assistant Giana mopped the floor.

"Yeah. That sounds good, but I gotta check wit' the boss 'cause we got a lotta work 'round here. Sounds like it could be a good payday, huh? That would get his attention. He'll be here in a little while. I'll call you back."

Lenny walked around Giana to refill his coffee.

"Nobody said nothin' about moppin' floors when I took dis job!" Giana rinsed out the mop.

Lenny Knuckles, or Lucky Lenny, as he was also known, grunted. He had been out late the previous evening distributing dental products to Sal's business partners. Lenny had earned one of his nicknames because of his uncanny ability to pick winners at the racetrack. Giana assumed the other one referred to his love life. She mopped closer to his desk.

"I look like Cinderella or somethin'?" She pushed at his feet with the wet mop and he lifted them.

Sal, in black silk shirt and linen slacks, entered the office carrying a brown paper bag. He shook raindrops off his clothes and stomped his feet to dry off his brand-new shoes. Giana turned on the espresso machine.

"Goddamn rain," Sal said, wiping the sides of his shoes with a napkin.

"I dunno WHY you wear doze bee-YOU-tiful shoes in dis weatha," Giana said. She blew a bubble with the gum in her mouth and poured a short cup of black coffee for Sal.

"Thanks for the espresso, but how many times I gotta tell you, appearances are everything! Get rid of the gum."

She blew another bubble, this time popping it for effect.

Sal did not want to argue with his bookkeeper. Tall, attractive, hourglass-figured, Giana was eye candy around the drab office. She was also the widow of a former business associate. Sal had asked Giana to do his books after her husband was found facedown in the gutter outside a nightclub. With three small children to care for and no formal education after high school, Giana was grateful for the job. Keeping track of Sal's business affairs turned out to be a straightforward recording of the week's take in an accounting notebook, which Sal kept locked in the office safe. Giana was not the sharpest knife in the drawer, but Sal did not want a certified public accountant keeping his financial house in order.

"Friggin' wife didn't fix my watch yet. I need a new one." Sal took five Rolex boxes out of the bag and opened each one on his desk.

"Wow." Giana reached out to pick up a box. Sal slapped her wrist.

"You know what this costs?" He slipped one with a platinum face around his wrist. "Whaddaya think?" He held his wrist up for Lenny to see.

"Nice."

"I can't decide between this one and the white gold."

Giana took a lap around the desk to check out the choices. Sal raised his eyebrows.

"I'm not touchin' nothin'! You want an opinion or what?"

Sal had to give her credit. For a single mom on a limited income, she had balls. He handed her a box.

"You put Sunday's game money in the safe?"

Giana gave Sal a do-I-look-like-an-idiot face.

"I'm making sure, is all. We got a lot of expenses around here, and it's important that the cash keeps flowing."

Sal sniffed the minty air.

Lenny sighed. "We had a little accident last night moving da inventory. Some mouthwash spilled. We wiped it up."

"Open a friggin' window, why don't you?" Vexed at the pungent reminder of his strained income prospects, Sal collected the watches and put them back in the paper bag, which he locked in a desk drawer.

"And why are cards lying around from Thursday's game? Why can't we keep this friggin' place neat?" Sal tossed cards from the poker table into the trash. "Control is critical, Lenny, especially in a complex operation like ours. No different from some big company. We start to get a little sloppy and some people might get the wrong idea."

Embarrassed, Lenny collected the chips left on the table and threw a few dirty napkins into the trash.

"Speaking of business interests, how'd your conversation go with that new card shop down the block?"

Relieved that the conversation changed to a topic that would draw attention to his strengths, Lenny explained.

"All good, boss. They got da message pretty quick. All it took was a coupla mean looks at da grandpa's wheelchair and one, two, tree, we had an agreement."

Sal was pleased with this news, though the feeling was short-lived. He opened the mail, and his credit card statements put him in a funk.

"Between the boss's points and my wife's being pissed off all the time, I'm going broke. We got to get new lines of business going."

Sal had a lot on his mind. His wife recently presented him with an estimate for a new in-ground pool. He had acquiesced to this demand after she found size-five panties in the back of his SUV. She wore a size eight.

Sal had not figured in decking around the pool during the argument about the panties. His wife also ordered imported tile for the coping as well as the patio. When the architect suggested an outdoor kitchen, Sal's wife ordered a stainless steel cooker and smoker. ("What the fuck's a smoker?" Sal inquired regarding the $2,500 add-on).

Sal took the newspaper from Lenny's desk and searched through the sports section.

"Let's see what Vegas says about the fight this Saturday. These fights are essential to our future, with that Park Ridge business going to Antonio's crew. I still can't believe the big boss gave it to another crew. That friggin' business is like an annuity stream."

"Anna who?" More familiar with instruments of physical commerce than financial, Lenny did not understand the analogy.

"Fuggedaboudit."

Sal had been counting on revenue from the North Jersey territory even before teak furniture had entered his wife's outdoor picture. With that piece of business having been reassigned to another crew, he really felt the financial pinch.

Sal sat down. "I don't get it. We been doing real good, especially with the playoffs."

He looked to Lenny for affirmation.

"Yeah," his number two responded.

"And I helped the boss with that situation in Atlantic City. In fact, we took care of the whole thing."

"Yep."

"And it wasn't an easy thing!"

"Tell me about it."

Lenny brought Sal an espresso refill.

"Boss, my cousin Tiny called. Turns out he picked up work over at Chemix International, and sounds like they got a cleanup job for us."

"Is that the company over by the river? How dirty is it?" Sal eyed Lenny curiously.

"Yeah, by the river. He works in manufacturing of chemicals and shit.

They had some kinda spill, and it's not so good for that new housing development they are building in the area. So, they need to make the accident go away."

Lenny thought he did a good job summing up the proposition.

"Sounds like it could be a big problem for a big company."

Lenny nodded. "Yeah. Poor slobs could lose their jobs if the company goes out of business."

"Wouldn't be great for our cash flow, either, dopey. Those guys are some of our regular customers. Where's your truck?" Sal asked.

"Out back. Are you thinkin' it might be a nice day for a long ride down to the shore?"

"I'm thinking that kind of work—doing a favor for a big company—that should be good cash."

"My cousin said his boss—get this, it's a woman that's his boss. I told him he was in the wrong line of work. Whateva. This boss lady is gonna be there in a little while, and we could work out the details directly wit' her."

CAROL PULLED UP to the plant after a thirty-minute drive at 80 miles per hour. Luckily, no cops were around to remind her of the legal speed limit.

"Where's Ethan?" Carol waved off the cotton mask Johnny offered her.

Johnny explained that Ethan had discovered the leak during an early-morning review of the facility. Mixing it up with the crater made Ethan a casualty, with chemical burns on his hands, feet, and knees.

Carol asked to be taken to the crater.

"Sure," Johnny said, pulling his mask over his mouth and nose.

"Tiny is down there," he mumbled through his mask.

"I can't understand a damn word you are saying." She ripped the mask off Johnny and threw it on the floor. "Don't you know anything about chemicals? The damage is likely already done. Don't be a sissy."

Carol marched toward the back of the plant. Johnny raced down the aisle after her.

"You said you wanted us to be creative, so it turns out Tiny has a cousin," he said.

"Who the hell is Tiny?" Carol asked.

Carol looked at the beeping phone she carried. Bob had been calling.

Screw that guy, Carol thought.

What bothered her most about this whole situation was that Bob knew about it.

Mr. Goody Two-Shoes is going to want to help fix this. "Urgh!" Carol exclaimed.

As they approached a hole in the floor, Johnny introduced Tiny, one of the workers who unloaded material on the dock. Johnny explained that, at his urging, Tiny had reached out to his cousin who worked for a local waste management company. The UMess=RMess Remediation team was on its way.

Tiny offered his hand but Carol ignored it. The phone in her pocket beeped again. She walked around the edge of the crater. A dark greenish slime covered the bottom. The stink was overpowering, and it made her eyes water. She took Tiny's mask from him and held it over her mouth.

"Pretty bad, huh?" Tiny carefully maneuvered around the hole.

"This?" Carol pointed forcefully at the crater.

"Uh, yeah," Tiny answered tentatively, looking behind him in case he missed another hole.

"It's not so big." Carol's nonchalance frightened both men.

Carol looked at the containers, now less full of waste thanks to the cracks and crevices evident around each of them. She took a step back and scanned the production lines around the area. She noticed that the lines were different from the ones her team had put in two years earlier, and she remarked on that.

"Bob's team put in new equipment about two months ago, when we revised the product line. Right above you here"—Johnny pointed to the beginning of the new line—"to that section over there." He pointed to a different end.

"The cable suspending that conveyor belt is made of steel, isn't it?" Carol asked.

Johnny nodded.

"I have to imagine if one of those cables snapped . . ." Carol snapped her fingers hard. Johnny and Tiny were puzzled.

"It would flip around with great force, enough to tear into any material in its way."

Johnny and Tiny looked at each other and then at Carol. They agreed with her assessment.

Carol stared at the production line and the cables more intently. She asked for wire cutters, strong enough to cut through the cables.

"Why?" Johnny and Tiny asked in unison.

She looked at them with contempt. Tiny went to get the cable cutters, glad to be away from the unpleasantness, to say nothing of the leak.

Recalling basics from her physics classes, Carol pulled a cart underneath the part of the new production line that was closest to the chemical waste containers. Tiny returned with the cable cutters. Carol instructed Johnny to climb on the cart and cut one of the longest cables.

"This one here," she pointed to a cable. "Based on its length, torque, and proximity to the containers, it ought to swing wildly in that direction."

Johnny looked incredulously at his boss.

"Someone or something is going to get hit with the cable as soon as I cut it loose." He thought she must not understand what she was asking him to do.

"Johnny, you have two bright—promising, in fact—children from one marriage, alimony payments to a loyal wife of twenty years, and a new family to provide for. Didn't you say your new wife also had young kids of her own?"

Tiny did not get where this was going. Johnny was afraid he might.

"If I had those obligations, I would be concerned about losing my job and maybe even prison time, given the damage to the water table in the surrounding community. Now, if this leak were caused by an accident, say by a break in the new production line, then Johnny and his quality team are not at fault."

Johnny started climbing the cart.

It took some work, but after a few minutes of cutting, tugging, and pulling, Johnny yelled, "Take cover!" and the cable snapped. The production platform shook a bit, but Carol had been correct about the trajectory. The cable swung and then landed wildly on and around the containers of chemical waste, punching a few new holes. Sparks flew from the speed and power released by the swinging cable as it hit the floor, tables, and walls in its unpredictable path. With every whip of the cable, Johnny and Tiny scurried like agitated rats in a maze.

Amid the commotion of the ricocheting cable, Sal slipped into the plant unnoticed. He approached confidently, walking straight toward the small group. Lenny followed his boss, albeit more cautiously, never taking his eyes off the swinging, sparking cable.

"Wow," Sal said. "Looks like the Fourth of July in here."

Sal unbuttoned his coat and handed it to Lenny. His silk shirt and charcoal-gray slacks were striking against the drab factory floor. Assessing the crater, Sal let out a long, thoughtful whistle. He stepped around the gaping hole in the floor while Johnny, Tiny, and Lenny stood back in amazement. Carol, standing astride a gently dancing cable, was clearly the boss lady to whom Lenny had referred earlier. Sal admired her cool, particularly in contrast to the fear in the eyes of the men. He extended his hand.

"Sal Scruci of UMess=RMess Remediation. We are in the business of solving other people's problems."

Carol gripped his hand and introduced herself.

Tiny whispered in Lenny's ear as he embraced his cousin, "Watch out for her."

Sal walked around the crater and looked at the three containers, dripping even more from the new punctures. While the others backed away from the burning sensation, Sal maintained eye contact with Carol.

"I can see you have a problem, Ms. Himmler."

Carol realized that it was past the time that Scott was to call her about that job with StreamLINE. She thought about her own phone, ringing away in the trash can in her office. She was growing weary of this problem.

"Great. So you'll get rid of—eradicate—this matter, right?" She brushed dust off her suit.

"Well, yes. We may have a solution for you. When do you need this done?"

Carol considered the question. He was either not bright or not finished with her.

"Well, of course, time is of the essence."

"Anybody aware of this outside your own outfit?" Sal asked.

"Not that I am aware of." Carol looked hard at Johnny, who raised his shoulders and palms in a how-do-I-know gesture.

"Going to take a few guys to move this stuff out."

Johnny asked, "Where will you take it?"

Carol glared at him.

"We got facilities just right for this type of spring cleaning," Sal explained.

Without speaking, Tiny mimed to his cousin, "South Jersey?"

Lenny's eyes told Tiny to shut up.

Sal continued. "Transportation, workers, storage. This adds up, you know. And there's got to be a premium for speed. We'd be putting off lucrative business opportunities to get this done for you."

"Can you move this out of here now and get this place cleaned up so it looks like new this evening?" Carol asked.

"Done."

"And can you make that go away?" Carol pointed to the crater.

Sal nodded that it would be done.

"It is what it is. Get it done. Johnny can settle up with you."

Sal offered his hand again. Carol took it.

"Pleasure ma'am. Look forward to doing business with you again sometime."

"What other remediation do you do?"

"We do every kind of cleanup you might need," Sal replied, smiling.

Tiny whispered to Lenny, "Yeah, and some you might not want to imagine."

Lenny smacked the back of his cousin's head.

Citing pressing business concerns, Carol hurried out to the parking lot. Johnny followed her.

"Here's the number for Ethan," Johnny said as he handed Carol a piece of paper.

"I have his home phone number at the office."

"This is his number in the hospital room. I thought you'd want to go by there today." Johnny explained that as far as he knew, Ethan should recover fine, after burn treatments and physical therapy.

"What? Don't you think we have more important work to do, Johnny, than bring flowers to someone who already has doctors and nurses waiting on him hand and foot?"

"Oh." Johnny was dumbstruck. "Who should call the reporter, then?"

"What reporter?" Carol asked.

"A reporter called and said she heard Ethan was injured in a work-related accident."

Johnny held another piece of paper with a different phone number on it. Carol grabbed that paper from him.

"Why do I feel like I am always pulling information out of you, Johnny?"

Johnny put the note with Ethan's hospital phone number back in his pocket.

"Here, give me Ethan's number too. Why don't you order a huge bouquet of flowers for his room. Sign the card from me."

Johnny had something else on his mind. He leaned on the car door but did not say anything.

Carol was eager to find out if StreamLINE was going to make her an offer. "What is it, for Christ's sake?"

"Carol, in Sal's business, we now owe him a big favor."

Carol's familiarity with organized crime consisted of an occasional mobster movie, news reports about gangsters and their paid-for politicians, and the practical ramifications of a random waste management strike. For Carol, "wise guy" was an over-the-top moniker for a bully who strong-armed bureaucrats and milked government operations. How hard could that be? Since she did not gamble, use drugs, or have an uncontrollable urge to satisfy any other base human desire, Carol was not worried about Sal, Lenny, his cousin Tiny, or any other member of the family.

Carol started the car. "Johnny, Sal Scruci is a businessman. I am sure we will pay highway-robbery prices for him to cart away this issue. That's favor enough."

Besides, by the time Sal comes back around to collect on his favor, I will be long gone, she thought. *Johnny will have to deal with Sal.*

Carol pressed the gas pedal and peeled out of the parking lot.

SAL INSTRUCTED LENNY and Tiny to move the containers into Lenny's truck.

"But boss, we don't have the right clothes for dis job. See what the chemicals did to that cement floor?"

Tiny nodded furiously behind his cousin.

"What are you afraid of? A little Clorox gets on your nice clothes? We made a deal with these people. 'U' mess is 'our' mess? Get it? Last guy couldn't do a job, we found a replacement for him when he had to go to the hospital. Remember that guy?"

The poisonous mix of chemicals in the air overpowered Lenny's low blood pressure, causing him to sway as he dutifully listened to his boss. *I don't need to be carrying that load out myself, fuggedabout the containers,* Sal thought as Lenny's swaying convinced him that this was a job for a larger crew.

Luckily, Lenny had a few cousins who spent their days shaking down gamblers. Bored with the thin traffic at the track given a light racing schedule, they jumped at the opportunity to make a few bucks. Sal was not happy with the extra cost, but he wanted out of that plant fast, before someone from the state got wind of the problem. He decided to allow the additional manpower, provided that most of the cousins' cut came out of Lenny's end.

Speaking of cuts, Sal thought as he sliced a few pieces of the snapped cable line.

"Souvenirs," he said in response to Lenny's inquiring eyes.

VII

O n her way back to the office, Carol called Scott Landing. He was exasperated.

"Where have you been? I've been trying to reach you! Tomas LOVES you! He wants you to start immediately, or as soon as possible. Whichever comes first." Pleased with his keen assessment of his client's needs—Scott knew Tomas would be moved by Carol's long legs—Scott patted himself on the back. He also figured StreamLINE's leadership team would eventually grow weary of Carol's hard-ass personality, so her looks would help, even if her severe beauty had something of an evil edge.

The StreamLINE leadership put together an extraordinary financial offer, which Scott detailed. Besides a generous base salary, a guaranteed bonus, and eye-catching stock awards, the proposal also included a company car, country club membership, and a luxury condominium to serve as Carol's corporate apartment.

"It won't be long before they're calling you 'Madame President,'" Scott joked with his candidate.

"I prefer simply to be called by my first name. I think that's more in keeping with the current cultural norms, don't you think?"

Scott did not allow himself to dwell on Carol's narcissism, nor the stunning ignorance that resulted from it. After all, without another ruthlessly focused candidate to present, he could not afford to look this corporate gift horse in the mouth.

"Simply Carol. I like it," he offered.

By almost anyone's standards, the StreamLINE offer was embarrassingly rich. However, Carol did not know how to be embarrassed. She wanted to make sure she did not leave anything on the table.

"Hmm. I love the company and simply adored Tomas. What a fascinating multinational character. Did you know he grew up in Spain? However, as my representative, you wouldn't presume that I leave the work I'm doing with my great Chemix team for that paltry offer, would you? I mean, I wouldn't want Tomas to get the idea that I am not a good negotiator . . .

Yes, Scott. I understand. That's why you are the recruiter and I am merely the talented executive . . . Yes. You do that. Go fix it for me and we have a deal."

Carol's next move was to express profound sorrow about her employee's condition—in a call back to the reporter. A youthful, female voice answered the phone.

Clare Woodard, editor of her college newspaper and president of the senior class, was fiercely committed to her responsibilities. Inspired by the sacrifices of wartime correspondents, the journalism student considered it an honor to keep a scanner in her dorm room. Earlier that morning, the normal crackling had been interrupted by a series of bloodcurdling screams in the background as an EMS technician radioed in a burn trauma en route to the emergency room of St. Alban's Hospital. Clare threw a sweatshirt over her pajamas, laced up her sneakers, and jumped into her Volkswagen Bug.

The ER nurses and doctors were too consumed with the victims of a city bus accident to notice the college reporter sneak behind Ethan's bedside curtain. However, Clare's probing inquiries were met with a consistent refrain thanks to the influence of mind-numbing painkillers: a long, loud snore. Ethan did return to consciousness long enough to tell her his name and position at Chemix. It was not much of a challenge for the ace reporter to trace Ethan back to Johnny and Carol.

The well-informed reporter recalled Carol's name and story from the newspaper clipping she had of Carol soldering a cable on a Chemix conveyor belt. An avid proponent of opportunities for women, Clare taped that picture, flanked by images of World War II's Rosie the Riveter and a thin list of female CEOs serving Fortune 1000 companies, to the wall above her desk. The picture of Carol assuming a typically male role, accompanied by an article on Chemix's next-generation facility, encouraged Clare's calling as champion of authentic leadership. She was pleased that Carol returned her call; to her it was further proof that the Chemix executive was an inspirational manager.

"Ethan Perrin is such a devoted employee. Yes, I meant to say Perrelle. Of course I know my employee's name. This has been a busy day."

Carol described "the mishap" as a minor spill that had already been addressed. Clare asked a few who, what, when, where, why, and how questions but sensed that another angle would be of greater interest to her readers. She pressed Carol for details on how she had guided her team during this crisis.

Desperate to get this reporter off the chemical leak story, Carol delightedly indulged Clare's interest in her managerial skills: "I believe in leading by example, Clare." She went so far as to hint at an exclusive on her next career move. Thrilled at the prospect of a groundbreaking business news story for her university newspaper, Clare jotted down Carol's fabricated examples of her executive courage and provided her contact information so that Carol could set up their next conversation.

Carol's second call was to her boss, Ed. She explained that the cleanup of a minor leak was already under way and that Ethan's injuries, while unfortunate, were the result of improper footwear. She also told him that, while they were not yet sure how it had happened, one of the cables securing the new production line had snapped and was lying in and around the damaged containers.

"I don't know what Bob was thinking, putting in those new lines," Carol said. "The facilities we had would have been more than adequate to support the new manufacturing processes. Maybe he's preoccupied. Have you heard the rumors that he is interviewing outside Chemix?"

Carol informed her boss that the DEP would conduct an independent investigation. She neglected to mention that she was assuming such an investigation would be launched once she informed the agency about the leaks—which she intended to do as soon as Johnny reported that UMess=RMess had scrubbed the evidence.

"By the way, this is the last mess I'll be cleaning up, Ed. I'm accepting an offer to join StreamLINE Corporation as vice president of operations. They are a progressive, risk-taking organization, and they value my experience. Good luck, Ed. For what it's worth, I'd keep an eye on Bob."

Before the close of business, Carol reached out to the editor of *Economic Week*, the most widely respected business publication in the country. Despite what she had promised Clare, Carol gave the exclusive interview about her career move to a reporter at this publication, setting herself up with national exposure as she assumed her new executive role with StreamLINE.

VIII

Despite admonitions about his blood pressure from the Canyon Plateau spa director, Stewart fell back into old, albeit successful, habits upon his return to everyday life.

As Iago leveraged his anticipated future wealth from TMC shares on fast cars and faster women, Stewart spun the CFO's absence from day-to-day business activities as part of a strategy to build relationships with investors. Stewart also stepped up Iago's coverage, working with TMC's public relations team to get Iago chosen as keynote speaker at another event, the Latin American Trade Exposition, conveniently held at a resort in Baja near where the senior financial officer had been fishing. The photo opportunity alone was too good to be missed. It put TMC back in the news, this time from an international venue.

In the meantime, Stewart decided to upgrade the open controller position to vice president.

"You've got to make the controller job sound bigger!" Stewart yelled at Charlie over the phone from the deck of his lake house, where he was helping his wife prepare for a dinner party they would host that evening. "You should mention in the job description that TMC has several patents on unique satellite technologies. And that we have a promising consumer business, in addition to large contracts with corporations and government organizations."

As he snapped at Charlie to get the executive search into higher gear, Stewart nodded to a florist who was offering centerpiece choices for his dining room table. He pointed to his preference, an arrangement of South

American roses and Asiatic lilies lying flat in a hand-painted pan of water. In the background, Stewart's wife, Mariellen, tossed overcooked meatballs down the trash compactor. A distressed caterer raced to intercept her carefully prepared hors d'oeuvres before they hit the blades. Stewart's father would be joining them for dinner, and the elder Narciss liked his meat cooked medium rare, full stop. In recent years, he had taken to carrying a thermometer in his jacket pocket. Mariellen had determined that these meatballs just would not do for her father-in-law.

An only child, Stewart was coddled by his mother, but Mariellen knew that her husband found it difficult to rise to his father's expectations. A man of few words, the elder Narciss chose the most painful ones to communicate with his offspring. When the lanky Stewart did not make the lacrosse team at Hightower Academy, his father commented, "No matter. Lacrosse is a sport for people who are coordinated." Accompanied by Junior, his new multicolored sphynx cat, Stewart's father retired to his study and the comfort of tangible operating reports for his family's business conglomerate. Stewart's mom withdrew to a large bottle of gin.

When Stewart's croquet mallet accidentally smashed the thumb of Rosewood Prep's team captain the day before the championship game, leaving Stewart without a pal in the entire school, his father remarked, "We won the championship all four years I was captain at Prep." He purchased a second, black and white, hairless cat that he named Precious Child (or Precious, for short). He buried his embarrassment at his son's clumsiness by reviewing advertisements for the signature product of the Narciss confectionery empire. The marketing campaign for Narciss Nuggets, the top-selling, nugget-shaped chewing gum, featured a family of three blowing bubbles into a circle formed by their clasped hands. Underneath the picture was an award-winning catchphrase: *Narciss Nuggets Breed Bonds*. Stewart's mother crashed her Mercedes coupe into a life-size marble replica of the successful advertisement on the front lawn of corporate headquarters and then checked into Cliffridge Cottage, the local sanitarium, for an extended rest.

With his emotional buffer AWOL, Stewart sought refuge in the manufactured communities created by the beachcomber movies of the

1960s—particularly appealing were the characters of the *Gidget* series. As he progressed from high school to university, he began to reinvent himself. A surfboard became his regular backseat companion, and his standard uniform consisted of flip-flops, sideburns, and bleached hair. A minor negative to his evolving look was the tangerine hue his hair acquired as a result of do-it-yourself dye jobs. Though the Great Lakes did not offer the athletic challenge of coastal waters, Stewart was still not much better at surfing than at lacrosse. Yet, the physical beatings inflicted by hundreds of pounds of water pummeling his body temporarily cleansed his psyche of his feelings of inadequacy.

Stewart applied the lessons from those waves to his management style, pummeling his team with sometimes unrealistic demands.

When Stewart complained that the executive search to find a controller was taking too long, Charlie reminded his boss that the last time TMC rushed the search for an executive, they ended up offering a job to N.O. Audette.

"We might have averted that situation if we'd taken a little more time on the process, Stewart. We didn't do a thorough reference check on Audette."

"Charlie, I personally conducted the references on Audette. The wife of TMC's audit committee chair sat on the board of a major municipal theater with him. She said he was delightful."

"Did we get references from anyone who worked for him?"

"Audette gave me the number for his controller, but that guy never returned my calls!"

Charlie thought better of reminding his boss that the controller may have been otherwise fixated at the time of Stewart's calls—specifically, to the floor of the stockroom.

"Just rewrite the job description so it sounds more impactful, Charlie. This VP position is a BIG role. For Christ's sake, we are growing at almost 75 percent a quarter. Stock options alone should be a great motivator to join TMC."

Stewart hung up to referee the escalating meatball altercation. His father would be arriving shortly.

"Mind the heirloom gladiolas by the sink!" he called to Mariellen.

With Iago successfully repositioned and Charlie leading the search for a controller, Stewart intended to invite his father and the cats to join him and Mariellen on their upcoming trip to the Caribbean, where Stewart planned to inspect island property for his real estate portfolio. His father had never owned property outside the United States. Aside from Cuba in the 1940s, Stewart was not sure his father had ever set foot in the Caribbean. As for the animals, though his father took great care of his pets—as evidenced by their unusually long lives—Stewart thought the cats would benefit from international exposure, too. He organized an itinerary that was sure to impress.

"Can you imagine? Fresh seafood every day for the cats. They're hardly getting that once a week at home," Stewart explained to Mariellen as he picked up shards of the dinner plates she dropped upon learning that Stewart wanted Junior and Precious, as well as his father, to join them on St. Bart's.

I X

Not even two weeks after Dandy's contingency plan was approved, the TV in TMC's cafeteria displayed cheering longshoremen just after they voted to strike.

The company's factory workers watched the news with great interest. A few of the hourly employees sighed as the longshoremen clasped hands and raised them above their heads in a sign of solidarity. There were murmurs of concern about what this would mean for TMC's workforce. Suspended shifts? Layoffs? The production floor manager assuaged their fears. Dandy, the undisputed supply-chain thought leader, had a plan, the manager told them.

Since receiving the text message in Colorado about the possible strike, Dandy had been working to align the necessary resources for TMC to successfully ride it out. First, he informed TMC leadership and his operations team that he had assurances, from long-standing contacts in the Long Beach Board of Harbor Commissioners, that the city council would not allow a work stoppage to last long. Second, he persuaded the board of directors to approve a large, out-of-budget expenditure to pay commercial air transport companies to fly component parts directly to U.S. factories from manufacturers in Asia. This work-around would enable TMC to continue production and delivery during the strike. Although it would decrease the operating margin, Dandy reminded the board of the assurances of the Harbor Commission—a short strike—and his own track record of successfully manipulating expenses.

Ted reached Stewart during his weekend on St. Barts and told him to work up a human resources angle around customer experience and the longshoremen walkout.

"If TMC is going to take a margin hit, we might as well let customers know what we are doing to ensure that they are not affected by this strike. And get back home pronto. I need you here to find a controller with a sharp pencil who can fix these profitability challenges. Iago is a useless goofball, even if he is the CFO."

Several of TMC's competitors contracted with air transport carriers, too, but for multiple weeks of service. Dandy directed his finance team to crunch the numbers and calculate risk in the event the strike dragged on. That analysis indicated that the cost of maintaining this expensive air-transport system for more than a week would erode margins almost completely. Although his finance team suggested that their competitors' strategy provided insurance against greater risk, Dandy thought otherwise. He trusted the outlook offered by the Long Beach politicians, people with whom he had fostered partnerships over many years as TMC's sourcing of product from Asia increased.

"The longshoremen live paycheck to paycheck. Besides, the cargo-handling companies are crying about the lucrative contracts the unions already have. They claim there isn't anything more to give the longshoremen," a Long Beach Harbor Commissioner told Dandy. "This strike will be over in a week."

When the strike moved to day ten, TMC's operations team scrambled to address the expanding backlog of orders missing critical chips, receivers, and connectors sourced from abroad. The commercial air transport companies functioned at full capacity and struggled to find additional aircraft to address burgeoning demand. Any additional airplanes enlisted came at a premium price, one that was passed along (times two) to the fastest bidder. TMC paid the exorbitant fees to get finished product to its customers in a timely fashion, just as Stewart's customer-experience campaign had promised.

X

S tewart often contrived personnel issues that required interaction with members of TMC's board of directors, thereby amplifying his power and influence, at least in his own mind. After the excursion to the Colorado ranch, Dandy's obvious attraction to Oneida became a focal point of conversations with Rick, the chairman of TMC's Compensation Committee and, as such, a board member critical to Stewart's agenda. Stewart reminded Rick that with Dandy directing the critical supply chain, TMC shares had increased in value despite the strike, which Stewart described as a short-term blip. Stewart casually mentioned that Dandy was making plans to see Oneida again. Rick responded enthusiastically to the suggestion that Dandy be introduced to Rocky Mountain organizations through which the TMC executive could shape a positive public profile.

"We'd like Dandy to feel special—to know that his leadership contributions are valued. Also, any free publicity will be good for TMC," Stewart told Rick.

With encouragement from Stewart, a wink from Ted, and the support of Rick's network, Dandy began inventing reasons to return to the Boulder facility. Rick presented Dandy to regional business leaders and real estate barons who had been seeking new blood for their philanthropic pursuits. Most critically, he swayed Oneida, his long-term houseguest, to give Dandy confidence that his interest in her was reciprocated. With Stewart suggesting that Dandy explore his talents, Rick's contacts pushing him to express himself, and Oneida physically taking him to the edge of his known universe, Dandy began to heed his own press—especially those articles that Stewart arranged to be printed.

AS THE STRIKE wore on into a third week, Dandy's finance team sought him for approval of additional expenditures to rent even more aircraft. Dandy had let it be known that, in the event he was needed on the coast for negotiations, he had set up a temporary office in TMC's Boulder facility (Colorado had more direct flights to California). At the same time, although Rick's ranch was quite a ride from the Boulder operation, Oneida convinced Dandy that he was needed in the mountains for some other give and take.

"Dandy ain't here," the Boulder plant manager bellowed over the clamor of late-morning production one day, during the only shift still operational as the strike wore on.

"Where the hell is he?" Ron Eagleman, the procurement team's finance manager, screamed into the phone.

"How the hell should I know! Did you try his cell phone, Ron? He's been talking about building an ashram for injured horses up around Telluride. Maybe he's out looking at property."

"He's WHERE? Doing WHAT?" Ron threw a paper clip at a co-worker in his office who had been encouraging him to take it easy.

"If you get ahold of him, you might tell him that the Ranchers and Racers Betterment Society has been calling here looking for him too. Seems Dandy's pledge of TMC stock options bought him a photo op in their newsletter."

Ron covered the mouthpiece as he whispered to his co-worker, "Some local ranching society wants publicity shots of Dandy because he made a big donation!"

His colleague shrugged.

"Did you hear what I said? Dandy Liege, who charged his team for breakfast doughnuts, gave money to an organization! I hear he has a hot girlfriend now, too! And the press treats him like the Seer of Supply Chain. My wife read an article in a cooking magazine that applied Dandy's principles to baking cupcakes. All the money he could make from TMC stock has gone to his head. We'll never get him to focus on our little problems now."

The Boulder plant manager spit a wad of chewing tobacco out an open window. He needed to get back to work.

"Try his cell, Ron. He's out there somewhere. And when you find him, tell him the production managers want to talk to him about our option grants, too." Then he chuckled. "Oh, I forgot. We didn't get any." The plant manager hung up and returned to the production floor.

AS MEDIA-COVERED EVENTS featuring TMC executives drew more investors to the company's shares, Rick had grown increasingly appreciative of Stewart's exposure strategy. He felt that, with a little more work, Dandy could have even greater impact. Though Oneida functioned as a life coach, Rick worried that her personal involvement with Dandy might lead to a conflict with Rick's interests in the long term. He knew a few partners at the executive coaching firm Executive, Heal Thyself and recognized in Dandy a textbook case. A life strategist from that firm mapped out a flowchart of activities that would provide Dandy with exposure to influential, and beautiful, people. Above all, they recommended that Dandy identify and champion a cause célèbre.

With Oneida, Dandy found a sense of fulfillment that he had never before experienced. She took him for the ride of his life. And, as their passion reached greater heights, so did Oneida's influence. Locals said she took his money for the ride of her life. Before his physical and psychological obsession with this muse, Dandy's greatest excitement had come from screwing a vendor on a large order. He felt indebted to Oneida for rescuing him from an operating-expense-focused existence, particularly when he considered his close call with the waitress at the Down On Your Luck Diner.

In Dandy's softening heart, and in his mushrooming investment portfolio, Oneida sensed a kindred spirit and the funding for her interests. She worked around, and with, his beefy awkwardness and encouraged Dandy to have confidence in the platform that his position in a prestigious company offered. And, now that Dandy had put TMC on the map, Oneida counseled him that he owed it to the public to contribute his talents to more worthy causes. She readily served up her favorites.

In a previous life, Oneida had been among a select group of people voted off reality TV shows after having endured life-altering trials. She had been in the lead on the *Exotic Chef* competition during one November sweeps week. However, the central ingredient (a rare Ecuadoran insect) in the aioli she liberally applied to her monkfish entrée disagreed with her digestive tract and necessitated a blood transfusion, interrupting her participation in the holiday show. When her protests about the dangers of extreme TV were drowned out by an inundation of cash filling the bank accounts of the shows' producers, Oneida partnered with other survivors to form a political action committee.

After getting a thumbs-up on the Reality/ActionTV PAC from his personal strategist at Executive, Heal Thyself, Dandy calculated that his financial involvement with Oneida's group would not put him on the hook for much more than the cost of a flight to Washington DC to draw attention to their injuries. In exchange, he thought this high-profile muckraking might solidify his position as an important, and compassionate, mover and shaker. Thus, on this particular day, it turned out that Dandy was not in the mountains but in Boulder, lunching with the R/ACT PAC at a health food café in preparation for his appearance before Congress, when his TMC finance manager tracked him down.

Dandy's lunch mates recounted, sometimes in painful detail, the exploitations they had endured at the hands of greedy television executives. He listened intently as Phillipe Montrashay, a strapping masseuse and last season's runner-up on the hit show *Knead Work?*, described treatments to relieve repetitive stress syndrome from his elbows to wrists after a season of rubdowns on a stable of thoroughbreds. A lack of muscle control led to more than one cabernet knocked back over his shoulder and onto the clothing of an unsuspecting bystander at his local watering hole, Leather Rainbows.

Ron reached Dandy as the first course, essence of tomato soup, was being served. Although he had been screeching at the Boulder plant supervisor, the finance manager realized that Dandy was still Dandy and, as creator of the secret sauce that propelled TMC's outlandish growth, was not to be pushed around. Ron swallowed a sedative before he made his pitch.

"Hey, Dandy. How are you, man?"

"Who is this?" Dandy demanded, annoyed at the interruption.

"Dandy, it's me, Ron."

"Who?"

"Ron Eagleman, your finance manager at TMC."

"Oh, Ron. Hi. What do you want?"

Dandy stepped away to talk as a waitress refilled the iced hibiscus teas around the table. Ron explained the issue as succinctly as he could, as it was clear that Dandy was irritated. Very logically, he laid out the pros and cons of the additional expense necessary to rent additional aircraft and keep production from slowing even further.

Dandy was appalled.

"You interrupt my lunch—er, meeting—with some trivia about this strike? Don't you think I've been in touch with Long Beach?! I know what's going on!"

Dandy's gaze returned to the table. Phillipe, whose biceps were almost as large as Oneida's, had coaxed another lunch mate to lie across the table so that he might relieve some of the pressure on her somatic nervous system. Dandy found himself envying the stallions whose tension had been released by Phillipe's amazing hands. Feeling suddenly flush and lightheaded, he requested a glass of ice water from a passing waitress.

The drug, and his instinct for self-preservation, having kicked in, Ron maintained radio silence.

"Hey, it is what it is," Dandy resumed. "Sorry about the margins, but TMC has room to burn a little capital. We have to be big boys and take this one on the chin. Go ahead and get the extra planes." Dandy rushed to get Ron off the phone, explaining that he was missing an important briefing for his congressional testimony later that week.

"No, not for TMC," he replied to Ron's question. "I am in a position to speak out on behalf of an oppressed group of people. Stewart arranged for me to testify before Congress on behalf of the R/ACT PAC."

Having approved the expenditure, Dandy returned to his meeting.

Ron hung up and reached for another pill, saying to himself, "Dandy Liege will be testifying before Congress. I remember when Dandy Liege wore shorts and tube socks to golf outings with customers."

LATE THE FOLLOWING week, Ron watched footage on the evening news of leaders of the longshoremen's union signing a multiyear contract worth substantially more in medical and vacation benefits than their members had hoped to achieve. Four had been the magic number of weeks needed to bring the municipality of Long Beach and the cargo companies to the bargaining table.

However, the demise of the strike did not signal an end to TMC's problems. Not even a week after the longshoremen returned to the docks, TMC and many of its competitors experienced unusual and inexplicable issues with cargo. Products and containers were damaged. Huge amounts of inventory went missing. Almost simultaneously, technology components appeared on the black market, temporarily forcing down prices on finished goods and raising longer-term questions about quality and product warranties. Interviews with longshoremen about lost or flawed goods were nonproductive, though a news segment captured the pique that the workers felt toward the technology industry.

"That direct sourcing from Asia was a BS scab move, as far as the workers are concerned," an unidentified union sympathizer was quoted as saying.

THE IMPACT OF the strike was far worse on TMC's profitability than Dandy's finance team had predicted. Ted and the board leaned on Iago to address the margin pain. When customers expressed annoyance with backlogged orders or product quality issues, TMC's sales took a hit and Iago's spreadsheets drew greater ire from senior leaders. Iago threatened Stewart with severe budget cuts, or worse, if he could not figure out a way to get Ted and the board off his back.

"Ted doesn't appreciate me, Stewart. After all, it could have been worse. Remember N.O. Audette? Of course, I don't have a controller to staple to the floor, do I? You better find me a buffer from Ted damn quick."

Stewart thought about all he had done to help Iago become CFO. Before the IPO, Iago, as vice president of finance, had been a senior finance executive, but Ted would not name him CFO. Tiring of Iago's lackluster personality and eager for a successful public offering, Ted concluded that TMC required a more media-appealing leader for the big job. He ordered Stewart to initiate a search for a top-notch chief financial officer. When the $200,000 executive search fee produced a murderous felon, Ted decided that Iago wasn't so bad after all.

But Iago was very much the realist. He and Ted had never been close, photo ops notwithstanding, so, while he readily agreed that this CFO gig was a great opportunity, he suggested that his efforts justified a handsome reward. With little time to go, Stewart worked up a new compensation scheme for Iago, complete with a hefty stock grant. He assuaged Ted's lingering concerns about his new CFO by reminding him that TMC's corporate controller was very strong.

Now, Iago, holder of the purse strings, was threatening Stewart. Yet, sensing an opportunity for a win-win, Stewart accepted this new challenge. He again pushed Charlie to step up the controller search and find a scapegoat for Iago, and he pitched Ted on the idea that all of the leadership team should participate in cost-savings initiatives. This plan took a little heat off of Iago and redirected some limelight on Stewart's strategic thinking skills. Ted's translation of Stewart's suggestion amounted to a mandate that each of his direct reports implement cost-cutting measures immediately to stem the rising, unbalanced, expense tide.

Under Dandy's instruction, the procurement team, experts at identifying cost-saving opportunities, devised an algorithm demonstrating several million dollars in savings throughout the year simply by flipping a switch. Because it had an instant impact, Dandy's recommendation to raise the thermostat by four degrees in all TMC offices was swiftly implemented.

"Why didn't I think of that?" Stewart muttered as he opened a window to cool down his sweltering office.

Each year, TMC, like many manufacturers, sought opportunities to enhance process and reduce costs by retooling factory machinery. Traditionally, this required a complete shutdown of operations for one week. Stewart's human resources team recommended an extension of the annual factory shutdown from one week to two in response to Ted's demand to find ways to reduce expenses. However, Stewart raised concerns about the resulting loss to sales if production were cut for two consecutive weeks. Also, he was worried about his quarterly bonus. The effect of his team's suggestion would not be experienced until later in the year, when the shutdown was scheduled to take place. And it would be limited to manufacturing employees.

Stewart wanted a plan that demonstrated human resources' influence more broadly—and straightaway. Therefore, he tweaked the timing of and the participants in his team's suggestion and added some statistics to support the proposal, gaining the attention of Ted and the board of directors. As soon as possible, according to Stewart's revisions, all middle managers, who outnumbered executives 2 to 1, would be required to shut down without pay for one week. According to Stewart's analysis, the mandated furlough would result in $2 million in savings. There was such enthusiasm for the program that the board agreed to visit it again on a quarterly basis.

"Think of it as an extra vacation week," Stewart advised as he organized unpaid time off for his own staff.

X I

Meanwhile, back in New Jersey, Sal was wrestling with operating issues of his own.

Kenny Logan backed himself into the corner of his media room, away from Lenny Knuckles's menacing approach. "Not the nose, Lenny. You've broken my nose twice in three years, and it's ruined my love life. I can't get anyone to spend the night with me anymore. I got those anti-snore bandages. I even spent a weekend at a sleep apnea center. Nothing helps." Kenny covered his nose with both hands.

"Here, break my arm," Kenny offered his left arm. "Or even my leg, if I owe that much."

Crash! Kenny hit the floor. Those early-morning workouts in the local gym helped Lenny's form. Sal's number-two guy considered the brass metal object between the fingers of his right hand.

These don't suck either, Lenny acknowledged.

Kenny stumbled his way up the leg of the card table and threw his forty-six-year-old, battered body across the top of it.

"*Please*, n-no m-more." He spit out a broken tooth.

Sal sat and watched TV coverage of the New York Mets' loss to the Atlanta Braves.

"These Mets. They break your friggin' heart." He looked at Lenny, who wiped his sweaty brow with a pillow from Kenny's couch.

"You a Mets fan or a Yankees fan, Kenny?" Sal bent over and looked sideways at the client who owed him $50,000, not counting the vig, a premium for doing business with Sal's organization.

"Wh-who d-do you . . . like?" Kenny managed a small, bloody smile.

"I like the Yanks, of course. They know what they want. They got a winning attitude." Sal poured himself a single-malt scotch from Kenny's ample collection. He looked at the bottle and complimented Kenny on his taste. He also took note of the high-end room furnishings, the projection TV, the upper-shelf liquor cabinet behind the Brazilian cherry wood bar, and the collection of fine art hung around the room.

"Nice setup you have here, Kenny. What line of business are you in, again? I have so many clients, I can't keep track of what they all do for a living." Sal sat on the far end of Kenny's chestnut-brown leather couch and put his feet up on a cracked glass–topped coffee table. He stirred the scotch with his pinky finger.

Lenny allowed Kenny to straighten himself out as he answered the boss's questions. He offered Kenny the pillow, which Kenny accepted and immediately raised to his bloody mouth.

"Th-thanks for watching the nose."

"Don't mention it," Lenny replied and got behind the bar to pour himself a drink.

Kenny held the pillow to his cheek and answered Sal.

"I do executive search," he mumbled.

"What?"

"Executive search," Kenny offered again, as he spit blood out of his mouth and onto the pillow. He found a piece of a tooth and put it in his pants pocket.

"What the frig is that? What, like you find executives that are lost? What, are their pictures on the side of wine bottles?"

Sal looked at Lenny and laughed. Worn out from the beating he gave Kenny, Lenny sat on a barstool and chuckled.

"How do executives get lost, anyway? Elevator lets them off on the wrong floor? They take the Lincoln Tunnel instead of the Brooklyn Bridge to work?" Lenny said, laughing again.

"Wait. Are you one of those guys like I seen in that movie where you go find executives that are kidnapped in South America?" Sal was truly curious. "I loved that friggin' movie."

"N-no." Kenny rinsed his mouth out in the bar sink. "I recruit executives from one company to another."

"You do what?"

"When a company like IBM needs a chief financial officer, they hire me to find an executive who does that same job at a different company. Then IBM hires them."

"You friggin' kidding?" Sal was intrigued.

Kenny thanked Lenny for the ice pack he handed him. Wincing from the cold sting on his sliced cheek, he shook his head no to Sal's question.

"You tellin' me that a company pays you money to find someone they know exists at another company so that they can hire them?"

"That's about it."

"So why do they call it 'search'? What are you searching for if you know it exists? And another thing, why doesn't your client pick up the phone and call the executive directly? What do you do that's so special?"

Kenny explained that there was more to it than simply finding the person. He needed to persuade him to leave his current job and take a new role with his client. Salary negotiations were crucial, too.

"Sounds pretty cool," Lenny offered.

"It is. Thanks," Kenny clinked glasses with the thug who, five minutes earlier, had knocked him under the card table.

"You must be tired. Here, take dis stool." Lenny handed the barstool to Kenny.

"OK, you lovebirds. We're having a conversation here, if you don't mind," Sal admonished Lenny, who backed into the corner.

"Let me get this straight," Sal continued. "Some company says, 'We need a president. Go get us one.' So you call presidents of other companies until one answers. Then you convince that president that he is better off being president of your client company than being president at his own company. That right?"

"That's about it."

"It's like George Steinbrenner hires you to go get the Yanks a great relief pitcher." Lenny chimed in. "You go to Mark Ellis of the Oakland A's and

say, 'George wants you to play for the Yanks.' What's that knucklehead goin'
to say, no?"

"Yes, Lenny. It's a lot like that." Kenny raised his glass again.

"Boss, he's like a talent scout for corporations." Lenny beamed, proud
that he had figured it out.

"Yeah, but Ellis playing for the Yanks I understand. Why would a president of one company want to be president of a different company? You
already are the top guy. What's the point?"

Kenny solved the puzzle. "My client will pay him more."

Sal and Lenny said together, "Oh."

"So you get a cut of this?" Sal's mental calculator was ready.

"Yes. I take a percentage of base salary and bonus."

"What's the percentage?"

"One-third."

"You get 33 percent of somebody's take-home pay?"

"And 33 percent of the bonus they get at the end of the year."

"Anything else?"

"Sometimes I get equity in the company, too."

"What? Like stock and shit?"

"Yeah, like stock and shit. Sometimes it's more shit than stock, with
the way these companies are performing lately. But once in a while it works
out. I negotiated one deal with a biotech company to find a chief marketing
officer before they went public. I took equity in the company instead of my
usual 33 percent fee. That worked out real nice."

"What'd you get from the deal?"

"This house. That pool out back that Lenny was going to drown me in."

"That's a nice pool. I was admiring that outdoor kitchen area."

"Top-quality appliances and rainbow-slate decking from Central
America."

"I noticed."

"Yeah. I'm pretty proud of my achievements." Kenny's smile revealed
the gap that Lenny's fist created.

"You gotta stay away from the ponies. What's the matter wit' you? If I had these digs, I wouldn't be throwin' money away at the racetrack." Lenny said, emphasizing his point with a loud whistle.

Kenny shrugged his shoulders. "It's in my blood. My grandma loved the greyhounds. When I was twenty-one, my dad bought me a quarter horse." He whistled. "Man, she was a beauty."

"You have your own horse? Why you bettin' on these ponies?" Lenny asked as he stabbed at olives in a jar.

"Lost her in a claiming race. Dad was pretty pissed off."

Sal walked around the room. "Let me get this straight. Companies pay you a lot of money to convince executives to take a job with them because your client is going to pay them more. Is that it?"

"That's about it."

Sal plopped back down on the soft, leather sofa.

"I still don't get it. Why would they pay you to do that? Can't they do it by themselves?"

Kenny asked permission to join Sal on the sofa. The barstool didn't provide the support his back needed. Sal granted permission.

"It's not that straightforward. Sometimes it's hard to find exactly the right person who can get along with the executives that are already in the company."

"People pay me enough money, I can get along with anybody," Sal said.

"There's lots of ways to solve problems," Lenny said. "Sometimes people who are hard to get along wit' go away."

Sal looked at Lenny.

"What? I was gonna say they just go away. They disappear in thin air or somethin'." Lenny finished his thought.

Sal was interested in Kenny's business model.

"So, if a company has a job, why don't people who want the job call the company? Again, why you?"

Kenny asked permission to loosen his tie. With permission granted again, he continued.

"Some companies aren't attractive. They need someone outside to help tell their story. Remember that CFO who killed two people when they found out he was stealing money?"

"N.O. Audette."

"That's right. That's right." Kenny was impressed with Sal's awareness of the corporate world. "Well, that CFO took out more than employees. He whacked VITE! Corporation's credibility. I know because they hired me to find his backfill, and the company tanked before I could finish the assignment."

"What's your crew look like?" Sal asked.

"Crew?"

"How many guys you got working for you in this line of work?"

"It's me, my bookkeeper, and sometimes I hire someone to help with research."

Lenny let loose another whistle. "Only three people, and you make enough for all this house? So how come we gotta come here every six months and tell you what's what?" Lenny found Kenny's lack of discipline annoying.

"All I own is in this house. The cash I make or can borrow I blow on the ponies and the ladies."

Sal gave Kenny's suit the once-over.

"What can I tell you? I like beautiful things." Kenny said.

Sal picked up a Waterford crystal bud vase that had been sitting on the fireplace mantel.

"How much this go for?"

Kenny took the vase from him. "This one is old. My grandfather bought it as a wedding gift for my grandmother to remind her of where she was born in Ireland. Took him two years to save enough for a deposit. The store owner pitied him, so he let my grandfather make weekly payments for some time thereafter, just so my grandmother could receive the gift on her wedding day. Our family treated it like a precious gem. When she died, I inherited it."

Kenny carefully placed the family heirloom back on the mantel.

"Very important to you, I can see."

Kenny felt ill at ease as he watched Sal reach for the vase again. Kenny was a former Golden Gloves boxer and judged Sal to be a very toned welterweight. Despite Sal's lighter weight class, Kenny's instincts cautioned him not to mess with Sal.

Suddenly, the Waterford crystal piece slipped through Sal's fingers and hit the floor, shattering. Incredulous, Kenny dropped to his knees to collect the slivers and chunks.

"That's got to be hard to replace," Sal said. While inflicting corporeal punishment made Lenny feel profoundly alive, emotional manipulation got Sal's juices going.

Sal looked at the expensive items around the room. "There's a lot in here that would be hard to replace."

Kenny wiped tears from his eyes. Despite the body blows he had taken, this was the first time he had cried all night. He re-formed the vase as best he could with the shards he collected. His hands bled.

"Why we gotta come here and beat the crap out of you for fifty grand, Kenny?" Sal was standing beside an original landscape painting by a long-dead local artist. He lit a cigarette. Kenny did not recall ever seeing Sal smoke a cigarette.

Kenny was more nervous now than when Lenny had beaten him. Yes, he had been able to purchase this house and the furnishings because of the successful marketing search, but that project had been hard to complete. He had not explained that it had taken twelve months and twenty candidates before his client hired someone. Sal did not know about candidate number seven, who, in the midst of contract negotiations, got cold feet and rejected the job offer. He also had not heard about the countless boring conferences Kenny had attended, seeking executives to take this job. Nor did Kenny speak of the endless and expensive power lunches to drag what turned out to be weak referrals from advertising agency executives. Kenny had taken to calling them powerless lunches.

The stuff in this room, his life, had been hard-earned. And he wanted to keep it. Yet, at this moment, it was painfully clear to Kenny that when you dance with the devil, it is the devil who leads.

"What do you want from me, Sal?" Kenny slid a pack of cigarettes off the coffee table and into his pocket.

"The question is what can I do for you, Kenny. Seeing as how you don't have the money you owe me, it looks like you will need a partner to keep up the lifestyle to which you have gotten yourself accustomed." Sal adjusted the artwork, which had tilted slightly left.

"What kind of partner?"

Kenny's business cards sat in a sterling silver container on the coffee table. Sal picked one up.

"The best kind. The silent kind."

XII

S tewart paced outside TMC's boardroom. He finished two cans of caffeinated soda while awaiting a chance to pitch his program, Equitable Equity, a compensation initiative popular with his own staff. He wiggled as beads of sweat tickled his back. The boardroom doors finally opened. He picked up his laptop and rushed toward the opening.

Cool air wafted out of the expanse of the conference room, operating off its own AC system that Ted controlled. The boardroom doors shut quickly behind Travis and Don—Tweadle-Dee and Tweadle-Dom—as they exited the meeting.

"Am I on now?" Stewart asked the EA to the chairman and the EA's EA.

"Oh. I forgot about you." Tweadle-Dee stopped in his tracks and considered Stewart. "There isn't time on the agenda today, Stewart. Buh-Bye." The executive assistants resumed their course. Tweadle-Dom took off his sweater, with the temperature outside the boardroom decidedly warmer.

"But I've been waiting over an hour, and you said I could give this presentation at last month's board meeting but then you bumped me. And it's hot out here." Stewart heard his voice crack.

"This is coming at a bad time," Tweadle-Dee said. "Ted and the board are not interested in distractions. We are at the end of the second quarter, and that means the sixth-month trading window opens. They do not want

ANYTHING to negatively impact the stock price now that they are within striking distance of trading their shares."

Uncomfortably warm, Stewart squirmed demonstrably.

"Fellows. I understand how critical this time is. In fact, I want to talk about the implications to morale once the trading window is lifted. We need to consider awarding additional stock grants to great performers before it's too late." Stewart took a folded sheet of paper from his suit jacket pocket. "I've got a list of those high performers right here, from operations through to HR."

"Would you stand still, Stewart!" Tweadle-Dee exclaimed, taking the list as Stewart ripped his tie from his sweat-soaked collar. "Dandy better not be on this list. They are upset with him."

The EA said that, based on Dandy's overly optimistic projections, TMC missed an opportunity to rein in expenses. On top of that, Dandy built up infrastructure assuming sales would materialize. "Ted thinks the thin air out west got to Dandy. Some on the board are hacked off at Rick for getting Dandy involved with that Yoda person."

"Oneida," Stewart corrected Tweadle-Dee.

"Whatever the reason, Dandy's procurement strategy cost us a bundle."

"Yeah! Is Dandy on the list?" asked Tweadle-Dom as he read over his boss's shoulder.

"The board did have a request of you, Stewart," Tweadle-Dee said.

"They did?" Stewart's eyes brightened.

"Yes. The exact quote was, 'What the hell is HR doing?' Specifically, they referenced the negative press about the strike, our issues with product quality, and the impact of all this on productivity. Stewart, we heard them use the 'A' word."

"Aptitude? Allegiance?" Stewart searched their faces for the right answer.

"Attrition!" Tweadle-Dee bellowed.

"Attrition!" Tweadle-Dom reiterated.

"You know, the whittling away of TMC's employee base and the resulting drain on our business. They are very concerned about a possible spike in ATTRITION! Isn't that word in the top ten of the HR lexicon?" Travis was baffled by the ignorance of his human resources executive. "Stewart, the board wants to know what the vision is."

"Vision?"

Tweadle-Dee and Tweadle-Dom stared in disbelief.

Regrouping quickly, Stewart offered: "As a matter of fact, we have an initiative under way on this very issue. Of course, I never thought it would be a problem, but Charlie insisted—I mean, I insisted—we be prepared."

"Where is this initiative? Can you present it at the next board meeting?" Tweadle-Dee asked.

"Yes! Yes! We can! I'll put aside this Equitable Equity presentation for another time, and we'll talk about attrition at the next board meeting! How wonderful!"

The executive assistants looked at him.

"I don't mean attrition is wonderful. Be prepared to be dazzled as we discuss our vision to fend off attrition!"

Tweadle-Dee and Tweadle-Dom started off in the direction of the corporate finance team. As the lockups were ending, opening the window for corporate insiders to trade their TMC stock, the board wanted to initiate a stock buyback program. They hoped that having the company repurchase its own shares on the open market would serve as a signal that management believed the stock was undervalued. This tactic could fuel investor confidence, providing support for the share price. The board was very keen on fueling support.

"We're in a hurry to catch the treasury managers so that they can initiate a buyback program before the end of the quarter. The rumor is, they negotiated a group rate on a party boat so that they could take their mandatory furlough together next week," Tweadle-Dee explained. "Oh, one more thing. Ted and the board want you to remember you work for a technology company, not one of those highfalutin consulting firms. Lose the suit."

"But it's European," Stewart replied meekly, unconsciously petting the sleeve of his underappreciated suit.

"Whatever. You need to represent the people of a technology company, not some Wall Street megafirm. The employees think you're stuck up. Get yourself a few golf shirts."

Stewart stood, his mouth open and chin hanging loosely. He had so wanted to step up the game of this leadership team. Ted himself had instructed Stewart to improve Dandy's uniform.

What do the employees have to do with anything? Stewart wondered.

Tweadle-Dee called over his shoulder as he hurried down the hallway. "They want that controller on board before the close of the quarter, too. We have to write off costs associated with the longshoremen's strike, and the board is concerned about a further squeeze on operating margin. They are not convinced that Iago has a handle on it."

Tweadle-Dom had been walking closely behind his boss, reviewing TMC's financial statements as he did so. He failed to see Tweadle-Dee stop short, so he bumped into him as he repeated, "Yeah, end of this quarter."

"Ouch," Tweadle-Dee pushed his EA away from him. "Get off of me."

Tweadle-Dom offered profuse apologies.

Watching the two high-waisted EAs waddle toward the treasury pit, Stewart considered the ramifications of a stock buyback on the value of his options. Coming to his senses, he hurried after the pair.

"How's the hair? Did the board say anything about my hair?"

XIII

The following Tuesday, Charlie entered Stewart's office. His boss stood in the middle of the floor, bent over a putter. He gently tapped a golf ball toward his side-turned shoe about three feet away, and missed.

"Shit." Examining five putters on his office couch, Stewart chose a new one that resembled the Space Shuttle.

"They say it's all in the feel of the club," he explained to Charlie, who waited patiently as Stewart took another shot. He banked a putt off a small fan under his desk and sank it deep into his shoe.

"Woo-hoo!" Stewart wiggled his hips with enthusiasm, having found a keeper.

"We got Ted a membership at that new club downtown." Stewart lined up another shot. "He's invited me and some members of the governance committee to play with him next month, so I've got to work on my game. It'll be great to get out of this office and cool off."

They both watched as Stewart's next putt circled the makeshift cup and rolled away. Stewart called his assistant and told her to cancel his calendar for the rest of the day.

"I have a lot of work to focus on. I can't be interrupted," he told her.

Charlie had news of his own.

With TMC coming up on that sixth-month mark as a public company and revenue and profitability forecasts still not looking good, Charlie knew that hiring a controller to address the accounting challenges was imperative. Senior executives would not be happy if it did not happen before the trading window opened. Savvy investors had questions that a company without a controller did not have good answers for. Thus, amply motivated to suffer through insightful questions about corporate strategy, concerns about a volatile stock price, and complaints about Iago's blatant sexism—all the while with Stewart dangling a quarterly bonus over his head like a desirable suitor waving mistletoe—Charlie found a capable candidate who was interested in the role.

"With a few days to spare, I believe we are going to close the controller search this quarter!" Charlie waved the resume of his successful candidate and did an animated dance in Stewart's office. "Mercedes said if we offer a fair compensation package, she'll take the job."

Stewart pulled the résumé from him.

"Wonderful news. I knew from the moment I met her that I would like that woman," Stewart said. "Her mere presence speaks authority and rigor around all things financial."

Stewart's comment confused Charlie, who preferred the plain speak of businesspeople to the flowery platitudes offered by his HR leader. Often such talk was camouflage for a hidden message, and half the time Charlie could not figure out what that message was. Mercedes was a strong candidate. Her financial depth and managerial experience made her a solid addition to the team, as well as a potential backfill for CFO down the road. Her references made note of her integrity, talent for working complex issues, and authentic leadership—critical skills in a dynamic organization, as far as Charlie was concerned.

He asked plainly: "What are you saying, Stewart?"

"Mercedes Rodriguez! She's qualified, interested, and willing to take the job. After being turned down by three other candidates, she's got my attention! Not to mention, she's female and Hispanic. Do you realize what a double-diversity executive hire could do for my bonus multiplier this quarter?"

"Mercedes's financial strength and leadership will be very good for our company," Charlie replied. He firmly articulated the value that Mercedes would bring to TMC, as opposed to Stewart's personal bank account.

"And Iago won't want to be in her skirt all the time," Stewart chimed in. "Brilliant move, finding a woman over forty for this role." Stewart gave Charlie a faux punch to the right shoulder.

"That wasn't the search strategy!" Exasperated, Charlie reminded his boss that he needed to speak with Iago about maintaining boundaries. Particularly, the CFO required a crash course in avoiding crass, or, worse, potentially litigious behavior before they were all dragged into court. They both knew that they could have filled this job sooner with another confident, strong controller candidate. However, that disarmingly attractive female candidate would have been typical prey for Iago's wandering hands, and she had not been amused with Iago's game of footsie during her interview.

But Stewart was not interested in scolding Iago. He needed to double the size of his human resources team if they were going to accomplish the work required to qualify for the ARD (Attraction, Retention, Development) Gold Cup Award presented by the local Chamber of Commerce. Iago was the guy who signed off on the budgets.

"Whatever," Stewart said. "Ted and the board are happy; Iago's delighted that they are off his case, and this hire will help us meet our diversity hiring goals for the quarter." Reflecting on his quarterly goals, Stewart grew quiet.

Thanks to recommendations from the Compensation & Benefit division of Evergreen Consultants, TMC executive base salaries were in the 85th percentile among similar companies. Moreover, in addition to the annual stock option awards that Stewart had recommended to encourage a risk-taking culture, the executives were eligible for a management-by-objectives bonus, which offered additional cash incentives on a quarterly basis. Stewart's MBO goals were tied to increasing representation, with regard to sex or ethnicity, on the management team. The more diversity on the team, the greater his quarterly cash payout.

"Any chance she might be a lesbian?"

Charlie did not respond, which Stewart interpreted as an answer. He reconsidered.

"Hmm. You're right. She could turn out to be bisexual. I don't think that counts toward my bonus goals. Double diversity is good enough."

Calculating the size of his quarterly bonus reminded Stewart about a Grand-Craft brochure that was on top of the mail on his desk. Picking it up to review, Stewart made a mental note to call the local dealer for the high-end sports boat. His wife had been embarrassed that their Cobalt Bowrider had not been the only one of its kind on the lake.

"Go work out the financial details with Mercedes, but don't give away the farm, Charlie. Not that she's likely to build up too much equity in the time she has left, given her age and all. Still, we want to be prudent."

Then Stewart remembered something Charlie might need to know about the deal with Mercedes.

"If anything comes up about France, it might be useful to know that I may have implied that someday Mercedes could be CFO of our French subsidiary." Stewart mulled over the engine choices on the newest Grand-Craft line.

"Er, I wasn't aware we had an operation in France," Charlie replied.

"Charlie, you must provide candidates with a vision. This company is growing so fast that by the time Mercedes is ready for a role like that, we'll have an entire division in France. Speaking of visions, go finish that work on *What's Your Forte?*. I'm eager to support this initiative for you."

XIV

S tewart set up a meeting to pitch the *What's Your Forte?* initiative to Ted and the board at the beginning of TMC's third financial quarter. This time, he did not wait alone. Charlie and Vera paced for him, anxiously awaiting the opening of the boardroom doors and Charlie's opportunity to present.

Although he had faced initial opposition to the idea of *What's Your Forte?*, Charlie had been determined to pursue the idea as he witnessed the culture of teamwork and resourcefulness that TMC forged in its early years being replaced with fiefdoms and self-preservation. As the employment market heated up, Charlie connected with other companies also interested in finding ways to ensure employee commitment. He spent hours benchmarking with those organizations to understand workforce motivation.

Vera, too, was intrigued. For several weeks she put in extra hours to work on this project, helping Charlie analyze and integrate the data.

Charlie was pleased when Stewart expressed interest in his effort, particularly because his boss had been one of the early opponents of the program. In fact, Stewart convinced Charlie that this project could be an opportunity to showcase his strategic thinking skills to the board, a key ally when promotions were up for consideration.

Charlie rightly assumed that the media attention around TMC's problems helped his initiative. Although fortunes had been made when the trading restrictions were lifted, many senior leaders were miffed that their realized gains were not as outstanding as had been originally forecast. Bad press had hurt the share price. A declining stock value also made employees more likely to quit, so there was vigorous interest in a program to stem attrition and establish a floor for the stock.

Charlie's detailed plan offered TMC several cost-effective means to spark creativity, engender loyalty, and invigorate the workforce. He saw Stewart's cost-saving idea, the mandatory furlough, as a short-term fix that undermined trust. Charlie's hope was that the board could be persuaded to take a longer-term view. It did not hurt that this meeting overlapped with the furlough of the compensation team that normally prepared materials for board meetings. The directors would have time to consider Charlie's proposal, since there was nothing else to look at this month.

According to Stewart, he had insisted to Tweadle-Dee and Tweadle-Dom that this project needed the visibility of the board. The executive assistants easily agreed, especially since Ted and the board had demanded to see something of this ilk anyway. However, Vera's access to Stewart's calendar meant that she and Charlie found out about the pitch and now stood eagerly by his side as Stewart contemplated a move to ditch them from the meeting. Clad in charcoal-gray T-shirt and dark slacks, Stewart appeared relaxed, even cool, as he stretched his arms across the back of the couch outside the boardroom.

"Why do you guys look so nervous?" he asked. "This board is made up of people like us. Underneath those expensive clothes, they have birthday suits, too. Except maybe that private-equity guy from Dubai. The way he saunters around here, you'd think his boxer shorts are made of solid gold."

Stewart paused and then added, "Hell. Maybe they are."

Stewart smiled at his team. Charlie and Vera exchanged nervous glances.

"But hey, you get the point." Not sure that they did, Stewart picked up a magazine.

Charlie and Vera settled down on the armchairs on either side of the couch. Charlie tapped his foot until he noticed Stewart's glare.

Finally, Tweadle-Dee and Tweadle-Dom swung through the boardroom doors. Stewart stood up and quickly grabbed the portfolio containing the printed presentation from Charlie. With a confused glance at Charlie and Vera, the EAs shook Stewart's hand.

"They are looking forward to hearing this presentation on your initiative, Stewart." The executive assistants smiled in unison as they escorted Stewart into the boardroom.

"I see you took our advice on the wardrobe," Tweadle-Dee whispered, admiring Stewart's business casual attire. "Good choice."

"Yes, nice shirt," Tweadle-Dom echoed.

Charlie and Vera watched as the boardroom doors closed on Charlie's chance to pitch the proposal he had spent the last several months perfecting.

Vera threw her copies of the presentation down.

"That son of a bitch. He never intended to let you make the presentation. He stole your work and will pass it off as his own. He makes me so mad I could . . ." Vera kicked the leg of the sofa.

"Ouch!" She took off her shoe and rubbed her injured toes.

"He's such an ass-kisser. You should hear how he angles himself onto Ted's Gulfstream. Once a month he comes up with an HR issue that has to be discussed in person. Just so happens, this issue turns up when Ted retreats to his country estate."

Frozen with defeat, Charlie heard little of Vera's tirade. He was the main casualty of Stewart's narcissistic hit-and-run, and his head grew heavy and his joints ached as the betrayal seeped in.

Vera continued to fume, going on about expense accounts, changes to Stewart's wardrobe, and his penchant for sucking up to anyone with influence.

"Tweadle-Dee and Tweadle-Dom are his new best friends. He has a picture of them hanging in his office. You know, the one where they won the three-legged race."

"Why do you work with him?" Charlie interrupted her.

Vera took a breath. She recalled the pep talk she had given to Dandy several months ago. She believed it then and, for the most part, she still felt the excitement of the TMC that she had helped to build over the years. However, there were compelling practical reasons as well.

"It's a good-paying job, Charlie. And I've been here a long time. I know how to get things done. I know where the bodies are buried and how to avoid the landmines. I'd hate to have to learn that over again somewhere else. Then, there's Christian." Vera pulled out a wallet photo of her son, a high school junior. The family picture captured Vera, her son, and Wilkerson, their cat, around a Christmas tree. She had preserved the cat while surgically removing the image of her ex-husband from the picture.

"Christian has an uphill climb with diabetes, but we are hopeful," she said "How about you, Charlie?"

Like Vera, Charlie already knew where the TMC skeletons were and, generally, how to maneuver around them. He was also the main breadwinner in his family, and TMC stock held promise for the future. He recalled his own family photo, in a frame on his desk. The picture, taken in the backyard of his parents' Philadelphia home, commemorated the twofold celebration of his dad's sixty-fifth birthday and the retirement of his parents' thirty-year home mortgage. The addition to their single-family row house, a sunroom paid for with contributions from Charlie's after-school job at an alarm factory and his brother's occasional shifts with his dad's employer, could be seen behind the rosebush in the corner of the picture. He thought about his career options versus the choices that had been available to his father.

Charlie enjoyed the work of building a team. He likened his responsibilities to being in front of the eight ball in a billiards game. While he may not have complete control over his moves, he was critical to the game. He explained this to Vera in more direct terms.

"I like to describe my work as helping leaders make the best possible decisions for their business. The company can't get the work done without me helping to hire and motivate our teams. So, I guess I feel like I am building something special."

But there were other reasons Charlie stuck around, too. He felt he had leadership talent, and he was ambitious to gain a platform from which to wield it. He had been encouraged by TMC senior management that he had the right stuff to be a future mover and shaker. It was logical that he could leverage his current situation into an executive role at TMC, and he assumed it would take less effort than to rebuild credibility and a network at a new company. It occurred to Charlie that the best way to treat betrayal was to cut out the source. While getting rid of Stewart would be nigh impossible, shedding some financial ties to the company would not be.

"But right now, I'm thinking I'll take a furlough," he said to Vera. "Maybe next week. While I'm at it, I'll dump some TMC shares, too."

TO: ALL TMC EMPLOYEES WORLDWIDE

FROM: STEWART NARCISS, VICE PRESIDENT OF HUMAN RESOURCES

RE: *WHAT'S YOUR FORTE?*

Team,

We are engaged in a battle for the hearts and minds of our customers. Each one of us brings a unique set of weapons to the crusade. It's time to showcase your expertise for the betterment of the company, our customers, and yourself.

With no further ado, I am announcing a grand scheme to exploit the gifts of our team: *What's Your Forte?*

This initiative will drive transformational change across the globe. The very act of sharing talents will reinforce our company's strengths and, once again, show the world the power that TMC can exude when we focus on the positive.

If you are eligible (i.e., your manager determines you have a talent to share) and haven't yet taken your furlough, please use that time off to contemplate your participation in this critical and urgent initiative.

Stay tuned for more announcements and updates.

Go Team!!

Stewart

X V

The next month, news reports of additional setbacks rocked the public's faith in TMC. In the past, proactive management of the purchasing function had made TMC's supply chain a force to be reckoned with. More recently, however, the lack of a visible, engaged captain at the procurement helm hurt that function as the team cut bad deals with multiple vendors and overpaid for supplies. Adding to the troubles, managers across the company overreacted to a spike in attrition and hired more people than were needed to run the business. This additional headcount expense did not help the bottom line. Adding fuel to these fires, many broad economic indicators, including consumer confidence, dipped precipitously, increasing anxiety among the board of directors.

Ted needed a scapegoat. Since so many of TMC's difficulties involved people, he determined that this was a human resources crisis. That, at least, was how he presented it to the board, teeing up Stewart's head in case things did not turn around. Stewart's knee-jerk reaction to the increased scrutiny was to suggest a workforce reduction. Despite warnings to keep that idea quiet and take a wait-and-see approach, news traveled fast around TMC.

Charlie had concerns of his own. The procurement team needed to discuss another urgent issue with Dandy, who had taken to turning off his cell phone. Charlie, one of several people trying to track down the vice president, knew that Stewart usually had a line on Dandy's whereabouts, so he headed for Stewart's office.

Before he got to Stewart, Charlie found Vera at her desk, wiping her eyes. An invoice for what appeared to be medical expenses totaling more than $12,000 sat on her keyboard. Vera covered the invoice with a folder and tried to change the subject by asking Charlie how she might help him.

"I think I should be asking you that question," Charlie said, handing her a tissue. Vera's eyes met his and she started crying again. She folded the medical invoice and put it in her purse. She explained that her "bottom-dwelling jerk" of an ex-husband refused to contribute to Christian's uncovered medical expenses.

"He said if I took better care of our son that Christian wouldn't have ended up in the hospital last month."

This was not the first time Vera's ex had been stiff with money, but TMC recently had required employees to contribute significantly toward the cost of health-care benefits. That hit Vera's bank account, not her ex's. Plus, she was concerned about job security. Mandatory reductions in operating expenses, compensation haircuts, and budget slashings made the whispers of a layoff all the more daunting.

"Ted's admin told me Ted is so exasperated by human resources that he was of a mind to get rid of all of us," Vera said next.

This comment got Charlie's goat. He was already angry about the fires that popped up due to a disengaged leadership team. Weeks into TMC's third quarter, Charlie himself had secured the hire of a strong controller (averting a public relations and financial reporting disaster); created a robust plan for rebuilding employee engagement (which his boss had passed off as his own); and successfully managed the bulk of TMC's training, employee relations, and staffing challenges (all of which were proliferating).

While Charlie was fixing TMC's problems, Dandy was largely absent and Ted was busy manipulating people and processes to prop up the stock price. But Stewart took the cake. He had been preparing executive talking points for media interviews; introducing C-level egos to civic and nonprofit institutions interested in their commitment (read: money); and lobbying Tweadle-Dee and Tweadle-Dom about the merits of his Equitable Equity program (which amounted to an enhanced financial reward for high-potential executives—a list on which Stewart's name was prominent).

"It's really hard to screw this business up, but somehow Dandy and Stewart and Ted managed to do it!" Charlie said. "With patents on several unique products and a client roster that reads like a who's who of the corporate elite, TMC business should be thriving. A reduction in the workforce won't solve the issues we are facing. Our challenges are going to require a change in the way we do business—and who does it."

All this negative discussion reminded Charlie why he needed to speak with Stewart. He entered his boss's office in a huff but was immediately confronted with another surprise.

"You cut your hair?"

Stewart looked up from the presentation he was tweaking.

"Hello to you too, Charlie. Yes, if you must know, it became a distraction to my golf swing."

Stewart had sought the advice of an image consultant in reshaping his look to comply with the mores of the "hip" technology industry. The consultant advised that facial hair was en vogue, but Stewart opted for a ponytail when his beard refused to cooperate. However, when the ponytail slapped Stewart as he was teeing off in front of an important customer during a TMC golf outing, Ted pulled him into the men's locker room and chopped it off.

"Where's Dandy?" Charlie refocused.

"Today he is speaking before Congress for the third time as a concerned citizen affiliated with the R/ACT PAC."

"Is this the group he got hooked up with because of that Olga person?" Charlie asked.

"Oneida. And yes, that's the organization and she's the woman, though this article in the latest issue of *Out of the Medicine Closet and Into the Weeds* magazine would suggest that a masseuse now carries the secrets to Dandy's ever-enlarging heart."

"Who, what?" Charlie forgot why he needed Dandy.

"Yes. It would appear that Dandy's celebrity status has made him feel very desirable. The attention certainly opened his world up in more ways than we counted on."

Stewart's father had discovered the story in this relatively obscure magazine. Distraught due to the passing of his cat Junior, the elder Narciss had become a late-night Internet surfer. He regularly pummeled his son with articles about the supremacy of the executive suite as well as updates on the successful careers of his former classmates. The previous evening he had attached the story referencing Dandy, along with another copy of the obituary for Junior, in an e-mail to Stewart:

"What is it that HR does again?"

Stewart handed Charlie a printout of the article from the magazine of alternative health for people with alternative lifestyles. The human resources manager read it out loud.

This reporter discovered Dandy Liege, the naturally hunky leader of supply chain activities for TMC Corporation, in a mountaintop village several hours' drive down the Baja peninsula. Under the tutelage of the local shaman, Dandy has been studying the medicinal properties of a regional herb, Supernatural Sage. The straight-talking executive described what compelled him and his life partner, Phillipe Montrashay, to make the treacherous journey to this remote locale.

"Super Sage is a painkiller with amazing restorative properties. Phillipe and I use this herb extensively at our ashram in the Telluride mountains, the Dandy Liege Palace for Pedigreed Ponies. Super Sage is not only useful in addressing injuries, but it's been proven to enhance speed and agility on the field. Not to be mistaken with the illegal advantage that steroids provide baseball players and bicyclists, this natural medicine could be the breakthrough needed to rescue many a promising racing career from the glue factory, a commitment my soul mate Phillipe and I have made to our thoroughbreds."

"Does this mean that Dandy dumped Ozona the horsewoman for a guy, Phillipe, and an ashram in Colorado?" Charlie was very confused.

"Oneida, and yes, that's my take on the situation. Though I can't explain the ashram. Who knew that Dandy could be so complex. The good news, as I pointed out to Ted, is that our leadership team is much more diverse now."

"How does Rick feel about this? Isn't he a major shareholder of TMC stock and a good friend of what's-her-name?" Charlie assessed this situation as a boneheaded move that could hurt TMC.

"He WAS a major stockholder, all right, until recently when he started dumping his shares. And not because he's angry with Dandy but because the stock price SUCKS! He blames Ted for that, and Ted blames me. It always falls on my shoulders, Charlie."

Stewart wrote a final comment to his speech for the TMC all-hands meeting that afternoon. He had chosen a black T-shirt and jeans with loafers as his relaxed, yet chic, look for the official launch of the *What's Your Forte?* initiative. "Why are you looking for Dandy anyway?" he asked.

Charlie explained that Ron needed Dandy because he had questions about a company that Dandy wanted TMC to purchase.

Dandy intended to preserve his connection to TMC and a regular, positive cash flow, particularly because his non-TMC pursuits offered no significant financial remuneration. He had his company spies and knew the board was incensed about the longshoremen's strike, the quality challenges, and margin pressure. Also, a part of Dandy missed the excitement of the workplace. He got a kick out of pushing people around, and the purchasing function provided many more prospects for that than humanitarian causes.

Stewart and Ted's plan to put Dandy in the limelight had backed TMC into a corner. Hemmed in by publicity shots and Dandy's conviction that a long-distance bark from his cell phone would make any employee or business partner bend, Ted and Stewart complained about the situation but basically accepted Dandy's status quo. The media hype around Dandy's achievements was so great, the CEO and his human resources leader were more concerned they would be taken for idiots if they let him go. On top of all this, Dandy was loaded up with so many stock options that TMC had taken away any impetus for him to seek employment anywhere else.

Because his temperature-control idea had generated immediate savings for the company and deflected some of the cost overruns arising from the strike, Dandy sought out additional, creative ways to add value to TMC— as long as he could do it from his mountain outpost in Colorado. Dandy's understanding of the supply-chain function and experience with the California port strike convinced him that a little insurance was in order. He reasoned that he could reestablish credibility with Ted and TMC's board by creating supplemental means of distribution for TMC's growing product lines. He identified a company that would serve as an alternative logistics supplier, should one more strike or some other calamity befall the company. He wanted TMC to buy it.

3RD Party Incorporated was a profitable, flourishing, and well-run logistics firm managed by a seasoned general manager, Don Freeman. Don recognized that his firm needed a significant capital infusion and the infrastructure of a larger company in order to grow. He also knew his reputation could command a premium for the business, which meant he would have to be part of any acquisition. This was fine with Don as long as his role within the new company allowed him to stay engaged with the logistics game he loved.

Dandy knew of Don's standing in the industry and was intrigued with the success that 3RD Party enjoyed. He also knew that for TMC to make a successful run at the company, he needed cash, and fast, because there was another, serious bidder: StreamLINE Corporation. Charlie was on the hunt for Dandy because the finance team needed him to complete the bidding process.

"Ron won't sign the capital request that Dandy needs to buy that logistics firm unless he speaks to him directly about concerns he has with the deal. But, until this article came out"—Charlie pointed to the magazine—"no one knew where Dandy was."

Stewart checked his watch and then walked out of his office with Charlie.

"Dandy knows what he's doing," Stewart said. "He's convinced Ted that this acquisition is the right move, and Ted has convinced the board that adding revenue quickly can move the share price up. Rick might actually get bullish on the stock again. I'll ask Iago to talk with Ron. No need to worry about the small print. This deal's already been approved at the highest levels." Stewart checked his teeth with his tongue for any lunch residue.

Stewart handed Charlie several poster-board props and asked him to carry them to the all-hands meeting. He did not want to ask Vera because she was in such a bad mood.

"Stewart, maybe this isn't the right time to launch *What's Your Forte?*," Charlie said. "Given the problems we've been facing lately and the slowdown in the overall economy, the employees might find it disingenuous."

"Nonsense. This is the time to buck up and be optimistic. You should be proud I've decided to champion this tool for the company."

Charlie bristled as Stewart patted him on the back. Together, they headed to the cafeteria, where the workforce was assembling for the meeting. Stewart walked briskly with his head held high and Charlie rushed behind him, arms full of posters.

"Besides, a reporter from *HR Enlightenment* Magazine will be interviewing me on this initiative next week," Stewart went on. "We have to deliver on this!"

"What about the rumors?" Charlie whispered.

"What rumors?"

"Reduction-in-force rumors."

"Who told you? I mean, who said anything about a RIF?"

"Stewart, the rumor mill is buzzing. The training team has stacked boxes of personal belongings outside the break room. You know how efficient they are. Each box has a tag with a name and phone number on it. Whoever gets RIF'd takes a box home; those who don't unpack."

"Charlie, you should use this opportunity to strengthen your leadership skills. Take advice from your own initiative. Tell the training team to be positive. These recent business challenges are a blip on the screen for TMC. We'll get through this. There will be no RIF."

"All I'm saying is that maybe it wouldn't hurt to hold off on the launch of an initiative around career development while there's a whiff of layoffs in the air."

Shaking off Charlie's concerns, Stewart pointed out the walls where he wanted the posters hung. He strode to the front of the cafeteria, enthusiastically waving to the assembled crowd like a newly elected politician embracing his constituents.

XVI

Eight weeks later, Stewart was in a panic.

"Vera, get Charlie down here right now!"

"What's up?"

"Don't you read the newspapers? We are plagued with quality challenges, lousy margins, and bad publicity. Our stock has taken a beating! In the last week alone we've experienced a 20 percent spike in employees requesting their retirement savings match in the form of stock in 'ANY other company.' That's a direct quote from the employee survey! The only good news is the stock buyback program kept the share price up long enough for the executives to recoup decent gains before the shit really hit the fan."

"Oh yeah," Vera muttered. "THAT is the silver lining in all this."

Stewart wished he could persuade Vera to assume a company-line philosophy. He had no objections to her work. It was consistently good. Nor could he criticize her work ethic. She was often first in the office and last to leave, and she always had her ducks in a row. But her take on most issues was from the viewpoint of lower-level employees: what would be motivating to them and how an empowered employee base would be beneficial for TMC overall. It drove Stewart mad that she never considered external forces, aside from customers. She did not understand how the stock market worked; the potential benefits a positive analyst's report could bring to TMC; why it was elementary to coddle, coax, and control the executive suite. When he finally resorted to outright bribery, in the form of accepted HR practices such as performance awards, Vera shared hers with the administrative staff by treating them to lunch.

Stewart had quietly put out feelers for a new assistant. To calm down now, he picked up a seashell he had acquired during his last vacation and listened to the sounds of the ocean as he pictured Ted's curvy secretary, dressed as a seafaring wench, answering Stewart's phone.

"Vera, one of the things I most appreciate about you is that you are not afraid to speak truth to power. Thanks for being my guiding light. Now, will you please get Charlie?"

Responding to the urgency in Vera's voice, Charlie reached his wife before she got to the restaurant where they had planned to have an anniversary lunch and told her to get lunch to go. He suggested she place an order for her dinner, too, as he sensed he would be working late.

It had been eleven months since TMC had gone public and, while it had been an eventful year, it was not exactly what Ted and the board had anticipated. Although the first-quarter results had been strong, the small fixes here and there were not enough to prevent the business challenges experienced in both the second and third quarters, which sent the stock into a tailspin. When Charlie arrived, Stewart explained Ted and the board's determination that a reduction in force was necessary to get the company back on track. When Charlie questioned the long-term viability of a corporate strategy that alternated hiring spurts with employee cutbacks, Stewart reminded him that a continuous pattern of expansion followed by reduction in the workforce had been a successful tactic that many technology companies used to stay competitive and manage operating expenses in 2000. Charlie said that the method made him feel more like a well-played accordion than an HR strategist.

"So, have you ever done one of these before?" Stewart asked Charlie.

"Have I ever done what?"

"Have you ever put together the plan for a RIF?" Stewart asked.

"Nothing major. We've had department reorganizations from time to time, and we had to let a few people go."

Stewart handed Charlie a pad and pen.

"That's more experience than I have. You are now in charge of creating the strategy for Operation Emancipation. That's our code name in case word gets out."

Stewart offered Vera's assistance with access to whatever sensitive information Charlie might need. The good news, according to Stewart, was that the cutbacks would not impact the executive team much. At Ted's request, Stewart had stepped up the media coverage of Iago. This strategy paid off; the CFO had just announced that he had agreed to join a private hospitality chain as chief operating officer.

"That exclusive I got Iago with *Economic Week* put him on the map," Stewart said. "That's how this hotel company heard about him. The buzz is they doubled his cash. He should be kissing the ground Ted and I walk on."

Mercedes Rodriguez would assume the senior financial role through this period of "rightsizing." This gave Stewart time to let the media inquiries die down before he hired a high-profile CFO for the company—Ted remained enamored with the idea of a big-name executive for that job despite TMC's black eye over N.O. Audette. The upside in the short term was that Ted had promised Stewart something extra at bonus time for having executed a solid succession plan in the finance department.

Stewart asked Charlie to keep him in the loop on the game plan and action items.

"I'll have to report to the board next week, so we should plan to review the outline no later than Friday," Stewart said. "Anything else you can think of?"

It was four o'clock in the afternoon and the sky behind Stewart was darkening ominously. Charlie could see flashes of lightning in the distance.

"Stewart, I may not be a senior executive, but this RIF strikes me as a drastic step. It doesn't even tackle the actual operational issues that have brought about our problems."

Stewart packed up his briefcase. He was not interested in having Charlie second-guess the executive staff.

"You're right. You're not a senior executive. By the way, you need to connect with the public relations team, too. One of our lawyers said something about the Third Disclosure Act. Mean anything to you?"

The Third Disclosure Act required that a decision about any material event, such as a 10 percent reduction in workforce, had to be publicly disclosed within five business days. Before Charlie could respond, Stewart continued.

"I'm sure you'll learn all you need to know about it from the lawyers. Well, the clock is ticking. I should get out of your way. Besides, I have to get to my final sitting with Alistair. The dedication for the TMC Hallway of Inspiration is next week."

Stewart left to meet the artist who would complete his official corporate portrait, the last executive painting needed before the dedication ceremony.

LATER THAT EVENING, Charlie and Vera tried to figure out how things had gone so terribly wrong. Despite the operations challenges, demand had flourished for TMC products. As U.S. and global customers realized the benefits and flexibility new product lines offered, sales took off. However, TMC was plagued with excessive fixed costs. The infrastructure created to support the growing company became an albatross. When operational and quality problems kicked in later, TMC was further weakened just as the overall economy began to soften. Then, negative press raised concerns about the leadership team. This hit the share price hard. On top of everything else, the *What's Your Forte?* initiative flopped as employees became more concerned with immediate job security. Ted and the board of directors' response to external pressures, declining share value, and rising operating expenses was typical. Layoffs were considered a fait accompli.

For Charlie, there was another answer.

"Dandy has not had serious public company experience before," he said to Vera. "He never faced the complications, or the scrutiny, that accompany this environment. As far as he's concerned, a few colorful expletives barked over a speakerphone should redirect any business challenge."

"Not to mention, he's living at an ashram, screwing a masseuse," Vera added. She did not think she was overstating things.

Acknowledging the obvious, Charlie reminded Vera that the loss of 3RD Party in a bidding war had been another kick to Dandy's standing, although Dandy had insisted that StreamLINE would rue the day they paid more than twice what TMC had offered.

"We need a supply-chain leader who knows how to handle complexity," Charlie said. "Someone who won't get wrapped up in the limelight."

"Someone who shows up for work would be a huge improvement," Vera offered. "Do you really think that a different supply-chain leader could fix our problems?"

"If the operational issues were addressed, confidence in our products would increase, margins should improve, Wall Street would have renewed faith in management, and the board wouldn't feel a RIF was necessary. Yeah, I think that's worth a shot."

The colleagues ruminated on how they might convince Ted and the board that Dandy had to go. The supply-chain function was revered like a religion around TMC.

"Charlie, they are already livid with Dandy because of all the problems that cropped up this year," Vera said. "All we have to do is speak with Tweadle-Dee and Tweadle-Dom. Let them convince the Board."

"Ahhhhh . . ."

"Yes. Imagine the possibilities. Tweadle-Dee and Tweadle-Dom taking credit for an HR resolution to the business challenges. They'll look like heroes. Despite their bonding experiences, I suspect they'd love to stick it to Stewart."

Charlie sat quietly for a moment. Vera knew her colleague liked to maintain the proper bounds of decorum. Her own world more often operated in shades of gray.

"You are not an evil person because you find the idea of outfoxing Stewart appealing. Think of it as helping to correct our fearless leader." Vera smiled.

Vera's point of view offered Charlie a reprieve. Still, accomplishing the task was another matter.

"But how to convince Tweadle-Dee and Tweadle-Dom?" Charlie mused.

"Pitch them on statistics and trend analysis and put the whole theory into a PowerPoint presentation," Vera said. "That'll get those MBAs' engines racing."

XVII

Vera leveraged her friendship with Ted's administrative assistant to circulate Charlie's PowerPoint presentation ("The Statistically Irrelevant Impact of a Workforce Reduction on the Future Valuation of TMC Shares") to Tweadle-Dee and, it could go without saying, Tweadle-Dom.

The Tweadles had questions:

"Charlie, can you substantiate this $42,000 average cost per rightsized employee for severance, medical, and outplacement services? How did you arrive at that number?"

"What research organization supports a 34 percent shift to the negative in a company's goodwill after a layoff of greater than/equal to 10 percent of its workforce?"

"What's the correlation between a company's reputation after a workforce reduction and its stock price?"

After grilling Charlie sufficiently about the numbers, the executive assistants were amply persuaded that this planned RIF was worth rethinking.

"But what's the solution to getting the stock price back on the right trajectory—up?" Tweadle-Dee asked.

"A lot of our operational problems stemmed from pressures on the supply chain," Charlie responded.

Tweadle-Dee and Tweadle-Dom gasped in horror at the implication. Charlie looked into their eyes and nodded, as if to say: *The first step is admitting you have a problem.*

Tweadle-Dom searched Tweadle-Dee's face for a reaction. Tweadle-Dee waved him away.

"OK, Charlie. You have my attention. What's your recommendation?"

Charlie, armed with third-party, objective data, presented a compelling case that the right supply-chain leader could bring enhanced value to TMC. It did not hurt that Dandy had been gone so long, he was more legend than reality to the workforce, most of whom had not benefited from the early stock gains largely credited to supply-chain innovations. Tweadle-Dee was swayed that the time was right to bring in a new executive to run this function. However, he was not sure the organization was ripe enough to pluck the old one out.

"This recommendation may be tough for Ted and the board to swallow, Charlie. Sure, they're unhappy. But firing Dandy after all he did for TMC? That would take guts."

Charlie had an answer for this, too.

"My guess is the board will follow Ted's lead. You have a way with words, Tweadle—I mean, Travis. Maybe you can convince Ted that investors will see him as a bold leader who can make tough choices for the good of the overall company. Of course, it might not hurt to point out that a board sometimes demonstrates its own bravery by decapitating the head of an underperforming organization."

ALTHOUGH IT FELT like an eternity, Charlie was summoned back to Stewart's office before the close of business the following day. He entered as Stewart was violently tearing up a picture of Tweadle-Dee and Tweadle-Dom winning the three-legged race at the last company picnic.

"Charlie, about that workforce reduction. We are going to put it on hold."

"Woo-hoo!" Charlie jumped up and down. As he offered a high five, his boss tossed the torn picture into the trash, put his foot in the trash can and stomped on the photograph.

"I'll never be more than a third leg to him."

An hour earlier, Travis Tweadle had stood right where Charlie was standing and reminded Stewart, per Ted's instructions, of the CEO's original mandate: "Make sure the executives get what they need when they want it. Make sure they have the right team to get the job done. Don't get in their way. And, if somebody screws up, get rid of them."

Acting as Ted's emissary, Tweadle-Dee went on to inform Stewart that Dandy had screwed up. It had been decided that rightsizing the organization would not actually fix the company's problems. Further analysis indicated that a change of leadership in the supply-chain function offered the best hope to address TMC's operational and financial ordeals.

"For what it's worth, Stewart, Ted and the board aren't very happy with the part you played in encouraging them to give autonomy to Dandy. They relied on your professional assessment of his leadership skills. Heck, they weren't crazy about your choice for CFO, either, but at least Iago's gone now."

Stewart sensed blood draining from his face. Only a short time ago, he had canceled a fishing trip with some well-to-do neighbors in favor of a visit to the Mall of America with Travis, an excursion set up to select a wardrobe for Stewart with which they could both be comfortable. Stewart's calculated intention was to sacrifice his apparel preferences for career advancement. He felt betrayed.

Tweadle-Dee continued.

"Dandy took advantage of our trust. He threw money at problems and clearly didn't have TMC at the top of his priority list. Look at these magazines." Tweadle-Dee tossed the publications onto Stewart's desk. "Every one of them has an article touting Dandy's ventures, yet TMC is barely mentioned. I thought executive publicity was also your responsibility?"

Stewart was familiar with the publications; he had arranged for most of the interviews. However, he was miffed that the board would hold him responsible for the content of the stories.

What about Dandy's congressional testimony for the R/ACT PAC? Stewart thought. *That was a good idea. Free publicity, too.*

"And what of that association with the Reality/Action TV PAC?" Tweadle-Dee said. "Several of our board members are investors in big media conglomerates." He threw a newspaper article about Dandy's appearance before Congress into Stewart's trash can.

"I feel compelled to tell you there was some talk about additional changes to the leadership team, Stewart."

"Why are they relying on my judgment of Dandy? What the heck do I know about the supply chain?"

"Not to worry. I convinced Ted and the board that this organization needs you, provided you can demonstrate your commitment to TMC by firing Dandy and finding a great replacement for him *tout de suite!*" Tweadle-Dee also asked Stewart to gin up publicity around Ted's bold leadership.

Before leaving, Tweadle-Dee instructed Stewart to call off the reduction in force. That's when Stewart had called Charlie.

"We are taking a different approach to solve the business problems," Stewart told Charlie now. "You have to fire Dandy."

Charlie stopped dancing. "Why me?"

Stewart studied Travis's smudged image now gracing his office trash. He remembered his father's allusion to a feature story on Ted in the Sunday

Business News. Included in the story was a reference to the responsibilities of the executive assistant. A sidebar article featured Travis and detailed his access to the powerful and mighty at TMC. Stewart himself had suggested the accompanying piece after Tweadle-Dee gave him access to the board to pitch the *What's Your Forte?* initiative.

Disdain dripping from his outsized lips, his father had asked, "Who is it you report to, Ted or the assistant executive?"

Bruised and brooding from his treatment at the hands of the CEO's lackey, Stewart made a mental note to eliminate the layer between him and Ted.

I have to protect my flank. I need better access to executives to influence them, especially before the likes of Tweadle-Dee and Tweadle-Dom get their plump hands on them.

Given all the press coverage, it would not be out of line for Stewart to call an executive search consultant and confidentially mention that the time was right to fine-tune the organization. He would consider it a personal favor if Tweadle-Dee were recruited into another company worthy of his talents. He planned to give up Tweadle-Dom too, for good measure.

Stewart mumbled under his breath: "What about loyalty? Why doesn't anybody value that?" He piled Dandy's magazines on top of the garbage in the trash can. "Someday TMC will replace Ted with another CEO. I need to make sure I am the leader of that selection process, so whoever we hire will be faithful to me!"

"What are you TALKING about?" Charlie broke in. "Are you suggesting I have to prove my loyalty by firing Dandy and Ted?" The whirlwind of information and shifting allegiances put Charlie on edge.

Stewart looked up.

"Firing Ted? Are you mad?" Stewart put the trash bin back under his desk. "With regard to firing Dandy, we both know I am better at the leadership stuff. You're good with the tactical issues."

Charlie collapsed in a side chair. Much as he knew this was the best decision for TMC, he did not want to be the one to fire Dandy. Besides the unpleasantness of it all, Dandy had a reputation for being a tough guy. It was impossible to predict how he might react to being told he was no longer necessary. Charlie liked his face just as it was. So did his wife. It occurred to him that Stewart might be more afraid of Dandy than he was. If Charlie had to stick his neck out to save Stewart's, it would not be cheap.

"Let's face facts, Stewart. This is a dirty job. Last I looked, I wasn't receiving any combat pay."

Stewart recommended that firing Dandy was a chance to showcase courage as one of Charlie's key leadership strengths. "Charlie, this would be a valuable growth experience for you."

"So would working for another company." Charlie let the threat hang in the air. He did not know where his burst of daring came from, though a picture of his wife yelling at him for allowing Stewart to push him around crossed his mind.

Stewart was not sure which was more frightening, confronting Dandy or doing the HR work himself if Charlie quit. Either way, he did not like his prospects.

"Come on, you know Dandy and I are good friends," Stewart said. "As a rule, I don't let friendship get in the way of difficult corporate decisions."

"Or blind personal ambition," Charlie mumbled. He was getting a little nervous. Another picture of his wife drummed in his thoughts; in this one she was lambasting him for threatening to quit without a backup plan in place.

However, when Charlie did not blink, Stewart accepted defeat. Charlie had played this hand well.

"Charlie, did I mention that I nominated you for a special, one-time stock grant of five times your annual award to show our appreciation for all your contributions?"

And for carrying your bags, Charlie considered. However, he really was not ready to pull the rip cord. And an award that size could substantially increase his "F-you" money. So Charlie swallowed the desire to dump this dirty work back in Stewart's lap and rationalized that terminating Dandy would be a good development step.

Stewart informed Charlie that the board of directors would not support any severance arrangement because Dandy's attention to non-TMC causes left a leadership vacuum that created problems.

"Plus, by the time he cashes out all the stock we loaded him up with, his net worth will be close to $50 million," Stewart said. "Even taking into account the palimony payments to Oneida, he's accumulated enough wealth to speak to congressional committees for the rest of his life."

"I didn't know that Dandy and Oneida had kids together." Charlie was again confused.

"Rick said as much to Dandy. A pregnant Oneida would be hard not to notice. You know what Dandy told him? 'Hey, Oneida's horses are like family to me.'"

XVIII

C harlie found the fresh mountain air of Telluride refreshing. He wished he were visiting Colorado under other circumstances. He shuddered as an image of Army Captain Willard motoring up the Nung River to whack Colonel Kurtz in *Apocalypse Now* crossed his mind.

The GPS on his rented Lincoln Navigator got him only so far, and then he had to call Dandy to get directions to his remote ashram. Having only just spoken with Vera, Dandy was reflecting on his long career when Charlie telephoned. Vera's call, to alert Dandy to Charlie's imminent visit, had reduced the sting of this impromptu meeting. Well accustomed to TMC techniques, having utilized them on occasion to manage his own team's headcount, Dandy took a deep breath and greeted Charlie pleasantly.

Charlie found the soon-to-be-former vice president of procurement observing as a yogi taught the downward dog posture to a filly with high blood pressure.

"Charlie. It's good to see you."

Dandy gave him a warm embrace. Charlie realized that this was the first physical contact he had ever had with Dandy. He'd received not so much as a handshake before Dandy built the ashram.

"Let me give you a tour." Dandy took Charlie through the barn, equipped with ten-foot-wide and almost as deep troughs to provide water therapy for its inhabitants. The front of the building contained a separate supply store where the yogi's tapes and books, as well as medicinal salves, were sold.

"Everything's a potential business to me, Charlie," Dandy nodded toward the cash register.

Several men in white cotton work clothes tended to the upkeep of the facility, sweeping out the stalls and laundering dozens of Egyptian cotton towels used to rub down the thoroughbreds after a therapy session.

"Putting in our own launderette has made a real difference to our bottom line," Dandy pointed out.

"These guys work for next to nothing, and it's an all-cash deal with them. There's more money to put back into the operation to care for the horses and less money coming out of my TMC proceeds." Dandy chuckled and slapped Charlie on the back. "Even in an ashram, the supply chain is important."

When Charlie asked how he got the idea for the ashram for thoroughbreds, Dandy told him, "I found I had a lot in common with the people out here in the mountains, despite the technological divide between us. I didn't come from money, and neither did Phillipe or Oneida, for that matter. Once I put that personal digital assistant aside, I could hear my inner calling, and it was a 'Neighhh.' Oneida heard it too. And then, of course, Phillipe. In fact, through Phillipe I found my true passion—in the ashram, that is."

Dandy stopped to scold an employee who was about to dump a cup of expensive, organic fabric softener in the wash. He pointed out the one-quarter mark on the measuring cup.

"Can't be too careful," Dandy explained, returning to the tour and his guest.

"I know why you're here, Charlie. TMC needs a VP of procurement who will be a predator and compete fiercely for TMC in the global marketplace.

I've come to realize that's not me anymore. I've been a fierce lion, and now I'm cultivating the lamb in me. Different skill sets. Opposing talents. You need to start an executive search for a new king of your jungle."

Charlie had lain awake all night thinking about how this conversation would go and what he would say. He was relieved that Dandy gracefully let him off the hook.

Dandy was a realist. He read the papers, heard the rumors. Losing the 3RD Party deal forced him to come to terms with moving on from TMC. Yet, he still had a little roar left.

"Of course, I have contributed significantly to TMC's success. It'd be a shame to throw away that legacy." Dandy paused and then added, "I'm sure Ted and the board wouldn't want other executives believing that their contributions might be tossed aside as the company is growing."

The board had acquiesced to the possibility of providing Dandy a financial incentive to move on—if absolutely necessary. Dandy's directions to take back roads up the mountain to the ashram had provided Charlie with an idea. He teed it up.

"I noticed an airstrip under construction on my drive up the mountain. Must be expensive to maintain the supply chain for a successful ashram. It would be nice if TMC's announcement of your intention to refocus priorities and pursue your dream of a shelter for battered and abused racehorses coincided with a contribution to the Dandy Liege Palace for Pedigreed Ponies," Charlie suggested.

"You were always full of creative ideas, Charlie. That's why I liked working with you." Dandy put his arm around Charlie's shoulders. "I like to think of our little hideaway here as a place where animals can rest, recuperate, and rediscover their inner foal."

Charlie followed Dandy's lead and inhaled a slow, deep breath as he took one long last look at the ashram. Yogis instructed a group of horses in advanced meditation while a shop clerk explained the healing properties of ginger and eucalyptus to a tour group visiting from a local assisted-living facility.

Dandy provided directions to the Denver airport as he walked Charlie back to his rental car.

"I almost forgot. I printed this article off the computer last night. Yes, we have technology up here." Dandy winked. "Seems Stewart's going to be feted by an HR organization for the *What's Your Forte?* initiative. They are recognizing him for innovation in the field." Dandy handed Charlie the article, which praised the program despite a lack of results.

"You know, I genuinely like Stewart, in spite of that weird Moondoggie thing he has going on with his sideburns. You remember that surfer character from the *Gidget* movies? But this initiative sounds like an idea you were trying to sell way back when. Watch your back, Charlie."

Dandy hit the hood of the SUV and waved as he walked back toward the barn. Workers were coaxing a fifteen-hands-high former champion racehorse named Daisy Lu into the trough for a water therapy session.

"Easy there, Daisy Lu. You know how much the yogi loves you." Dandy patted the anxious animal.

Charlie drove down the mountain and back to his own reality. Dandy's admonition reconfirmed that the bloom had definitely come off the touchy-feely HR rose. Stewart was not to be trusted. But, then again, Stewart's cowardice created opportunities. Whacking a powerful executive made Charlie feel, strangely, very much alive. This rite of passage reawakened his self-confidence and his ambition for leadership. It also widened the crack in TMC's hold on him.

Charlie's thoughts returned to work and TMC's need for a supply-chain executive who had experienced the growing pains of a large, public company. He considered the choices. A woman might bring a new perspective to the company. Catching another glimpse of the airfield as he descended, Charlie found his thoughts flooded by the manufactured crises of the past year. He considered that one month still remained before TMC closed the books on its second first year as a public company and shook his head.

"Hell, she couldn't be worse than our current cast of characters."

THE BIG PICTURE

X I X

S al cursed and hung up the phone. An espresso machine, a case of Barolo wine, Giana's bookkeeping notebooks, and three stacks of size-eleven sneakers replaced the leather-bound bookends, single-malt scotch, and laptop computer that had previously occupied the bar area of Kenny Logan's media room. Remnants of communications systems and computer parts that Lenny was not able to offload were stashed in a coat closet. Kenny explained to his cousin in Long Beach that his connections were more interested in prescription drugs than obsolete computer compo-nents, but his relative would not take the electronics back. For Sal, the closet contents were a reminder of another failed business venture. Not good.

"I don't know why I ever agreed to take this house off your hands. This place is a mess. The pool drained more of my money than my wife and all her sisters put together," Sal yelled at Kenny, who was on his cell phone negotiating an offer package with a candidate.

"Where do you want these, boss?" Giana entered through the patio doors carrying another stack of sneakers.

Giana, chewing gum, blew and burst a bubble. *Crack.*

"For crying out loud, Giana. I been telling you to step it up. We are not in the backroom of a bar anymore! Does this look like a rinky-dink opera-tion to you?"

Giana took a look around the room.

"Sal, it looks like a media room wit' a bunch of shit in it."

Sal's wife was on his case because the hot tub was not working and her sisters would be visiting that weekend. The pool guy said the part necessary to fix it would not be in until Monday. Sal was already getting a headache over the scene he anticipated with his wife.

"Would you get rid of the friggin' gum, please?"

Kenny threw his phone on the floor. Over time, he found himself avoid-ing polite questions about work, as it was difficult to describe and he often did not want to recall the specific details of his daily grind. He sought solace from persistent depression by eating the pasta dishes that Giana shared with the office. The extra 30 pounds he carried activated his latent arthritis, which precipitated an addiction to sleeping pills. He was so out of sorts that he was more often a no-show at family functions. The effects of almost four years as Sal's business partner had taken a heavy toll on the executive recruiter.

"People, please," he beseeched Sal, Giana, and Lenny, the latter of whom had been reading the horse gambler's bible, *The Racing Sheet*. "You were supposed to be silent partners. I can't concentrate during these negotiations with talk of mothers-in-law, hot tubs, who scratched in the seventh race at Aqueduct, and the constant buzz of that espresso machine!"

Kenny walked across the room to the bar.

"And what the hell are all these sneakers doing in here! Are we in the warehouse business now or what?" He knocked a stack over.

Sal took a deep breath.

"No, WE are not in the warehouse business. Lenny and I are using those sneakers to supplement the income from this partnership we bought into. We'd be happy to discontinue the consumer products line of our operation if this executive search business you bragged about was actually making some friggin' money."

Sal stood in front of Kenny. Though Kenny was physically larger, he had an instinctive fear of Sal.

"Sal, sometimes you hit a dry spell, but there is opportunity out there. I have lunch with an old client next week. He's moved to a different company and has to build a leadership team, so we are going to talk about hiring some people for him."

Sal eyed Kenny suspiciously.

"How come I didn't know about this lunch?" Uninterested in expending more energy than necessary, for a long time Sal had left Kenny alone to run the executive recruiting business. But when Sal's big boss found out about the work Sal had going on the side, he wanted his cut. This negative impact to cash flow spurred Sal to get more involved in executive recruiting, under the theory that more recruiters would result in more fees. However, the quality of the work suffered with Sal's engagement, so Kenny had begun keeping him out of the loop.

"This client is a private guy," Kenny said. "He's a low-key person. It'd be better if I met him alone to pick up the business." Kenny took a deep breath.

Sal remained calm, never losing eye contact with Kenny.

"And we're meeting at Neptune's Diner for sandwiches. Not a big lunch or anything," Kenny added.

"Neptune's Diner over off Route 17? What kind of friggin' lunch is that? Amelio's Restaurant is where you take a client to lunch," offered Lenny.

Sal returned the focus to the issue of making money. Kenny had said they might make a $50,000 fee on the sales vice president search he had been working. Sal had a knack for remembering details.

Kenny picked up his cell phone from the floor.

"That's the deal I was trying to negotiate. The candidate is playing hardball. I'm not sure I'm going to be able to convince him."

"Why don't I take a shot at it?" Sal asked.

Naturally, Kenny was hesitant. Negotiating with candidates was not Sal's strong suit. They usually found him intimidating. In fact, Kenny and Sal's executive search firm had developed a reputation for union-style arm-twisting.

"Sal, this negotiation is at a delicate point. This candidate has several reasons why he might not take the job, not the least of which is that his wife is resisting the relocation."

"So we can help them find reasons they should move, heh?"

Sal suggested there would be no harm in someone else taking a shot at swaying this candidate. "Introduce me as the senior partner. That kind of clout should carry weight."

Kenny noticed that Lenny had started polishing his brass knuckles and dutifully, but regretfully, obeyed. He called Dylan McBride, the leading candidate for the job, introduced Sal, and handed over the phone.

"What's his name?" Sal whispered, his hand covering the mouthpiece.

With anxiety running through his veins like fluid in a hot car motor, Kenny handed Sal the candidate's resume and repeated, "Dylan McBride."

"I get along famously with the Irish," Sal whispered before he uncovered the receiver. "Hey, Dylan. How's it hanging?" Sal winked at Kenny and motioned for him to sit down on the couch.

"Yeah, yeah. Kenny and I, we been in business some time now. We got a few interests together and he respects my judgment, see, so he asked me to talk to you about what a great deal our client is offering you."

Sal covered the mouthpiece again and whispered, "What's the name of our client?"

Kenny reminded him that they had been hired by All American Finance Advisors. He asked Lenny to pour him a scotch. Lenny looked at Sal, who motioned that he should comply with the request. Lenny filled Kenny's glass, but he was not happy about it. It was one thing to fill Sal's glass. It was something else to fetch drinks for the rest of the crew.

Kenny, Lenny, and Giana listened to Sal pitch the candidate.

"Yeah, of course I understand this is a big move. I made a few big moves in my time. I can sympathize. Lots of responsibility comes with a promotion, but lots of shit comes with staying lower on the totem pole, if you know what I mean ... All's I'm saying is progress is good. Good for you, your family. And your progress is good for me and my family, too." Sal chuckled at his own joke.

Sal responded to McBride's point of view. "Yeah. Yeah. I get that. Whateva. Let me ask you something, Mac." Kenny cringed at the picture of this well-heeled sales executive hearing himself referred to as Mac.

"What's your take-home pay today?" Sal scribbled a note and threw it at Kenny, who opened the scrunched-up paper. On it, Sal had written: "What's the offer?"

Sal listened as Dylan objected to the question.

"It can make a lot of difference, Dylan. Tell me what you're making today. No, I don't need to know about the benefits. Just the cash ... The difference is, if you can make more money at our client company, it's plain stupid to turn down the job."

Kenny asked Lenny for a refill. Sensing the tension swell in the room, Lenny complied without a ruffle.

"Yeah, sure there is more to this career move than money." Sal put his hand over the telephone receiver and mimed to Kenny: Is this guy a dope or what?

"Sure you need to think about your future. In fact, I am encouraging you now to think about your future, you get me? As I see it, Mac, your future and my future are very much entwined. And I clearly see this job with my client in your future. *Capisce?* What's that? You don't like my tone? . . . I don't like your stupidity, but what can I say? My client likes you, so I got to work with you . . . Mac, I'm not trying to do anything. This is for real. I got to deliver you so we can do this nice, or we can do this the hard way. Up to you in the end . . . What the fuck?"

Sal turned to his audience.

"The son of a bitch hung up on me."

Sal copied Dylan McBride's home address from his resume onto a piece of paper. Kenny had assumed the fetal position in a corner of the room. Sal handed the paper to his enforcer. "Here, Lenny. He chose the hard way."

Kenny let out a loud moan, then vomited.

"What now?" Sal looked at Lenny and Giana and shook his head.

Giana got out the mop.

"BUT DYLAN'S A local bigwig in the Republican Party. Are you sure he said he wants to move to the Left Coast?"

Kenny spoke to his client from a leased Volvo 850, his Jaguar having been repossessed. This was only the latest in a growing list of modifications he had had to make since the number of associates in his business had expanded and revenue had decreased.

"He actually said that he wanted to get as far away from Jersey as possible? Yes, I heard you, but I'm not sure what Dylan means by 'brute.' . . . Maureen, all partnerships have ups and downs. Is it really necessary to get a lawyer involved? . . . How much are his medical bills? Whew! That's a lot of money. Did he get a second opinion? . . . I'm not suggesting he's a liar,

Maureen. I want to be sure the right protocols are followed. After all, does anyone really use their pinkie toe?"

Before hanging up, Maureen Atkinson, the director of human resources for All American Finance Advisors, offered several colorful suggestions for what Kenny and his partners might do with their pinkie toes. Kenny did not have time to mull over this unpleasant encounter. The phone rang again. This time it was his bank, informing him of a margin call on his corporate account. When he inquired about his personal portfolio, the bank clerk confirmed that his checking account was in overdraft status. He hurried to the office, determined to stand up to Sal this time.

Giana was holding down the fort, applying nail art to her manicured tips while Sal and Lenny made the rounds, collecting the weekly vig from their business associates. She greeted Kenny and returned to her grooming. Kenny went to the bar and started tossing magazines and papers and cans of illy coffee around.

"Giana, where do you keep our business records?" Kenny asked.

When they started working together, Sal had advocated a reduction in overhead. "Consider the savings in operating expense," he'd said. "Giana is doing the books for my business operations. We can add this recruiting business as a simple line item and eliminate additional cost by getting rid of your bookkeeper."

Kenny had been extremely suspicious and even more concerned about the ramifications of mixing his books with Sal's, but Sal presented it as an offer he really could not refuse. After his encounter with Maureen, he felt more like a worked-over customer service representative than an adviser to senior executives. Imagining himself an Eliot Ness to Sal's Al Capone, he resolved to bust Sal's operation wide open. When Giana approached him with a number two pencil and bookkeeper's notebook, he nearly fainted. Hopeful, he suggested that they simply view the financials on her computer.

"I tried to bring Sal into the Renaissance age with the latest and greatest computer," Giana replied. "But he said, 'If it was good enough for my grandfather and my father to use notebooks, that's good enough for me.'"

This revelation confirmed Kenny's fears. Giana continued.

"Personally, I think it is because his dad was a child of the big depressions. Y'know, at the turn of the century, when people lost all their money and had to bargain with their clothes to get food. That's where they get that expression: They lost their shirt. Did ya know that?"

Giana allowed a small smile, impressed with what she thought to be her knowledge of financial history.

Kenny asked Giana to pour him a libation as he pored through the books. There were not many entries and, of those listed, several read "misc."

Giana explained: "Miscellaneous. Like when there is nowhere else to put it."

While the miscellaneous entries were upsetting, most were for under $1,000. However, there were two recent entries for $25,000 each. Giana explained that these were cash outlays that Sal had asked her to withdraw and put into envelopes for him. He had not explained what they were for. Giana assumed it was for travel and entertainment.

"After all, I seen Sal's credit card bills. I guess you guys gotta do a lot of entertainin' in dis racket."

"Sal has credit card expenses in addition to what you have recorded here?" Kenny unbuttoned the top button of his shirt and took successive deep breaths.

"Sure!" Giana looked surprised that Kenny would question Sal's expenses. The color was draining from his complexion, and Giana fanned his face with her notebook. "Eva meet his wife?" Giana did not wait for a reply. "If that woman has one fur coat, she must have five! And the shoes! Gorgeous shoes, but they are wasted on those feet. With all that money, you'd think she'd get her bunions fixed."

Kenny reached for more scotch, but the bottle was empty.

"A favorite of Lenny's," Giana explained.

He opened the only alcohol left, a bottle of sambuca, and took the entire bottle to the couch with him.

"No, thanks." Kenny waved off Giana's offer of a glass, took a deep swig of the licorice liqueur, and started punching numbers into a calculator.

SEVERAL HOURS LATER, with the room lights glaring and Kenny snoring through a small pillow, Sal shook his partner awake.

"Hey. What the frig is this?" Sal hit Kenny on the head with a notebook that had been on the coffee table.

"Huh? What?" Kenny roused from a heavy sleep the sambuca had rendered. His head throbbed.

"This. Here. Who let you see my business? I'm going to bean you, Giana." Sal collected the books and locked them in the short safe behind the bar.

"It's my business too," Kenny mumbled.

"What?"

Kenny attempted to stand up, but the full effect of all the alcohol hit as he shifted his weight. With Lenny behind him, Sal grabbed Kenny by the shirt collar and pulled him back up onto his wobbly feet. Giana, who had been browsing magazines, silently left the room.

"Who the frig do you think you are? This is my business you got your curious eyes on, you understand?"

Kenny felt the warm breath and fierce strength of his partner. He willed himself out of his drunken stupor.

"I-I-I got an overdraft call today. And . . . and we lost the All American Finance Advisors account."

Sal was dumbfounded at the news of the account loss. He dropped Kenny, who fell onto the couch.

"That friggin' guy. That friggin' coward. I told him to take that friggin' job. He didn't take it, did he?" Sal turned toward Kenny.

"No. He moved."

"What the fuck? What do you mean he moved? Where'd he go?"

Kenny mustered all his mental strength to answer Sal without insulting him. Though Sal was a few years older than Kenny, his natural physical edge defied time. Kenny did not want to get beat up again, although it occurred to him that a beating now might not be so bad, given the alcohol cushion running through his bloodstream.

"Dylan objected to what our client described as 'heavy-handed tactics' by the executive search consultant."

"Heavy-handed? That coward doesn't know heavy-handed! Somebody had to slap sense into him. The client was offering him a 25 percent increase in base salary! If McBride couldn't see that, he's too stupid to work for that company."

"He objected to that, too."

"Objected to what?"

"Being called 'stupid.'"

"How the frig can you get through to some people?" Sal asked, his head in his hands.

"Well, our client expressed great concern about the candidate experience that McBride had. There was also discussion around who should pay for Dylan's trip to the emergency room."

"Because of one dumb-ass candidate, so stupid he walks away from a 25 percent increase in cash, we lose the account?" Sal was livid.

"Yep."

"Wasn't that our only account?"

"It was the last one we had."

"You want I should go over to that client and tell them what for?" Lenny wanted to be helpful.

"No!" Kenny and Sal barked simultaneously.

"Hold on. What about the company over by the river that was looking for a lawyer to head up their legal team? We can get that job." Sal suggested.

"Yes, Gallagher Trucking. I did think we were a shoo-in until, that is, the president inquired about our experience in the legal field. I don't think Lenny's detailed list of run-ins with law enforcement was exactly what the president had in mind when he asked for representative work."

One look from Sal and Lenny recoiled to the back of the room. Removing his suit jacket, Sal placed it carefully over the sidearm and then sank into the supple leather of the couch.

"Nice suit," Kenny said.

"Thanks." Sal stared at the wall in front of him.

"Don't think I've seen it before."

"New. Last week."

Hopeful, Kenny asked, "Fall off a truck?"

Thoughtful, Sal turned to look at Kenny.

"Oh, no. Not one of those. Paid full price at the mall."

"Fuck."

"You can say that again. Brought my wife shopping with me, too."

"Fuck, fuck." Kenny buried his face in his hands.

"Yep."

They sat quietly for a few moments and considered the problems facing their business.

"So what were you doing with the books anyway?" Sal asked.

"I was trying to get a clearer picture of our financial situation. We need to determine what we have and what we owe and work out a plan to save the business."

Kenny paused before continuing. What did he have to lose?

"What's the $25,000 outlay for, Sal? That's a hell of a lot of money."

Sal explained that the $25,000 payment was tribute to the boss.

"I thought I was in business with you, not with your friggin' boss, too."

"Hey, don't dis the famiglia," Sal responded, not loudly but firmly. "Besides, it ain't me but Lenny you got a bone to pick with."

Lenny lowered his head.

"How's that? Is his grandma on the payroll, too?" Kenny asked.

"You don't know all I do for our partnership, Kenny. I kept this operation quiet for a long time, see. But what happened is Lenny's cousin is fiancé to the boss's granddaughter. Did I mention Lenny has a lot of cousins? Big family. Anyway, Lenny let his tongue run at his cousin's engagement party. Told his uncle, his cousin's father, all about the great operation we set up and what a cash cow this recruiting business was." Unable to resist a little sarcasm, Sal added, "Lenny's also a pretty good liar. Whateva. Naturally, the uncle, who wants to look good for the big boss, tells one of his guys, who tells the boss, who calls a meeting with me looking for his vig."

"Why does he get a vig?"

"Like I said, you can blame Lenny the Mouth over there. I love the boss but I got inclinations to agree with you, seeing as how we're taking all the risk in this entrepreneurial endeavor."

Giana, who had been listening from the safety of the next room, piped up, "I thought he was called Lenny Knuckles?"

"Well, now we need to call him Lenny the Mouth!" Sal yelled so she would hear through the wall.

"We need to get cash flow into this business fast," Kenny redirected the conversation.

"That's right. Dis is a time for leadership and productivity," Lenny readily agreed, wanting to move the discussion off of his error. "Who else you know that will give us work?"

As Kenny considered the possibilities, Sal imagined other angles.

"You know, these companies hire a LOT of executives. And they got a lot of executive search firms working for them," Sal suggested.

"What are you getting at?" Kenny asked.

"Would they really know the difference if we sent in a bill for placing George Steinbrenner as a VP of something or other?"

"What company hired him? I thought we lost our account?" Lenny was confused.

"Pick a big company and send them a bill. How could they prove we didn't place George? Would some accounting clerk really know that vice president so-and-so doesn't work at their company?" Sal tested the idea with Kenny.

In spite of the mess they were in, Kenny had standards. He was appalled.

"You want to send in a bill for placing someone who doesn't actually work in that company?"

"Well, if you have a moral issue with it, Mr. high-stakes gambler, we don't have to make up a person. Pick an exec who already works for the company and pretend we placed him."

Kenny held the near-empty sambuca bottle over his open mouth and waited for the last drop to run down his throat.

"I'm telling you, the accounting department won't know the difference."

Sal picked up the current issue of *Economic Week* and leafed through the pages.

"Here, take Dean Nelson, VP of finance." He paused to read an article. "This is interesting. This guy saved his company a lot of money by 'streamlining operations.' Any company would be happy to get him. Yeah, he would be a good placement. In fact, we could place him a few times."

"Jesus, Sal. If you're going to make up a placement, why not go for broke and pretend we placed a female executive? People might get the impression we know what we're doing. Hell, it might actually improve our reputation!"

"Huh?" Lenny was getting a headache.

"Sheesh." His sarcasm having failed to drive home his disgust, Kenny fell into the comfort of his increasingly worn couch.

"OK, if it's gals you want," Sal continued to look through the magazine. "Hold on a minute." He had an idea.

"Lenny?"

"Yeah boss?" Lenny kept his distance.

"Remember that job we did for your cousin many years ago?"

"The one we did for Sonny the Slip or the one wit' that window cleaner who had the accident?"

"The cousin at the chemical company. They had that awful spill that needed remediating. Remember, UMess=RMess?"

"Oh, yeah. I remember. We drove to the South Shore."

"Whateva. We don't need to bore Kenny with the details of the job. Remember that lady who was in charge of that plant?" Sal looked at Lenny to see if any of this was registering.

"Yeah," Lenny remembered. "But when we returned to her place of business we was told she moved on to a different company in another state. I think she moved to the middle of nowhere, didn't she?"

"Moving cross-country is one way to cover your tracks. I read about a guy—Bill or Bob Somebody—took the hit for that mess. The local community board practically ran him out of town when they found out what leaked into the groundwater. That was a brilliant setup. People could stand to learn from her."

"Dat lady was scary, boss."

"I like doing business with people who know what they want. Now, Kenny, don't companies in the middle of nowhere need executives, too?" Sal looked at Kenny, who was running his finger inside the lip of the sambuca bottle. Kenny focused hard to make the four images of Sal merge back into one.

"What kind of organization is it?" Kenny burped out his response.

Sal went to his desk drawer and pulled out a folder that contained information he had been collecting on Carol Himmler. In the plain folder were articles from newspapers and regional business publications about her meteoric rise at StreamLINE.

"StreamLINE Corporation. They're a logistics company in California. Not exactly the middle of nowhere, but it ain't New Jersey, either. Whateva. She's been in the news for doing good at her company. 'Rising young star' is what they called her."

"Wow, boss. You've been keeping tabs on her, huh?"

"Lenny, I never lose track of anyone who owes me a favor."

"That job was a long time ago. Why didn't we call in the favor sooner?"

"You shouldn't squander a chit, Lenny. Sometimes it takes a little time for the right opportunity to pop up."

Sal rifled through the papers until he came across what he was looking for: a slip with Carol's office and home numbers on it.

Knowing that it is harder to refuse a favor in person, Sal's first call was to a travel agent.

X X

As the United States moved toward a service-oriented economy in early 2004, industries that could move material and finished goods faster, cheaper, better were in great demand. Carol Himmler leveraged this trend to put as much distance as possible between herself and the remnants of her junior executive days at Chemix. She rode the momentum straight to the chief operating officer position at StreamLINE, the number two role in that well-regarded freight and logistics company.

Beth Carrington, who had been working for Carol since the COO joined StreamLINE, knew that her boss abhorred waiting. On this morning, as the executive suite prepared for a board of directors meeting the following day, Beth jumped when Carol's phone rang. Beth could hear Carol's bark before she got the receiver to her ear.

"The stupid Jag dealer didn't install the right software on my new GPS system. I can't find the building where this meeting is to be held."

Well accustomed to these outbursts, Beth instantly pulled up a local street map on the Internet and asked Carol: "OK. Now where are you?"

"Beth, if I knew where I was, I wouldn't need your help, would I?"

Beth fumbled a response.

"Forget it. Don Freeman will be there. He ought to be able to handle this situation. He was CEO of his own company before I acquired it, after all. Call Don and tell him to go ahead without me. I am a good thirty minutes away."

Carol hung up and dialed her salon. She now had time before her hair and nail appointment to fit in a deep-tissue massage. The dinner with StreamLINE senior management and the board of directors was that evening, and the quarterly board meeting would take place the following day. Carol anticipated that the board would be giving her the once-over as a candidate to succeed Chuck Goodfellow, the current chief executive officer. She wanted to maximize her opportunity for success, and she always looked healthy (read: young) after her tissues had been sufficiently manipulated.

The board of directors had been particularly solicitous of Carol since the acquisition of Don's company, 3RD Party, had doubled operating margins and increased revenues immediately by almost 30 percent. Another plus was that Don actually had hands-on logistics experience, a critical leadership skill for a company in the transportation business—and a familiarity Carol had not yet acquired, having cut her StreamLINE teeth primarily on strategy and corporate development projects.

Having grown tired of running the show and finding himself far from the supply-chain activities that he loved, Don had been open to overtures from Carol and others interested in purchasing his company. He found the alignment with StreamLINE's business activities and culture more compelling than any other options. It did not hurt that Carol persuaded the board to pay a premium and wipe out the competition also bidding for 3RD Party. One troublesome side note to the purchase was that, as longtime operations guys, Don and Chuck were intrigued by the same supply-chain problems. Carol found their evolving friendship irritating.

With Don's expertise on hand, Carol had the time to do the big-picture maneuvering with the board that was so central to her ambitions. She argued that Don's company should be the first in a series of acquisitions that could enhance StreamLINE's position in the logistics industry. However, Chuck mounted resistance to her recommendations for expanding the company. None too affectionately, Carol labeled Chuck's methodical, organic approach to corporate development the Tortoise Tactic.

Before Carol could complete the call to her salon, her phone rang again. She glanced at the caller ID before answering. It was Beth's number. Perhaps there was a change to the dinner plans that evening. She took the call.

"What is it now?" she shouted.

"Carol Himmler! How are you?"

Taken aback at not hearing Beth's voice, Carol was unable to place this caller. She stammered a "Hello."

"Carol, it's Bob Smith of Chemix. Remember me?"

It had been a while since Carol had departed Chemix, and as she left an investigation into the chemical leak was under way, the by-product of a story by an enterprising young journalist. While he found it difficult to understand how, exactly, the cable had snapped, Bob admitted that evidence at the scene supported the conclusion that it had created the breach. He also could not deny that his team had put in those production lines. Chemix was fined $5 million. It might have been even more damaging financially for the company, but, as the reporter noted, Carol epitomized grace under fire and addressed the immediate danger by quickly remediating the area. Johnny Egan might have said Carol remediated the evidence, but job security and family obligations refocused his priorities and his conscience.

Chemix senior management decided that someone had to take one for the team, especially since local officials were calling for heads to roll. Bob's was presented, minus his pension benefits and any financial gains resulting from Chemix stock awards. Additional media references had been so negative that Bob's employment prospects amounted to a part-time role in his brother-in-law's house-painting business and some janitorial work.

"If anyone asks about your past, tell them you recently got out of prison," his wife's brother had instructed Bob to say to prospective painting customers.

More recently, Bob's nine-year-old daughter, Cecilia, had been diagnosed with leukemia. That happened to coincide with a significant jump in interest rates that put a huge dent in the market for home equity loans. The home-improvement business hit the wall. Bob's brother-in-law, who had six mouths of his own to feed, reduced the painting staff to himself and a twentysomething high school dropout.

So, with a resume that looked like a patchwork quilt of odd jobs spanning the past four years, Bob reached out to his old cronies at Chemix for help to find a job with medical benefits. Someone had suggested that Bob reach out to Carol, now a big shot at StreamLINE.

"Bob Smith? From Chemix? It's been a long time. What do you want?" There was not a lot of time to beg the Parisian-born salon owner to wiggle in an extra spa treatment.

Bob had been genuinely eager to hear about his former colleague's success at what he recognized as a powerful company. And, since he was in the dark about Carol's part in the downward spiral of his career, he had been looking forward to catching up with her. It was obvious, though, that Carol was not as interested in hearing about his life.

Who knows? Maybe she has a kid who is dying too, he thought.

"Well, Carol, I appreciate that you are a busy executive, so let me get right to it. I noticed that StreamLINE advertised for a director of lean operations. It sounds like you need an executive with engineering and manufacturing depth who can eliminate waste in operating processes. I don't know if you recall, Carol, but I managed a few plants at Chemix before I took over the engineering responsibility. I—"

"Oh, Bob. Oh, I really don't think so. You see, operations in a logistics firm is different from the work we did at Chemix. We are integrating quality into all we do at StreamLINE. I really don't see how your experience would fit in." Carol hoped to get Bob off the phone. Her salon was so busy these days.

"Oh, but I worked for a logistics company early in my career. You may not know that. I do have familiarity—"

"Yes, I see," she interrupted him again. "Well, Bob, I am not involved in that level of hiring activity, so I wouldn't even know who to recommend you to."

Bob tried a different tack. "My daughter, Cecilia. She's sick."

"Oh, I am sorry to hear that. What is it? Is she allergic to something?" Carol clicked to the next track on her CD of ocean sounds, but waves crashing on a rocky shoreline was not what she wanted to hear. She hit the track advance again. *Jesus, this music was supposed to be relaxing*, she reflected.

"Leukemia. Some days she can't get out of bed. But still she dreams of becoming a doctor. Do you remember that time she showed up at the office in that doctor costume? She's had a stethoscope around her neck ever since," Bob chuckled warmly.

Carol could not summon up a greeting-card sentiment for a preteen with leukemia. She decided that a moment of silence would imply sincere concern, so she let a pause hang in the air before she spoke.

"Oh, Bob. I am SO sorry to hear that. You must be sick with worry." Carol flipped the track advance again on the CD player. She pictured that annoying Jag salesman who sold her this car.

Where is that friggin' song? Carol's irritation returned.

"Well, it's not easy. But she has been such a blessing, and we are grateful," Bob responded.

"Yes, of course you are. I would be happy to get your resume into the right hands at our company. Send it to my assistant, Beth Carrington, and she can make that happen for you."

"Thanks, Carol. Your support means a lot."

"There must be some way a charitable contribution can help. I want to help you, Bob." *And get you off the phone. My masseuse is never available after lunch*, Carol thought.

Bob felt ill at ease, but he could not tell if it was his own or Carol's discomfort he was sensing.

"Well, we are planning a fundraising dinner," he said.

"Yes, of course you are. You must give Beth that information as well. Maybe StreamLINE, er, I can fund the cocktail hour. I'll have to check that leukemia is on our list of approved charitable causes and, if it is, you'll have the best cocktail hour ever." Pleased with her suggestion, Carol moved to bid her former colleague goodbye.

"I am running to a meeting with a vendor who has a unique process. It is hard to get an appointment, so I must be off. You know how it is. Call my office line and Beth will take care of everything." Carol hung up and again punched the salon's number into her phone so that she could confirm her coiffure appointment and beg the owner to add a massage to her treatments.

Her phone rang again after she tweaked her salon appointments. *Now what?*

X X I

Later that afternoon, Sal presented Carol with a box of cannoli he had purchased and transported from the pastry shop around the corner from the now-shuttered Chemix plant.

"I wasn't sure you could find the good sweets we have in Jersey out here, so I went to that bakery near the plant where we did that favor for you." Sal made himself comfortable in the chair across from Carol's desk.

"Yes, you mentioned that favor when we spoke on the phone. So sad that my colleague created a situation that led to those leaks. I understand the young man who discovered the problem had to have four skin grafts.

What a shame." Suspicious, Carol moved the box of pastries to the side of her desk.

"Yeah. Too bad for the young man and your friend. Whateva. Carol, in my business a favor is a favor. It's a handshake between honorable business-people." Sal reached for the box of cannoli and opened it.

"Here, try one. I bet there's nothing this good on this side of the Mississippi." He smiled graciously at Carol. Watching Sal take a bite, she accepted the cannoli.

Wiping powdered sugar from her lips, Carol acknowledged that the cannoli were, indeed, delicious. She carefully placed the cream-filled pastry, with a light impression of her lipstick, back in the box and asked, "What business are you in these days, Sal?"

"My business interests have expanded since our last deal, Carol. I've taken on a partner whose expertise has been placing executives at fine companies like yours."

"How did you meet your partner?"

"Carol, in my line of work you meet all kinds. Kenny—that's my partner—well, turns out he had an awful gambling habit. He came to owe large debts to associates of mine. He was really in a jam." Sal offered Carol another cannoli. She declined.

"Kenny's a good guy. Just a little weak around the horses. And the card table. Roulettes, too. He's not as bad with the one-arm bandits, but I wouldn't leave him alone with three lemons in the kitchen."

Carol's desk phone rang. As she reached to answer it, Sal gave her the subtle but powerful impression that he should not be interrupted. She pressed the speaker to let Beth know to hold her calls during this meeting.

"Anyways, as I was saying," Sal continued, "Kenny couldn't come up with the cash to cover his note, but he was good for it because he had receivables for several hundred thousand dollars. When he told me he got paid that much money to move suits around from company to company, I said that was the best scam I'd heard in years. You didn't even have to get your hands dirty." Realizing his faux pas, Sal corrected course. "Now since I got into the business, I understand how critical it is to have the right leadership! So I bought into Kenny's partnership."

"What role does Kenny play in the business today?"

"Tough break that guy got. The stress of the recruiting business got to him. He's out on what we HR professionals call LOA. Leave of Absence for the layman. Kenny's resting at a place in Vegas. My friends are looking after him out there."

Carol had no intention of giving business to this gangster, but she assumed it would be prudent to meet with him, given the threatening undercurrent during their earlier phone call.

"Congratulations on your good fortune, Carol. I wonder what your boss would think if he found out what really happened in that Chemix plant."

She was eager to move the meeting along.

"Sal, I think it's admirable how you are assisting this degenerate. What did you say his name was?" Before Sal could answer, Carol continued, "Whatever. It's great that your interests have expanded. While I'd be absolutely delighted to give your executive search firm a shot, we don't have any executive openings that need filling right now." Carol took a folder out of her desk drawer and shoved papers into it.

Standing up to signal the conclusion of the meeting, Carol believed it would be wise to end this conversation on the right note.

"Perhaps there could be a project down the road. The human resources professionals make the decisions about these sorts of things." Turning her back on Sal, Carol put the folder in the credenza behind her desk.

When she again faced him, Carol was surprised that Sal, looking quite relaxed, had not yet stood up. He reached across her desk, took the box of cannoli, opened it, and again offered one to Carol. Irritated at Sal's naïveté about corporate meeting etiquette, she took the box of cannoli from him and firmly put it down.

"Sal, while I appreciate your taking the time to fly out here to meet with me, you must understand that I have pressing business issues to attend to right now."

Carol felt a strange sense of dread as Sal stood up and walked toward the window behind her desk.

Maybe I pushed too far. He might leak that story about the Chemix spill after all, she worried.

Sal carefully positioned himself behind her desk, leaning against the credenza.

Goddamn Johnny Egan probably didn't give him enough money, Carol fretted.

Carol sat down in her chair and turned to face him.

"What a beautiful view out your window. Is that a horse farm?" Sal asked.

What does he want?

"Where?" Carol got up to look out the window. Sal pointed to the white picket fence enclosing a circular field beyond the row of colonial-style homes in the distance.

"I guess it is. Never noticed it before," she responded.

"Never noticed it?" Sal moved directly behind Carol. He was not a big man, but with him standing so close, she felt his presence powerfully.

"Carol, you are too busy. You've got to stop and smell the roses. Or at least look out the window once in a while."

Carol wished Beth would buzz her with a mundane issue so that she could cut this short, but she had already told Beth not to interrupt her.

"By the way, I ran into that old colleague of yours, Bob Smith." Sal smiled as he returned to his chair. "Funny thing. He lives near the bakery where I bought these cannoli."

Carol sat down again and faced Sal.

"Interesting," she said. *Maybe Bob's call this morning wasn't a coincidence.*

"Shame what happened to his career after he was blamed for that environmental disaster in the Chemix plant. He never found meaningful work again. I understand he did odd jobs as a house painter and janitor. That is, until the school he was cleaning found out he was responsible for the spill that contaminated the drinking water in that town. Did you know that three kids in the local school have been diagnosed with leukemia, Carol?"

Carol shook her head.

"Yep. One of them is Bob's kid. He must feel like shit, don't you think? I wonder how he pays for his daughter's medical care, being unemployed, that is."

Sal looked directly at Carol as he spoke.

"You know what Bob says? He says that plant was one of the safest. He found cable from the production lines that he believes was cut. His guess is that somebody sliced those lines, and then they hit the containers hard enough to snap a hole in them. Sounds preposterous, doesn't it?"

Carol sat silently.

"He wanted the state authorities to investigate his sabotage theory, but when they asked for evidence, the cables were nowhere to be found."

Sal placed his briefcase on Carol's desk, opened it, and dumped cable lines on last month's productivity report.

"Oh," Carol sighed.

"They might have looked something like this." Sal handed an eight-inch piece of cable to Carol, explaining that Tiny, Lenny's cousin, had been preserving the material and the story of what really happened in the plant.

"You remember him? He's the one who asked us to help you with that favor."

Carol handled the piece of the production line, considering her options.

"Where I come from, one good turn deserves another. It makes for good business," Sal pressed.

Cornered by her own history, Carol did not take long to devise a plan.

In response to a slipping growth rate, StreamLINE's board had asked the members of the executive team to step up their game and drive expansion at the eighty-year-old firm. The directors would be deciding on a few proposals, one of which, submitted by Carol, requested funds to build a corporate development team. This team would support the acquisition strategy Carol recommended to grow the company. And, Carol believed, this strategy would strengthen her candidacy to be the next CEO. She did not want anything to get in the way of an affirmative vote on that agenda item. Sal's threat had to be neutralized.

"You know, Sal, there may be executive search work here for you, after all. I'm pitching the board of directors on a new direction for the company. If I am successful, we'll have to hire an executive to lead a corporate development function—we don't have this experience in the company."

"Sounds promising."

"Yes, it does. Though, mind you, it needs approval from the board. We'll need money to staff the department and a kitty to purchase acquisitions. On top of all this, our CEO is old-school. He thinks we can grow the company organically, one step at a time. You can't get the multiples that Wall Street demands these days unless you think big and act boldly."

"Once you have approval to build the team, we can get started on the search for this executive," Sal said.

"Theoretically, yes."

"I'll prepare our first invoice, which, by the way, is payable upon receipt."

Feeling the power settle a little more evenly in the room, Carol stood up and moved around her desk toward the door. Sal followed her.

"Let's get the approval on my proposal first."

She held the pieces of broken assembly line in one hand and offered the empty, faded green briefcase to Sal as she opened the door.

"Consider it a souvenir, Carol. I have others."

Carol didn't know if Sal was referring to the briefcase or the cables. Either way, it did not bode well for her.

"I sense ours will be a very consequential association, Carol."

Sal winked at Beth as he left the office.

CAROL RECOGNIZED THAT she had gotten lucky with the acquisition of 3RD Party, especially after a bidding war had raised the cost of that transaction. She needed something more to spur momentum in her favor so that the board would anoint her as heir apparent, something they had been reluctant to do so far.

The weakest link in StreamLINE's leadership chain appeared to be the weighty lifestyle of Tomas Severe, chairman of StreamLINE's board. Manipulated correctly, Tomas's precarious personal situation, aggravated by whispers of another divorce, might be just the ticket to encourage the board to choose her strategic plan for the company and, ultimately, choose Carol to succeed Chuck.

Aside from the financial leverage it might provide Tomas, if StreamLINE were on a loftier growth trajectory, as per Carol's proposal, business publications would become more interested in covering the relatively quiet company. Carol assumed that she would receive some of the additional publicity. She did not see her long-term career in the logistics industry. Yet StreamLINE presented a respectable platform from which she might leap to a sexier company, one offering money, benefits, and prestige commensurate with her contributions. And it would be sweet to be the CEO of StreamLINE before such a leap.

Therefore, Carol focused like a laser on persuading Tomas, especially since she suspected her influence with Chuck to be on the wane. She had sent her proposal exclusively to the chairman, who called her immediately after he reviewed her recommendations.

"I'll take it to the board, Carol, and we'll drive this as an agenda item at the quarterly meeting. This is good work. The financial assumptions you have made appear to be sound. It looks like we could get several times today's valuation if we added the service tiers you recommend."

Carol set up the chairman to have her back at the board meeting: "Yes, we can, if we are smart about it. We must be careful not to overpay in this hot market. That's why we need to hire an expert to report to me on acquisition strategy."

XXII

"**M**arinated figpeckers, mind you! Henri is SO to die for. Such a treasure after that misadventure with our last chef, Gilles."

"Figpeckers?" Private-equity titan Tomas Severe chafed at the cocktail chatter about personal chefs. Normally he might have led the repartee before StreamLINE's quarterly board meetings, but tonight the chairman of the board had a lot on his mind, so he relinquished control of the discussion to accomplished raconteurs Lulu Earl and Bubba Oberlin.

"Small birds, darling. Small birds." Scion to the Earl Widget fortune and chairwoman of StreamLINE's compensation committee, Lulu delicately, yet purposefully, reminded Tomas of the distance in their respective upbringings. "Délicieux." Lulu pressed her fingers to her lips and blew a kiss to the gods of food and wine.

"We should have a cook-off, Lulu," Bubba said. "Your Henri's haute cookin' against my Maria's down-home, feel-good-all-over fixings." Bubba, new to the board of StreamLINE, chuckled at the image of his Louisiana-reared, mama-taught, don't-mess-with-my-apron cook giving a culinary whoopin' to Lulu's French-schooled, uppity-crust, flown-in-ingredients-only chef.

These people have way too much money and time, Tomas thought as he drifted back to the conversation he had had with his financial adviser around his upcoming, and likely hostile, divorce. Tomas's wife held powerful evidence of his infidelities. Although Tomas's attorney advised him to hide assets before papers were filed, his decidedly ethical financial manager would only support shedding property to raise cash for a quick settlement. With his personal life already enough of a mess, Tomas sided with his upright financial manager. Regrettably, a recent series of bad bets left his portfolio full of undervalued companies. Selling anything in the near term could put his personal circumstances, already overwhelmed by the upkeep of multiple residences, a Kentucky horse farm, and a vineyard in Napa Valley, at grave risk.

Tomas had grown up on the streets of Barcelona. With a head for math and a persona for persuasion, the street urchin charmed the local Catholic church into funding his education; the area tennis club into bestowing employment; and the jaded, affluent wives lunching at said club into discarding the restraints of their matrimonial vows for a few hours. Years in the financial markets, particularly with high-risk, highly leveraged transactions, had, until lately, served Tomas well. All the same, his affinity for leggy, brunette cocktail waitresses never waned. He should have presumed his current wife would have been suspicious, given that she was once a leggy, brunette cocktail waitress herself—one whose canoodling behind the bar of an East London pub precipitated Tomas's divorce from his second wife.

Tomas's mind wandered to the business proposal that Carol had sent him. He had been intrigued with Carol's recommendations to expand StreamLINE's footprint rapidly through a series of acquisitions. Her first one, of 3RD Party, had certainly added value. An even bigger StreamLINE might command a greater premium if Tomas sold his shares, a transaction he was considering more seriously as wife number three intensified her denunciation of him.

Leaning back into the soft leather of the bar lounge chair on this evening of the board dinner, days after his review of Carol's proposal, Tomas stirred his martini with a speared olive. He smiled appropriately at the banter between his fellow board members but did not engage them. When a StreamLINE board member uttered something ridiculous, causing him to shake rather than stir his libation, a splash of vodka hit his black-onyx, platinum pinky ring. *Patience*, he told himself as he wiped his hands with the restaurant's monogrammed cocktail napkin. *More flies with honey.*

The lubricating effects of the top-shelf vodka were beginning to find their mark as Tomas listened to Bubba, a former CEO himself, make a compelling argument in support of yet another strategy for StreamLINE. Don Freeman had outlined a design for organic growth, one that suggested steady, but more predictable, revenue and earnings for existing business divisions each quarter. While his plan did not hint at the upside to stock valuation that Carol's approach trumpeted, Don's proposal called for job creation *with* the revenue curve, not ahead of it, leading to tighter management of operating expenses.

This guy makes a lot of sense, Tomas considered.

Tomas listened keenly until a vision of his divorce attorney knocking on his skull crossed his mind.

"Mierda! I almost forgot," he murmured.

"What!" exclaimed Lulu, who was unaccustomed to the street talk of Barcelona's indigent neighborhoods.

"*What* is the right question," Tomas said, composing himself. "Bubba, we value your insights. However, I would argue we should not overlook the compelling proposal Carol has submitted. The valuations in this industry are lower than they have been in a decade, making any company, including

StreamLINE, a cheaper acquisition target. Wouldn't it behoove this board, as representatives of the stockholders, to return their investment, and confidence, sooner rather than later? Let's build StreamLINE into something big quickly or risk becoming an acquisition target ourselves."

Before Bubba could respond, Lulu lent her perspective.

"Tomas, darling, this board is supportive of Carol. Indeed, she has proved to be a good investment for StreamLINE. However, one thing we have never been able to lock down is her level of commitment."

Tomas was surprised to hear that; he always found Carol to be hard-driving and committed to StreamLINE's success, as long as it was linked to her own.

"She certainly says she is committed," Lulu continued. "But I've often wondered about her allegiance in the long run. Every business goes through ups and downs. Might her loyalty fade if StreamLINE's fortunes weren't as great as her own ambitions? In other words, is she with us for better or worse?"

Bubba offered, "She does seem a bit self-centered."

"That vanity keeps her focused on achieving good business results," Tomas interjected. "What's good for her is good for the company, too."

"At the end of the day, Tomas, the company's excellent results haven't hurt her recognition in the business press." Lulu referred Tomas to a recent issue of *Economic Week* with Carol, among other young female leaders, on the cover.

"I'll remind this board again that StreamLINE and its shareholders have benefited from the symbiotic nature of that relationship," Tomas said, reinforcing his position.

The six board members nodded in agreement on Carol's contribution to the company and their own coffers.

"If she wants to be the feature story someday, StreamLINE must do very well. Carol is exceedingly motivated for success," Tomas continued.

Despite Tomas's stance, Lulu felt momentum for her agenda.

"Tomas dear, we all agree that Carol has been an outstanding asset to this organization, and we are incredibly grateful to you for bringing her to the company. However, ever since she arrived at StreamLINE, Carol's been pushing for bigger positions. The ink isn't yet dry on her strategic plan for one area of the business when she asks for more. I think I can speak for the rest of the board when I say that we'd feel more secure about Carol's allegiance if she were to demonstrate a long-term commitment to almost anything."

All of the board members had had their share of meetings with Carol, and there was general agreement around the table on this point.

"You can learn a lot about somebody from what they value," Bubba said. "Carol and I got to talkin' 'bout family stuff in our last one-on-one meeting. That's real important where I come from. Did you know she doesn't own a pet? Not even a pet rock. Hell, the plants in her office are on life support."

"How long will her relationship with StreamLINE last if her acquisition strategy puts pressure on operating expenses?" Lulu queried her fellow directors.

Fancying herself a woman of discriminating taste and exposing a not-well-hidden agenda as chairwoman of the conservative Relations Matter PAC, Lulu pressed on: "And, what would investors think about a nonattached female CEO in a company with deep-rooted conservative traditions? Think of the ramifications to the stock."

Tomas found her opinions discriminatory rather than discriminating.

"You're telling me that if Carol gets married, you'd support her plan?" Tomas said.

"Desire is the best way to ensure commitment," Lulu smiled at Tomas.

Tomas noticed Carol, Don, and Chuck entering the restaurant. Before the board rose to greet StreamLINE's senior executive team, Bubba seconded the proposal:

"Wouldn't hurt her loyalty to us if she was tied down with a few rug rats to feed and college educations to fund."

XXIII

I n a preemptive move intended to generate support for his choice as heir apparent, Chuck rose during dinner and proposed a toast to the leaders who would take StreamLINE into the future.

"I want to congratulate our team for the outstanding business results of the last quarter. Not only have we increased revenue again, but we also continue to benefit from efficiencies in our core business areas."

A round of applause and a few "hear, hears" went around the table. Chuck raised his glass a second time.

"Don, your innovations in supply-chain technology and creative leadership during great change in this industry have been a beacon of light for StreamLINE. Congratulations on the superior results." Chuck beamed at Don, perceiving in this executive a younger version of himself. Although he had stood in opposition to the acquisition of 3RD Party—largely due to Carol's mishandling of the transaction and the resulting bidding war— Chuck capitulated in the end, appreciating the value to his company, which was driven in large measure by Don's unique talents.

Sitting next to Chuck, Tomas cleared his throat forcefully. When he had gotten Chuck's attention, Tomas's eyes locked with the CEO's, and he directed their mutual gaze to Carol.

"Oh, and yes, to Carol. Carol, thanks for bringing Don and his team to StreamLINE." Chuck raised a glass to Carol, who returned the gesture, a smile beginning to defrost her facial muscles.

"Act fast." Carol heard herself murmur.

"What's that, Carol?" Tomas threw support to his protégé.

"Tomas, I was agreeing with Chuck. How lucky StreamLINE was to have had the additional revenue and margin that the 3RD Party organization brought to our portfolio of services."

Carol's effort to gain control of the dialogue continued. " . . . a portfolio that will grow stronger still with more acquisitions, including ACME Distributors, with whom we met this morning."

Chuck gave Don a look of surprise. Don subtly shrugged his shoulders to indicate he did not understand Carol's reference. Chuck questioned Carol.

"What did you think of the ACME presentation today, Carol?"

Assuming that Don, who reported to her, would back her up, Carol looked at him as she answered. "Uh . . . it was compelling."

"Compelling. That's interesting." Chuck paused to take a sip of wine and decided to keep going. "What exactly did you find compelling?"

Carol scanned the table to see if anyone else might want to jump in. A fleeting image of her hairdresser discussing hair colors momentarily caught her attention. The Jaguar salesman who sold her the GPS system came to her mind, too. She made a mental note to upbraid that salesman as soon as possible.

"Well, the whole thing, actually," she finally responded to Chuck's question. "Everything about the business model, financial structure." She looked around again for a lifeline. None was offered. "And the leadership team, of course."

Chuck had become suspicious of Carol's ambitions, particularly because her contributions to StreamLINE consisted largely of presenting smaller companies in the supply-chain industry that might be candidates for acquisition. While Chuck acknowledged that acquisitions might be worthwhile as part of a strategy to augment specific offerings, he derided Carol's strategy of acquisition for acquisition's sake. His view was that her approach might gain revenues in the short term but, in the longer term, did little more than acquire other companies' problems.

"What strengths did you see in their leadership team?" he asked Carol.

Sensing that Chuck was trying to trap her, she punted to Don.

"Don, you know these guys best. How would you describe their leadership attributes?"

Delicately walking a tightrope between his boss and his boss's boss, Don offered his views on the ACME management team, as well as that company's business model. He felt that ACME warranted further review, particularly in light of their pioneering, and patented, logistics software.

Don's position somewhat vindicated Carol's points without flying in the face of Chuck's obvious inquisition.

"Thanks, Don. I came away from the meeting with similar observations," Chuck said. This revelation shook Carol: Chuck knew that she had not been at the meeting.

Time to change the subject, Carol thought.

"I'd like to remind the board that we need to consider the proposal to create a new executive role in support of StreamLINE's progress," she said. "A vice president of mergers and acquisitions would research target companies, negotiate deals, and assimilate the new brands into StreamLINE. This is a position, and a strategy, that many organizations have utilized to enhance shareholder value."

There were murmurs of agreement around the table, led noticeably by Tomas, who propped up Carol's suggestion with fist-pounding and a few cheers.

Chuck had also been made aware of Tomas's shaky personal affairs. He was concerned about the influence those circumstances might have on Tomas's judgment, particularly now that the chairman's company, the Severe Fund, controlled 51 percent of StreamLINE's outstanding shares. He also worried that Carol's personal appeal might blind his chairman to the holes in her leadership profile.

"There is another way to grow the company," Chuck responded. "Given the groundwork that Don and his team have laid, we might consider leveraging our strategic advantages through an alliance with ACME Distributors that would give us access to their software."

Now that he had regained everyone's attention, Chuck spelled out his idea. "By combining the efforts of these two strong organizations, we provide Don and his team with the right resources and relationships needed to make a step-function change to our model and expand the business immediately. I suspect the ACME leadership will also see this as a win-win situation. Don, would this type of arrangement marry well with your plan for organic growth?"

Carefully selecting his words, Don agreed with Chuck. "An offshoot of this type of relationship," Don added, "is that we get the chance to kick each others' tires before we are tied to a long-term relationship like a merger. We might even realize some benefits in the first quarter."

There were louder murmurs around the table.

Bubba led the applause for this try-before-you-buy plan. Carol shot quizzical glances in Tomas's direction, but he ignored her exaggerated coughing and pounced on an idea. He suggested that the company embark on both paths simultaneously.

"Don, you take the initiative with the ACME people and set up that partnership. Let us know what you need from the board to make that successful. Carol, you seek out new companies for StreamLINE to acquire. Let's revisit this idea of a new executive to handle mergers and acquisitions later, once we see what acquisition targets pop up. Meantime, we have a two-pronged approach to advance the business." Tomas slapped Chuck on the back.

"One of these strategies would have to be successful, so either way, StreamLINE benefits," he continued. "How's that for a win-win?" Tomas smiled at his fellow directors and the StreamLINE executive leadership team. Much as he ultimately favored a strategy of quickly acquiring revenue, he ignored Carol's frown because this arrangement hedged the rather large bet he had on the company.

TOMAS TOOK CAROL by the elbow as they stood up after dinner.

"Stay and have a drink. I want to discuss something with you." He directed her toward two empty chairs in the lounge area.

Lulu crossed her fingers and waved them at Tomas.

"Is this something we can cover in a conference call, Tomas?" Carol smiled at him, but he sensed tension. She had witnessed Tomas swinging the board in his favor on previous occasions, and tonight she was disappointed that he had not supported her recommendations more forcefully. In fact, Carol had been so convinced that Tomas could sell her plan to the board, she had had no compunction about rearranging her schedule in favor of a more comprehensive salon session that morning. After all, a future CEO needs to exude confidence in everything, including skin tone.

Tomas was satisfied that he had made the right call. What could be better than both Carol and Don working on plans to increase his investment? However, he had some coddling to do to get Carol in his pocket in the event she became the lead in this horse race. And he knew the coveted CEO mantle was the lever to assuage her ego. But, just in case Carol did not come out ahead in this contest, Tomas made a mental note to set up a lunch with Don as soon as possible.

"Carol, you know I believe in you. Your proposal is a great scheme for building shareholder value. In the meantime, given the love that Chuck clearly has for Don, doesn't it make sense to keep him busy? He is your direct report, is he not?"

Carol nodded.

"And wouldn't Don's achievements speak well of your ability as a leader?" Tomas was familiar with the annual performance reviews of all senior executives. Building and sustaining teams was an area in which Carol had often been noted as weak.

Carol bristled at an ancient memory of Ed Simmons's insinuation that she was not a good manager. Tomas was right; Don's triumphs would reflect well on her.

"So, if both Don and I are successful in our projects, you could still convince the board that I am the right leader to succeed Chuck, right?"

Tomas knew Carol was not much for small talk.

"Look, Carol, that would put you in a good position to be the heir apparent to Chuck. But there is something else." Tomas teed up the agenda item succinctly.

Carol slapped an open palm on the bar, demonstrating passion around what she felt was rightly hers: the executive brass ring at StreamLINE.

"Like what? I've already brought more value to this company through one acquisition than anyone else has in years! And I've been working on the . . . er, suggestions that Chuck recommended during my performance review."

"Carol, the board has confidence in you as a leader. This is all good. However, let's consider the makeup of this board: veteran CEOs like Bubba and socially conscious personalities like Lulu. Both want long-term stability for StreamLINE and for the investors they represent. After my stake, they are the largest institutional investors."

"Stability? Stability?!" Carol inadvertently knocked over Tomas's drink. The bartender ran over with a towel. Tomas looked to convey an apology as Carol, either not aware it had happened or unconcerned, continued ranting.

"I have given years of my life to this organization. I have required my teams to work long days with minimal resources! I have consultants and investment bankers on contract to bring us good ideas and identify processes to improve. And for what? To watch as my brilliant plan takes a back seat to the second-rate ideas of AN OPERATIONS MANAGER?"

"Carol, Don built and ran his own company, for God's sake." Tomas checked his watch. If he could move this conversation along, there would be time to work in a call to a sultry customer-care operator working the graveyard shift. He had developed a regular late-night steamy dialogue with the untraceable, virtual sexpot after his satellite TV blew out.

"Look, Chuck's been married to the same woman for forty-three years," he continued. "That's what this board is used to. They are very old-school. Lulu wants to maneuver in a certain social milieu. Bubba thinks that family commitments will keep you focused on the business of StreamLINE."

"Tomas, I'm a plain speaker. What exactly are you saying to me?"

"They want you to get, and stay, married, Carol."

"You don't get married and stay married, Tomas." Carol could not help herself. "Do they doubt your loyalty?"

"As long as I keep money in this company, they don't care who, what, or how many times I marry."

Carol sat without speaking for a few minutes. Tomas shifted his weight in the lounge chair as the silence between them sank in. He considered how much time he should give her to think. Not enough and she would not take the recommendation seriously; too much and she might get angry and quit. When the bartender bought the next drink, assuming Tomas was striking out with Carol, he cleared his throat. Carol spoke first.

"For this strategy to work, we have to move fast."

Nodding, Tomas pulled a handkerchief out of his pocket and pretended to cough. The less said the better, in this circumstance.

"Convenience has to be considered," Carol continued.

Tomas watched Carol intently. On the verge of what seemed like a second lengthy pause, his mind raced for something encouraging, yet noncommittal, to say.

"Of course, he'd have to be good-looking and successful!" Carol added.

"Certainly!" Tomas hoped he sounded supportive. Then he recognized the pensive gaze he often saw Carol take on as she worked through complex business issues.

"Are we sure it has to be a man?" Carol asked with genuine curiosity.

"Carol!"

"I've seen the way Lulu looks at me, social milieu or not." She picked up a handful of lightly salted Virginia peanuts from the bar and popped them into her freshly Botox-laced mouth. "We need to have all the data points correct from the beginning."

Carol pressed more peanuts against her swollen lips. Her long, silky black hair seemed particularly luscious as Tomas considered the idea of Lulu and Carol en flagrante. The customer-care operator could wait.

"How about Don?" Carol continued.

Now Tomas took a breath, and a handful of peanuts. "Well, he is good-looking, successful, and terribly convenient."

Carol was encouraged that Tomas saw things the same way. "In one move, I could appease the board and neutralize the competition."

"There are wrinkles to this idea, however." Tomas said, signaling for another drink. This was going to be a long conversation, but not for the reasons he had originally considered. "It would appear to me that Don is happily married and might not be considering divorce. And I can't prove this, but I have a gut feel about it: I get the sense he despises you."

"Hey, this would be a sacrifice for me, too. I haven't heard you come up with anything yet."

"Carol, I am encouraged you see the professional advantages to this initiative, but there is no deadline."

"Tomas, my CEO clock is ticking. The board may not have a deadline, but I do." Carol finished her gin and tonic. "Besides, how much time will your wife give you before her lawyers ask for a settlement?"

Impressed with Carol's knowledge about his affairs, Tomas made a mental note to find out who in his circle had spilled the beans about his divorce.

"What about one of those professional dating services?" he suggested. "I had a friend who met his second and fourth wives through one of those organizations. He was quite pleased with the return on investment."

"I might as well have a headhunter find me a husband." Carol asked the barkeep for a glass of ice water. But her flip remark gave her an idea. "Tomas, if you can get the board to agree to hire the mergers and acquisitions executive I want for my team, I'll engage a search firm and ask for a two-fer."

Tomas was confused. "What's a two-fer?"

"We'll have StreamLINE pay the executive search firm to find the corporate development executive I want, and we'll ask the same firm to introduce me to prospective suitors for free. So again I am creating value for StreamLINE, because we wouldn't pay a fee to find me a husband!"

Tomas tried to figure out how the company would save money by not having to pay to find Carol a husband. *No matter*, he thought. *Carol seems accepting of the board's recommendation and has a strategy to get it done. That's more than I can say for many of the executives I've worked with.*

Reasoning that the costs involved in hiring a new executive would be a pittance compared to the potential value the executive could deliver for the company, Tomas assumed he could convince Chuck that this addition to Carol's team was a good idea. Plus, nothing about this new executive position flew in the face of Don's proposal, which clearly had Chuck's support. Tomas had not pushed this issue during the board dinner because it seemed extraneous to his agenda. Now it appeared beneficial, as leverage with Carol.

Generally, executive searches took about three months, during which time Tomas figured that Carol could woo a suitor, get married, and implement her plan to build the company through acquisitions. That would give Tomas time to court specific buyers for his investment in StreamLINE. He thought about how he might stall his wife's attorneys.

Carol interrupted Tomas's reverie with an intriguing consideration: "We have to have the right search firm for this type of assignment."

"Got to be a professional who has good instincts about people if we are going to ask them to help you find Mr. Right," Tomas suggested.

"Yes. Instincts. It can't be someone who stands on some high moral ground or we won't get the speed we need to consummate this deal."

Taken aback by Carol's indifference to the integrity of the executive search professional required to secure her a soul mate, Tomas spilled his drink in his lap. The bartender shook his head in exasperation as he handed a stack of napkins to Tomas.

"Carol, the search firm must have the moral muscle to identify only the most distinguished and socially connected mates for you." He patted his slacks with the bar napkins. "You don't want to get stuck with a deadbeat."

Carol picked through the peanuts in the dish on the bar. "Right. Muscle. Connected. Dead."

Except for the "dead" comment, Tomas felt they were making progress.

"Choosing the right search partner will be critical, Carol."

"I know a guy."

Having reached détente with Tomas, Carol shook his hand, grabbed her coat, and asked the maître d' to fetch her car.

XXIV

"There's been a little hiccup." Carol chose her words carefully. Speaking from her newly rearranged office—her desk now sat in a corner facing the door and across from the window overlooking that horse farm—Carol felt safer talking to Sal with no room for anyone or anything to get behind her. It also helped that there were multiple states between them, as Sal was back in New Jersey.

"Hiccup? What's a hiccup?" Sal did not understand. "Is that like when someone is unexpectedly detained? Or is it like a little problem?"

Carol did not know what a little problem meant in Sal's world. It could mean anything from an overnight stay in the clink to a business partner gone missing. Carol's penchant for directness took over.

"Look, I have the chairman of StreamLINE's board in my pocket. He is going to persuade the rest of the board and the CEO that we need to hire an executive who can build the company through acquisitions."

This sounded like good news, so Sal was confused again.

"I don't get it. Everyone will support you? I get paid to find you this new executive. How is that a hiccup?"

Carol tried to sculpt the right message.

"Tomas, our chairman, has to work the board."

"So this Tomas, he takes the board out for a nice meal, talks about the family and commitment. Abracadabra, everybody's good, no?"

"Sal, it doesn't work exactly that way—though it's not too far from what you've described, interestingly." Carol laid out the business plan that she and Tomas had discussed.

"Wow! You would be positioned to be the next CEO. That's excellent news, Carol!" Sal considered the fees he could make if Carol got the top job and was in control of the entire company.

"Yes, it's good, but it's not locked up yet. You see, the board is rather old-fashioned."

"You gotta be kidding me. After all the press you been getting, they still want a man in that top job?" Sal feigned indignation.

"No, no. They've read those articles too!" Carol smiled as she considered that even this mobster was aware of her accomplishments. She scribbled the name of her publicist on the calendar. It was time to discuss an angle for a new article.

"Sal, the board consists of seasoned business and community leaders who feel that the next CEO of StreamLINE should present permanence and fidelity in all aspects of her life. Like marriage, for instance."

Disgusted with Lenny's inherent sloppiness and disappointed that Giana was not more of a homemaker, Sal cleaned the handle of the espresso machine with the only available tool, his linen handkerchief. "Marriage and family. That's important in my business, too, Carol. I get that." Sal examined the coffee grime collected on his handkerchief.

Carol considered the feminist arguments she could make, but, more narcissistic than ideological, she had come to terms with the board's request and now simply wanted to fulfill the mission.

"Yes, well, the bottom line is I need to get a husband pronto. Tomas will push the board to pay a search firm to find the new executive I want if the same search firm will also help me find a husband for free."

"Carol, if that's a hiccup, then my executive search firm specializes in hiccups. I can find you a hubby, no problem. All my business connections are men. Make a few calls and find you a good guy, no sweat. Would help to know what you like. You don't strike me as one of those picky women, Carol. Are you?"

"Of course I am! We are talking about a significant other. I'll have to put up with him until death do us part. Or at least as long as I remain with StreamLINE."

Sal backed off to restart the dialogue. "How long might that be?"

"That will all depend on how well the StreamLINE stock performs over time."

"OK, so let's say it's a few years. Long enough that this guy must be something special. Why don't you give me a sense of what appeals to you?"

Carol chuckled as she considered the job description for a husband.

"Well, we gotta start someplace," Sal said. "What do you like in a . . . what did you call it? Significant other?"

"You mean besides the obvious?"

"Carol, one girl's tiramisu is another gal's cannoli. Why don't we start with the obvious and take it from there?" Sal noted a trail of coffee stains in the Berber carpet, leading to a depression in the couch which, even from across the room, clearly outlined Lenny's physique. A necktie was strewn across the back of the couch.

Friggin' slob, Sal winced.

"He HAS to be handsome."

"What? Oh yeah, your guy. Goes without saying."

"I'd prefer he were connected in some way. Politics, government, maybe. Not a businessperson. I don't need the competition."

"Carol, you've come to the right search firm. I am connected and I know who else is, too. What else?"

"I don't need a parasite feeding off my bank account. He needs to have money of his own."

Sal carefully considered his response.

"Carol, in a partnership there is always a give and take. You give; somebody else takes. In a marriage it's much the same. People have to see the benefits all around. Take a handsome guy in politics, which, if you ask me, is somewhat redundant. Now, this handsome, politically connected guy, he got where he got because of some skill he has. Maybe he's a great baby-kisser. More likely he's a great ass-kisser. He's learned that there's a quid pro quo."

"Quid pro quo? What does this have to do with finding a husband?"

"It has everything to do with your finding a husband who is handsome and connected." Sal explained that it was unlikely that these particular characteristics also came with a bank account, and that good looks and social connections need a regular diet of cash flow—the more regular, and sizeable, the better. "He'll be willing to trade his good looks and invitations to a social circuit for your money. It's a straightforward business deal."

Sal assumed this logic would appeal to his practical-minded client.

"What is this going to cost me, Sal?"

"Hey, nothing for my time. I'll benefit from knowing I found you the best partner to live out a happy and productive association, at least as long as StreamLINE shares continue to increase in value. But for the guy—well, it all depends on how high up the food chain you want to go. State representative won't cost you much, but I'm not sure how you'll benefit from his contacts. I'm thinking we are at the federal level. Representative. Senator maybe."

Sal contemplated the choices.

"Hey, how about a judge?" Sal's cousin had a cousin whose wife worked for a judge at the Second Circuit Court in New York City. The judge was so unhappy in his marriage that he had been spending a lot of time away from home, in an Atlantic City hotel. That's how Sal got to know him.

"Very sharp guy. Handsome? Wow. I'd marry him, that is if I was a woman and needed a husband with connections. He might not hit your bank account so hard, either, since he's been around a while."

"How old?"

"About fifty-five, fifty-six years old."

"Fifty-five! I'd need a long-term-care insurance clause in the prenup, Sal."

"He's a young fifty-five. He jogs fifteen miles a day. You should see him running around the casinos. Guy has a heart that just won't give. He'll live a long and healthy life. Might live a happy life, too, once he jettisons his current wife in favor of my preferred client."

Carol had a meeting with Chuck shortly. She intended to discuss an acquisition target with him, so she needed to wrap the discussion up.

"Sal, no need to schmooze me further. You've got the search—both of them, assuming you pass muster with our CEO. He'll need to meet you first before he signs off on spending the money."

"Tell me when and I'll be there."

"I'll call you this afternoon, once I secure a time on Chuck's calendar. It'll be in the next few days. By the way, no need to mention the search for Mr. Right when we are speaking with Chuck. He only needs to know about the executive search."

XXV

Chuck wiped his nose for the umpteenth time. He reached for a bottle of aspirin in the top-left drawer of his desk. His arm brushed a picture of his four-year-old granddaughter, Lillie, running up the big-girl slide at her preschool. A bright smile filled his face. He was so in love with little Lillie.

"Everything I do, I do for you, Lillie."

But the virus Lillie had shared was getting the better of Chuck. He sneezed three times in a row. As he rose to pour himself a glass of water with which to take the aspirin, the constant sneezing made his head hurt, and his reflection in the window, a slouched version of his normally erect frame, shocked him. The toll of the past few years had worn on his seasoned parts.

StreamLINE, his granddaddy's legacy, had paid a tremendous price for the revenue and margin growth of recent financial quarters. The workplace camaraderie that Chuck and his family nurtured had been replaced with cynicism and infighting among the business functions. It did not escape Chuck's notice that this behavior began not long after Carol's arrival. He did have to give her her due, however. She brought Don and 3RD Party into the fold, which cleared at least one of the hurdles the board had placed in front of him. This acquisition added revenue just as the directors were clamoring for a bigger, faster StreamLINE. Don also represented the leadership qualities Chuck valued, which was particularly helpful as the board encouraged him to identify his successor.

As he shuffled back to his desk, Chuck thought about his board. Despite Tomas's agreement that Don should investigate options with ACME, he worried about his chairman's objectivity. Whispers of Tomas's personal and financial concerns were growing more numerous. Plus, rumors of Tomas's affairs were regular watercooler banter—lately accompanied by discussion of the poor track records of his racehorses.

Chuck's entire body grew achy.

Maybe it's the flu, he reflected.

A mix of the virus and cold medicines made Chuck's thinking fuzzy, and his thoughts drifted to happier memories of Lillie running around his house.

"ACH-OOOOO!"

"God bless you, Mr. Goodfellow," Chuck's assistant called through the intercom system. "Can I get you anything?"

"No, thanks. I've got all I need in here, though I may not stick around all day."

"OK, sir. By the way, Carol called and asked if she could stop by to discuss the corporate development project with you. I told her you were pretty open today."

"Confound it! That woman wants to spend more money to hire an executive to do a job she should be doing herself."

"I'm sorry, sir. I didn't get all of that."

"Nothing. I'll see Carol." He turned off the intercom system.

We certainly don't need to add the expense of another executive salary, bonus, and perks, Chuck thought.

Chuck was still rankled with Carol for wasting his time earlier in the week on a lackluster acquisition target. More and more, Chuck wondered if Carol's job wasn't unnecessary overhead.

"Why would I want two of them?" he mumbled as he reached for his vitamin C.

LATER THAT MORNING, Carol and Sal entered Chuck's office unannounced because his assistant had taken an early lunch. Carol had been unsuccessful at persuading Sal to wear a sports jacket, and a fierce glare of sunlight reflected off Sal's shimmering gray suit. The glare rendered Chuck unable to make out the features of his guest, other than a medium build and full head of dark hair.

Do I know this guy? Chuck wondered as Carol introduced Sal.

"Nice to meet you, Sal." Chuck noted a strong grip and felt a fleeting, though unmistakable, sense of doom.

Chuck longed for the good old days when StreamLINE was a private company. His dad was the president, his granddad led a board that comprised bankers, lawyers, and other investors from the local community, and Chuck was in charge of the freight division. Everyone, from the truck drivers to the board members, pitched in as necessary to make the company successful.

However, at this moment, he experienced a strange foreboding as he faced the board's likely choice to succeed him. He evaluated Carol as a shrewd, but not bold, executive. He saw her as successful at managing up but lousy at managing down. He also suspected that she was quite comfortable pitching others' ideas as her own. He worried about how the company and surrounding community would fare with Carol in charge. His only child, a daughter who was an artist, had no interest in the business, so the Goodfellow leadership bloodline would die upon Chuck's retirement.

"AYY—AYY—AYY-CHOOOOOOO!"

"God bless," Sal said.

"Gesundheit," Carol chimed in, moving a box of tissues closer to Chuck.

The force of the virus hit Chuck with that sneeze. His sinus cavities filled again, putting pressure on his eyes, which teared up.

"Excuse me," Chuck said, wiping his nose again. "I've seen better days."

"You poor thing." Carol poured Chuck a fresh glass of water. "Would you like me to ask Beth to bring you tea? That always helps me cure a cold."

"I'm afraid my granddaughter Lillie brought the flu bug to our home. I've got a touch of that."

"Little aches and pains all over?" Sal joined the conversation.

"ALL over." Chuck acknowledged.

Knowing what was at stake and wanting to put his best foot forward, Sal offered, "Maybe we should come back another day, when you're all better."

Carol ignored Sal's comment and didn't give Chuck a chance to agree. She needed to get her projects under way ASAP. She pulled out three copies of a presentation her assistant had prepared.

"Chuck, I asked Sal to join us so that we could create an action plan around hiring a mergers and acquisitions executive. Sal runs a successful executive search practice. In fact, he did work for me back at Chemix years ago."

"I see." A pause filled the room as Carol awaited questions from Chuck. She sensed a need to prime the pump.

"Chuck, we are prepared to take you through our game plan to secure the best executive candidate for our merger and acquisition effort. Under my direction, of course."

"Of course." Sal supported her.

"Of course." Chuck did not sound as supportive.

Carol placed one copy of the presentation on Chuck's desk and opened it up to page three. She provided Sal with a second copy and used the third to direct the meeting.

"On page three, you can see where we've explored the benefit of business growth through acquisitions. In every example"—Carol used her pen to direct Chuck's eye to the examples in the presentation—"revenue growth and margin improvement is accelerated with each acquisition."

Chuck reached for his pearl-barreled fountain pen, a Christmas gift from devoted employees, to jot notes in the margin of the presentation. The pen would not work. He shook it.

"Carol, this is interesting, but I don't see how these examples guarantee that same value creation for a business like ours. Did you take into account, for example—"

"Please flip to page five for a look at how this program really hits its stride," Carol broke in.

Sal flipped to page five for a look. Chuck sneezed. Carol pushed forward with her pitch.

"Now for the best part. This data indicates that the costs associated with each acquisition drop significantly if the acquiring company has its own in-house acquisition team."

Chuck strove again, in vain, to write a note on page five of Carol's presentation. He had been using the pen a lot recently. He looked it over.

Maybe it's out of ink, he thought.

Sal offered his pen, which Chuck accepted, placing his own fountain pen on top of his desk.

Carol compared the stock valuations of acquisitive companies with market capitalization similar to StreamLINE's. Chuck sought to interrupt her, but his throat was raw and his voice weak. Carol ran with this advantage.

"Chuck, this is the information we've been hoping to find to support this initiative. Imagine the shareholder value." Presuming she knew how to motivate her boss, Carol continued. "Think of the families who've worked here for generations. Imagine how those hardworking people would benefit from outrageous valuations of StreamLINE stock."

Chuck took a swig of water and blew his nose. His muscles and bones ached. The room was beginning to sway. Again, he struggled to speak. Again, Carol stopped him.

"A Ferrari in every garage. That could be our motto!"

"That's your idea of a motto for StreamLINE? Carol, sometimes I wonder what planet you're on!" Chuck was so angry that he choked on his words. His family had maintained a strong tradition of hiring locally. Chuck attended dozens of graduations, weddings, and anniversary parties each year. He felt a kinship with StreamLINE employees, which they reciprocated. And, while many of them could appreciate an exceptional sports car, this was a community that put first things first.

"I know this community," he said. "These families want their kids to grow up healthy and happy." His voice persevered. "They want to send them to college. Maybe a few will go into the service. They'd like to grow old watching their grandkids play in the backyard."

Chuck paused to catch his breath and drink more water. He cleared his throat. His voice down to a whisper, the CEO focused all the attention and energy he could muster on Carol.

"Do you know this company, Carol? I mean really know it, care about it, and care about the values we hope to espouse?"

Carol stood still, unclear why her motto had elicited such a strong, negative reaction from Chuck. Her complete ignorance of his workforce, the community, and StreamLINE values struck Chuck hard. He pounded the desk with his fist. Coughing violently, Chuck rose. He reached his arm out toward Sal. Sal also rose and shook Chuck's hand.

"I'm sorry this has been a waste of your time, Mr. Scruci, but I can't allow this expenditure at this time."

Carol interjected.

"But the board of directors approved—"

"I know what they said, Carol. I'll talk to them. I don't think spending money on a search to find an executive who will lead a strategy I fundamentally disagree with is the right appropriation of our funds. Maybe when I'm gone StreamLINE will go in this direction, but as long as I am around, we do not need Mr. Scruci's assistance to hire any more executives. Especially when we may have more than we need already!" Chuck motioned for the two of them to exit his office. Carol left without another word. Sal nodded his head to Chuck and walked confidently out of the room.

XXVI

"Well, that was completely frustrating. Tomas told me that the board supports this action. They understand what hiring this new executive means in terms of value creation for the business." Carol and Sal walked back toward her office. Chuck's dismissal incensed Carol. *How dare he expel me from his office!*

She looked at Sal. "He's right about one thing, you know."

"Who's right about what?" Sal was annoyed. Carol did not have this situation under control. Sal would never handle a meeting with his boss that way.

"If Chuck weren't in the picture, we could launch the search and hire this new executive." Her opinion was that she had brought more leadership to StreamLINE in a few years than Chuck had in the previous twenty. She fumed. *Who does he think he is?*

"What are you getting at?" Sal needed clarification.

"I personally presented this idea to the board. Tomas Severe, our chairman, assured me that there was support for this proposal. Chuck is so old-school. So conservative. He won't take the risks that are necessary to grow StreamLINE. I'm telling you, this board is going to take him out."

"How can they take him out? Isn't he a made guy?" Sal asked.

"This is an independent, risk-taking board. They are not beholden to any CEO. I'm telling you, Chuck Goodfellow is not long for this company." Carol shook her finger at Sal, trying to get him to keep up with her.

Suddenly, a college intern carrying a finished model for a new logistics facility came around a corner. With the huge model blocking his view, the intern did not see Carol. Carol's pique clouded her vision and she, too, missed the opportunity to avoid a collision.

The model broke her stride and focus, hitting her first on the forehead. Sal caught her as she stumbled. The intern endeavored to regain balance and steady the model, but he tripped over Carol's outstretched feet. The intern and the model fell to the floor.

"AYYYYYYY!" came the collective cry.

Carol saw the intern lying on top of broken plastic pieces.

"That better not be my model!"

Flashes of long evenings with the architect, declined party invitations, and a late-model Corvette he had been coveting crossed the intern's mind as he viewed the scattered pieces of his project.

"Pick up this crap and get out of my sight. What a clod you are!" Carol yelled at her intern.

Sal steadied Carol as she rearranged her suit jacket. He kicked a few plastic shards out of their way and gave Carol a slight nudge in her lower back.

"Let me get this straight. The board is OK with you starting this new business, for which you're going to need to hire a big-time suit, for which me and my associates could get paid a nice finder's fee, and your man Chuck is standing in the way of all this and he's NOT the board's guy?"

"That's about the gist of it. It'd be great for all of us if we didn't have this problem. We could move ahead with my game plan and add revenue to StreamLINE almost immediately."

Sal stared into Carol's eyes.

"So, you're saying all we need to do is eliminate the problem? Then everybody's happy?"

"Harrumph. The solution sounds so simple, doesn't it?" Carol winked at Sal.

Feeling the need to feed her own fury, Carol invited Sal to accompany her. "There's a coffee shop downstairs. You can buy me lunch." She pressed the down elevator button.

When the elevator arrived and the doors opened, Sal gently encouraged

Carol to enter it. "I'll catch up with you," Sal said, his voice deep but faint. "I left my pen in Chuck's office."

With one foot in the elevator, Carol turned around as if to exit. Sal prodded her back in.

"I can take care of this myself."

The doors closed and Carol, not understanding why she obeyed Sal, pressed the button for the floor with the café.

Across the hallway, surrounded by plastic bits and through a steady stream of tears, the intern snapped his model back together.

THIRTY MINUTES LATER, Carol heard police and ambulance sirens.

Likely heart attack. That means another position to fill. Where will I find the time? Carol sighed.

There had been no sign of Sal. She finished her mocha latte.

How dare that hoodlum stand me up! Do I have a sign on my back that says 'kick me'?

Carol reached her arm around her back to check.

This day couldn't get any worse, she thought.

Carol gathered up her things and stepped in front of an older woman awaiting the elevator with a tray full of hot drinks. When the elevator arrived and the doors opened, the woman asked Carol to hold the door for her. Carol pressed the button to close the doors instead.

The elevator bypassed Carol's floor and brought her to the sixth floor instead. "What the hell is going on with our elevators!" Carol bellowed, furious at the incompetency of the facilities team. She stepped out onto the sixth floor, the location of Chuck's office.

Immediately, Carol was accosted by loud cries. Several seasoned executives were openly in tears. The office receptionist was breathing into a paper bag. One executive with a reputation for indifference—his nickname was Dr. Freeze—choked on his own vomit in the corner. A security officer spoke quietly with those StreamLINE employees who were able to communicate. A group of police officers arrived on the next elevator. One officer approached Carol.

"Who are you?" He looked her up and down.

"I'm Carol Himmler, chief operating officer. What the hell is going on around here?"

"Ma'am, would you please step over here and lower your voice?" a newly arrived detective warned Carol. "You're making the witnesses more upset."

The officer explained that, upon returning from her lunch break, Chuck's assistant discovered a pearl-barreled fountain pen sticking out of her beloved boss's chest. Chuck had stopped breathing by the time his assistant entered his office to retrieve the documents she had left for him to sign.

Carol felt herself drifting toward the floor. Before she hit the ground, she heard the officer say: "We'll need to know when you last saw your boss, ma'am."

Boom.

XXVII

Beth took the cool, wet cloth from Carol's forehead and dabbed her boss's cheeks. The police officers had carried Carol's unconscious body to a couch in the conference room, where Beth was attending to her.

As her boss began to stir, Beth discerned fear, then uncertainty, concern, and finally peace on Carol's face. In her relaxed state, Carol dreamed of a large bear in a shiny, charcoal-gray suit approaching her. As he raised his giant paws to attack her, she noticed that his fingernails were pearl-barreled fountain pens. Her dread turned to relief when she realized that the bear was not after her but rather after her father. About that time, Beth detected a smile on Carol's face.

"Carol. Carol. Are you OK?" Beth's voice reached her. Carol willed herself to wake up, coughing as she came around.

"Would you like water?" Beth leaned over with a glass of cold water at the ready.

Carol pushed her mind forward. "What happened?"

"You fainted when you learned that Chuck—that wonderful man—" Beth began to cry.

Carol looked with disgust at her own assistant crying for a man whose lack of support Carol would not miss.

"Give me that." She sat up straight and grabbed the water from Beth.

Carol's cell phone rang. She felt around in her pockets and located it. She barked into the phone, "Where are you?"

Beth attempted to reapply the cloth to Carol's forehead. Carol pulled the towel away from Beth and tossed it into the trash can.

"Stay right there." Carol hung up abruptly and stood up.

Beth beseeched Carol to sit down and rest. "This is so unsettling, especially considering how close you were to Chuck."

Carol picked up her purse and jacket. She told Beth to hold her calls. In all of the commotion, none of the law enforcement personnel noticed Carol leaving.

CAROL FOUND SAL sipping espresso in the back of the coffee shop, within easy reach of the rear exit.

He nodded almost imperceptibly as she approached. He looked around and behind her.

"What the hell did you do?!" Carol raised her voice.

Sal motioned for Carol to take the empty seat beside him.

"You said there was a problem," Sal whispered.

"There are ways, and then there are ways, of eliminating problems, Sal!"

"Old habits die hard, Carol. So, who can I send my first invoice to?

We've gotta start that search. You need all the extra help you can get, now that you are down one." Glancing regularly at the door of the coffee shop, Sal was eager to get out of the area.

"We can't start a search now! The whole company is in disarray! Nobody knows which end is up. The board needs to choose a new leader, and there will be an investigation into the mur—uh, unfortunate passing of Chuck. Killed by his own fountain pen, to boot!"

"That was a pretty pen. But, no reason to stay down in the dumps, Carol. Life goes on. You have a business to build. So do I. Let's get this project started and deliver results for your company. Who knows? If you demonstrate the leadership the company needs during this crisis, maybe the board will make you CEO with or without a husband."

Sal's statement resonated with Carol. He wiped espresso drippings from his saucer.

"Sal, what about the investigation? The police will figure out you had an appointment with Goodfellow."

"How can they? You brought me by when his assistant was out to lunch. What's her name, by the way? I saw a picture on her desk. If that was her, she looks like the kind of gal who is going to need consoling."

"This is not the time for dalliances with the bereaved administrative assistant of the man you—how do you say it, Sal? Whacked?"

Sal wiped his mouth with a paper napkin. He carefully opened the wrapper of the chocolate accompanying his drink.

"It's business, Carol." He looked coolly at his client.

"What are we saying? Sal, I don't see how we can do any business together. I could be implicated."

"Nobody saw anything. His secretary was on lunch and you were in the coffee shop. You've got an alibi, and—" Sal pointed to the three baristas behind the counter— "witnesses."

"I can't have anything more to do with you, Sal." Carol prepared to leave.

Sal placed the chocolate wrapper delicately on the saucer of his coffee cup. He stood up slowly and buttoned his suit jacket.

"This is the second time I've got you out of a jam, Carol. Your debt is growing. But, that's OK. I like you. You're a lot like me. Ambitious, smart. It makes business more palatable if you share interests with your partners. Don't you agree?"

Sal jotted down the name and personal phone number of a high-ranking U.S. senator. The matchmaker had arranged an introduction for Carol. The senator was looking forward to showing her his horse farm that weekend.

"Take it from me. I've experienced more of these setbacks than you have. It's temporary. The police will eventually close the investigation. The important thing is to get back to work, Carol."

As Carol held the paper with the senator's phone number, Sal went out the back door.

XXVIII

Nothing significant turned up during the investigation into Chuck's death. For a while, there was talk of a disgruntled employee run amok, but no one could identify any truly disgruntled employees at StreamLINE. Another rumor circulated that Chuck could not imagine how life could get any better, so he decided to end things on a high note. Without compelling clues to continue the inquiry, the police closed the case file.

Given the nature and suddenness of Chuck's death, the board decided it would be prudent, and would help mitigate further disruption, to select Chuck's successor from inside the company. That would send a positive message to the employees, the customers, and the financial community. Carol and Don were the only contenders.

Don was vastly qualified but so broken up by Chuck's death that the board had great concerns about putting the entire company in his hands. By contrast, Carol demonstrated strength and objectivity during this tragedy. She pressed her team forward and kept the focus on the business. She even convinced a few smaller companies to be acquired by StreamLINE, throwing in enhanced life insurance policies for the executive officers as a bonus to sweeten the deals.

Carol was quoted in the national press after StreamLINE reported superior financial results the fiscal quarter following Chuck's passing: "The important thing for me and the StreamLINE team was to get back to work. How else to take one's mind off this misfortune?" Newspapers across the country ate it up. A laser-focused female executive driving a business forward despite the greatest challenge in a company's history was too much for the media to pass up. General business and financial magazines tripped over each other to get interviews with Carol.

The board chose Carol as StreamLINE's next CEO. To create a handsome package that would assure Carol's continued commitment, they dropped the marriage requirement, moving it to the "wouldn't it be nice" category. Still, they did not want to break the bank over Carol's compensation. Tomas's divorce was not yet final, and Lulu's charity calendar, and therefore StreamLINE's external financial obligations, was robust.

However, the exposure Carol was receiving put her on a short list of top leaders that executive recruiters followed. So, aside from a base salary that would make a big-league baseball player blush, Tomas and Lulu decided that backdating a few stock options would put Carol out of reach of hungry corporate predators. Carol accepted StreamLINE's offer, complete with built-in financial gains courtesy of the unique stock options, and assumed the CEO reins—for as long as she presumed respectable before her next rapacious move.

STRATEGIC PLANS

XXIX

I n the last quarter of 2004, the overall U.S. economy was hitting on almost all cylinders. Consumer spending was on the upswing and capital investments surged.

Over at TMC Corporation, Charlie's replacement for Dandy fixed the operational issues that had plagued the procurement and fulfillment functions. In his years steering those teams, the multitalented Jim Collins had introduced new ideas and discipline. These changes got the margin and revenue ratios back on the right track, which was necessary to reinvigorate the company. One inadvertent consequence of Jim's charismatic leadership was that Charlie had renewed vigor for his mission at TMC.

The upbeat economic conditions, along with the adjustments to process and operations, resonated well with TMC's customer base and stakeholders. Sequential quarters of positive earnings encouraged a growth spurt. TMC expanded its global footprint, increased revenues, and created healthier margins by means of a series of acquisitions of communications services companies. Jim's expansive career history included building solutions for large corporations, so he took a lead in these deals, too. The transactions were grouped together under a new Solutions division that TMC reported on separately within the financial statements. Jim managed this amalgamation of disparate entities so expertly that the assumption of the general workforce was that he would add this division to his portfolio of TMC responsibilities.

Wall Street traders and hedge funds tracked TMC Solutions results carefully. They drove the stock share price to a new high with each uptick in revenue or increase in margin. Positive media exposure was another by-product of the good results. TMC was increasingly looked upon as an employer of choice and Jim as a desirable mentor. The TMC workforce began referring to Jim as "our next CEO."

It did not escape Stewart's notice that, as business results improved and employees were happier at work, his job got easier. Driven by increased opportunity as well as optimism, workers from the factory floor to the executive suite had fewer complaints.

Jim's generous spirit extended to Stewart, in whom he found redeeming value. Stewart felt better about himself when he was in Jim's presence, juxtaposed with feeling like an abused spouse after his meetings with Ted. Jim encouraged Stewart to participate in decisions about the business and his team. Flattered beyond his expectations, Stewart sang Jim's praises at every stop and made extra efforts to expose Jim to the press. He often joked with his colleagues that when they traded a Dandy for a Jim, they got a jim-dandy in the bargain. The goodwill surrounding Jim spread like an infection all the way to the boardroom.

Ted had also been quite pleased with Jim's results—that is, until the board began to circumvent Ted, seeking advice directly from Jim on a wide assortment of business issues. When more than the occasional publication referenced Jim as Ted's heir apparent, the CEO feared a threat to his one-man rule. A practical person, Ted knew he would eventually be replaced. But it was one thing to be backfilled as CEO, the person and timing of Ted's choosing. It was something else entirely to have his influence pale before his very eyes. Therefore, Ted called in a long-standing IOU with Hugh Hangerone, a headhunter who had a successful history of tweaking the executive roster when Ted was of a mind for change. A revolving door of expensive executive talent had cost TMC a ton in search-firm fees over the years, and Hugh was the main beneficiary of Ted's succession-planning process. Lucky for Hugh, he could settle the score in one fell swoop.

Therefore, after some major projects were completed, Ted added another executive search to Charlie's workload. Dandy's famous successor was squeezed out in a power play of Ted's design and Hugh the headhunter's execution.

XXX

I n addition to workforce planning, assuaging employees' grievances, and reorganizing a company now worth $10 billion, Charlie was charged with increasing female representation within TMC's leadership ranks. Specifically, Stewart, who was now senior vice president of the renamed human capital management function, challenged his team to win "Shattered," the prestigious Department of Labor award bestowed upon those organizations that best enabled women to smash the glass ceiling.

This admirable initiative had its roots in a fundamental desire to change behavior. However, the behavior Stewart was interested in changing was more familial than corporate. He convinced Ted that capturing "Shattered" would be good for business. But he also fervently hoped that TMC's winning this award might take his father's mind off an unfortunate incident overseas.

Stewart had recently returned from a trip to the Middle East with his father, his father's favorite sphynx cat, Precious Child, and Stewart's boisterous girlfriend. Precious, who had been diagnosed with feline leukemia, demonstrated no improvement after multiple chemo treatments. So, in a further effort to build bridges, as well as put a little distance between himself and his bitter divorce from Mariellen, Stewart agreed to accompany his father to Egypt to consult with a veterinary oncologist specializing in radical cancer treatments for the bald cat varietal.

Over the course of their marriage, Mariellen had accepted her place as second fiddle to Stewart's dad but had taken umbrage to sharing a backseat with his father's cats. When they decided to divorce, Stewart's lawyer urged him to give Mariellen their vacation home and as much cash as she needed to pay off that mortgage, allowing Stewart to make a clean break. "But whatever you do," his lawyer advised him, "don't give up the future value of the TMC stock options." So Stewart parted with half of his $2 million in the money market account as well as the lake house, but the TMC stock options remained on his side of the divorce balance sheet. On the drive through the Nile River Valley, his new girlfriend, Vivianne, assumed Mariellen's place in the rear seat beside Precious.

Although the breed originated in Canada, it was rumored that Egypt had a greater affinity for the sphynx cat, so the foursome set out to seek the wisdom of the ages to save some of Precious's nine lives. Stewart intended to investigate potential investment properties along the way, too. After a particularly hot and tiresome day of assessing real estate near the Nile delta, Stewart retired to his room for a eucalyptus steam and hot stone massage utilizing fragments of the pyramids. The big-hearted Vivianne encouraged the elder Narciss to enjoy a long nap before dinner. She promised to feed and care for Precious as Stewart's father dozed.

Never having owned a pet, Vivianne was unfamiliar with the finicky behavior of cats around food. She found Precious underwhelmed by, even refusing, her dinner. Vivianne attributed a lack of interest in the sushi to the extremes of the local climate.

"I know what you need, honey." Not realizing that the maid had forgotten to replace the outtake valve cover after cleaning the bathtub, leaving a pipe-sized opening through which circulating water could be vacuumed out, Vivianne placed the purring kitty into her tub. No sooner had Vivianne turned on the whirlpool motor than Precious's tail got sucked up into the valve with great force. Were it not for her hefty hind quarters, evidence of a cat life very well lived, she might have become a major obstruction in the plumbing system of one of Cairo's finest hotels. Vivianne corrected the situation without delay so that the only palpable outcome of the mishap was that Precious lost flexibility in her now-longer tail.

"Probably lucky she didn't have any hair on her tail or it could have been a lot worse," an embarrassed Vivianne offered as she handed the sopping-wet cat to Stewart's very wide-awake father.

His spa treatments having been interrupted, Stewart assessed the damage. He bought an Egyptian cotton pillow, hand-embroidered with pink and lavender camels, from the hotel gift shop for Precious's precious parts and filled a suitcase with designer dresses for Vivianne, which, along with their new owner, he placed in a car bound for the airport.

The next morning, Stewart accompanied his father and Precious to the first of several experimental treatments she would receive to combat her cancer. They conducted the remaining days of the vacation in silence.

When he returned to his office, Stewart found the application for the "Shattered" award on his desk. He thought it might be just the ticket to regain his father's confidence in his leadership abilities. To qualify for the "Shattered" honor, a company needed a minimum of $10 billion in revenue and a woman in at least one of the top five executive roles. As a result of a multiyear, double-pronged strategy of acquisitions and organic growth, TMC had the necessary revenue. However, no women were in any such leadership positions. According to award guidelines, the company had two months to change that, and Stewart was determined to do so. Charlie worked overtime to make sure Stewart hired the best talent, with or without an award at stake.

Late one afternoon at TMC's headquarters, Charlie was conducting research around possible executives to consider when he came across Carol Himmler's name on the list of skyrocketing leaders featured annually in *Economic Week* magazine. An accompanying article depicted her rescue of StreamLINE Corporation. The story described how she harnessed her team's energy to advance the business after the murder of a member of that company's founding family. In spite of the reporter's insinuation that an early-afternoon skim mocha latte was an odd alibi for an exceedingly driven executive, Carol's story checked out.

With that question put to rest and a litany of acquisitions in her first months as CEO increasing the strategic significance of StreamLINE, Charlie deemed Carol a solid leader. Out of the blue, he called her and pitched the opportunity to oversee TMC's supply-chain function, both the procurement and fulfillment departments—the position Ted had forced Jim Collins to relinquish.

Driven more by his well-honed appreciation for the opposite sex than the strength of Carol's supply-chain skills, Ted had a clear ulterior motive when he decided to hire the physical beauty largely because he thought that it would be fun to have Carol around.

Desperate for his father's admiration, Stewart pushed Carol to start her new role ASAP, ensuring that TMC would meet the deadline for the "Shattered" award competition. So, six weeks after her name caught Charlie's eye, *Economic Week* interviewed the newest member of TMC's executive team.

This time, Clare Woodard would conduct the inquiry into Carol's departure from StreamLINE and budding new adventure as the senior vice president of the supply chain for TMC Corporation. After completing her baccalaureate degree, Clare had climbed the career ladders of increasingly larger newspapers. Her progressive reporting and keen skill in crafting a narrative eventually led to a desirable byline at *Economic Week*. She worked her way up to a prime reporting gig, covering two pillars of the American economy: technology and communications.

Carol could not put her finger on how, but she had the sense that she knew Clare. The accomplished journalist did not remind Carol that she had broken a promise for an exclusive story years ago. Experience and maturity reinforced the lesson that having something on her interviewee often gave Clare a powerful edge. Experience taught Carol that reporters work in sound bites, so she had several at the ready. Among them: "I believe that superior leadership and teamwork are how great things get done."

However, this reporter was not interested in capturing sound bites. Clare had an in-depth understanding of StreamLINE's financials. She kept Carol on the defensive and quizzed her relentlessly about the viability of the acquisitions, starting with 3RD Party. Clare wondered aloud about StreamLINE's debt exposure. Her unstated but clear intimation was that Carol overpaid for the acquired companies.

Carol was surprised at Clare's style of rapid-fire questioning. It made her uncomfortable, especially since she assumed this would be a softball interview to sell a few magazines. She sought to steer the discussion to the initiatives she ran, the businesses she built. After Clare's particularly grueling probe into Chuck Goodfellow's murder, which left Carol's surgically enhanced facial muscles pinched like a puffed pastry, Clare turned to the decision to join TMC. While the technology conglomerate was certainly considered a success story, Carol would not be assuming the top job.

"I think our readers might find it odd that you left the CEO role at

StreamLINE for a divisional responsibility in any company," Clare said. "Are you running from something, Carol?"

Relaxing her lips, Carol offered a rationale. "Clare, it's not about the title. It's all about the contribution one can make to the life of an organization. StreamLINE is ready for new blood. And I'm ready to sink my claws into something else." Immediately, Carol regretted her word choice.

Carol also could have said that this was the chance to be among the top five executives of a very hot technology company—one that had seized the attention of Wall Street. But what she would never say was that the TMC job was an opportunity to exit StreamLINE while the getting was good. Based on their earlier interaction, Clare correctly presumed that Carol did not want any career black eyes, which StreamLINE might become if the company did not successfully navigate around the next twelve to eighteen months. The reporter undertook different angles to get at this point, but Carol would not give an inch.

"It's time for StreamLINE to take a new course with a different leader, just like I will be an injection of fresh, raw thinking at TMC," Carol said.

Clare felt in her bones that there was more to the StreamLINE story than Carol let on. She took another shot at it.

"I noticed that you awarded the executive search for your backfill at StreamLINE to an unknown firm. Why make that choice when there are so many better-recognized executive search firms who would kill for that assignment?"

Tempted to pepper her answer with more accolades about her achievements, Carol decided that, since Clare had already made strategic mincemeat of many of them, it would be best to wrap things up quickly.

"I must tell you, Sal Scruci can execute. Those other search firms are just pretenders."

When the interview was over, Carol sensed the relief of having dodged a bullet. Yet, *Economic Week*'s cover illustration of a miniskirt-clad, high heels–wearing vixen ripping TMC's balance sheet in two was not the image the new TMC executive had hoped to portray when she told Clare that she was ready to "tear into another challenge."

JUST WEEKS INTO Carol's tenure, Stewart asked the corporate communications team to send a photograph of Carol holding the "Shattered" trophy, a Plexiglas plaque with a crack running out to four corners from the center, to Ted and each member of TMC's board of directors. He sent another one to his father, with a handwritten note acknowledging the elder Narciss's personal successes in shattering corporate barriers. A week later, a box arrived at Stewart's office. The contents included the hand-embroidered Egyptian cotton pillow that had once softened Precious's blow. Pinned to the dead center of the pillow: the photograph of Carol holding TMC's "Shattered" trophy.

XXXI

TMC's success and its stock price continued to skyrocket through 2005 and 2006. The executive team was inundated with job queries from executives at competing companies who wanted in on the action. This flood of resumes gave Stewart an idea.

With the executive-assistant buffer gone—Tweadle-Dee was now the chief operating officer at a major real estate investment trust, and Tweadle-Dom, citing his experience in behavior modification as a junior executive for TMC, landed a job in the animal husbandry department of a large university system—Stewart worked directly with Ted. Given the media buzz around an escalating corporate war for talent, the human resources function was gaining recognition. Stewart manipulated this rising awareness to his benefit, likening HR to the role played by the supply chain earlier in TMC's history.

"TMC's secret sauce today is our workforce, Ted—the folks who fill up the parking lots by seven o'clock in the morning and toil past midnight to keep our name at the top of the charts. We have to be as vigilant about managing this capital as we do all our other assets."

In a series of meetings, Stewart nagged the CEO about hiring an executive to drive talent-management processes. Stewart backed up his request with data on the structure of human resources departments at companies with similar revenue and expansion patterns. The upshot was that the HR leaders at those companies each had their own talent-management executives. Stewart felt it was only fair that he get one, too. What better evidence of his importance than an executive on his team who would be responsible for hiring executives? And what better guarantee that Stewart would own the planning process to fill future leadership openings, particularly the next chief executive officer?

This idea had some appeal for Ted. Ever since Jim Collins left, the board of directors had been pressuring him to build succession plans so they would know, and could shape, who would lead TMC down the road. However, having narrowly averted the acute career threat Jim posed, Ted was determined to control the process, and outcome, of any succession planning exercises. So, rather than jump to support Stewart's play to advance his own influence, Ted worked his Rolodex to generate ideas of possible successors to tender to the board. Dandy's opinions still carried weight with some members of the board, so Ted's efforts eventually led to a conversation with the well-networked TMC alum.

Ted and Dandy had maintained frosty relations since Dandy went off the reservation, literally and figuratively. Ted had half expected to be told to take a hike, especially if his former vice president harbored any resentment at having been retired. The CEO was therefore surprised when his past procurement chief pleasantly responded to his inquiry. They talked about the old days. Dandy was clearly well informed about the current state of the company and asked insightful questions about the business.

He told his former boss that he had warm feelings for TMC and wanted to do anything he could to help attract capable succession candidates. What Ted did not know was that ever since Dandy and Phillipe decided to scale back their investment activity and plan for a family, Dandy found himself with more time on his hands—and less cash coming in. In Dandy's eyes, this request for a favor presented a business opportunity. He told Ted that he was happy to dust off his contacts and make a few calls on behalf of TMC. Ted instructed Stewart to run down Dandy's candidate recommendations.

Stewart began receiving regular e-mail and articles from Dandy, offering suggestions for prospective CEO candidates but mostly advice and counsel on business issues. Stewart's inbox swelled with comments, articles, and spreadsheets, all tailored to business opportunities for TMC. Also, given that they had remained friendly, Stewart occasionally visited with Dandy at his ashram. The former TMC executive used Stewart's weekend retreats to further bend his friend's ear.

Interacting with Dandy called to mind his successor, which pained Stewart; he missed Jim. Mutual trust, respect, and camaraderie were absent from Stewart's relationship with Ted, and Stewart had felt closer to his goal of consigliere when Jim was in the picture. The injury from that disappointment deep, Stewart wanted assurance that it would not happen again. Dandy's suggestions were not helping.

"Ted, you've opened a can of worms," Stewart said. "It's nice that Dandy feels so good about TMC, but my team can't process all the suggestions he sends me. He hasn't come up with one good candidate for CEO, either. Maybe we should ask him to focus his enthusiasm on college recruiting. That would allow us to hire a professional talent manager to help with our executive-succession planning."

When he got an invoice from Dandy for services rendered, Stewart thought it was a joke—until he got the second statement, with a notation that the first was thirty days past due.

Some things never change, Stewart thought.

Stewart shut Dandy's executive search practice down.

Having successfully leveraged a wild goose chase to push the memory of Jim to the far recesses of the collective minds of the board, Ted began to appreciate the possibilities Stewart's talent-management executive would present. The CEO also calculated that Stewart's executive might help with another predicament.

Thanks largely to the contributions of her predecessor, Carol had made a mark on the organization in her two years with TMC. However, she was fixated on amassing greater power, which made Ted an active gatekeeper of her ambitions. This increased his headaches and left the CEO chilly to her considerable allure. Balancing his libido with other resources, Ted eventually learned to seek gratification from her business results.

With Carol's career appetite never satisfied, Ted teased her with a steady diet of fattening and influential responsibilities. Then, after putting it off as long as he could, he promoted Carol into TMC Solutions as its new general manager early in 2007. His assumption was that this position would keep Carol's motivation high because it placed her in an advantageous spot from which she might succeed him.

According to TMC literature, the Solutions division provided the services that enabled large institutions and middle-market business customers to transform their communications environments. Often as not, this amounted to fixing problems caused by the original equipment manufacturers, an assembly in which TMC was an important participant. Increases in customers' discretionary spending budgets and greater penetration of multinational markets fueled noteworthy growth in this segment. Largely due to the strength of the operating margins in this division, TMC stockholders profited handsomely.

The visibility of the Solutions general manager would also help Ted determine if Carol had the mettle to step into the top job when he was ready to step out of it. He admired her single-minded focus to be chief executive. She reminded Ted of himself in earlier days, when his strategic initiatives were built around his personal ambitions and used to eliminate any competition. He thought she had the most machismo of his direct reports. Her leadership style intimidated or outright frightened large swaths of the employee base, including many of her peers. This kept everyone else on their toes and, for the most part, out of his hair.

These attributes were strong positives, in Ted's view. He thought she should be a contender to succeed him. Nevertheless, and despite her ascension within the TMC hierarchy, Ted remained determined to retire on his timetable, not anyone else's. Therefore, he recognized in Stewart's talent-management executive an opportunity to create a horserace of executives who might succeed him. And buy himself more time.

FOR HIS PART, Stewart attributed Carol's enthusiasm for his talent-management initiative, which she voiced persuasively at Ted's staff meetings, to be an acknowledgement of the idea's strength. But he was blinded by his ambition to increase his influence and a taste of the role a true consigliere could play from his interaction with Jim. Carol had her own reasons to encourage Stewart's talent-management agenda. She wanted to leverage the board's pressure on Ted and stealthily orchestrate a coup so that she would be chosen as Ted's successor. Therefore, she introduced Stewart to the savior of her own staffing conundrums: Sal Scruci.

Stewart desired a talent-management leader whom he could manipulate, making Charlie's evolving independent streak a material weakness in his candidacy for this position. Thanks to Carol's rose-colored description of Sal, Stewart thought he would be the perfect partner to fulfill his mission to find a candidate impressive to the executive team but not so smart that he would threaten Stewart's influence. Carol knew Sal would be her best ally in her mission to be TMC's next CEO. Plus, as Sal often reminded her, she still owed him.

After a lackluster process, which constituted calls to outplacement firms asking for recommendations of recently fired or otherwise failed human resources leaders, Sal found the perfect candidate for TMC vice president of talent management: a corporate-credentialed, overeducated, French-speaking recruiting manager whose wife's trust fund was running low. Stewart made Harry Habet an offer he could not refuse because his wife would not let him. It was the only offer he got.

Carol buried a negative, and unsolicited, reference, tendered by Ann McManus, the new CEO of Colreavy Consulting. Colreavy was a multinational advisory firm where Harry allegedly made his recruiting "bones." She was thankful that Ann had called her and not Stewart, who Carol reasoned would not have had the nerve to ignore the opinion ("Doofus is about the nicest word I can think of to describe Harry"). Carol assured this prestigious business leader that her comments would be duly noted by the powers that be. Secretly, Carol was delighted that, albeit unintentionally, Ann had endorsed her own view that Harry was the ideal candidate to drive her agenda.

XXXII

Harry kissed Vera's cheek and exclaimed, "You've been a tremendous asset throughout this interview process, Vera. We are going to make beautiful recruiting music together."

As he stepped into the Town Car, Harry took a deep breath and looked around long enough to ensure that someone might notice his confident, pin-striped, power-broker pose—one he struck to communicate the importance of his new role as leader of the talent-management effort at a maturing Fortune 200 Company. Vera delicately pushed Harry off her shoulders and into the car. He slid the executive contract she had given him onto the seat next to him and closed the door. He lowered the window. "Ta-ta, girlfriend. Tell Stewart I'll talk to him next week."

Vera kept her hand at waist level and waved him off. "Buh-bye," she spoke through pursed lips. As the Town Car turned the corner, she wiped both cheeks with the back of her hand.

"Yuck!"

BACK AT HER desk, Vera covered her hands with disinfectant gel. As she picked up the phone to confirm the travel itinerary for yet another candidate interviewing for a different leadership job with the company, a giddy Stewart interrupted her.

"So, what did he think? Any issues with the contract?" Stewart's palms felt sweaty. He rubbed them together and nervously bounced his eyebrows.

Vera turned carefully in her desk chair and slowly raised her eyes to meet his. She allowed a pregnant pause to fill her office cubicle.

"What? What? Carol has been on my case to find somebody to lead talent management!"

"How could you hire that weasel?" Vera turned her back on Stewart, who had a flashback to a neophyte reporter pushing back on Dandy about TMC's poor judgment call on N.O. Audette all those years ago.

"Vera, Vera, Vera. Harry Habet ran the executive-staffing function for a global software company. He also has business-development experience from his consulting work."

Largely inured to Stewart's arrogance, Vera dialed the travel department.

"And, and . . . he speaks French!" Careful not to sit down because Vera had a practice of placing sharp objects in his path to register disapproval with a decision, Stewart spread his feet apart and let his hands fall to his waist, his bobbing head betraying the confidence he had hoped to exude.

Vera turned around so violently that her chair kept spinning long after she stood up.

"That California software company with an office full of part-time programmers in Minsk doesn't constitute *global*. One of his references said he wanted to fire Harry after he lost a critical account, but his wife's family connections protected him. Every word that comes out of his mouth is contrived, and WE don't have any offices in FRANCE!" She slammed her pen down on the desk and turned her computer on.

Aside from her opinion about Harry's value to TMC, Vera was miffed that she would be expected to support Harry while also continuing her work for Stewart.

Puzzled, Stewart asked, "How'd you know about the reference?"

"If you don't want me to manage your calendar, you can take away my access to your e-mail."

"Carol has it on good authority that that reference was all washed up. Besides, Harry's a ranking member of Executive Search Professionals, a best-practice organization of executive recruiters."

"And that means what?"

Stewart stomped his feet. He did not want this upstart messing around with his plan to be consigliere to the next CEO. Stewart and Ted had maintained a détente of sorts, as long as Stewart kept Ted's executive team in good standing. But Ted never took him into his confidence, and Stewart wanted more. The memory of his dad's unsolicited advice played incessantly in his head:

"If you can't be the guy running the show, at least be in his inner circle. That's where the money and influence are."

While the prestige of the human resources profession was not as noteworthy as that of general management, Stewart did not have to make the quarterly numbers, either. Plus, he was well positioned to benefit from a mounting interest in HR. A closer relationship with the next CEO would really step things up for Stewart. He reasoned that he would control the outcome of a search for Ted's successor through his puppet, Harry.

"Look. This is all beside the point," Stewart barked at Vera. "Harry's credentials support the expectations we have, especially given our global plans for the Solutions division. And Carol, who's considered by many to be our strongest general manager, thought Harry was unique."

"Carol said 'unusual.'"

"If you must mince words, she said 'uniquely unusual.' She also said he was exactly what she needed to finish her agenda here."

"And that doesn't frighten you?" Vera asked.

Stewart stood like the proverbial deer in his assistant's headlights. Carol's plans actually did frighten him, on some strange, visceral level.

Vera liked to make the best of things, particularly when there was no other way.

"If we're lucky, maybe Harry won't last that long. I've seen executives come in and out of favor around here like members of a mob crew."

Stewart stomped his feet again. Vera shrugged her shoulders in mild apology.

She picked up a pile of mail and handed it to Stewart. On top was the latest issue of *Economic Week*. The magazine contained the first in a series of articles by Clare Woodard on innovation in the workplace. Stewart figured prominently in a photograph complementing the story, which referenced TMC's human capital strategy. In her account, Clare described TMC's initiative to build a talent-scouting team as "aggressive and compelling." Stewart had anticipated, correctly, that this program would generate decent media attention.

Clare's report on recruiting and motivating talent included optimistic quotes from TMC employees and senior leaders, all of whom Stewart had handpicked. In general, Clare found TMC to have a corporate culture that mixed determination with vision and teamwork. Those interviewed felt the company had matured from its start-up roots. They were confident about its future prospects. Many spoke with substantial knowledge of the industry, the competition, and TMC's game plan for success. They also expressed pride in their work, as well as in the company's support for individual ambitions—the *What's Your Forte?* program had received a second life when TMC's operational misfortunes turned around.

On the whole, Clare's article was upbeat and encouraging. Independent research data supported that Stewart and his human capital management team were on to something. Clare did raise a caution, however, with regard to Harry Habet. The executive hired to attract, retain, and develop TMC leaders had a résumé with more job hops than an Easter bunny at an egg hunt. Her finale laid it out plainly:

"Only time will tell if Harry has the right stuff to discern if TMC's future kingpins are people of substance or empty suits."

Several national human resources organizations took note of Clare's article. One of them nominated Stewart for its coveted Character of the Year award. Although the CoY competition was fierce and included the human resources executive who created a groundbreaking poll to measure executive optimism, Stewart secured the votes necessary to capture the title and showered new accolades on the TMC leadership team.

XXXIII

A pit bull roamed inside the fence of a dark and otherwise deserted construction site along a river in northern New Jersey. With no one around to hear him, the guard dog may have been overkill for the future condominium project, but the crew had warmed to having him around.

Lenny Knuckles sipped hot coffee behind the wheel of his Cadillac Escalade. From this vantage point, he watched for signs of activity that might interrupt his job. Michael Vacanti, the newest member of Sal's crew, snored in the front seat next to him.

"Fuckin' A." Michael's sleeping habits did nothing to enhance Lenny's opinion of Sal's choice for consigliere.

Eager to balance the cycles of his commercial activity, Sal coveted the interstate distribution business leading south and west out of North Jersey. The big boss approved Sal's plan, provided that Sal could strike a deal with central Philly, a territory run by Michael's uncle, a man to whom Sal's big boss owed a bigger favor. There was incentive to support the partnership; a marriage of the two families could create efficiencies in the lucrative trucking trade. Sal's opening for a consigliere was the sort of role that could help Michael earn his bones, return the favor Sal's boss owed Michael's uncle, and secure the success of the enterprise. It helped that Michael, a well-educated, good-looking guy, reminded Sal of the constructive characteristics of his last consigliere.

Lenny had received a tip that a huge shipment of pedestal sinks would be dropped at this location Friday afternoon, for installation to begin the following Monday. Sal arranged for a truck from the new partnership to redirect the sinks late Friday night. At the last minute, the driver came down with the flu.

"Michael, need you to give Lenny a hand tonight," Sal had said.

"No prob, boss. Seen this type of action before. Any heat gonna be there, Len?"

Lenny looked at Sal. *Heat?*

"Like, I need to bring any extra tools?" Michael tried to explain.

"Tools?" Lenny asked.

Sal looked up from his cappuccino. "Michael, do what you'd normally do, whateva that is."

"I'll pack knuckles, Len, just in case." Michael gently tapped his colleague with a mock one-two punch to his bicep.

Now, as he sat in his car and plotted an approach to readdressing the sinks, Lenny watched Michael's tongue roll out and in and wondered what Sal saw in him.

"What's he got that I don't?"

This time Lenny's voice startled Michael, who reached around frantically in his jacket pocket for his gun. When he found it, he shot a hole through his jacket and into the glove box.

"What da hell?" Smoke rose from the dashboard in Lenny's six-month-old car. "I still got payments to make on this vehicle!"

Michael rubbed his right shoulder, which ached from the recoil. "Sorry, man. I thought we were being attacked."

"Attacked! Attacked! When's the last time you been attacked by an all-wheel-drive vehicle? I was gonna give this car to my ma!" Lenny took the napkins from his coffee run and wiped soot off the dash.

"Your ma with the seeing-eye dog?"

"How many ma's you think I got? The point is, how's she gonna drive wit' a hole in the car now? She'll get cold." He tried to stuff napkins into the hole in the glove box, but most of them spilled out, smoking.

"My friggin' arm really hurts," Michael said.

Lenny looked at the consigliere, who was covered in soot and small pieces of polyester from the taupe dash trim. He took the gun out of Michael's shaking hands.

"Good for you this piece you got is a piece of shit, and a small piece of shit at that, or more than your shoulder would be hurtin'." Lenny glanced in the general direction of Michael's groin and raised his eyebrows. Michael placed his hands over the family jewels and involuntarily gulped.

"How we gonna do this thing now, you bein' laid up?" Lenny was fuming. And concerned. He had promised the best sink to Sal for the bathroom renovations his wife required.

Michael regrouped.

"I can do this, man. I'm OK." He reached for his gun, which lay on the car seat between them.

"AWWW!"

"Fuck me!" Lenny got out of the car to investigate the new bullet hole in his side panel. Although the bullet had pierced the bodywork, the car was operational. Michael wobbled out to take a look.

Lenny took wire cutters from the trunk. He shook his head and mumbled as he crossed over to the fenced construction site across the street. Michael approached and Lenny took another set of keys out of his pocket.

"We gotta get a move on. See that truck on the side street? Think you can drive it over here without puttin' a friggin' hole in something?"

Lenny cut through the fence.

"This is gonna be a long friggin' night."

XXXIV

The right leadership had been so indispensable to TMC's success and the need for it so crucial to Stewart's expanding personal agenda that he decided Harry would not be enough. Besides, Stewart could not be sure Harry was any good. He wanted an entire team dedicated to recruiting executive talent. Harry would be the window dressing and Stewart's executive foil if one turned out to be necessary. But his best manager would be required for the actual work.

Stewart emphasized the critical and visible role that this talent-management team would play in the company's ongoing success when he discussed his plan with Charlie. He suggested that Charlie should narrow his focus in order to maximize his level of influence in the ever-larger TMC.

"You don't want to be spread too thin, Charlie."

He likened Charlie's "taking one for the team" to flexing like an executive does around competing business issues. Also, Stewart made a play to what he thought was Charlie's ego.

"Charlie, I know I can count on you to put your nose to the TMC grindstone."

Charlie had not been enthusiastic about giving up some of his broader human resources duties to focus specifically on executive staffing. Plus, TMC did not have a great track record of allowing employees to relinquish responsibilities. Rather, jobs just tended to get bigger as employees took on new roles. Nor was Charlie excited when informed that Harry, to whom he would now report, got the vice president title. Stewart reassured Charlie that his moment would come.

Over time, Stewart and Charlie had developed a little dance. Just as Charlie reached a moral impasse or career breaking point, Stewart would tease him with the promise of a future executive role. To strengthen his hand, he occasionally made up some accolade about Charlie's work and falsely trumpeted it to a member of the board or senior executive. When that was not enough, and it increasingly was not, Stewart massaged the situation with another TMC equity award, as he did this day.

So, with his own, albeit smaller, set of golden handcuffs getting tighter, Charlie stuffed his self-respect in his back pocket, handed over his general human resources duties, and accepted responsibility for the executive staffing team.

FOUR WEEKS AFTER accepting an offer of employment from TMC, Harry straightened his cashmere jacket and waited outside the main entrance of the hotel where he had established residency, not yet having found a house worthy of his standing. He brushed a muffin crumb from his navy slacks, allowing the couture symbol on his high-priced loafers to show as he did so. Harry was pleased with his wardrobe choice, which he deemed an impressive, and visible, framework through which to conduct his work as a selector of executives. He looked around for the car service that would deliver him to his first day of work.

Finally, his driver arrived.

"Sorry to be late, sir, but traffic is a bear at eight o'clock in the morning. It'll be a long ride to the office, too, in case you want to alert anybody."

"No issues there. I'm a VIP at TMC. The consigliere of talent, if you will." Harry dropped his Tumi briefcase to the floor of the car and climbed in. "They will wait for me."

PER DIRECTIVES FROM Stewart, Vera filled Harry's calendar with a strategy session on the company's employment brand, lunches with various business leaders, and a conference call that very morning with Stewart and his direct reports. Harry's onboarding would be quick and intense. *Hit the deck with a face-plant* was the slogan the training manager devised for the initiation.

Stewart hustled down the aisle to Vera's desk, mumbling into the Bluetooth device hanging off his right ear. The global HR leadership conference call was already under way.

"Where IS he?" Stewart mouthed to Vera, who extended her hands out, palms up, and smirked "beats me" with her body language.

Harry knew enough about TMC's blue-collar culture that he did not want to be spotted being chauffeured to work in a Town Car. He had the driver drop him off at the back entrance of TMC headquarters. Once inside the building, the new leader of talent management made his way to the front desk and called Vera from the lobby.

Her cheeks full of Harry's air kisses, Vera led him to his office, rattling off the day's agenda as she did so.

"You've missed the monthly global HR leadership conference call, but you are early for your one-on-one meeting with Charlie Watkins, your top HR manager."

After they walked into his office, Vera pressed Charlie's personnel file into Harry's belly, hit the start button on his laptop, and demonstrated how to set up the voice mail on his telephone.

All giggles, Harry asked, "Coffee? Light, no sugar."

Vera pointed a long, straight finger in the direction of the bathroom.

"Caddy's Java Jungle is opposite the restrooms." Eyes wide, she gave Harry a hard, frozen smile. As she walked away, he called after her.

"Vera, is it typical for staff to wear flats around the office? Shouldn't we dress it up a bit for the executives we are recruiting?" Harry smiled as his eyes fell to Vera's feet.

"If TMC is going to require—and pay for—a uniform, I'd be happy to buy my shoes from Jimmy Choo. The café is still beyond the restrooms."

XXXV

To ensure that he would not get caught between an employee and a hard place if cash ever became tight again at TMC, Stewart leveraged research by human resources think tanks that indicated that employees were almost as motivated by a positive work environment as by compensation.

As noted by Clare Woodard's recent article, out-of-the-box activities were encouraged by the TMC human capital function. So, taking a page (literally) from his local diner, Stewart decreed that the company would have daily specials, or motivational activities for employees that, with the food service company's grudging agreement, corresponded with menu offerings in the cafeteria.

Every Monday was Rio Rhythms theme day. A pear-shaped woman in a snug red leotard and matching skirt demonstrated the samba to eager students in one corner of the cafeteria while "The Girl From Ipanema" softly cooed through the speaker system. Charlie picked at the breakfast buffet as he worked through the details of a financial offer for a sales executive.

"Show me MORE money, MaryAnn," he bellowed over the music and into his cell phone. MaryAnn Briscay, TMC's compensation manager, listened attentively on the other end of the line.

Reaching for queso, Charlie's silk tie dipped into the papaya salsa.

"Shit." He wiped the food off his tie.

"No, not you, MaryAnn. I got salsa on the fifty-dollar tie my wife bought me for our anniversary." He carried his food away from the buffet.

"What's that? No, I didn't realize that's the role ties originally played. Hope my wife finds that interesting."

With one hand around a piece of traditional *fuba* cake, Charlie furiously scribbled numbers on a napkin as MaryAnn outlined a compensation proposal. Charlie had been hiring so many executives lately that he had come to scheduling compensation discussions with MaryAnn anywhere they could fit in his busy calendar. Discussing incentive compensation over corn porridge, though, was a new low. His stomach told him so.

"MaryAnn, why don't we give this executive what he wants and front-load the restricted shares? ... Yeah, break it up so that more stock vests in the early years ... Yes, I think that will appeal to him. Do you think we can get it approved?" Charlie wiped the last of the porridge from his lips and popped an extra-strength, cherry-flavored antacid into his mouth.

"Great. On my way up to see you now."

Charlie bounded up the staircase, two steps at a time.

"Yes, I ate fast. Got a lot on my plate besides breakfast tacos. After we close this deal, I meet my new boss. Then I have to see what Carol's got brewing."

RUNNING TMC SOLUTIONS, the most profitable and fastest-growing segment of the company, was a clear feather in Carol's cap. Ted communicated to the workforce that her promotion to this position was a reward for the cost-cutting and process improvements she brought to the supply chain. He repeated the accolades, emphasizing his part in Carol's career development, in his petition to be the chairman of a nonprofit organization dedicated to promoting women in sports—a platform to greater political influence as well as to nubile female athletes. As charities went, it was a personal favorite.

TMC Solutions had carried the company's earnings for most of the past ten financial quarters. Record revenues in the Solutions division also spawned a hiring spree, the infrastructure necessary to support continued development. The future of the business segment looked very bright. In addition to long-standing corporate accounts, there was ample opportunity to expand TMC Solutions through access to emerging markets in Eastern Europe and parts of Asia. The country of Turkmenistan was particularly promising.

TMC stock had risen almost 300 percent over the past 24 months, largely on the results of this Solutions division. But sustained success hinged on a delicate balance of operating expenses and revenue growth.

As Charlie wrapped up the offer for his sales executive and Harry discovered Caddy's Java Jungle, Carol delivered a presentation on the current state of TMC Solutions to the companywide TMC leadership team. The executives in the room had accumulated colossal financial gains on their TMC stock. However, their stock grants could not be exercised until the end of the year. If the stock price tanked before the grants matured, any financial windfall could blow away.

On this particular day, the relatively new leader of the Solutions segment informed the group that TMC's success could be in jeopardy. Carol detailed a Solutions loss for the quarter as well as ongoing issues, such as operating expenses out of proportion to revenue growth, that had the potential to impact the full year. She had been running the division for the past three quarters. It appeared she would be holding the bag as it experienced its first trouncing.

Anticipating a negative reaction to this news, the Silk Screw, a nickname the procurement department awarded her, went on the offensive. Her recently clipped hair offered a more militant and, Carol assumed, powerful look in this testosterone-heavy company. She also calculated that the shoulder pads in her fire-engine red suit jacket gave her 5-feet-8-inch frame more of a commanding-officer appearance. Her nostrils flared ever so slightly, her eyebrows grew closer together, and, through carefully selected language, she positioned her plan for recovery. Carol directed a laser pen over the large screen on the front wall of the conference room. She focused the group's energy on a slide in her presentation that outlined a shortfall in revenue.

"Our assumptions and accompanying infrastructure growth were based on projected revenue anticipated from the contracts we signed with customers," she said. "The revenue miss is the result of poor controls in the bids and contracts process."

Pin-dropping silence. Her next slide clearly demonstrated that, unless addressed, operating expenses would continue to outpace revenues, and margins would deteriorate further.

"What ideas can this leadership team offer the Solutions division to ensure proper controls are in place going forward?" Carol's blanket pass-the-buck tactic was not picked up by anyone. Time for an executive Hail Mary.

Carol pointed to another slide, with colorful graphics, that suggested a huge potential in new business. "This data, compiled from discussions with the Solutions sales team, is encouraging. Clearly, the business opportunities are abundant. We simply need finance to get its house in order. Wouldn't you agree, Vince, that your team dropped the ball on financial controls?"

All eyes turned to Vince Kumar, finance director of TMC Solutions, who was responsible for bids and contracts, among other things. Preferring the "rip the bandage off" approach to business challenges (rip it off quickly and move on), when no one else stepped into her trap, Carol fingered Vince as the threat to the obscene wealth that everyone in that room felt was rightfully theirs. Puzzled by discrepancies in his copy of the presentation and the conclusions Carol's version raised, Vince stammered incoherently as he tapped numbers into his calculator. The vice president of marketing, who was scheduled to take delivery of a $175,000 scarlet-red Spider Ferrari, threw his pen cap at the back of Vince's head. Vince considered himself lucky when he noticed that the marketing executive held a stainless steel coffee container in his other hand.

Having recently joined TMC from PRU (PartsAreUs), a component supplier, Vince knew Carol from her work within the supply-chain operation. Though he had no prior experience in companies that provided communications solutions, three months earlier Carol convinced him that they were the right team to lead this successful division. Vince, in turn, persuaded his wife that a relocation from San Antonio would be a great move for their budding family.

Vince stuttered through an explanation as the rumble from the crowd amplified. Carol scanned the room and found Charlie against the back wall. Her eyes met his and she gave him an almost imperceptible nod. Almost imperceptible, that is, to anyone but Charlie, who had been providing human resources support for Carol since she arrived at TMC. Charlie pulled out his Blackberry and began a note to Amanda Albright, an executive-search consultant who had developed a robust practice in replacing TMC executives. The subject line of Charlie's note: "Dead Man Walking."

XXXVI

The following week, Stewart was in Washington DC for the annual meeting of the Positive Executive Attitude Society, whose motto was "Give PEAS a Chance." He leaned out the window of his taxicab and whistled with admiration at the Washington Monument.

It'd be impressive to have a miniature replica of the Washington Monument on my bookshelf, he thought to himself. *Note to self: Convince PEAS board that we need an award to recognize positive behavior. As its optimistic architect, I could be the first recipient of the Monumental Manners Medal.*

It occurred to Stewart that this was yet another benefit of his association with PEAS. He pulled a nail clipper out of his briefcase and began preening himself. Startled out of his personal grooming routine, Stewart fumbled for the cell phone vibrating in his pocket. He hit the speaker button.

"Hello, hello," he called out as the taxi driver zoomed around a corner. Stewart brushed a few nail clippings onto the floor of the cab.

"Stewart? It's Randy Kimble. How the hell are you?" Stewart was happy to hear from his former Evergreen Consultants colleague. They had started their careers together supporting a client in the import/export business. Randy had made a career of consulting. Today, he was a senior partner with global responsibility at Colreavy Consulting.

"Doing fantastic, Randy. In DC for the annual PEAS rally. Are you here too?"

Randy, calling from his San Francisco office, explained that he was not able to make it. He also articulated waning interest in the organization since its founder, with wrists sliced, had checked into a spa for a lengthy holiday.

"No one said it would be easy to maintain a positive attitude, Randy," Stewart admonished his friend.

"OK. Actually, I'm calling about your recent hire, Harry Habet."

"Oh, you read about my groundbreaking leadership-development work. Honestly, all the attention from the press is a little embarrassing." Stewart recalled the battles he had had with TMC's corporate communications team to persuade them to get the word out about Harry's new executive role. Randy was highly influential in corporate America. If he was aware of TMC's talent-management initiative, Stewart had been right to have held his ground.

"Harry will help us pick the winners out of the field," Stewart gloated. Secretly, given Harry's fondness for fine-tailored clothing, the HR leader also felt fashion vindication. With Harry on the team, Stewart hoped to resurrect a few expensive suits that had been mothballed way back when.

"Why didn't you call me before you hired him?" Randy asked. "Our last CEO was exploring a shot at running for governor, and Harry's wife's family made a contribution to his fundraising efforts. In exchange, we hired Harry to be recruiting manager for our financial division just when the global economy was exploding with capital-markets activity. All he had to do was stay out of the way of the recruiters, who were well compensated to hire the best talent. Harry was so incompetent that he pissed off just about anyone he came into contact with. It got so bad that one morning I found an effigy of Harry hung upside down outside our main entrance. The best way we could protect him from his own incompetence was to fire him."

While this news was not welcome, it was certainly not the first time Stewart had heard something like this. In fact, unwelcome warnings about Harry's clumsiness had dripped in from a variety of sources. However, Stewart had lobbied hard, building a coalition of support for this critical hire—critical to Stewart's personal agenda, at least. He needed to protect his work. He had a response ready.

"So, you're telling me that he has his own style and is not afraid to make the tough calls."

"What? No, that's not what I'm saying, Stewart. After we canned him, Harry packed his business suits, and any lingering self-awareness, and became recruiting director for Tek-Biz, the software concern. I heard he hired a personal trainer and put a tanning bed in his office to look the Palo Alto part. Ask him about that bruise on his left arm. I understand the CEO turned Harry's tanning bed into an iron press when Harry screwed up a big hire."

"Hey Randy, what's that? You're breaking up . . . can only get every other word. Hey, if you can hear me, thanks for the reference. I'll call you next time I'm in San Fran. We'll do lunch. Haha. I love that expression. Buh-Bye."

Stewart tossed the phone into his briefcase and wiped his brow. He closed his eyes and slowly exhaled.

XXXVII

L enny had decided to keep quiet about the hole in his Escalade since they managed to get most of the sinks out. *Talking wouldn't do any good anyway*, Lenny judged. Michael had Sal's ear, and the interstate distribution business had picked up, benefiting everyone. But, one Monday afternoon a few weeks later, Lenny was in the office with Sal when his boss expressed impatience with Michael.

"Why does it take so long for Michael to collect?" Sal was counting the protection money that Lenny had collected earlier in the day. "I'm hungry." Michael had offered to pick up lunch after completing his morning rounds.

Lenny floated a trial balloon.

"When we did those collections last week, he seemed a little nervous."

"Like what?" Sal was a man of specifics.

"Like those Turkmen almost didn't hand over the money. Like that nervous," Lenny said.

Sal grew pensive. Michael's constant chatter was annoying and he always had a story when something was late or missing. Michael's uncle was not quick, either, to return calls when Sal asked for intervention on some trucking matters. Then again, the cash flow from the distribution business looked like it should get brighter during the holiday season.

"Anybody can have a bad day, Lenny," Sal reminded his longtime associate. "I remember when someone else was starting out." Sal gave Lenny a wry smile.

"Got to cut your teeth somewhere," he added, locking the money in the safe.

XXXVIII

Although Carol and the TMC leadership team held Vince responsible for what could amount to a multimillion-dollar loss, she let the dust settle on Vince's departure for a good month before summoning Harry and Charlie to her office to discuss his replacement.

Devoid of family pictures or vacation scenes, Carol's office had the coziness of solitary confinement. Her desk was empty of all but a notebook, pen, and Blackberry. At a whiteboard hanging on a wall, she drew her future organization chart as Harry and Charlie took notes.

"Little chilly in here, guys. Think we can get the heat turned up a bit?" Harry smiled coyly at Carol while rubbing his biceps.

Carol took off her jacket and returned to the whiteboard.

"So, here are our critical requirements: a global sales executive and a finance leader for our business segment. In our planning session, the executive team determined that the finance role should be upgraded to a divisional CFO to bring on board the leadership heft that this business requires. As you know, Charlie, because you hired him, Vince was actually a controller, and not a very good one, it turns out." Carol drew a box around "Division CFO" and a solid line from that box to her name on the whiteboard, emphasizing that the finance leader would be a direct report to her.

Tapping into his self-perceived strengths, Harry sought his baritone voice, thrust his worked-out shoulders back, and, chest high, dived into the cool waters again.

"When Ted spoke to me during our recent lunch, he asked me to follow up with several big-time executives he knew. They might have referrals for us."

Carol's support of Harry, along with the positive references that Stewart constructed, had put his candidacy over the top with the hiring committee in spite of what Ted termed his general goofiness. Now that Harry was aboard, Ted wanted to get the board of directors off his back. The CEO had given Harry the particulars on a few people outside TMC who Ted felt had leadership capabilities the company could benefit from—in the future.

Aware of Ted's ultimate motive and desiring more specifics, Carol moved her chair closer to Harry's.

"Well now, that sounds promising," she prodded.

Misunderstanding Carol's intentions, Harry felt his body temperature rise.

Focusing on the task at hand, Charlie pulled out the job description for Vince's role and handed each of them a copy.

"We should retool this and make sure we are all on the same page before we reach out to any candidates," Charlie said as he scratched out verbiage he assumed was no longer applicable: "Candidate need not have worked in a solutions business previously."

Charlie was eager to get these open executive positions closed quickly because employees in the Solutions division were restless. Carol's approach to managing the business challenges had been to cut "nonessential" head count, which provided license for her to run roughshod over her team. The number of complaints logged by TMC Solutions employees was only slightly eclipsed by the number logged by the supply-chain team the year before, when Carol ran that function. Complaints from the Solutions team might have been higher were it not for a great external demand for these professionals. However, workers voting with their feet was not deemed a sustainable strategy for managing employee relations, so Charlie opted for an influx of inspirational leaders.

Carol's concentration shifted to the Rolodex in her mind. One after another, she pictured the executives in whom Ted might be interested. She wondered whom Harry would be calling. She needed to find out.

"Charlie, we have to pitch senior-level executives on the opportunity to be part of a global-solutions business. Dealing with ambiguity is critical, so let's not quibble over a job posting. Any candidates come to mind, Harry?"

Blushing, Harry nodded affirmatively and winked at Carol.

"We had a similar situation when I recruited Tim Arnes to be the CFO for Tek-Biz. We needed solid financial controls to support a promising international expansion. I put together a search strategy based on three bullet points, and Tim accepted our offer. Matter of fact, I heard through the grapevine that Tim might have outgrown Tek-Biz. I'll give him a call."

"Sure, Harry. Great idea." Carol moved closer and smiled more brightly at Harry. Tim's experience did not sound like the profile that would interest Ted. She thought of other executives outside TMC. She wondered if Harry might try to recruit the chairman of the Italian food conglomerate whom she and Ted had met at a corporate leadership seminar.

Handsome, tall, wealthy. Ted plays golf with him almost once a month now, Carol contemplated. Then she reconsidered: *The board would never go for his accent. Maybe Ted prefers that Navy SEAL who runs the paper manufacturer. Ted is such a pushover for the armed-forces types.*

Carol kicked herself for leaving her grandfather's military pins when she departed Africa. *They would have impressed Ted*, she thought.

Carol mulled over additional prospects Ted might deem worthy of a shot as his backfill. She knew that Harry took credit for a substantial increase in the number of diverse executives in senior leadership positions at Colreavy Consulting. Determined to derail the competition, she pounced on an opportunity to impress Harry and move her hidden agenda forward.

"I can see why Stewart brought you on board, Harry." Carol gave him the million-dollar grin that she reserved for the most important TMC customers. "As you know, I've made a commitment to diversity in this business. We should seriously consider our own Emily Harris as a candidate for the Solutions CFO job."

"Great idea to promote from within," Harry took the bait. "Sends the right message to the troops."

Harry smiled his own seven-figure grin right back as he and Charlie got up to leave the office. "Carol, don't worry about a thing," Harry said. "We've got recruiting under control."

Carol bid Charlie adieu but asked Harry to stick around.

"Harry, let's strategize about how you might approach these contacts Ted gave you, so we can maximize the usefulness of the interactions. For the good of the Solutions business, that is."

XXXIX

A few days later, Charlie sat in front of his computer, transfixed by his workload. A paralyzing tension gripped his core, and his fingers locked on the computer keyboard. He closed his eyes.

Inhale . . . exhale . . . inhale . . . exhale . . .

Because of the Solutions earnings shock wave, the recruiting team experienced a tsunami of new work as TMC scrambled to bring in new executives who might add value immediately and help turn paper riches into cold, hard cash at year's end. Leadership positions that were not filled quickly were perceived to have a negative effect on TMC's ability to prosper, which in turn had a negative effect on Charlie's ability to thrive.

Opening his eyes, he wrote down his priorities for the morning. Then he returned to his computer and started working. Likening answering his e-mail to at bats for a baseball player, Charlie hit a few singles. Once in a while, he took the time to answer the e-mail equivalent of a double or triple, but he did not yet attempt any home runs (e-mail with attachments). After ninety minutes and one coffee refill, he was ready to tackle a spreadsheet.

Let me get the worst over with first, he thought, opening an attachment from finance. The financial analyst for the procurement team had sent Charlie an e-mail questioning his request for a large expenditure. Charlie wanted the funds to initiate an executive search to find someone to back-fill Vince (whose official explanation for his recent departure was "personal reasons"). The financial analyst supported her argument against what she deemed an outrageous cost with an attached e-mail from her own boss, the procurement controller, Emily Harris. In her haste to move this action item off her plate, the analyst failed to realize that, earlier in the long e-mail attachment, a gun was still smoking.

The first note, way down in the string, came from Vince and contained comments on an executive summary on business results.

Carol,

Attached is the presentation for tomorrow's meeting. These results are disappointing. Not likely to be received well by the team. Someone wrote long-term contracts without considering currency, infrastructure, or tax impact. TMC Solutions is about to experience negative margins. On top of that, we cannot recognize revenue for several quarters based on the way a number of deals were structured.

Who approved these contracts?

Vince

When Carol forwarded the e-mail to Emily, who had worked directly for her when she ran the supply-chain function, she wrote two words: *Fix this.*

Subsequent messages specified Emily's actions with her team to address the contracts. The same finance analyst who started the communication to Charlie had identified the root of the problem: "Appears loss is largely connected to Q4 contracts where revenue/profitability guidelines weren't followed. Isn't this the same quarter we made the big push into professional care? We hired a ton of people."

Because of the size and complexity of the deals, and the potential exposure, the procurement team had been asked to review the contracts. Carol had signed all of them.

Charlie choked as he recalled Carol's campaign for Emily to be the next Solutions finance leader. TMC's Corporate CFO, Rupert Bhein, had complained bitterly to human resources about it.

Stewart told me that Carol had pestered Rupert about promoting Emily Harris. Would Emily be rewarded with a bigger job for cleaning up a contracts mess that Carol, not Vince, created? Charlie wondered.

Charlie visibly stiffened as he reviewed the document attached to the e-mail string. Although it carried the same title, this presentation was different from the one Carol had delivered to the executive team. Specifically, this one contained a longer list of questionable contracts, many predating Vince's employment. Conveniently, they had been omitted in the version Carol shared with TMC leadership. Charlie recalled Vince's comments during his exit interview. At the time, Charlie had considered them the bitter rants of a disgraced executive. Cast in the light of this new information, Vince's words suddenly seemed prescient: "Carol plays this company like a card shark in Vegas. For those of you remaining around the table, I hope someday the house will get even."

Way back when, Carol was quite eager to hire Vince. Was he intended to be her fall guy all along? Charlie had a lot on his mind.

X L

"Somebody doesn't have things under control on the Philly end of this operation, boss. Insult to injury, my wife's new fur was on one of those so-called lost trucks. All due respect, why does this have to come out of my end?"

Sal held a small glass of red wine in his left hand and the cell phone in his right. He delivered his message with composure, but his grip on the wine glass strengthened as his boss, with equal self-control, persuaded Sal to eat these mistakes.

"Yes, boss . . . the beginning of a long partnership. I get that, but . . . Yeah, I understand there are bound to be hiccups so . . . Forget and move forward? . . . OK. I'll talk to Philly."

Crack.

Sal wrapped his bloody hand with a bar towel.

"Nothing. A little glass broke . . . Yeah, I know what I have to do." He hung up with the boss and called Michael.

"I need you to call on those Turkmen again. They stiffed us last week. Need you to make it right."

SAL'S CELL PHONE rang as he headed west on the parkway in the direction of his girlfriend's apartment. After the usual and customary platitudes to Sal, his local mob boss, the proprietor of a neighborhood restaurant delicately apologized to Sal for not being able to accommodate his consigliere and their friends for dinner that evening. Unfortunately, Michael's tab was adding up faster than it was getting paid down, he explained.

"Sal, I would have spotted Michael the dinner, but we ain't Atlantic City over here." The restaurateur reasoned that soon the consigliere's patronage might impact the size of the envelope that Sal received each Saturday night.

Sal inquired about specifics: the amount Michael owed (large); whom he was with (the Turkmen); and where he went afterward (a college basketball game). Sal booked a birthday party for his wife and hung up.

Sal changed course and drove to the sports arena where Michael was entertaining the Turkmen in a skybox. Michael hoped a display of American skill on the basketball court, together with an overdose of flattery and hard liquor, would persuade these street thugs to hand over the money they owed Sal. After all, three weeks of allowing himself to be bullied by them had not produced the money.

When the younger of the two foreigners, Aganiyaz, noticed Sal, he stood up excitedly, dropping warm Brie on his designer knockoff slacks.

"Halo, boss! Thank you for these great accommodations!" He smiled broadly at Sal.

Taken by surprise, Michael smiled reflexively.

Aganiyaz was indeed impressed by the attention, the likes of which he had not seen since competing Ashgabat street gangs vied for his membership. And that was when scraps of ham could turn an allegiance in Turkmenistan's capital city. He wiped the appetizer from his pants and thanked his patron again.

"I love America. In Ashgabat, if we were late on the vig, somebody would shoot us. In America, they feed us. I love America!"

Michael introduced his guests to his boss. The elder Turkman, Saparmurat, did not rise to shake Sal's hand. He pushed his suit jacket behind his back to allow easy access to his firearm. Sal remained standing, taking in the contents of the room while two college basketball teams played an exhibition game on the court well below them. Michael poured him a drink from the bar. Sal took it.

"We were discussing business, boss. These guys are running an operation out of New York that has potential. They need a little money to get started. What did you call it, Saparmurat? Angel assets?"

Saparmurat corrected his host. "Angel investors."

"Zat so?" Sal picked at the hors d'oeuvres on a plate by the bar. The second quarter was just beginning, and the sizeable tray of food was almost empty.

"Yeah, boss. Saparmurat was telling me that we'd have our money soon as they unload the first shipment." Michael further explained that there was a promising opportunity to double their money if they invested the vig in this new venture.

"Really? Well, I've got a better idea. Why don't we get our money that's due us now and we won't have to break anybody's legs?" Sal stared purposefully at Michael.

Saparmurat, not only senior but also smarter, knew a good hand when it was dealt. He did not have the money he owed Sal, nor was he close to getting it, but his intuition told him this confrontation was more about Michael than about the vig. He accused Michael of setting them up.

"Please! This is insulting. What do we look like, Russians? We come here in good faith and you shake us down? Yolly will hear of this!"

This was altogether too much for Michael, who spilled his soup. While he had never met him, Yolly's reputation, and well-known 400-pound physical mass, preceded him. For a moment, Michael forgot about Sal.

Michael did not know that Yolly stood to profit handsomely from a transaction between TMC Solutions and Turkmenistan's government, a deal that Sal had arranged for a small fee. Sal was not concerned that the deliverymen had been offended. Besides, he sensed that Saparmurat had accurately read the situation and was grateful to have an excuse to get out of there. In terms of the money they owed, the right look from Lenny Knuckles would convince these hoodlums to come up with the cash.

Aganiyaz followed his compatriot out of the skybox, stuffing hors d'oeuvres into his pockets as he did so.

"So now we don't love America?" he asked as they headed toward the exit.

After they left, Sal called Lenny and put Michael on the phone.

"Here. Tell Lenny where he can find those two waste products so he can get my money."

A WEEK AFTER his meeting with the Turkmen, Sal arranged to meet with the boss to tell him about the phenomenal potential for interstate trucking in the northeast. Lenny had cousins lined up to help build the business in Boston and Connecticut. The missing piece of the distribution route was upstate New York, but Lenny remembered another cousin, twice removed on his mother's side. Having lived off the state since a car chase with New York state troopers had gone awry, he would be coming home soon and looking for work. New York looked promising.

Three weeks later, Sal met with the boss again. They sipped espresso at another social club, this one on the corner of a busy intersection in Hoboken. As car horns competed with yapping shoppers and the occasional expletive of a frustrated delivery truck driver, the heavyset boss finished a second napoleon while Sal made very clear that his new business venture was succeeding.

Sal spelled out how the northeast corridor business had been more lucrative in three weeks than the North Jersey–Philly run had been in three months. Also, no trucks or drivers had gone missing. The boss was impressed with Sal's operation and, particularly, his quick reversal of what could have been a downturn in the business. Sal's leverage of Lenny's contacts also met with the boss's approval.

"I believe it's healthy to encourage Lenny's entrepreneurial spirit," Sal said.

Stewart's human resources lingo had rubbed off on Sal. He could barely contain himself. *I've seen Stewart work this on guys smarter than the boss, so what do I have to lose?* Sal considered.

"And provide leadership opportunities for him," Sal added.

The boss agreed it was not easy to manage personalities, which was largely what their business was about, when you boiled it all down.

Man, this crap really works. Sal was feeling good.

The boss acknowledged that Sal efficiently handled this transition to a new distribution model. Not a drop of blood had spilled. That was notable.

Sal went for broke.

"As you of all people know, boss, it isn't easy being innovative in the best of times, never mind when you have business issues or partner troubles. You got to have the balls to make the calls, so to speak."

The boss readily concurred as he sipped his espresso.

"And when change is needed, it's critical to move fast. Mediocrity can eat away at the whole organism," Sal added.

The boss was delighted with the greater financial returns the new distribution route was generating. Also, he too had tired of the incompetence evident throughout the Philly operation. He agreed that developing the right team, providing opportunities for leadership, and being open to innovation were as important as having a strong number two in the organization. The boss gave Sal permission to send Michael packing.

XLI

Ted tried to call Harry from Pebble Beach, where he was playing golf with Rick Robertson, chairman of the powerful governance committee on TMC's board of directors. Rick also had felt the sting of disappointment when Jim Collins, his personal favorite to succeed Ted as CEO, departed TMC for ostensibly greener pastures. Intensely focused on ensuring a smooth transition of leadership, which would help secure the equity position his family held in the company, Rick's constant badgering about succession planning affected Ted's performance. By the sixth hole, the CEO had sliced three drives.

When he reached the back nine, Ted excused himself. He intended to step up his game, no matter his opponent, so he called Harry to find out where things were with the external succession candidates. When Harry could not be located, Ted called Stewart and read him the riot act. Bristling from the latest setback with his father, Stewart was determined not to disappoint Ted.

Stewart had taken to inundating his dad's e-mail box with positive press releases and upbeat analyst reports about TMC. He sent pictures, too, chiefly when he received an award on behalf of the human capital management function. He got no response—not so much as a smiley face. His most recent attempt at communicating his successes was met with: "This is an automatically generated delivery status notification. Delivery to the following recipient failed permanently: Preciouschild001@narciss.com."

Worked up from Ted's browbeating, reminiscent of so many his father had delivered, Stewart marched to Harry's office. Finding it empty, he cornered Vera and deputized her to relay the riot act. His next step was to introduce himself to the candidates in whom Ted was interested. Stewart placed a call to each candidate and explained that, due to business commitments, he would send his emissary, Harry Habet, to discuss TMC with them. While he assured the contenders that they would be in very good hands with Harry, Stewart also provided his personal cell phone number.

He wanted to make certain that if any of these candidates was eventually chosen to run the company, they would remember how gracious and helpful Stewart had been.

And, because Carol appeared to be the most likely internal candidate to succeed Ted, Stewart hedged his bet. He worked media contacts to gain more exposure for her. After speaking with all the candidates and a few reporters, Stewart hurried to complete an application for Ted to nominate him as *Corporate Consigliere of the Year* for the Business Select Society.

Later, when Harry returned to his office, he found Vera booking him a flight to Los Angeles, where he would interview several of Ted's candidates.

"Stewart stopped by. He wants to make sure you know how to handle those executives that Ted recommended," Vera called over her open office wall to him. "He said they could be pivotal to TMC's future."

"Pivotal?"

"Specifically, he said to tell you not to insult anyone."

Harry declared, "What impudence! I know how to behave with top business leaders!"

Vera reminded Harry of an earlier mishap, when Stewart served as keynote speaker at the Asian-American Exchange Summit, an organization dedicated to building bridges between Asian professionals and top companies. Harry attended the event with the express purpose of drafting new, warm bodies into TMC's middle-management fold, an area experiencing huge spikes in voluntary attrition as promised promotions and large equity awards failed to materialize. The revelations about the state of TMC Solutions' business had not helped, either. With so many managers exiting the firm, executives were concerned about not having enough people to get the work done. Stewart convinced his colleagues that Asians had a reputation for hard work and self-reliance, the latter of which also was in demand as resources were increasingly curtailed at TMC. But Harry's mission was something less than a smashing success.

"You asked Hui Hosang, the Taiwanese-born sales vice president for Pearl's Couture Clothiers, what his American name was!" Vera reminded him.

"Who knew the Japanese were so touchy?"

"Taiwanese. And Stewart was mortified when you used the walking cane of the retired chairman of the Asian Bar Association as a prop for the limbo dance."

"But that old goat looked like he was having such a great time sliding across the floor on his belly."

Vera was silent.

"OK, OK," Harry relented. "I'll be on my best behavior when I interview Ted's guys. What time is my flight to LA?"

Vera dropped a copy of the completed travel reservations on his desk.

"Any chance I can wiggle onto Ted's jet for the trip west? It'd be great for business. The quicker I get there, the more time available for interviews." Harry considered the possibilities of riding in style to the West Coast. He imagined top-shelf bourbon served in fine crystal, a personal chef catering to his culinary whims, and the latest Hollywood release showing on the flat-screen TV.

Vera weighed the consequences of hitting Harry upside the head. It occurred to her that she once had similar inclinations regarding Stewart. She determined that it would not help and could backfire—the TMC scholarship committee might not look favorably upon the parent of an applicant attacking a member of the executive team—she tabled the idea, at least until the college scholarship recipients were announced.

Charlie stopped by her desk. "Did you get the latest *Economic Week* magazine yet?" he asked.

"Here ya go." Vera handed her colleague the magazine. "Don't forget to bring it back when you are done. Harry hasn't read it yet."

"Vera, I've seen the budget," said Harry, who had overheard. "Let Charlie keep that copy and we'll get another subscription for me."

Exasperated, Vera threw an imaginary punch in the direction of her boss.

This is not the time to be spending the corporation's money frivolously, be it a ride on the corporate jet or a duplicate magazine subscription, she fumed to herself.

"Don't know what company you work for, Harry, but as long as I work here, you'll share magazines," Vera told him.

The finance team had taken to a regular reading of their own riot act as business expenses continued to eclipse TMC's growth rate. Ted's response to this operating expense–driven crunch was a demand that executives reduce costs in their respective areas. Once again, Stewart identified a grand-scale initiative that would address the entire workforce. Or, as he put it, "bring efficacy to efficiency and, in the process, make employees healthier."

Stewart's recommendation, an extreme adjustment to the company contribution to employees' health-care benefit, hit Vera's out-of-pocket expenses immediately. The home equity loan she had taken out to help her son Christian pay for higher education was now needed to cover higher health-care premiums.

To offset the deleterious public relations associated with this change in benefits, Stewart persuaded Ted to fund after-work sports teams. The employees who participated in these healthy-lifestyle activities were rewarded with cash payments to their health-care spending accounts. However, sports did not rank high on Vera's native inclinations. She was particularly piqued by Harry's insensitivity about expenses because the cash payments accumulating in her account were wiped out when her volleyball serve sent two people on an opposing team to the medic.

TMC's growing pains left Vera with the sense that the original corporate mission was fading. The workday was more often drudgery than anticipation. She found herself keeping her head down when previously she might have raised it to offer help. Her one solace had become a regular Monday morning coffee with Charlie. He bought the lattes and played barista-keep to Vera's concerns.

Eager to get out of the middle of Vera's argument with Harry, Charlie took the magazine back to his desk. He flipped to the "Career Transitions" section on the back page. This column listed executives who were leaving companies or moving up into new leadership roles. He scanned the page for good leads for TMC's open positions.

Looks like that networking company E-Zents lost their sales leader. I wonder if the company will reorganize. Might be a good time to go after their top sales-people for our Solutions opening.

Suddenly, Charlie let out a piercing whistle. Startled, a few colleagues in the area shouted at him to keep it down.

The *Economic Week* cover story was about politics and the oil and gas industry: "Is there Middle Ground in the Middle East?" Charlie referenced that in his apology to co-workers. "Sorry. This article says oil could get to $200 a barrel!" As visions of carpools and garaged SUVs crossed their minds, his colleagues sighed collectively.

Clare Woodard, who had become a standard-bearer, regularly harangued corporate executives about their poor performance. Charlie's whistle had actually been in reaction to a new alarm the reporter had sounded:

> Struggling Tek-Biz CFO Tim Arnes was released from his lucrative, two-year contract following the announcement that the company would report a decline in earnings. This would be the third sequential quarter of "less than spectacular" performance, to quote the CEO. An anonymous Tek-Biz executive had this to say about his former financial leader: " . . . Tek-Biz is a complex business model. We had great expectations of Tim. But, the company needed a Ginsu blade to surgically cut operating expenses. Tim's more of a butter knife." Where are the gatekeepers as another tightly wound tech concern unravels at the hands of mediocre management? Note to human resources professionals: How about a little less focus on king-making and more on ego-breaking, business-building, leadership?

"Ouch!" Charlie whispered to himself.

Whenever an opportunity to do so arose, Harry had touted Tim as one of his top executive placements. In fact, at Harry's urging, Vera had been organizing interviews for Tim with the TMC leadership team.

Could Harry have known what was going on at Tek-Biz? Does he owe Tim? What the heck is going on around here? Charlie worried.

Charlie knew this kind of press would not be good for business. Plus, having lost sleep trying to figure out what to do about Carol's manipulations of the business and her employees, Charlie was not about to invite in someone else who might screw things up further.

This place has gone from the ridiculous to the unethical. Somebody's got to make a stand, he decided.

No longer wondering about the leadership skills Harry might have that he did not, Charlie walked down to his boss's office to show him the article and explain why he was going to scuttle Tim's interviews.

Maybe it's time to think about a new line of work. After all, what's next? Charlie sighed.

X L I I

Newspaper on the table, hot coffee in his mug, Harry struck his most intense posture, chest and chin high, biceps taut. He stared intently out the restaurant window. He hoped that Adam Fleming, CEO of the successful IT services company Y-U, would arrive soon. Looking impressive was hard on his abdominal muscles.

Adam, who also served on the corporate board of the British petro-chemical conglomerate PETRO PLC with Ted, would be exiting Y-U at year's end. Ted's notion was that Adam might run strategy for TMC, a platform from which he would be well situated to compete in a horserace with Carol for the future CEO perch.

Ted respected the contributions Adam made on the PETRO board. Also, from the sidelines, he had witnessed Adam's hands-on leadership as Y-U grew tenfold in five years. Adam was widely regarded as a bold executive who knew how to shape and nurture a successful team. Ted hoped that a move to the much larger TMC might have the career cachet that would appeal to Adam. He was certainly of the ilk to give Carol a run for her money and, in so doing, provide Ted an extended leadership stay.

Harry considered it his good fortune that Carol also knew of Adam and offered pointers about how he might handle this accomplished executive. Recognizing Adam from the many news articles in which he had been featured, Harry waved to the clean-shaven, powerfully built CEO as the latter entered the restaurant. As the former Marine lieutenant approached the table, briefcase swinging delicately against his broad, pin-striped frame, Harry purposefully checked the time on his platinum Movado timepiece.

"Late for something?" Adam pulled out a chair and sat down without shaking Harry's outstretched hand.

Harry gaped at his empty hand. Awkwardly, he stated, "Oh, no. Not at all. Flew into town specifically to meet you. Have all the time in the world. How the hell are ya?" Harry reached around to slap Adam on the shoulder.

Adam's military training kicked in and he forced his chair back.

"What the . . . ?" Adam pushed Harry's arm away.

Sensing the interview power shifting in the wrong direction, Harry recouped.

"Let's get right to it, shall we, old boy?" Harry began as a waiter handed out menus.

Eyeglasses sitting on the bridge of his nose, menu open in his lap, Adam looked intently at Harry.

"You'll be needing a place to land after you exit Y-U, and we need your IT strategy experience and contacts." Harry waved the waiter off.

"I thought we were going to eat."

"Adam, my motto is never let food get in the way of a good meal." Harry laughed heartily.

Adam called the waiter back and ordered a sandwich. He sighed heavily as his attention returned to Harry's pitch.

"Adam, we are revitalizing our business! Never in my executive history have I been so excited! The guy, or gal, who is chosen to create and execute the strategy for TMC is going to be on the forefront of communications technology. He, or she, will create and implement the strategy that the entire organization will live or die by." Harry smiled and waved a finger at his guest. "So it better be a good one."

Taking his eyeglasses off, Adam focused on the half-filled water glass in front of him. Reflecting on his long relationship with Ted, he finally said, "Harry, I'm here out of respect for Ted and the fact that I believe that TMC is in a fantastic position to prosper from the intersection of technology and communications."

Adam paused thoughtfully and then continued. "I think the best way to move this forward for both of us is for you to tell me more specifics about the job."

"What do you want? A position description?" Harry asked.

"Yes! That strikes me as a reasonable place to start!"

"So passé, don't you think? I mean, come on! We are going to be making history here." Harry sat back in his chair and took a sip of coffee. "Can't capture that in a simple job description."

"Why don't you tell me what you'd like to discuss then, Harry."

"Image, Adam. Let's talk image. How's the wife? Pretty hot, I bet."

BACK IN HIS hotel room after an abbreviated lunch, Harry typed an e-mail message to Ted:

TB,

Met Adam Fleming. Great elder statesman but not a natural leader. Socially a bit stiff. Recommend we pass.

HH

Harry reviewed his reflection in the mirror. He decided that a few days in the sun would even out the skin tone considerably around his black eye. A little makeup would take care of the rest. He lay down on the bed and placed a rare rib eye steak over his injury.

XLIII

C arol had been under the ever-critical eye of the TMC leadership team since she revealed that the wheels had been coming off the Solutions division bus. With so much at stake, from goodwill to stock value, everyone wanted to get this part of TMC back on track. Carol knew her career depended on it. Disposing of Vince bought her only a little time, so she worked every other angle to resuscitate the division, from hiring executive bench strength to organizing the large transaction with the government of Turkmenistan. Who might have imagined that a simple dinner of pasta and meatballs with Sal and his associates could lead to such a significant Central Asian opportunity for TMC? Carol was not happy about Sal's insistence on a finder's fee for the introduction but rationalized that his charge was somewhat less than the fees a Wall Street firm would have billed for a similar transaction.

Although enthusiastic about diversifying his business interests, Sal was never completely comfortable with reported income, particularly as it was subject to tax. On the plus side, setting up a corporation to which TMC's accounts-payable team could send his fees lent an air of credibility to his operation.

Charlie had the marching orders to build the Solutions executive talent bench. Emily had assumed the financial leadership post for the division, and that took some of the heat off. (When Emily denied Charlie's request for funding an executive search to fill the role and Tim's candidacy was scuttled, Rupert Bhein succumbed to Carol's pummeling and moved Emily into the job.) Still, Charlie was worn out by Carol's relentless demands. He made arrangements to review a new crop of candidates with her and, hopefully, get Carol off his back.

Charlie toyed with the idea of feeling her out about Vince's departure. Although his findings were not yet corroborated, Charlie could make a compelling case that Carol terminated Vince to conceal her mistakes and protect her career. However, desiring to protect his own career, he thought it wise not to confront her head-on. He could get in a lot of hot water if his assumptions were wrong and maybe even more if they were correct.

But he definitely intended to use this meeting to suggest a strategy that would mitigate the opt-out practice that continued to pervade the Solutions division workforce. He reminded Carol that, only in the past week, fifteen salespeople had jumped at the chance to take advantage of a lack of focus. They formed their own company to compete directly with TMC Solutions. Wisely, Charlie did not mention that yet another, anonymous employee had initiated what was quickly becoming a popular blog: *Death and the Maiden: How the Silk Screw'd Up the Solution.*

"That damn Vince!" Carol shouted. "Our credibility has been compromised, and people are walking out on me because of his incompetence!"

Carol's condemnation of Vince provided Charlie with an opening.

"Do you think the company gave Vince a good shot to succeed, Carol?" A nervous smile passed across Charlie's face.

"Who?" Engrossed in her current problems, Carol glanced up from organization charts with more boxes empty than filled.

Charlie's tie felt particularly tight. He adjusted it. Golf shirt and slacks were his normal business attire, but on this day he had three executives interviewing on the TMC campus, so he had dressed up. Despite his wife's admonitions to lay off the heavy foods and get into the gym, he challenged his suit jacket, a size medium, with his extra-large build.

"I mean, should we have given him the boot so quickly?" Charlie finally answered. "After all, was he the only one responsible for structuring the contracts that created our problems?"

Charlie watched the shoulders of Carol's herringbone jacket rise slowly and fall deeply as she considered his question. Her nostrils were flaring. A slight change in expression fleetingly passed over Carol's face. Although he had barely noticed it, never had the expression "if looks could kill" held so much personal meaning for Charlie. In a moment, he knew he had gotten too close. He fell on his backup plan: open an escape hatch.

"I mean, given the expense of hiring and training, I have been thinking about what we might do to mitigate the costs associated with onboarding new executives. For example, should we see if an executive might be a better fit in a different part of the company before we let him go?"

Suddenly, Carol's office felt very chilly.

"Or is that just a bad idea?" he offered.

Through a frozen smile, Carol suggested that it was an "inspired idea. Why don't you work on that option with the legal department?"

Carol found a reason to cut their meeting short.

"So sorry, Charlie. I forgot I have a meeting with a customer."

Charlie left her office, the button on his well-worn jacket symbolically popping off as he returned to his desk and released his breath.

"Cooked goose," he later told his wife who asked, when she called to make dinner plans, what he felt like.

XLIV

Emily hated to admit it, but her team had taken this Turkmenistan deal as far as they could. U.S. Government compliance regulations as well as last-minute nits from the TMC legal team had held up the process long enough for TMC's major competitor, XLNZ, to wiggle in with a lower bid.

She told Carol the news. Her large deal was in jeopardy.

"It's Turkmenistan, for crying out loud," Carol responded. "Send a treasury manager over there with a briefcase full of cash."

Carol took a set of keys out of her purse. Bending down, she unlocked the bottom drawer of a credenza in the back of her office closet. She pulled something that looked like cable out of a faded green leather briefcase and handed the now empty bag to Emily. She had held on to Sal's briefcase in case she ever had a need for it.

"Here, use this one. It can't be traced back to us."

X L V

S al's cell phone buzzed in his tuxedo jacket pocket. He checked the number display, glanced at his chips as the roulette dealer spun the wheel, then glanced at his companion, a thirtysomething brunette a little the worse for wear. He removed her gin and tonic from the table and asked her to watch his position.

"How ya doing, Carol?" Sal moved away from the din of the gaming tables so he could better hear his client.

"Where are you? What's that noise I hear in the background?" Carol was often curious about Sal's other business interests.

Sal stopped outside the ladies' room. *Might as well enjoy the view*, he thought.

"I'm investigating a new business opportunity," he answered. Lenny Knuckles and a cousin were in an Atlantic City hotel, not far from the casino, meeting with three gentlemen who had arrived earlier in the day from South America.

"Sounds like you're in a casino." Carol let a pause hang between them. So did Sal.

"I hope you aren't too busy with your other business, Sal, to work on my account."

"Never too busy for my best customer, Carol. By the way, how'd you like that bandleader I fixed you up with last weekend?"

"Your research team has got their work cut out for them, Sal. Turns out he was more of a follower. A groupie on the R & B circuit, to be specific. He took me to a crowded, smoky bar where a brat with a braided beard mangled his horn and my ears. When we got up to leave, your charming bandleader realized he left his wallet at home."

"Carol, be fair. He's got a great voice, and a very promising future."

"Let's just say I'm not the groupie type. For someone whose job is to marry up talent with the right team, your results are diverging very far from my requirements."

"Whateva. You got another project like StreamLINE?" Sal never missed an opportunity to ingratiate himself with Carol.

"I haven't forgotten. This isn't the same kind of project, Sal, but it does require urgency. I need to start a search to find a general manager to lead TMC's Solutions business."

"Carol, last time I looked, that was your job." Sal winked at twin twentysomethings in short skirts and midriffs entering the restroom. They giggled and waved back.

Carol explained that the Solutions business, the jewel in TMC's crown, had issues that needed addressing before she would be able to move on to her next leadership role. Her game plan was to hire an executive who could help her fix the problems. With a successful turnaround to her credit and her backfill as Solutions general manager identified in this new executive, Carol would be well-positioned to succeed Ted as CEO.

"Alternatively, if the business continues to go south, we've got an executive to sacrifice for the loss."

"Good plan." Sal appreciated Carol's strategic thinking, which was more than he could say about most of his business associates. She got things done, too. In fact, Carol executed with the best of them, as far as Sal was concerned. She used Sal and Stewart to do her dirty work, but it was good-paying dirty work, so Sal did not complain.

"I'll send you a resume of the guy I want to hire for the job."

"He's got general management experience?"

"He's a good-looking sales executive. Wouldn't know how to run a business if his life depended on it."

Sal understood that Carol did not want anyone interfering with her agenda, which she made more clear as she described her ideal leadership team: Emily, her handpicked finance executive, would take care of bids and contracts; this sales executive would be responsible for new business; and Carol would continue to oversee the entire division as general manager until she had accumulated enough gravitas to bump Ted.

Sal waved at the twins as they left the bathroom. They giggled again. His eyes followed them into the roulette area.

"So, I'll call Charlie and get the paperwork started for this new search," he said. Eager to return to gambling and the twins, Sal wished to wrap up the call.

"No way. I don't want Mr. Goody Two-Shoes mucking things up."

"Oh. OK." He waited. He knew Carol had a plan.

"This is exactly the type of situation we hired Harry for. Besides, I need an excuse to keep tabs on what he's up to."

XLVI

"Regular pickup time or something different this afternoon, Harry?" Harry's Town Car driver pushed keys to advance his cyber-soccer team down the electronic field on his cell phone. "Yes!" The driver had scored.

"I have a lunch meeting today with Carol Himmler, the exceptionally successful leader of our Solutions business. We'll be discussing candidates for her confidential executive searches," Harry said.

The driver nodded and continued moving his players.

"Yes. Regular time. Buh-bye." Unable to engage his driver, Harry jumped out of the backseat.

Having just returned to the office after his recruiting excursion to Los Angeles, Harry listened attentively as Vera read a litany of messages.

"And Ted wants you to call him about your meeting with Adam Fleming."

"I sent him an e-mail on that guy already. Nice chap, but not the leadership ilk TMC requires. None of them was, in my estimation."

"Wouldn't know about that. Could you sign this for me? I have an interview in thirty minutes." Vera smiled at her boss. The close-up with Harry revealed differences in skin tone around his eyes. "Are you wearing makeup?"

Harry ignored her question and looked over the form Vera handed him.

It requested approval for her to interview for a different job within the company. Puzzled, he asked for an explanation.

"This signals your approval for me to interview for that admin job we discussed last week."

"Did we discuss you taking a new job? I don't recall that, Vera."

"Sure. Remember, I told you that Suzette's position had opened up."

Harry scratched his head. "I think I remember that conversation but not that you would be applying for the job."

Vera put the pen in Harry's hand and held it securely as she physically encouraged his signature on the dotted line.

"Sure we did. I mentioned that, much as I'd miss everyone, it's time for me to rotate into a new job. This opening is perfect for me, and I knew you'd understand my desire to learn new skills, being an HR leader and all. Thanks so much, Harry."

Having maneuvered a sloppy signature out of her boss, Vera exited Harry's office pronto. Putting on her hat and coat because the interview was in another TMC building, she reminded Harry of his lunch engagement with Carol.

"Nice hat," Harry noted sarcastically as Vera walked toward the exit.

Charlie passed by as Vera adjusted her yellow cotton cap. Overhearing Harry's comment, he considered his co-worker's hat and remarked with enthusiasm that he, too, liked it.

Vera smiled and winked at Charlie.

Harry whispered, "You *like* that hat?"

"I do. I think it's great."

"But it's so not couture!"

"That may be exactly why I like it. I like the message it sends to the world: 'Take me as I am.'"

Harry reconsidered the hat. "Well, it sure doesn't say, 'Don't you wish you were me?'"

CAROL WAS ENGAGED in a business call when Harry arrived at the quaint and quiet off-campus spot that she had suggested for lunch. She motioned for him to join her and waved the waiter over to order a drink, all without missing a single point with the customer on the call. Harry watched in amazement as the sheer force of her personality drove the restaurant wait staff to high attention.

Harry read the menu several times before Carol completed her call.

"Hope you like this place, Harry. Laguna's is one of my favorite restaurants." Before Harry could respond, Carol called the waiter back and ordered a turkey club, hold the bacon, and cold salmon salad.

"You'll love the salad. It's the best in town."

Carol got right to things with Harry. In spite of its balance sheet challenges, the Solutions division had close to a 50 percent growth rate in Europe and Asia. While ultimately good news, the complexity of this services operation was significant, and international expansion did not make it any easier to manage.

"Emily is cleaning up the mess that Vince created with those professional care contracts," she said. "And thank God you had insider information on Tim Arnes. Charlie would never have known what was really going on behind the scenes at Tek-Biz. Imagine the trouble we'd be in if Charlie had pulled off his plan to recruit Tim."

Still nervous about the role he played in trying to enlist Tim into TMC's fold, Harry froze.

Carol continued, emphasizing her concern that the Solutions business was going to get only more complex. "Charlie has done an OK job, but do you really believe he is the best man, I mean recruiter, for a global, dynamic business like Solutions?" Carol removed her glasses and placed them on her bread plate.

Harry needed Charlie. He had to turn Carol's opinion around or risk having to do the work himself. That had not turned out so well at his last employer, so his rule of thumb was to avoid as much actual work as humanly possible. He also had vowed never again to keep a tanning bed in his office.

Carol went on, teasing Harry: "As I—we—consider the talent we'll need for Solutions, the sense is that we need a more senior HR person to build our leadership team. An attractive, sophisticated recruiter who knows about power and heft." She leaned in to face him directly. The aroma of her perfume surrounded him. Harry's cheeks burned bright pink.

"But Charlie's the best recruiter I've ever worked with," he said. "Do you know that last week he closed three—"

"Doesn't Charlie strike you as too deliberate? Plodding, even? I need someone who is agile, Harry. Someone like you," Carol interrupted him.

Harry had been concerned about the heart palpitations he often experienced during meetings with Carol, but now he attributed his heart spasms to the sexual tension between them.

I wonder if she's come to terms with it? he asked himself.

Carol buttered Harry up further by suggesting that Charlie could learn a lot from working with him.

"I hope you see that capability in him," she said.

It might simply have been the residual effect of the punch he took from Adam, but Harry attributed his lightheadedness to this unspoken thing between him and Carol.

"Harry, you're so accomplished. I'd like to work directly with you on all our executive hiring requirements. Together, you and I will make a passionate team. Charlie would be a third wheel."

Carol moved quickly while Harry's head was still spinning. "Maybe you can tee this up in our meeting with Charlie this afternoon." She moved closer to him.

"Today?" Harry gulped.

"The sooner the better to get you fully engaged and into the cadence of our business." Carol looked into his eyes and lightly touched Harry's hand. She took a business card out of her portfolio and slowly slid it into Harry's hand.

"As you know, Sal has a knack for solving people problems. He's waiting for a call from you." Carol's potent perfume overloaded Harry's senses. He rubbed his face and neck with a napkin.

"Now that that's settled, how can I help you?" Carol asked. "Has Ted recommended any other executives for big TMC jobs? I might know them and be able to put in a good word."

After his clash with Adam, Harry wanted as much intelligence as possible on the people Ted asked him to evaluate. He did not need another black eye or any other broken body part. Grateful for her offer and the opportunity to spend more time together, Harry pulled out a notebook and shared with Carol the names of executives to be interviewed the following week.

"Carol, we have to keep this between us."

"Harry, I have never been accused of indiscretion. Look, here's our lunch. Bon appétit."

XLVII

"Charlie, how the heck are you? C'mon down to Carol's office and let's talk strategy."

"Harry?"

"Yeah, man. Carol and I had a great lunch at Laguna's. That bruschetta was the best ever. Carol, where do they find those tomatoes?" Harry spoke to Charlie from Carol's office phone.

"So you want me to come down to Carol's office to look for tomatoes?"

"No. To discuss recruiting strategy." Impatient, Harry hung up. *Maybe Carol has a point about Charlie after all*, he considered.

Hearing both of their voices as he approached, Charlie noticed that they became quiet when he entered Carol's office.

After an awkward pause, Harry offered his chair to Charlie and seated himself on the edge of Carol's desk.

Carol teed it up.

"We have a great strategy this year, team."

Carol pulled out her latest plan for the Solutions group. She explained that her reasoning revolved around the need for more sophisticated leaders, particularly those with global experience. Then she smiled at the recruiting team.

"Sounds exciting, Carol," Harry said, quickly smiling to demonstrate his level of excitement. Charlie had an inexplicable urge to bolt.

"Carol, given the plans you have for the business, sounds like you need full-time attention on your talent-acquisition requirements," Harry suggested.

Charlie sensed a shoe dropping.

"Maybe Carol needs a senior executive recruiter dedicated completely to the Solutions division, Charlie."

Charlie stammered. "Wh-, wh- . . . what are the . . . depends on the hiring forecast. Besides, I am the senior executive recruiter dedicated to the Solutions business." Charlie regained his composure, somewhat.

Carol did not say a word. She shifted her gaze from Harry to Charlie and back to Harry again.

"Charlie, given the burgeoning activity in the Middle Market group, maybe it isn't your fault that you haven't given Carol's recruiting needs the attention they warrant. Don't you agree?" As he was speaking to Charlie, Harry looked at Carol to confirm he was setting up their agenda correctly.

Harry's accusation stunned Charlie. His mouth opened and closed but nothing came out.

"I don't harbor ill will toward you for favoring the Middle Market group, Charlie," Carol chimed in. "You must be overwhelmed trying to get a fire under that team." She rolled her eyes at the incompetence of a rival internal division.

Harry patted Charlie on the back. "Let's just call it, Charlie. You've done great work for Solutions, but it's time for you to move on."

Carol stood up and forced a smile, one that conveyed the meeting's end.

"Well, now that that's settled, I'll ask my assistant to set up time for us to map out these executive requirements, Harry." She politely gestured toward the door of her office.

The insult of being shown the door without so much as an opportunity to defend himself against an incorrect, and profoundly unfair, accusation made Charlie's head swirl. In fact, as far as Charlie was concerned, Middle Market was the group that could have had a legitimate beef, because Charlie spent most of his time filling the executive holes that Carol's management style created in TMC Solutions. Harry chatted away next to him as Charlie walked back to his desk, trying to process what had occurred.

"This is going to be a big year for you, Charlie!" Harry raised his palm to give Charlie a high five, but Charlie declined the invitation. Awkwardly, Harry waved his outstretched hand to a few employees he did not know who were passing in the hallway. The employees looked at one another. No one waved back.

Suddenly, Charlie had a visceral recollection of the e-mail he sent to an executive recruiter the morning that Carol fed Vince Kumar to the wolves: "Dead Man Walking . . ."

"Don't you get it, Harry? If Carol could screw me now, after all the work I did for her, what makes you think she wouldn't screw you later?"

"Charlie, the Middle Market business needs a seasoned veteran like you. You can do for them what you did for TMC Solutions." Noticing a loose link, Harry fiddled with his David Yurman cuff links.

"Carol has got you doing her dirty work, Harry. Mark my words. She will be your undoing."

"Don't take it personally. This is just business."

"Don't fool yourself, Harry. If this is anything, this is personal." Charlie broke away from Harry and left the building.

LATER THAT AFTERNOON, Charlie found Stewart in the cafeteria enjoying Surfin' Safari theme week. Employees wearing 3-D glasses were hooked up to video terminals that simulated wave-riding. Charlie watched as a friend of his took a tumble as a virtual thirteen-foot wave crashed over his head. Unfortunately for Charlie's friend, the bruise to his knee was real.

Stewart looked at ease among the twentysomethings, especially wearing his "Don't Worry; Hang Ten . . . Or As Many As You Have. TMC Is an EEO" T-shirt. Despite Stewart's desire to rescue his hand-tailored suits from the closet, the casual protocol of technology fashion was persuasive. During this war-for-talent period, Stewart recognized that a component of his power base bubbled up from the workforce. As long as the general employee population preferred down-to-earth qualities in their leadership, T-shirts seemed a better fashion bet.

"Stewart, have you got a minute?"

Stewart stepped onto his skateboard.

"Sure, Charlie. Always have time for my best recruiter." Stewart skated away, waving to the employees in attendance. Charlie ran after him.

"Stewart, I need to bring something delicate to your attention." Carol having forced his hand, Charlie decided his own flank needed protecting.

"I have an e-mail string here that indicates that Vince Kumar may not have been responsible for the screwup in TMC Solutions." Charlie handed Stewart a hard copy of the messages on which he had been, accidentally, copied.

"What? Solutions practically carried the company for the last several years. If there is more of an issue going on there, we have to investigate! Carol will not stand for any shenanigans!"

"Stewart, you are not going to believe this." Charlie directed Stewart to specific comments as Stewart read the e-mail exchange. Carol's remarks had been underlined.

Stewart's face turned from indignation to confusion to questioning and finally to realization as the full effect of the e-mail sank in. Then, in a flash, Stewart slipped into HR camouflage and Charlie could not read him at all.

A few human capital managers skated by. Stewart waved at them, crumpling up the note with his other hand. Some surfer dudes gave him a virtual high five as Stewart made a shot into the wastebasket with Charlie's note.

"Wha . . . what are you doing?" Charlie ran to retrieve the paper from the trash.

Stewart noticed a crowd of employees roasting marshmallows in a corner of the cafeteria. He called to Charlie as he skated toward them.

"I am a beach bum, Charlie. I roll with the flow and I flow with the roll. You ought to try it."

XLVIII

Vera balanced the financials for the Solutions business on two cups of hot coffee. Carol's assistant, Jill, waved from her desk and asked her how she was.

"How'm I doing? I'm supposed to be adding value to our company by researching companies and candidates, but instead my goofball manager has me fetching coffee. How does it look like I'm doing?" Angry that Stewart had scuttled her plan to escape to another part of the company—Vera and Charlie were Stewart's insurance that the talent-management work would get done—Vera forcefully opened the door to the conference room with her hip. A waft of cigar smoke surprised her nasal passages and she choked.

Sal, surrounded by the dense cloud emanating from his Saint Luis Rey, held a lighter as Harry puffed and rotated his own cigar around the flame. Sal explained to his TMC client that he had taken time off from the executive search business the previous quarter to focus on an interstate trucking enterprise. Having recently dumped his interest in that partnership somewhere around Philly, he stated that his team could easily handle several large projects for TMC in addition to the sales-executive search about which they were meeting.

When the cigar was fully lit, Harry took a long draw on it and choked.

"Don't inhale," Sal said. "Let the taste linger in your mouth, then blow it out."

Harry tried again. His cheeks swelled with cigar smoke.

"I thought you said you were a cigar aficionado?" Sal puffed on his five-inch-long cigar.

"I am," Harry said, then coughed twice. "I am—" (two more coughs) "—more accustomed to the Cubans."

"You're still going too fast." Sal demonstrated a long, slow drag. "The top Cuban producers fled to Honduras and the Dominican Republic, so the best cigars are coming out of those countries now." Sal was put out that he brought these cigars to impress Harry when a simple newsstand brand would have done nicely. He made a mental note to add a charge for miscellaneous expenses to his next TMC invoice.

"You're not allowed to smoke in this building!" Vera was appalled at the latest example of Harry's conspicuous consumption, let alone his brazen disregard for others' welfare. Well-informed, thanks to her vigilant management of her son's health, Vera knew that secondhand smoke was a leading contributor to many illnesses.

"Vera, relax—" (Harry coughed twice more) "—and pull up a chair. Have you got a cigar for my gal Friday, Sal?" Harry pulled a piece of tobacco from between his teeth. Vera, not so politely, declined the offer and hurried out of the room, slamming the door behind her.

"I don't get it, but Charlie wants to take her under his wing and teach her recruiting," Harry said. "I wouldn't waste my time, she's such a moody you-know-what." Harry had turned a cold shoulder to his assistant upon discovering small German roaches cohabiting in his corporate apartment after he had asked Vera to set up housekeeping for him.

Eager to kick off this first project for Carol in an impressive manner, Harry turned his laptop on so that he might immediately e-mail Carol with comments on the candidates Sal presented. He had already reviewed the resume of one candidate, Jack Peterson, and was predisposed to find favor with him. Jack was a Floridian, and Harry was hankering for a getaway by the beach. Harry repeatedly punched a few keys to gain access to TMC's intranet so that he might move the meeting tempo, and his personal agenda, along.

Sal held the cigar between his teeth as he rifled through papers to locate a physical copy of Jack's resume. He found it and dusted a smudge of ash from the corner.

"Here you go." He handed the resume to Harry. "Jack Peterson is absolutely qualified for this Solutions sales job. Great guy."

Harry took shorter puffs and pretended to review the resume, but his concentration was on his computer's inability to connect to TMC's network.

"I have so much data on this system, it can take forever to boot up," he said. Frustrated, Harry shut down his system and resorted to pen and paper for note taking.

"I don't know about computers. What kind of data you got that would slow down your system so much?" Sal blew circles with his cigar smoke.

Considering it a reflection of his executive status within the company, Harry bragged about his access to all the personal information required to process a newly hired executive, such as home address and Social Security number.

"I should really clean up this system. I inherited information on every executive hire TMC has made in the past three years. This little computer also contains confidential information about my team, like performance appraisals, even system passwords. All of it sitting on my laptop. Imagine if that fell into the wrong hands!"

Picking up the laptop, Sal commented on its heft, or lack thereof.

"Not very heavy for something that has all that info in it."

"Technology is amazing. Is this an accurate address for Jack in Florida?" Harry inquired as if he had not previously known.

Sal indicated that it was. He repeatedly lifted Harry's laptop with one hand as he detailed the trappings of Jack's Sunshine State lifestyle. He recommended that TMC meet with Jack as soon as possible because Sal felt he would not be on the job market long.

"I think I should see him in his natural element before we fly him here." Harry stubbed out his cigar and waved the smoke away from his watering eyes.

Enjoying the draw on his Saint Luis Rey, Sal said they could fix the schedule so that Harry would be first on the interview roster when Jack was in town.

Harry pressed the issue, annoyed that Sal did not pick up on his drift. "I want only the best candidates to meet our team. I should go to Jack, kick his tires, so to speak, before we spend the money to fly him in to meet Carol and Ted."

"Do you think you can do that tomorrow?"

Harry gave Sal a look of confusion.

"Jack's scheduled to meet with Carol and Ted the day after tomorrow here in your offices," Sal said.

This was confounding. Harry felt he should be calling the shots.

"It's the way Carol wants it. After all, she's our client," Sal added.

Harry stuttered and then choked on the residue of cigar smoke that surrounded him. "But it's my job to evaluate the candidates."

"Nothing personal, Harry. It's just business."

Anticipating that he would interview Jack in Florida, Harry had had his travel agent book him a room at an oceanside resort and put a deposit down on a series of motocross classes. His mind raced through the plans he would have to change. *Shit.* "That deposit is nonrefundable," he murmured.

Sal packed up his briefcase, a little heavier now than when he first entered the conference room, and left a copy of Jack's interview schedule.

"Harry, trust me. You're gonna love this guy."

XLIX

Stewart reread the telegram.

"Wishing You Well. Stop."

He had not actually believed his mother would join him at the Washington DC dinner being held in his honor. He had relayed the invitation, and mention of the president's congratulations on his award, through his mother's nurse at Cliffridge. But he had hoped for a return phone call, not this three-word greeting.

Stewart mailed his father's invitation to the elder Narciss's lawyer. The message requested that he join his son at the Kennedy Center for the Performing Arts, where the president of the United States would recognize several executives for outstanding contributions in their respective fields. Stewart was to be recognized for an accumulation of initiatives over many years. His application contained too many projects to list on the official invitation, so the all-encompassing "et cetera" was placed after brief mention of game-changing programs in workforce planning and executive development. Additionally, the president nominated Stewart to sit on the Council of Human Capital Advisers, a new government commission organized to report on positive trends in employee relations.

Stewart had been intent on filling his table of ten with the highest-ranking executives available. Getting one's picture in national newspapers was generally considered good public relations, and it had not been hard to fill the table. He pointed this out to his father's lawyer when the esquire informed Stewart that his dad's social calendar was too demanding to accommodate his gracious invitation.

Stewart's phone rang a few times before it registered with him.

Not many people have this number. Who could this be? Stewart wondered.

Adam Fleming was on the line. Stewart had given his number to Adam and had assured his availability at any time and for any reason. Without any niceties to soften the blow, Adam informed Stewart that he had decided to accept the top job at a TMC competitor, Consumer Electronic Services. Several factors had led to his decision, but Adam was mainly interested in sharing one: his lack of confidence in TMC's human capital management process, generated by Stewart's having sent "that clown" to interview him.

Adam delivered his message in his typically succinct style. "If I'd had a guy like Harry in my platoon, men would have died. I'm a winner, Stewart, and you've got a loser evaluating your next generation of leaders. That's FUBAR."

Adam hung up.

Stewart felt the discomfort he often experienced when his father used to talk to him. He looked at his mother's telegram and the Kennedy Center gala invitation. He wondered how many senior executives used lawyers to broker family conversations. He doubted his father had even read the announcement about his achievements.

What do I have to do to impress him? Stewart wondered. Though wounded that his father had declined the invitation, interactions, or the lack thereof, with his father were also aggravating to Stewart.

Stewart's thoughts returned to the gala. Ted, who also had a "very pressing" conflict, had begged off. And, unaware that Stewart had not played any role in the machinations that led to his TMC termination, Jim Collins discarded his invitation. Stewart could not allow himself to dwell on this unrequited friendship, which was another distressing blow to his self-worth. But it called to mind a more immediate threat to his ambitions.

What do I have to do to impress TED? Stewart was feeling provoked.

He pulled a notebook from his top desk drawer. On the first page was a short list of possible future CEO candidates that Harry had been asked to evaluate. Stewart ran his pen down the list and found Adam's name on it. He scratched it out, as he had done to all of the other candidates whom Harry interviewed. He read Harry's comments next to the candidate names, insights such as: *I'm as open-minded as the next guy, but if we are going to hire a woman, wouldn't we want a pretty one?* and *How much seasoning do we want? This cat has slippers older than me.*

The only candidate on the list without any notation was the one internal prospect. Ted wanted Harry laser-focused on external candidates. The CEO suspected that Harry's work ethic might falter if he knew there were an internal possibility, so Stewart never informed Harry that Carol was also under consideration.

Stewart thought about damage control. Ted needed to demonstrate some effort on succession planning to the board, and his options were shrinking. The CEO would be particularly angry that Stewart's direct report screwed up Adam's candidacy. On the other hand, Carol was emerging as a solid backfill in her own right. In spite of that unpleasant public relations incident in Turkmenistan, she had rallied Ted and the board to complete the negotiations with that sovereign government, resulting in a large, positive impact on revenues. Stewart wisely counseled Carol to pay the ransom to get the treasury manager home safe and sound, if somewhat battered. The only time throughout the entire ordeal that she became angry was when Stewart insisted she could not fire the treasury manager for dereliction of duties. Her opinion changed when Stewart pointed out that it might be tricky to account for what the manager was doing in Turkmenistan with a green leather suitcase full of cash.

Yep. Carol appreciates me. What else can I do to impress HER? Stewart considered his options.

Stewart determined that he had to persuade Ted to move Carol to the top of the CEO candidate list. That should not be too hard, considering that hers was the only name left. Still, it would not hurt to get Carol face time with Rick Robertson, whose large voting bloc put his name at the top of the list to be the next chairman of the board.

But she's got to believe it was my idea to name her as Ted's successor, he reasoned.

Since Harry was in charge of talent management and was working closely with Carol, Stewart reasoned, she might assume that Harry had persuaded Ted to make her his heir apparent.

Got to do something about Harry. But what? he wondered.

Stewart opened the bottom drawer of his desk and pulled out a worn, leather-bound scrapbook. He opened the book to a clean page toward the back, uncapped a glue stick, and affixed his mother's telegram to the page. He flipped through the rest of the book and reviewed the notices, cards, and telegrams his mom had sent over the years. The occasional photograph of Cliffridge residents romping around the grounds, attendants running behind them to ensure that IV lines did not cross, brought color to the otherwise black-and-white contents. Stewart returned his scrapbook to the bottom desk drawer, securing the mementos of his personal life with a lock and key.

L

With her CEO clock still ticking after a few months of toying with Harry, Carol decided it was time to purge her trail.

"Emily and her finance team worked overtime to straighten out the mess Vince created. Thank God for Emily's dedication!" Carol unceremoniously plopped into one of the Queen Anne chairs Stewart kept in his office for guests. The HR leader had been meticulously examining his face for wrinkles when Carol interrupted him. He put the cap on his antiwrinkle cream and returned it and his mirror to the top desk drawer, careful not to expose the eye rejuvenating ointment, skin toner, and a small, round container of peach blush.

"Seriously, Stewart. She should be on the high-potential list for the finance function." Carol also put in plain language her appreciation for Emily's handling of that deal with the government of Turkmenistan. "No thanks to legal," she made note.

"Will you talk to Rupert Bhein about Emily?" Carol encouraged her colleague to appeal to the corporate CFO about rewarding Emily's efforts. "He wouldn't give her a better title when we moved her to the Solutions team. Controller doesn't begin to describe her contributions."

Carol leaned across Stewart's desk, cutting an imposing figure in a steel-blue pantsuit. She went on. "I don't understand what that guy has against Emily. He promotes other, less-qualified people over her. Have you talked to some of our finance executives lately? They have a maniacal focus on budgets, financial reporting, and operating margin. Not a risk taker in the bunch. For example, look at that has-been on the corporate finance team, Mercedes Rodriguez. Not one creative function on her calculator."

"What about Mercedes?" Stewart felt self-conscious. At every opportunity he had flaunted his involvement with this executive hire. "Of course, TMC hired her years ago, when we were a smaller, much less complex company." He covered his bet in case the rumor mill, churning the tide against Mercedes, had not yet caught up with him.

"I don't know what you were thinking back then, Stewart. Mercedes is all facts and figures. No massaging the details with her. Just like Rupert. Good thing I came along to take control of—I mean, play a role in recruiting around here."

Stewart picked up the two Chinese exercise balls he kept in a box on top of his desk. According to his masseuse, they were great stress reducers. He rolled them around in his hands.

"My sense is that Rupert favors people who are like him," Carol said. "That doesn't strike me as fair, Stewart."

Stewart liked the chime that the metallic balls made as they turned over in his palm. He took a deep breath.

"Stewart, would you please put your balls down and focus on my issue?"

"Always do for you, Carol." Stewart placed the balls back in their box.

Carol stood up and paced before Stewart's desk. Her long strides caused her to turn around after just a few steps. Caution rose within Stewart as her footsteps resounded throughout the office.

Are Carol's nostrils flaring? he worried.

Stewart reached for the Chinese balls again. Carol frowned. He put his hands, ball-less, in his pockets.

"Did you know that Emily is multitalented? She worked in the health-care field before joining TMC," Carol continued to build her case.

Stewart picked up a pen and jotted a note to himself: Talk to Rupert about Emily.

He put down the pen and looked up. Carol's intense body language indicated that she was not done with him. Besides, a simple e-mail indicating Carol's desire to get Emily promoted would have sufficed, which, they both knew, was what she was demanding.

"There is something more delicate we have to discuss, Stewart." Carol sat down again.

"If this is about the theft of our executives' personal information, we are conducting an investigation to find out how Harry's laptop disappeared."

Carol learned of the missing data as all affected employees had, from a memo Stewart penned explaining that a laptop that contained the personal data of many employees had been "misplaced." She had been among the lucky ones; her information had not been compromised. Several of her peers, however, were working their way through serious cracks in their financial integrity, including invoices from shopping malls in Buenos Aires and a host of sordid activities that registered under a sports and entertainment category on their credit card statements. The vice president for government sales received a call from the Bureau of Alcohol, Tobacco, Firearms, and Explosives, asking why a guy who had never even been on a camping trip suddenly felt the urge to open accounts at gun shops around the country.

Fortunately, lower-level employees were unaffected; the damage had been limited to the executive suite. Yet, coincidentally, Charlie's hard drive crashed a few days after Harry's laptop had gone missing. Although the

IT team was able to fix Charlie's computer, they could not save any of the e-mail, files, or other data Charlie had on his computer before the crash.

"It's not about that," Carol said to Stewart. "My team has been disappointed in the customer experience they've received from the talent-management department." Because all of the usual suspects, and a few novel ideas, for heir apparent to Ted had been shot down thanks to her regular coaching of Harry, Carol wanted to act swiftly.

Stewart reminded Carol that they had moved Charlie to the Middle Market group, as she asked them to do.

"I'm not referring to Charlie." After Carol's meeting with Charlie, it had not taken much digging for her to find out that he had been snooping around about the Solutions contracts. Stewart had folded like a cheap suit when she pushed him for information about what Charlie might know. Now, with Charlie's e-mail history having been vaporized, and with it the evidence of Carol's wrongdoing, she assumed that this threat had been eliminated. Besides, someone would be needed to conduct the staffing work once she had Harry removed. Carol itemized grievances she had specifically with Harry, from his insipid personality, which her team found wearisome, to concerns that his disparaging comments motivated candidates to work for the competition.

"Harry could hurt our business if the 'A' players don't want to be on the TMC team, Stewart."

She also intimated that Harry had made inappropriate advances toward her, which was a complete fabrication.

"I can handle myself, but I worry about other, more impressionable women," Carol said. "And, did you see this article?" Carol pulled out Clare Woodard's latest piece in *Economic Week*, about Tek-Biz's disappointing results. The report hinted that the Securities and Exchange Commission might initiate an investigation into financial statements filed on CFO Tim Arnes's watch.

She shook the article in Stewart's face. "This executive was a loser, and Harry wanted us to hire him for the top finance job in the Solutions division. Good thing I nixed that idea."

Stewart gently pushed the magazine away from his face and blinked.

I wonder why Carol is suddenly so eager to get rid of Harry. Not that I'd look a gift horse in the mouth, he considered.

"Clare Woodard is a nationally recognized business journalist," Carol went on. "This article is going to get people checking into things, Stewart. What if Harry was caught up in something bad at Tek-Biz?"

Stewart carefully calculated his next move. *It will look better if I defend my guy*, he thought.

"Harry was not responsible for the financial function at Tek-Biz, Carol. Besides, look what he's done for us. He got Jack Peterson to take the Solutions sales job."

"Oh, Stewart! We needed a general manager in that job and he hired a salesman. Anyway, Sal Scruci was the real muscle behind the Jack Peterson hire." Carol used the occasion to put in a plug for Sal, hoping that additional executive search fees would loosen Sal's stranglehold on her. "You have to admit, Harry's a little slow. After all, how did he misplace his laptop in a conference room?" Carol pushed her agenda.

Stewart's main concern, when he had hired Harry, was that he might gain the confidence of TMC's leadership team and usurp Stewart's authority. As Harry's "uniquely unusual" personality and notable screwups were becoming legendary, Stewart's initial worry now appeared unfounded. However, a new risk emerged that could still threaten his leadership credibility. Given the spreading recognition that Harry was a nincompoop, people might start asking why Stewart had not yet gotten rid of him.

They might wonder if I'm losing my touch, Stewart worried.

Stewart realized that whatever her true motivation, Carol's abandonment of Harry might be his best exit strategy.

I can advance my agenda and erase a leadership liability from my record, he reflected.

Still, Stewart assumed that playing a little hard to get might strengthen his hand.

"Carol, if we let Harry go, I'll have to add talent management to my other commitments. Do you realize how many HR organizations I belong to? And the awards! I probably don't have to tell you that the application process for those awards is a lot of work."

"You can do talent management in your sleep, Stewart. In fact, you could get more sleep if you'd just convince the board that I should be the next CEO."

Stewart picked up on this cue. "The board does appreciate my counsel, Carol."

Although this meeting was playing into his hands, Stewart felt his heart race. Despite warnings from his doctor to get Carol fired or suffer extreme consequences to his personal well-being, Stewart could not predict the type of relationship he might enjoy with an unknown chief executive.

My stock will go up in her eyes if I do her this favor.

The call from Adam Fleming had confirmed that Harry had to go, but, until now, Stewart had not worked out how. There was no reason to discuss those details with Carol, though.

Why disabuse her from assuming she owes me?

Stewart opened his desk drawer and looked at Ted's list of CEO candidates. As he circled Carol's name, it occurred to him that he could not have planned this meeting any better.

"You make a compelling argument, Carol. It will require a great sacrifice on my part, but your business interests are paramount to our team's success. If Harry stands in the way of your ability to be productive, then I will assume responsibility for the talent-management function myself."

Carol leaned across his desk and took a Chinese cloisonné ball from the box. She rolled it around in her palm as she had seen Stewart do.

"Great sound. Do these really relax you?"

L I

When Charlie received a request to meet with Stewart, he assumed that Stewart had reconsidered the information about Carol's involvement in the Solutions contracts fiasco. It occurred to him that perhaps Stewart had needed a little time to check things out. After all, the situation raised serious ethical, and possibly legal, implications for TMC—not to mention the damage it would cause to the credibility of its leadership team.

There's enough incriminating evidence that even Stewart couldn't ignore it forever, Charlie thought.

Whatever the reason for the delay, Charlie felt relieved. The stress of recent TMC affairs made him realize that no amount of equity would be enough to keep him in a potentially disastrous situation.

Charlie rethought the interviews he had set up with an executive-search firm interested in hiring him.

If Stewart is going to stand up to Carol, I should stay here and support him.

The idea of turning everything upside down and rebooting TMC's culture appealed to the idealistic human resources manager. Plus, the visual was amusing.

If there are going to be fireworks, I don't want to miss them. Charlie was secretly thrilled.

Charlie approached Stewart's new administrative assistant.

"Howdy! I was fixin' to call! I wasn't sure you had seen my invite to this meeting, and Stewart said to git 'er done, so I sure am glad you are here." South Texas native Beverly Hicks breezed by her printer and picked up a report Stewart had requested.

"He's waiting for you in there." Beverly smiled in the direction of Stewart's conference room.

Charlie found Stewart searching the stories in *HR Info Line*, a quarterly newsletter centered on human resources systems support, for an article on IT security that referenced TMC's human capital team. His feet were perched up on a table, revealing python-skin cowboy boots. Since Beverly joined his team, Stewart had incorporated a University of Texas championship belt buckle, several pairs of jeans, and the boots into his wardrobe.

"Take a load off, Charlie." Stewart folded the newsletter and motioned for Charlie to move a large conference chair closer to him.

Charlie found the chair unusually heavy, so he simply pushed it forward a bit.

"No, closer, closer. Let's take advantage of this time together to have a real intimate chat."

Stewart encouraged Charlie to push the high-back, bulky chair very close to him. Charlie placed it directly to the left of the conference table, careful not to hit his boss's feet, which had not moved.

"That's better. Hey, you look winded. You should make sure to hit that gym regularly, for all of us. We need you to be healthy. Beverly, bring in water for our boy, Charlie, would you?" Stewart called to his assistant through the open door.

"This chair is heavier than it looks." Charlie wiped his brow as he got comfortable. He thanked Beverly for the bottle of water.

"Charlie, I admire you."

Charlie unconsciously sat taller in the cushioned chair. "Well, uh, thank you. That's nice."

"No, I mean it. It's not easy to speak truth to power. Takes a certain kind of mettle." Stewart gently tapped his chest with a clenched fist. "In Beverly's hometown, they'd call someone who does that a real cowboy." Stewart smiled and slapped his boots.

"Well, thank you, Stewart. Actually, I was concerned about bringing that issue up, given all the senior people involved. And then I got a little spooked when all my e-mail went missing."

"Yes, yes, I can understand that," Stewart said, looking puzzled. Charlie told Stewart that he felt better about it now, given Stewart's support.

"Yes, yes. Of course, of course," Stewart's look turned to one of caution.

"So, what do you need me to do? I imagine we'll get legal involved at some point."

"Well, Charlie, I'm hoping that won't be necessary, but I'll defer to your guidance."

"My guidance?" Now Charlie was baffled.

Stewart placed his feet squarely on the floor.

"Sure. After all, we're hoping that Harry will be persuaded to leave TMC quietly."

"Harry? Is Harry leaving the company?" Charlie asked.

"Haven't you heard the scuttlebutt about his big placement at Tek-Biz? Tim Arnes, the CFO that Harry hired, might be indicted!" Stewart explained, with indignation, that his sources said that Arnes had been woefully underqualified to be chief financial officer of any company. As far as Stewart was concerned, it called into question the qualification process Harry used to evaluate candidates.

"Thank God Carol cancelled our interviews with Arnes, or we might have hired him based on Harry's recommendation," Stewart said.

Charlie took a deep breath. *Aha, Carol's fingerprints are on this one, too.*

"Stewart, look, I've observed behaviors on Harry's part that seemed naïve, maybe even quirky. Not that I would say it, but some employees have described him as goofy. So, your concern about his judgment may be warranted, but, at the end of the day, the CEO and board of Tek-Biz made the decision to hire Tim."

"Based on Harry's recommendation!"

Charlie wondered how this situation got so turned around. Here he was, defending the boss who had partnered with Carol to undermine him. However, whatever justice there might be in Harry's comeuppance, this situation just did not sit right with Charlie. He stood up.

"But that's not grounds for dismissal from TMC, Stewart."

"Charlie, you are right. That's why he's being let go for having falsified his employment application."

"What?"

Stewart explained that, after the Tim Arnes situation surfaced, he hired an external security firm to investigate Harry's background. That firm turned up discrepancies on Harry's application. Of special note: While talking with anonymous sources, the private eye learned that a number of Colreavy partners had lost confidence in Harry while he worked for that consulting firm. They confirmed that he had been fired from that job.

"That certainly was not on his resume!" Stewart said.

Charlie paced purposefully.

"Remember Adam Fleming, Ted's referral for the strategy job? Harry annoyed him so much that Adam took the top job at Consumer Electronic

Services. One of our largest competitors! Ted was so angry, he was fit to be hog-tied. Good thing I persuaded Ted to hire Carol years ago. Now that we have identified her as Ted's future backfill, the board has taken the heat off Ted."

When Ted's golf handicap hit an all-time high and no clear successor had been identified, Stewart successfully nudged Ted to move Carol to the top of the list of candidates for consideration. Stewart supported his suggestion with evidence of Carol's latest accomplishment for the company. A largely cash business, the Turkmenistan partnership had also generated ample margins, the kind that could bury blunders for a long time coming. This international collaboration pulled the Solutions business out of the weeds, which pulled TMC stock out of the muck. These results, and the lack of other candidates, made for a compelling argument. The following weekend, Ted shot a seventy-two, which was final confirmation for the CEO that the search for his heir apparent was over. Stewart was ecstatic. Everything was falling into place for him to become the top adviser to the next CEO of TMC. All that was left to do was to bring in his cleanup hitter.

Charlie sensed that the weight of Harry's transgressions had built a case that Harry could not overcome. Charlie realized he might never know the whole story, but he sensed that Stewart, and particularly Carol, now officially in line to succeed Ted, had made up their minds.

Looks like Carol played Harry like a fiddle, Charlie said to himself.

"When are you going to tell Harry?" he asked Stewart.

"Now, Charlie. It seems to me that the new leader of talent management should make his own decisions on when to fire someone on his team." Stewart leaned back in his Herman Miller ergonomic chair and placed his cowboy boots back up on the table.

Mystified for the second time during this short conversation, Charlie asked, "Have we hired a new leader to replace Harry?"

"Well, that depends. Are you ready for the job, Charlie?"

Stunned, Charlie sat back down.

"You're offering me the VP job?"

"Now, Charlie, vice president is big. Let's start with a lateral move, see how things progress. Maybe we can talk about a promotion in a few years. In the meantime, we are preparing an increase to your typical stock grant."

Charlie paused and then laughed, quietly at first. He lost himself, and his laughter became louder and heartier—so hearty that Stewart could not help but join in.

"What's so dang funny?" Stewart asked between chuckles.

"I am," Charlie said, giggling.

"You are?" Stewart guffawed. "'Splain, please." Stewart laughed again.

Charlie coughed to settle himself down. Clearing his throat, he answered Stewart.

"I really thought you called me in here to discuss what to do about Carol's cooking the Solutions contracts. And I said Harry was naïve!"

"Yeah, you called Harry naïve!" Stewart agreed, giggling.

Charlie placed his hands flat on the conference table, leaned in and looked the head of human capital management directly in the eye. Flashbacks of Charlie's most memorable TMC experiences shook his senses as if he were waking from a deep sleep. He felt the chill outside the boardroom as the doors closed behind Stewart, carrying his *What's Your Forte?* presentation; his olfactory glands picked up the memory of the compost heap about halfway down the mountain from Dandy's ashram; he heard Vince's wife cry in the background during his call with the finance executive to work out the details of Vince's severance package; and he saw the skid marks across his new shoes left by Stewart's skateboard during the Surfin' Safari demos. Even his inner voice played a tape of his wife pestering him to confront Stewart about the empty career promises.

In a painful moment, Charlie felt how these indignities had punctured his self-esteem. The stark awareness of his in-the-money stock options burying his principles was suffocating. He recognized that he needed to confront himself, not Stewart.

Charlie also saw that it would be an impossible task to extricate TMC from self-inflicted treachery and restore the culture to the purity he remembered from its early days. That was particularly apparent because his earlier attempts to inspire this leadership team around any higher purpose now appeared to have been a profound waste of time.

Unless Stewart and Carol make a concerted effort to change, things will get worse around here, he thought.

Suddenly motivated to make up for lost time, Charlie determined that he could save himself.

"Stewart, you need someone unique for that job." Charlie paused. "Someone who will get his hands dirty. I'm probably a little too clean-cut. Wouldn't you agree?"

Stewart was astonished. Fresh off the heels of a merger with a German communications conglomerate, TMC was now one of the largest communication-technology companies in the world. Was Charlie actually turning down a shot to run executive recruiting at a Fortune 100 company? Could it be worse than that?

Would he leave me high and dry to do the work myself? Stewart wondered.

"I've been thinking that it's time to make room for a new human capital manager to serve you and TMC," Charlie went on. "Yep. That rolling and flowing thing. I'm not streaming in the same current anymore."

In spite of how well it was constructed, Stewart's expensive chair could not support his entire body weight tipping back. He and the chair landed on the floor with a loud thud.

Beverly ran in, her blonde locks bouncing furiously. "What happened? The ground shook and sprung a few times. Felt like it does in the rodeo bleachers back home. Reminded me of when Uncle Roger fell off that buck and got pinned against the wall. Are you OK?" Beverly propped Stewart up on the floor.

"Good luck with those internal executive moves, Stewart." Feeling much stronger, Charlie easily moved his chair back into its original position and left as Stewart, with Beverly pulling him up, issued orders to get executive recruiter Amanda Albright on the phone.

WORKING AT HIS mahogany desk in his new wood-paneled office at CCA Executive Search, a global executive-search firm, Charlie came upon the latest issue of *Economic Week*. The magazine featured Carol's successful turnaround of TMC's Solutions group. The main headline stated: "Mission Very Possible with Carol Himmler at the Wheel." A secondary headline asked: "Is There a Female CEO in TMC's Future?" A photo captured Carol shaking hands with the chief information officer of BOING Transportation. Her black pin-striped suit and silk blouse, accentuated by her dark hair, lent a sinister air to the scene.

"The only thing missing is a machine gun and a bag of cash," whispered Charlie. Remembering the treasury manager's misadventures in Turkmenistan, he added, "Well, maybe not the bag of cash."

In the background of the picture, a TMC Solutions communications center in Turkmenistan operated to support BOING. The caption read, "TMC and BOING Transportation going global together."

The article, by Delilah Fabrikant, Clare Woodard's colleague and chief rival at the esteemed magazine, related the sharp reversal of the Solutions group's fortunes, particularly the noteworthy increase in large contracts from Central Asia. Emily Harris, the recently anointed CFO of this business segment, was quoted in the article: "Once we had tighter controls around the contracts process, we were able to recognize additional revenue almost immediately. Those controls will support substantial growth going forward."

A picture of Emily smiling confidently while her assistant punched figures into a calculator provided the visual support for this new era of control. At the end of the article, the reporter included a picture of Stewart accepting a U.S. Department of Labor award on behalf of TMC for being the "Most Fun Place to Work." Wearing a tie-dyed T-shirt, Bermuda shorts, and flip-flops, Stewart held a huge glass trophy of a happy face. Underneath the photograph was a caption: "Positive employee attitude equals good business for TMC."

And, only six weeks after declining the opportunity to succeed him at TMC, Charlie caught a mention of Harry in the "Transitions" section of the magazine, in the midst of a list of executives making career moves:

Harry Habet takes over as second-in-command of executive staffing for Tech Friends, the global social networking company, after a long and arduous search led by executive search veteran Amanda Albright. Interviewed during a youth rally in Paris, new Director of Talent Habet offered: "With my knack for selecting natural leaders, our customers can rest assured that the mundane details of their personal lives will be accessible to the most socially networked talent in the world!"

Charlie cut the articles out and pasted them in his TMC scrapbook, next to newspaper tombstones announcing the executives he had hired over the years. Closing the book on that chapter of his career, he wrote a message to himself inside the back cover of his scrapbook: "The End . . . ?"

LEGACY

L I I

On a typical Georgia day, sunny and warm, a light breeze occasionally ruffling the sleeves of golfers, Sal purposefully sliced his drive off the seventeenth hole on the course at Augusta National Golf Club.

"Aw. Thought I had that," Sal said to Ann McManus, CEO of Colreavy Consulting. With a recommendation from Carol, a pitiful golf game, and discounted fees, Sal hoped to win Ann over as a new client for his executive-search practice. If all else failed, it did not hurt to be playing Augusta.

Sal whistled at Ann's drive, 180 yards, straight down the middle. He placed his driver back in his bag. Surreptitiously taking a swig from his flask, he followed Ann down the fairway to her ball.

What a friggin' world, Sal thought to himself. *This woman tells CEOs all over the globe what's what, but she wouldn't be playing this golf course if her husband wasn't a member. Still, lucky break for me that this was where she wanted to play.*

"That was an interesting list of candidates you submitted to lead our international business, Sal," Ann said.

"Glad you had a chance to review that. Anybody on that list we can take a whack at for you?"

"Well, I was intrigued with one of the names. Nick Defeussener. Compelling background, lots of Asia experience, like we asked for." Ann took out her five iron and set up her shot. "But, unless we were just looking for a body to slip into the box, I suspect we'll have to move on to other people on the list." She hit the ball again.

Sal was confused.

"Here." Ann tossed an obituary notice at Sal. "I cut this out of the International News. Nick Defeussener's funeral was held last week in London. How could you do this?"

Reading through the newspaper death notice, Sal said, "Whoa. This isn't one of mine. Says right here he died of natural causes."

Now Ann was confused. "Didn't your research team put this list together?"

"Oh, you mean the list. Yeah, we put the list together. Hey, whaddaya want from me, everything?" Sal winked at the CEO of one of the largest consulting firms in the world. She did not return the gesture.

Sal and Ann finished the course without further discussion of prospective candidates, dead or alive. Ann directed them straight from the eighteenth hole toward the locker rooms so they could freshen up.

Sal's cell phone rang. He stepped outside to answer the call.

"Who's this? Alex! How the hell are you?" Sal was surprised to get a call, out of the blue, from this TMC executive. He had successfully placed Alex Martin a few months ago. By all accounts, Alex should be drinking from a fire hose, both excited about the business opportunities and overwhelmed with the amount of work.

This cannot be good, Sal thought.

Alex explained that he had been sick.

"I heard you were a little under the weather. Nothing a few vitamins couldn't fix, I'm sure," Sal said. "I got a connection who can get bulk vitamins real cheap. Tell me which ones you need. B6? B12? Hell, I got a trunk full of vitamin C. I could get a case of that delivered right to your door tomorrow."

Sal nodded at two older southern gentlemen walking into the clubhouse. He moved farther away to allow for privacy.

Alex pressed the nurse call button on his hospital bed. The IV machine was beeping loudly and continuously. It got on his nerves. The nurse did not answer the call, so he hit the button again.

"What's that noise?" Sal asked.

"Sal, I'm in the hospital. I've got an IV in me."

"All the better to get the vitamins into you fast. That's great news!" Sal struggled to sound encouraging.

Alex panicked. "Why aren't any nurses responding to this goddamn beeping?" He pounded on the call button. "Sal, I haven't been able to digest red meat or anything with wheat in it since the third week of employment with TMC. I've gained thirty pounds. Before I joined TMC I ran every morning for fourteen years straight. I was fit! Last week I had an intestinal blockage, and they rushed me to the emergency room. They took a large section of my colon out. In addition to everything else, my doctors are concerned about the spike in my blood pressure."

"Your colon out? Wow. Is it allergies?" Sal hoped.

"Allergies? Yeah, Sal, I'm allergic to TMC." Alex threw the nurse call button across his hospital bed, forgetting for a moment that it was connected by a line to the bed. The large button flew with such force that when it reached the end of its line, like a bungee cord, it swung right back and clocked Alex on the head.

"Ouch!! Goddamn it! Where is the NURSE?"

TMC managed cash flow like Sal managed the point spread on college games: tightly. The company still owed him money for placing Alex, and it was unlikely they would be inclined to pay the balance due if Alex was conducting sales calls from a hospital bed. Sal was determined to focus Alex on the positive.

"Hey, I saw those pictures of your property. It's beautiful. The creek is picturesque. Great area for the kids to ride their horses. The house! What can I say about that? It's gorgeous."

Alex was quiet. The stars around his head eventually stopped circling. He took a deep breath.

"Sal, the pressure at TMC is more than I can handle."

If Alex quit TMC now, Sal would either have to do the search over again or give all the money back—he had a six-month guarantee on this executive's placement. Sal's was a cash flow–neutral business. Returning the money was not an option. He breathed a small sigh of relief that the Maserati was in his wife's name.

"Alex. Let's talk about your bank account. How's that looking since you joined TMC? Those seven-figure bank statements can make most any problem go away."

"Sal, this company, this culture, Carol! She gets where she's going on the backs of others. I want out while I still have some internal organs in working order. I submitted my resignation."

"OH NO! C'mon, Alex. You think you're the only guy with problems?

Think of the team you are letting down. Think of the name you'll get in the marketplace for cutting and running. Who'll pick you out of a crowd after this? And what about me, for chrissake. You didn't even want this job when I first called you. I coaxed and pounded and headlocked you all the way! What about my work and my efforts? You weak scumbag!"

Several club members, their sensibilities offended, looked away.

"Another hedge fund gone south?" one golfer asked another.

Alex, well-mannered to the end, thanked his executive-search consultant for his hard work and handed the cell phone to a nurse who had finally arrived. Then he passed out.

A caddie jogged by. Sal whipped his phone at the kid.

"OW!" The caddie tripped and did a face-plant into the hydrangea bushes.

"Fuck me," Sal whispered. He walked toward the clubhouse wondering how to pitch Alex as a candidate to Ann McManus.

L I I I

Carol sat in front of her plasma screen computer display and watched, with amazing clarity, the precipitous drop in the price of TMC stock and, with it, the decline of her ownership stake in the company. Shares in the technology sector were taking their biggest pounding in a long time. She clicked over to the financial news headlines on another website to seek guidance on how to improve her personal financial picture. The title of the first article did not provide any comfort: "Fifty Out of One Hundred Economists Predict U.S. Recession (Assuming We Survive the Credit Crisis)."

Not good, she reflected.

She clicked again to a web page of stock listings. One week earlier, before the earnings announcement, TMC stock had been trading at a fifty-two-week high of $33 per share. This morning, egged on by skittish investors in Asia, the stock opened below the previous day's closing price. Currently, the shares stood at $27.17. A ticker running along the bottom of the screen read: "Product Obsolescence, Scandals, and Miscues Force Tech Consolidation."

Again, not so good.

She checked the stock market again: $26.75 per TMC share. Carol returned to the web page, this time looking for stories specifically about TMC. The first headline jumped out at her.

"TMC Leadership Creates More Problems Than Solutions."

Definitely sucks. Note to self: fire that good-for-nothing publicist. What doesn't he understand about spin, for Christ's sake?

Carol read through the article defaming her leadership at the helm of this multibillion-dollar communications technology and solutions firm. She could not believe the really bad luck and worse press the company had experienced since she took over as CEO. Jack Peterson was not the sales genius he purported to be and was even weaker as a general manager. Multinational opportunities languished and new service offerings lacked definition. Alex, hired to replace Jack as GM, spent more time in the hospital than visiting customers, thanks to Carol's unyielding quest for market share. What had been the most promising division in the entire company, TMC Solutions, was now squarely, and once again, in need of a turnaround.

Meantime, TMC's competition launched aggressive campaigns and ate TMC's lunch in the middle markets area. Product-quality issues returned after Carol instructed the procurement team to play hardball with vendor contracts, so customers from the average Joe to the average CEO turned again to the competition. These ordeals were exacerbated by the fact that TMC was now a much larger organization, with a bigger global footprint. On top of everything else, as Carol assumed the reins of TMC during the summer of 2008, the Economic Optimism Index experienced its third-lowest reading in its history.

With Carol focused on the entire company, the board wanted her to hire a strong number two to help manage the enterprise. Carol agreed; she wanted someone to hold the bag if she were unable to turn things around. The Solutions division yet again provided the best spot for this executive.

Not only was a general manager required there, but also Carol figured that the visibility of this operation offered the best option if an executive sacrifice were called for.

Sal and Stewart better get someone to take Alex's place fast, she thought. *I need a fall guy.*

Ding. Ding. Carol's computer sounded an alert about downward movement in TMC's share price. Her personal stockbroker, Long, Champs & Downs, sent a message: "NOTICE: TMC share price has reached your predetermined alert price of $26.00 per share or lower."

"Shit."

Carol returned to the news stories to see how the press treated her presentation at the previous day's annual meeting.

"More Questions Than Answers at TMC's Shareholder Meeting."

Carol knew if that kind of coverage continued, she risked losing the confidence of the board. The situation called for sacrifice.

Ding. Ding. "NOTICE: TMC share price has reached your predetermined alert price of $26.00 per share or lower."

Carol checked the ticker symbol for TMC stock: $25.97.

She clicked on TMC's corporate directory in her computer and scanned the list for her direct reports.

"Time to fire someone."

LIV

Stewart's incessant preening annoyed Sal. He needed Stewart to focus on solving this executive search so that Sal could get paid. He pulled down and away from Stewart's face the mirror that Stewart held.

"Tell me again. Why don't you want to hire Michelle Kline for the Solutions job?" Sal asked his client, to whom he was increasingly joined at the hip.

Stewart took a fleeting look at his lip line before putting the mirror away. *Those Botox treatments were all Carol billed them to be. So what if I never sip another bowl of gazpacho.*

"Based on an initial exploratory discussion with Michelle, I think she could bring strong leadership skills to the team," Stewart responded. "Of course, the position that we are looking to fill is a critical one. We would need to go a lot deeper before making a decision on any candidate. Having said that, I saw enough potential in her experience to support more detailed follow-up."

Sal was more confused and frustrated. Stewart's comments made it sound like Michelle was a good candidate—maybe.

"You want to hire her or not?" Sal asked.

"Do you remember Marie Sancredi? We hired her to run IT a few years back. Great pedigree. Finest educational credentials. Brand-name employers before she joined TMC. Michelle reminds me of her. She talked a good game but never delivered much. She was always running off to a ballet recital or T-ball game for one of her kids. Michelle has kids the same age."

Sal pursed his lips and shook his head as he considered Stewart's pig-headed logic and blatant discrimination. Sal had not been offended by the comments. He simply had his own priorities. The top one was getting cash flowing, and fast. If he thought arguing with Stewart might make a difference, he would have pretended to have principles.

He decided not to reveal his exasperation. TMC had an insatiable appetite for hiring executives, which Sal was delighted to help them find, for an outrageous fee. Business had picked up considerably when Carol became the CEO and got rid of any executive who would not fit under her thumb. This cash cow was likely to continue, too, as long as Sal held on to that piece of cable from the Chemix job years earlier. He also had made a practice of sending Carol a pearl-barreled fountain pen as a Christmas gift each year.

However, success with TMC had not come easy. To provide for these new executives (salaries, bonuses, stock, smartphones, secretaries, company cars), Ted, and later Carol, had to fire a few old ones. And that was the crux of the matter. TMC's reputation preceded Sal's pitch. The more fired executives, the harder it became for Sal to sell new ones on joining the company.

Plus, Sal had sacrificed some of his best business associates, those rich in one type of resource and indebted to Sal because of some type of vice, as suitors for Carol. She managed to manhandle most dates, often before dinner entrées were served. Even Giana complained.

"Sal, why do you waste your time setting Carol up wit' our top customers? Not for nothin', that woman is a you-know-what. I realize our customers are degenerates, but they are still nice people."

Sal's take had been that every date he arranged reminded Carol of her debt, and that had been good for business.

Carol eventually canceled their unwritten contract by finding and marrying her soul mate without Sal's help. Nevertheless, Sal would continue to drink from the same well that Carol poisoned, as long as the money was good. Therefore, when he got a live, interested candidate on the line, Sal did all he could to sell that candidate to TMC. Today, sequestered with Stewart in the latter's TMC office, Sal was pitching candidates to fill the Solutions general manager role left vacant by Alex's sudden departure.

Acknowledging that Michelle Kline's candidacy was a lost cause, Sal slid the resume of his next candidate, a fifteen-year veteran of Colreavy Consulting, across the table for Stewart to review.

"You know this guy?" Stewart asked as he read through the candidate's accomplishments.

"I got to know him playing in a foursome with Ann and her husband. Great handicap. Smart, too. He's a hell of a guy."

"Uh-hrump." Although they had been working together awhile, Stewart still took occasional offense at Sal's use of colorful language.

Sal's business partnership with Stewart flourished with Carol's voracious requirement for new executive blood. Their friendship advanced under the shared agita (a colloquialism Stewart enthusiastically acquired from Sal) they experienced as a result of Carol's mounting demands. The higher she rose up the corporate ladder, the more unreasonable her expectations were, so much so that Stewart and Sal began meeting monthly when she was named president and CEO of the $20 billion TMC. Several bottles of wine often accompanied multicourse meals followed by sambuca-laced espresso served with a dessert sampler. Stewart charged his portion of these sessions against his health-care savings account, under the mental health code. Sal charged them back to TMC, under miscellaneous recruiting expenses. This particular morning, as he sat amid the mess that Stewart's office had become, Sal craved more comfortable surroundings.

"Isn't Colreavy Consulting one of your clients?" Stewart found the resume intriguing.

"What the fuck," Sal shrugged as he pushed aside an empty to-go coffee cup to make room for his papers.

Stewart glared at Sal.

"Ex-CUSE me, Mr. Narciss." Sal was annoyed with Stewart's pretense of formality, especially since he had once witnessed Stewart use the ficus trees in the bar of a local restaurant as a latrine. That was after a particularly brutal week with Carol, so Sal had given him a pass.

Sal explained that Colreavy Consulting was not a client like TMC. He told Stewart that if they liked this guy, he would work it out with Ann McManus.

"Colreavy has got so many consultants running around the country that half the friggin' time they don't even know who works for them," Sal said.

Stewart considered elevating the conflict-of-interest discussion, but since it would have been a purely philosophical exercise—his own principles were slaves to his career ambitions—he dropped it. TMC was really hurting, and Colreavy Consulting was a company with much fatter margins.

Sal's right. Colreavy won't notice one fewer partner, Stewart reasoned.

"Remember, Sal, we need someone who can lead transformational change."

"I thought you guys were going to downsize the Solutions division anyway."

"What do you think transformational change means? The first action a new GM will have to tackle is rightsizing the workforce by 25 percent—the right 25 percent. That's where HR comes in," Stewart offered.

"Don't worry," Sal said. "I checked him out. Don't want another wuss like Alex in here. Friggin' guy." Sal had had to pay a personal visit to the Maserati salesperson to seek some leeway on the lease payment schedule.

The salesman had not seemed to be concerned that Sal was in a precarious financial situation when Sal explained it over the phone. The face-to-face meeting made all the difference. That and the new cigarette burn below the knuckles on the salesman's right hand—the one that maneuvered the stick shift.

Sal organized his papers alphabetically, tapping the stack on the conference table to align the edges. "We'll get this guy in here next week for interviews," he said, and put the stack into his briefcase.

"We are having a going-away party for Rupert Bhein at our local watering hole," Stewart said. "Why don't you join us?" Stewart referred to the retirement party for TMC's CFO, a onetime "rising star," as Ted had called Rupert when he hired the talented finance executive.

Stewart called in his new assistant, Kristie, and introduced her to Sal, explaining that Beverly, his former secretary, had quit to follow the rodeo circuit with her bull-riding boyfriend. "Kristie, what time does Rupert's celebration begin?"

"That's been cancelled," Kristie informed them matter-of-factly.

The thirty-seven-year-old assistant arched her back against the door of the conference room in a mock stretch. Obtuse to all but the bluntest of flirtations, Stewart fixated on this new information.

"Why? I was looking forward to sending Rupert off with a bang after all he contributed to TMC." Stewart's touchy-feely radar was on.

"Carol was concerned that the press might get wind of the retirement party and interpret that Rupert's departure was voluntary, and then they might further interpret that he wasn't responsible for the shithole we are finding ourselves in these days." Kristie stopped to take a breath. "If THAT happened, somebody might start calling for Carol's head instead of Rupert's." Little had Rupert suspected that he would become a falling star under Carol's leadership.

Sal joked, "I'm assuming none of this was in a memo from Carol?"

"Jill Jackson, Carol's assistant, is one of my best friends." Kristie reached for the coffeepot in front of Stewart to refill his cup. She winked shamelessly at her boss.

Stewart calculated that the cancellation of this party might scuttle his chance of capturing the *mHre* award. This award, sponsored by the National Association of Human Executives, recognized a human resources leader who exhibited life-affirming treatment of executives forced to exit a company under less than ideal circumstances. Noteworthy circumstances ranged from misappropriation of corporate funds and/or other illegal activity to embarrassing personal scandal (first-time divorce did not make the cut unless one of the parties named in the divorce proceedings was not human). The acronym, which stood for "most *Human* resources executive," called attention to the oft overlooked and thankless task of making a bad situation look good, or at least less awful.

"Kristie, get Lisa Links from our public relations team on the phone. We have to make sure Rupert's departure is linked to the revitalization of the business. It would be good if Rupert shared a personal humiliation with a national business reporter."

"Well, at least you've got somebody to console you in all this brutal turnaround activity," Sal winked at Stewart as Kristie left to carry out his request.

"What?" Stewart's preoccupation with TMC problems clouded his perception, particularly when it concerned the come-hither signals from his newest assistant. He stared at the opening he had created on his bookshelf for the *mHre* award.

"Tough times, huh?" Sal asked.

Stewart let out a long sigh. "You have no idea."

The combined impact of unrelenting increases at the gas pumps, the financial services calamity, and a U.S. dollar on life support hit TMC's business hard. The only good news was that this perfect economic storm came on the heels of a massive exodus of dissatisfied TMC middle management. While the remaining employees were stretched by additional responsibilities, Stewart rationalized that at least TMC may have averted a mandatory workforce reduction, a public relations nightmare the company did not need. He did not view the transformational change necessary for the Solutions division as a pending reduction in workforce but rather a reorganization around business priorities.

Stewart explained that the executive search they were doing was one of several initiatives the leadership had embarked upon to revolutionize the company. Another had to do with a makeover of TMC's brand image, including alterations to the advertising campaign. Together, these activities were viewed as compulsory to a successful turnaround of TMC's fortunes. Sal seemed unfazed as Stewart listed his responsibilities.

"You do know that she named me chief administrative officer and put me in charge of our new advertising campaign when she fired our marketing vice president, don't you?" Stewart asked.

"Big britches to fill, Stewart." Sal knew it was easy to get under Stewart's skin.

"You probably wouldn't understand, in your line of work, what it takes just to process all the employee grievances we get weekly," Stewart sighed.

"Sure I do. I may not have mentioned this before, but I ran a construction crew way back when. Had a bunch of workers submit a grievance over some safety thing."

Surprised and somewhat impressed, Stewart asked Sal how he addressed the situation.

"I asked whoever wanted to be on the committee investigating this safety complaint to take a ride with me so we could discuss it."

"What happened?" Stewart asked.

"Funny enough, nobody wanted to be on the committee after all. Guess the workers figured it out for themselves."

Stewart wondered how well Sal's approach might work at TMC, but the image of employment lawyers surrounding his workforce turned him against the idea. His labor-relations team just did not possess Sal's finesse.

"Back to the business at hand," Stewart said. "Carol herself is leading the reorganization of the Solutions division until you and I have victoriously landed a new general for that business."

"Revolutionize? Victoriously? You sound like you are at war, Stewart."

"This is a war, Sal. The battle is waged every day in the newspapers and in the living rooms of our customers!" Catching sight of his hairline in the gleam off his metallic coffee cup, Stewart licked his thumb and forefinger and adjusted the part in his hair.

"Living rooms? Is that going to be part of your ad campaign, Stewart?"

"Conference rooms, living rooms, whatever. Hostilities are all around us. The financial markets are unfairly pounding TMC stock, our competitors are leading a crusade against us with OUR customer base, and our own employees are blogging against us in cyberspace!"

Sal cleared his throat. He read the newspapers. He had his own concerns about Carol's ability to maintain the confidence of the board as the stock price fell, competitors lured customers away, and employees lambasted TMC leadership. He noticed a stain on his freshly dry-cleaned suit jacket and sighed, fastidiousness having become another fatality of his association with Carol.

"Stewart, I'm going to talk to you like a friend. You guys sat on your laurels for too long. You have good products and services, but when the customers asked for something different, you thumbed your nose at them. Your competitors gave customers what they wanted. Your competition's stock value isn't going down. It's going up. And I've read what TMC employees are saying about Carol and the rest of the leadership. That can't be helping your position with customers OR the financial markets."

Stewart and his TMC executive colleagues were not accustomed to being challenged.

"What's your point?"

Sal looked at Stewart carefully before responding. "What does the board think of Carol and all these business problems, Stewart?"

"The board is all over the place. Every time they get fed up with Carol, she redirects their focus to the latest deal or she expands internationally. Those tactics often mean additional revenue in the short term, which they like. Not to mention, it would be hard to find a replacement for her. We're not exactly an attractive company to work for these days."

Sensing an opportunity for more search work if the board decided to replace Carol, as well as a chance to ingratiate himself with people even more influential than the CEO, Sal pursued Stewart's line of thinking.

"So the board is discussing these issues?"

"How should I know what they discuss? I'm considered Carol's guy, so even Rick doesn't include me in the loop anymore," Stewart lamented. "This is just my take on things. That, and I read some notes that one board member unintentionally left in the boardroom after the last meeting."

TMC's business health was tenuous, and Sal was determined to protect his franchise. If the board vacillated about Carol again, Sal wanted to be there to help figure out a solution and find a new CEO to lead the company, for a substantial fee. There might be a way to leverage the HR leader to do the dirty work.

Hell, Stewart might end up looking good in the process, or at least thinking he looked good, Sal figured.

"Stewart, do YOU think Carol is the right executive to turn TMC around?"

"Sal, you've got to dance with the one that brung you."

Sal straightened his tie and adjusted the sleeves under his suit jacket. He decided a lesson about influencing the board to his and Stewart's mutual benefit was in order. Assuming that this strategy would be better served with lots of alcohol, he invited Stewart to join him for a drink.

"We have a lot to discuss, like starting a search for a new CFO now that Rupert is gone," Sal said. He held the door as Stewart exited the conference room.

Stewart informed Sal that they had already identified a new CFO. Though Carol had lobbied TMC's board to promote Emily into the position, citing the lucrative partnership with Turkmenistan among her many contributions, the board favored its own candidate.

"Carol felt that no one would understand how to manage TMC's books better than Emily, but the board overruled her. She was pretty much in shock, since she's not used to the board pushing back. But I guess they meant it this time when they told us to get serious about making improvements."

Stewart explained that Carol eventually came to her senses, increasing the top line by buying a small but significant competitor. Then the board issued a gushing press release about her achievements.

"Still, they stuck to their guns and promoted Mercedes Rodriguez into the corporate CFO job. Of course, I had to agree with the board. I remember when we hired Mercedes many years ago. I knew she would be a great talent."

L V

V era called Sal's office to confirm the interviews that Harold Bohner was to have the following day. In addition to meetings with TMC executives and one member of the board, the Colreavy consultant would spend a few hours with an industrial psychologist who would help the TMC team determine overall fit with the organization. Vera worked with Sal's office to line up all the details of these meetings and to ensure that Harold's candidate experience was excellent.

Giana was responsible for the logistics on Sal's end. She often worked with the clients to secure travel arrangements and provide local community information to their spouses.

"I like dat part of the business. I get real personal-like wit' the guys and the wives," she would report to Sal when he complained about the heft of the phone bills.

After working with her on arrangements for dozens of candidates, Giana grew to trust Vera over time. She appreciated the hard work Vera did to make sure that anyone who visited TMC had a good day, from offering coffee in the morning to supplying important information about the company and the industry. She sympathized with Vera's personal situation and valued the details Vera shared about her family life. Giana rejoiced with Vera when her son Christian had a good day, and she was sad when his illness kept him from participating fully in life. Eventually she trusted Vera with intimacies of her own, including the particulars of her husband's unfortunate demise.

"Vera, it was awful. I had to pick up his personal effects at the police station. A cop turned a vanilla envelope upside down and poured the stuff onto a desk. His beautiful Versace sunglasses, ruined. They had blood all ova them. It was heartbreakin'.

"But the worst was the cover picture in the newspaper. He was lyin' in the gutter wit' his hands together under his head like a baby in a crib. He woulda hated that."

Vera spent the remainder of the day working on the agenda for Harold's trip to TMC headquarters, trying to push the image of Giana's husband in the fetal position, blood pooling around his glasses, out of her mind.

LV I

"These aren't the numbers I asked for!" Carol threw the pro forma projections in the trash can.

Mercedes retrieved the financial statements from the wastebasket as Stewart explained what the finance executive meant to say.

"Carol, we understand these aren't the business results you wanted, but these numbers speak accurately to the results of our business."

Stewart noticed a small stain on the sleeve of his jacket. Long work hours, diminished benefits, and rumors of an Employee Stock Ownership Program–bailout of TMC—utilizing employees' 401K contributions to fund operating cash flow—led to a bombardment of tomato juice–filled balloons as Stewart had walked from the parking lot to corporate headquarters. Last week employees hit him five times in front of the main entrance. Today, only one rubber weapon glanced his arm. Still, the blemish provoked him.

I had hoped, when we built that tranquility pond off the break room, that the employees would lay off the pranks, Stewart thought.

Carol pulled the papers from Mercedes and looked through them again.

"This year's focus was supposed to be around centralization and consolidation. Translation: profitability! Not more operating expense, greater net loss!"

Carol wondered what the board's point of no return was. *I'll have to suffer through another Palm Beach boondoggle to placate them.* She winced.

Her desk phone rang.

"YES?"

Carol's face changed from fiery red to pink and her voice softened noticeably.

"Clare, what a nice surprise." She cleared her throat as she addressed Clare Woodard. The top business reporter had not always been easy on Carol, so the CEO assumed that this conversation would not be a walk in the park. Around TMC, Carol blamed Clare's impartiality for some of TMC's drop in market-cap value. The journalist's glowing reports on XLNZ, a major competitor whose stock price had tripled in the past year, certainly had not helped.

Carol's suspicion intensified as Clare mentioned that she was researching an article for her magazine's next issue.

"A quote?" Carol said. "I wasn't aware you were working on an article on TMC." Carol's nostrils flared. She motioned at the executive team sitting across from her to find out what they could about Clare's story angle while she answered questions from the popular correspondent.

"Well, yes, the past few quarters have been challenging, but also exciting! We are about to launch a bold advertising campaign that will extend TMC's reach into the marketplace."

Carol listened warily as Clare teased her with noise from the grapevine.

"No, Clare. Rumors of layoffs are greatly exaggerated. We simply have a unique opportunity to reorganize the company to better align with our customers."

She concentrated as the reporter suggested items of concern for investors.

"Yes, these are times for a steady hand at the helm."

Clare had an additional observation.

"Of course I mean my hand, Clare! . . ."

"GRRRRR . . . Jill!" Carol shouted at her assistant, having carefully closed out the conversation with the reporter.

After placing a call to Lisa Links on TMC's public relations team, Stewart hovered around Jill's desk. He followed her into Carol's office.

"Lisa is all over this, Carol," he said, attempting to defuse the explosion already under way.

"It's too late," Carol said. "Clare went to press. She didn't need a quote from me. She had already formed her opinion after talking with several executives who used to work here."

Carol recalled a conversation she had had with an executive recruiter the previous week. Certain she would be among the finalists in the executive search for a CEO for Kiddles Corporation, the consumer-products giant, Carol had fantasized about the compensation prospects. Kiddles had a reputation for breaking the bank when it came to hiring great talent. Kiddles's stamp of approval also would help to mitigate any noise about her ineffectiveness at TMC. So determined had Carol been to make a career move to this hip, youth-oriented company that she allowed her hair to grow longer and consulted a Generation X personal shopper about her wardrobe.

When the executive-search consultant informed her that the Kiddles board had grave concerns about her leadership style after having spoken with several TMC alumni, Carol rebuked the search consultant for wasting her time on such an amateur company. She detailed her own grave concerns about the search committee's "lack of balls." Then she called Stewart and ranted at him to get her nominated for "some executive of the year award!" She thought that would fix the "bony asses" of the Kiddles board.

"Urgh," Carol sighed, and her eyes began to tear. Stewart interpreted this as a sign that Clare had gotten to his boss.

Maybe Carol's not just a cold, insensitive bitch, he thought to himself as he handed Carol his handkerchief.

"Goddamn it, Jill. I told you to refill the prescription for my allergy medication. My eyes welled up so much from this hay fever, I was afraid I might cry when I was talking to that sniveling reporter."

Stewart felt a sudden, sharp chill throughout his body. Feeling weak, he sat on the edge of Carol's desk.

Carol dabbed at her eyes with a tissue and planned her next move.

"You're likely to get a call from her too, Stewart, so let's get a legal opinion. And don't sit on my desk!"

"Why does she want to talk to me? I'm only human capital management around here. Not important. Not running a business division into the ground. Just inspiring the workforce. Encouraging career development."

Stewart instinctively reached for his pulse. He remembered his doctor's warnings about the dangers of working with Carol.

"Would you please stop whimpering! It's so annoying. Why doesn't your doctor prescribe something for your blood pressure?" Carol asked as Stewart reached into his pocket for his portable blood pressure gauge. He attached it to his finger.

"Stewart, you can't take that out each time we have a problem, or I might as well make you a standing reservation in Barone General Hospital."

The local medical facility had been renamed after a large TMC donation in memory of the company's founding chief executive. Ted had expired prematurely, the casualty of a deadly mix of Caribbean rum, coconut oil, call girls, and Viagra. The death certificate cited the cause of death as complications due to circumstances. Out of respect for Ted's fourth wife, and with the assistance of another TMC donation to the regional law enforcement benevolent society, the details were omitted from the official police report and the press release announcing Carol's ascension to the CEO throne.

Carol now had the dubious distinction of being the only two-time CEO who had captured the brass ring on the heels of the untimely, and somewhat unusual, demises of her predecessors. While a few curious TMC minds poked around for a link between Carol and Ted's passing, her honeymoon served as an ironclad alibi. Sal was mad at himself for having missed this opportunity, as bumping off Ted would have been a surefire way to double down on Carol's debt to him.

Carol yanked the blood pressure gauge off Stewart's finger and threw it in the trash. Stewart lunged for his lifeline, but Carol blocked him.

"Jill, call my doctor and tell him I need a prescription for Valium," Carol instructed her assistant. Jill dutifully wrote it in her pad. Stewart looked longingly at the trash bin.

Carol doesn't need a sedative, though she inspires that need in others, he thought.

"What do you need Valium for?" he asked.

"It's not for me; it's for you," she said. "I want you to take one pill thirty minutes before we have any meetings from now on." Carol clicked through her contacts database to find the phone number of TMC's external counsel.

"But—but—but . . . we have meetings all the time!" Stewart panicked again, his pulse quickening.

Carol dialed the lawyer's number.

"Trust me. In about a month you'll be thanking me. I bet the Valium will even help your blood pressure problem."

Carol tapped her fingers on the desk as she waited impatiently for TMC's lead attorney, Lars Frankel, to answer his phone. Finally, someone picked up on the other end.

"Lars. It's Carol. We need your help . . . Yeah, hello to you too. Whatever. We have a situation. That snake Clare Woodard called to goad me about a story she's going to publish on the declining value of TMC stock. No, we can't stop it, but we do need to think about our counterspin. More imperative, she mentioned a conversation she had with Tomas Severe, the chairman of the board of StreamLINE when I was president of that company . . . Yes, exactly . . . No, the case was never solved . . . Lars, we are getting off the point. Clare intimated that she was working on another story about companies that offer backdated stock options to motivate executives. Yes, I am aware that TMC's board would never approve that type of compensation, Lars, but again, you are not listening."

Carol enlightened the external counsel on her version of the story that would serve as the basis for Clare's pending article. StreamLINE's board had been concerned about stabilizing the organization after Chuck's tragic death. Carol was asked to take the top job, but she harbored concerns about the board's long-term commitment to the company, so she had one foot out the door. According to Carol's rendering, the board pleaded with her to stay for the sake of the employees.

"The employees meant so much to me," Carol said. "It was clear that they needed an emotionally resilient leader, especially at that time."

To lock in the deal, the directors provided a handsome compensation package, including backdated stock options. At that time, the procedure of dating an employee stock option prior to its actual grant date was not viewed with disdain. Rather, the opportunity to bestow additional compensation upon executives by walking back the calendar and fixing financial rewards was characterized as discounting, enabling compensation managers and corporate counsel to sleep at night. Backdated stock options were no longer in vogue after the SEC had taken to investigating the companies, and the boards, that offered them.

Carol grimaced at Stewart, who held his wrist, counting heartbeats per minute.

"Anyway, if backdated options aren't illegal, what's the fuss?" Carol continued. "Hmm . . . falsifying documents to conceal the backdating from investors? Nope. Don't know anything about that."

Although everything about her TMC pay had been disclosed to the public through the company's annual proxy statement, Carol suspected that Stewart was likely to get a request from Clare for additional information. She requested that Lars prepare Stewart for an inquisition from this reporter.

Stewart sat cross-legged on the floor of Carol's office practicing a deep-breathing technique he learned from a yoga instructor on Dandy's ranch. As he pulled air into his lungs, Stewart recalled a recent visit with his old friend. Dandy was grateful for the company, as Phillipe had been spending all his free time preparing for the birth of their twin sons, carried by two surrogate moms in Mumbai. Dandy and Stewart had listened in on a conference call as Phillipe fired questions about diet and exercise at the ob-gyn who was managing their pregnancies. Stewart commented on the clarity of the international communications.

"You really should look into outsourcing," Dandy suggested, assuming there might be money to be had if TMC outsourced through his connections.

Dandy also encouraged Stewart to cash in his TMC chips and join him in an investment fund focused on paradigm-shifting nanotechnology. Stewart found the idea compelling, but he was not in the financial stratosphere like Dandy—a consequence of bad real estate deals and even more troublesome adjustable-rate financing; an acrimonious divorce; three gold-digger girlfriends; and a current wife with an insatiable thirst for all things cashmere. Thus, having ordered a twin jogging stroller for the family, Stewart returned home with strict instructions from the yogi for how to maintain a stress-free lifestyle in a techno-crazy world.

Now, sitting on the office floor as Carol spoke with Lars, Stewart pushed the air out of his lungs and TMC worries out of his mind.

Suddenly, Carol grabbed hair from the top of his head and pulled him up and out of his daydream.

"Yes, I'll have him call you later today. Bye. Yeah, thanks, too." She hung up with Lars.

Carol picked up newspapers and magazines that had been sitting on her desk and tossed them at Stewart.

"Make sure you make a call to Lars a priority. In the meantime, Mr. Chief Administrative Officer, what the hell is going on with our advertisements?"

The last edition of *Commercial Week*, the foremost publication for advertising and marketing, contained a list of top advertising campaigns for the quarter. TMC was not on it. There was, however, an article citing technology industry marketing statistics, distinguishing brands that were up from those that were down, and theorizing why TMC's advertising was so lackluster.

"This article says we have more problems than our customers do, that even our ads don't inspire confidence," Carol said. "In fact, it implies we can't be trusted!" Disgusted, Carol tore the magazine in two. "I don't understand why the board resists putting me in TMC advertisements. Look at my face, Stewart. It exudes trust!"

His thoughts had not yet caught up with his body, yanking notwithstanding, so Stewart decided not to comment on what Carol's face exuded. He moved slowly into a chair by her desk. The breathing exercise gave him a feeling of repose in spite of Carol's rant.

"Carol, do not fear," he said. "We have the solution at hand."

Stewart was proud of his work on TMC's new brand identity. He placed on Carol's desk two storyboards containing images and slogans for the company's new advertising campaign. The first depicted an elderly gentleman purchasing cell phone hardware at a local electronics store. The old gent happily handed over cash with one hand and placed his other hand on a box clearly defined as a TMC product. The slogan read: "Wish You Had the Right Partner? TMC: Technology You Can Lean On."

The second advert featured the same gentleman. He posed as a corporate manager catching a midafternoon nap as TMC Solutions worked successfully in the background. The catchphrase read: "Wish You Were Here? TMC: Technology You Can Sleep With."

Carol studied the mock-ups of the advertisements. Inspiration did not jump out at her.

Eager to pitch his concept, the outcome of hours of creative discussions with their advertising agency, Stewart picked up the first storyboard.

"Carol, Jill, imagine your mother or custodian . . ." (*Does Carol have a mother?* Stewart thought.)

Carol's angry eyes told him to get to the point.

"Imagine the confusion they might feel entering an electronics store, not knowing where to start or how to solve their problem." He looked at the ladies to see if they were connecting with this. Jill sensed Carol's impatience, so she urged Stewart along with her eyes.

"What company can offer clarity in the midst of this uncertainty? Yes, Carol, what company can be trusted to solve problems? TMC!" Stewart smiled as he held the storyboard high.

"Are those rays of sunshine peeking through the clouds that are parting above the old man's head?"

"Yes, Jill. How astute of you to notice. The clouds were my idea."

Carol took the storyboard from Stewart and searched it again.

"Do I know him?" Carol asked, pointing to the character in the advertisements. "Do I KNOW this guy?"

"You may. Tell me, do you get a warm and friendly feeling from him, Carol?"

Carol stared fiercely at Stewart. He recognized the telltale twitch of her nostrils just before an outburst.

"When I want warm and friendly, I used to look at my bank statements,

Stewart. Since that's been screwed up, I'm not getting warm and friendly from much. What are you talking about?"

"I, I feel warm and friendly when I look at him," offered Jill, meekly.

Stewart double-checked that he had a clear path to an exit and then focused his pitch on Jill.

"Do you recognize him, Jill? From your childhood?"

Jill examined the two boards carefully. As she did so, a smile of recognition crossed her face.

"Mr. Wishes! It's Mr. Wishes!" Jill jumped up and down. Stewart grabbed her hands and jumped with her.

"What are you two going on about?" Carol asked.

Stewart explained that Mr. Wishes had been the star of a TV series roughly thirty years earlier. The character traveled around the country and made wishes come true for destitute families.

Carol put one hand on Jill's shoulder and the other on Stewart's to stop the bouncing. "Our customers are among the richest companies in the entire world," she said.

"Carol, we have to reposition TMC so that we can prop up the valuation," Stewart replied. "That means we need a new way to talk about the business. Mr. Wishes encouraged a community to believe! He embodied trust. Mr. Wishes will stimulate enthusiasm for TMC products!"

"Yeah!" Jill jumped again, her recollections of the TV show palpable.

Carol wasn't convinced. "I don't know about this guy."

Stewart took Carol through the focus group results, which indicated a favorable response to qualities such as faith and trust. For Stewart, these results confirmed that the ad campaign would improve TMC's image. It was natural to predict that sales would increase from there. Stewart gave Carol a light pat on the back. Her look of disdain encouraged him to pull away.

"I HOPE you're right," she said.

"Carol, there is nothing to lose and so much to be optimistic about!" Stewart collected his storyboards and raced back to his office to officially launch the new advertising campaign, "One Word: Trust."

LVII

Carol was busy tweaking the ratios of revenue to margin one particularly tense morning when Sal came by to discuss Harold Bohner's candidacy for general manager of the Solutions division. Jill was away from her desk and, with no one around to show him in, he knocked firmly on the CEO's office door.

"What is it?" Carol did not look up, as the financial juggling commanded all her attention.

Hearing only silence, Carol finally turned to see Sal standing at her door.

Over time, Carol had grown to appreciate what Sal could do for her. His straightforward, no-nonsense approach was a breath of fresh air compared to the second-guessing and cover-your-ass penchant of her own leadership team. When she looked at it from that perspective, she felt they could have a positive partnership. That is, until she could figure out a way to get rid of him.

"Hey, Sal. I liked that guy you sent in here last week. Ann McManus will probably have a cow if we hire him, which I intend to do. But that's her problem. Think we can get him?"

"I'm sure you can with the right compensation package. He's done with waiting in the wings for Ann to step down. So I guess this means he did well with that company shrink you made him see."

"That shrink is Stewart's latest ingratiation with me and the board. Another expensive way to show how HR adds value. I don't get why we have to pay a psychologist to ask an executive a bunch of questions that don't have anything to do with our business."

Sal conveyed Harold's sentiments about the visit with the industrial psychologist, which included questioning about high school achievements and failures. "Friggin' high school! All's I remember about high school is, that's when I started my entrepreneurial career."

Carol and Sal always danced delicately around his other life. Carol once told him that as long as he stayed out of the newspapers, they could be successful business partners.

"So anyways, Harold passed the test?" Sal asked.

Carol opened her credenza and removed Harold's psychological assessment. She opened it to page three and scanned the verbiage, which listed his strengths as visionary thinking and team building. The report made special note of the candidate's strong competitive bent.

"The one concern raised is that his personal style can tend toward overbearing," Carol said. "The commentary suggested that he may like to keep subordinates under his thumb. 'Pinned down' is the exact phrase that the psychologist used. It all sounds good to me. There are a few employees around here I'd like to pin down to get better results." Carol tossed the report to Sal, who caught it and began reading.

"Be advised that I told that mean-spirited, so-called journalist, Clare Woodard, that TMC had identified an executive to run the Solutions business and assist me in the company's transformation. Don't screw up this hire, Sal."

Sal placed the psychological report on Carol's desk. "So I'll get with Stewart and we'll work up a good offer."

"Yeah, get with Moondoggie and do that," Carol laughed. Sal looked at her askance.

"Come on. Don't tell me Stewart doesn't remind you of Moondoggie, the character from the *Gidget* movies. Consistently tan, he wears golf shirts two sizes too small to make him appear toned. He's usually carrying around a sports board of some sort, playing the crowd for popularity points. Hell, I never know, one month to the next, what color his hair is going to be. I had to reintroduce him to members of the board at the last annual meeting because he had grown sideburns and bleached his hair again. He rolled the dice one too many times with that hair, though. One of the directors doused him with a pitcher of water. She thought he was on fire."

Sal rolled his eyes. He had done what he could to encourage Stewart to dress and act like a real man. Sal leveraged his style to drive his personal agenda, in spite of some sloppiness that had crept in lately. While he recognized that Stewart was also a pragmatist when it came to dressing for success, Sal could not for the life of him relate to Stewart's agenda.

Stewart's dress portrayed a desire to ingratiate himself with various constituencies. And the HR leader tweaked his self-image as changes in fortune and power structures occurred over the years. But his regular reinvention of himself sometimes pushed the envelope of social acceptability. To Carol's point, he had a recurring affinity for surfboards and flip-flops, particularly when the stress was intense. And Sal had suffered through Stewart's gangsta-style dress phase, when an inability to cinch his belt properly led to more than an infrequent mooning of restaurant wait staff when they stepped out for a meal. But the straw that broke the camel's back was when, during Stewart's recent dive into metrosexual couture, an obliging hostess suggested that Sal and Stewart might be more comfortable in a secluded, romantic booth in the back of her establishment. The sting of that embarrassment left an unforgettable mark on Sal.

Yet, at the end of the day, Stewart had been a true partner to Sal. He ran interference for Sal's people if they hit a roadblock in working with TMC. And he made sure Sal got paid, even if it did sometimes take a while. When Sal thought about the distribution business and that Philadelphia crew, he considered Stewart a very good asset in comparison.

"I'll agree there is a resemblance, Carol. Not for nothing, Moondoggie always got the girl." Sal smiled at his client.

"Yeah, well, sometimes Stewart's search for the fountain of youth can get on my nerves." She stopped laughing. "Whatever. Tell Stewart to hang up his surfboard and get that offer started. By the way, I'm assuming you've checked references so we aren't going to have a repeat of the Alex Martin debacle."

LVIII

T he following week, Vera sat at her desk with a hot cup of coffee and the newspaper. Turning to page four, she noticed the TMC display ad featuring the former Mr. Wishes. It was in the business section, so this was the ad that pictured the office manager character, confidently snoozing, comfortable with his choice for technology. Recognizing the actor in the advertisement, Vera quickly dialed Stewart's number.

"Somebody better let Stewart know what he's done before this turns into another mess," she said to herself.

STEWART RUBBED HIS eyes and yawned. The previous evening, he and a team of human capital managers worked late to scrub "the list," the secret roll of employees whose jobs would be made redundant in the next round of layoffs. The business leadership had decided that jobs would have to be cut to mitigate operating expenses for the quarter. Carol demanded that the organization downsizing be completed quickly. She desperately wanted to make the numbers that the financial community was anticipating. Although several managers, cut to the employee bone already, fought hard to maintain the jobs, the leadership rationale was that they could always rehire when revenues bounced back.

Long days, starting with stale breakfast doughnuts and ending with cold pizza, were showing in the bags under Stewart's eyes and the love handles around his waistline. He felt the loss of sleep acutely this morning. Sal handed him a cup of black coffee.

"You guys are going to need an espresso machine in here if you keep slashing the payroll," Sal suggested.

Sal was once again back at TMC headquarters, this time to make Stewart concentrate on putting together the offer for Harold. Though Sal was sympathetic to Stewart's workload, his patience reached its end when Harold said that because TMC had been dragging its feet, he would interview for a general management job with XLNZ, a major competitor. Sal's Maserati installments were not any less expensive, and his wife's anger-management program, which amounted to marathon shopping at prominent malls, did not show any signs of abatement. So Sal purchased another plane ticket, threw a calculator and Harold's cell phone number into his briefcase, and flew to TMC to get Stewart to focus on creating an offer proposal.

"Do you remember the summer of forty-two?" Stewart asked Sal as they took a break from the calculations.

"Yeah, it was a great movie. Coming of age and all that."

"No. I mean August of 2006, when TMC shares were at forty-two. Executives practically offered us money to hire them." Stewart smiled at Sal as he recalled the good old days when TMC was respected by the investing public, feared intensely by its competition, and keenly sought after by executives looking to capture a brass ring.

"Ah, those were the days," Stewart continued. "Now we have to pay Bohner triple his cash package at Colreavy just to get him to the table. But what's the point of remembering the good old days? Let's get this offer over with. I'd like to get him on board, and Carol out of my hair, as soon as possible."

With all the activity and long hours, Stewart had forgotten to charge his iPhone. He pulled out a plug from his briefcase and connected the phone into a wall socket in the conference room. Immediately, the electronic device indicated that he had messages. He listened to them. In addition to several from Carol, there were three from Vera, who had asked him to call immediately. With Harry gone and Charlie now working for the dark side as an executive-search consultant, Stewart had no choice but to promote Vera into a recruiting position—provided she did her own administrative work. Stewart knew that Vera understood what his workload was like. She should know better than to leave one message like that, never mind three. He called her first.

"I saw the advertisement in today's paper," Vera, anxious, jumped into the conversation with her boss.

Stewart took a deep breath before responding. While he was pleased with the enthusiasm his newest executive recruiter was demonstrating for the marketing campaign, this was exactly what could exasperate him about Vera. Calling to congratulate him on his advertising campaign as he was under the gun to put together a handsome offer for an important senior executive revealed how naïve Vera could be. However, Stewart's executive coach advocated a softer touch in his dealings with employees, especially now, with employee morale suffering under TMC's business challenges.

"Uh, Vera, that's great. Thank you. But maybe you could find another time for us to discuss your appreciation of the advertisement. If there is nothing else—something essential, perhaps—that you need to discuss, Sal and I will be getting back to this very important offer for Harold."

"Well, I was wondering if that guy in the ad was the same actor who played Mr. Wishes in the TV series *Family Values*?"

"Yes. Good memory, Vera. *Family Values* was a wonderfully wholesome show, and it demonstrated the principles that TMC is all about."

Vera, now in her mid-forties, was old enough to remember, with fondness, the television program, which promoted community and goodwill. However, she shared with Stewart a mild concern she had around the age of the TV show compared with the ages of the customers who purchased TMC products, especially since *Family Values* had not even been in reruns for more than a decade.

"Many of the managers who are purchasing our products today are barely thirty years old," Vera said. "They don't know Mr. Wishes from Dr. Doolittle. If they don't know who he is, how can it resonate with them?"

Stewart grew irritated with Vera second-guessing his advertising brainchild. "Vera, your know-it-all attitude blinds you to the possibilities of this marketing campaign. You'll see what a success it will become for TMC."

For the sake of TMC, as well as the long-term value of her 401K, Vera hoped that she was wrong. But she told Stewart that her greater concern was about a different aspect of the ad campaign's central character. She hoped that the buzz about Mr. Wishes's behavior with participants on his TV show was not true. But the evidence was persuasive, she noted.

"What evidence?" Stewart was eager to cut this conversation short.

Vera clicked "send," and multiple newspaper articles shot through cyberspace to Stewart's inbox. The commentaries referenced a clothing-optional holiday party Mr. Wishes had thrown for the award recipients of the *Family Values* series. Allegedly, when several older people opted to remain clothed, Mr. Wishes grew incensed and threw them into a tub of vodka. The police were called. It was a big scene at the time. Someone was photographed, from behind, running away from the party. Confirmation of a mole on his lower back might have exonerated him, but Mr. Wishes sat on the evidence. Eventually, he was found not guilty of public indecency. However, the publicity disrupted the show. It was taken off the air.

"I'm sending you an article now that talks about the court proceedings," Vera concluded. "It was thirty years ago, so maybe it won't make any difference to our customers after all."

THE FOLLOWING DAY, representatives of the Oldie But Goodie Political Action Committee formed picket lines in front of TMC headquarters. Exasperated by TMC's insensitivity to the plight of their constituents, as evidenced by TMC's print and broadcast advertisements featuring Mr. Wishes (the television campaign launched the morning of the protests), the PAC issued a statement:

> OBG is dedicated to commemorating its membership's contributions to all aspects of society. Our members hold positions of great authority across the country, as business elders, grandparents, significant pools of disposable income, and large voting blocs. The fact that TMC Corporation would choose as their spokesperson an individual with such questionable character as it relates to such a broad and important swath of the American public is beyond comprehension. How can people trust TMC with their technology requirements if they would not trust the company with their grandparents?

Confronted by TV news crews as he entered TMC headquarters, Stewart pulled a page from his management-consulting days. He took umbrage at the allegations of TMC's insensitivity the bystanders were shouting at him. He explained that TMC was a fierce supporter of old people everywhere. Furthermore, he told the media minions that "seasoned employees" made up 8 percent of the company's workforce (he assumed he could back into that statistic later). Lying about his own age, he offered himself as proof that the advertisements were not in keeping with TMC's values. He vowed that the person responsible for this blatant disregard of such a vital component of the TMC family would be fired tout de suite.

Later that morning, the print and broadcast ads were pulled, Mr. Wishes wished he had never heard of TMC, and Lisa Links packed her personal belongings in a cardboard box.

"I'm not even in the advertising department. I work in public relations." Tears streaming down her face, Lisa tried in vain to explain to the human resources android in charge of her termination that she had nothing to do with the marketing campaign.

The HR generalist insisted that Lisa's termination was not related to that episode. It was simply a strategic reduction of the workforce.

"Nothing personal," the android said, checking messages on her Blackberry. "There's not enough time in the day," she mused about this compulsive habit as Lisa loaded boxes onto a dolly provided, gratis, by TMC.

L I X

Sal enjoyed a long drag on his cigar. This night had been a long time coming.

Eager to recover quickly from a tarnished corporate image, Carol and Stewart pushed the process to get Harold on board. Sal persuaded Harold that his client's interest was real, and he persuaded Carol and Stewart that they had to roll out the red carpet or lose Harold to the competition. Vera quickly put together an Oklahoma weekend for Harold and his wife, complete with spa package, school interviews, and high-priced wining and dining. The getaway having fulfilled its purpose, Sal was asked to meet Harold upon his arrival home to the New York area and present him with an offer letter, making official a deal the parties had agreed to the previous evening.

With great fanfare, Sal handed over the proposal from TMC and asked the Bohners to join him for a celebratory drink at the Cigar Box Bar. Harold's wife begged off; the children and the house needed her attention after her long weekend away.

Sal ordered a round of top-shelf, single-malt scotch—the least he could do given that Harold had saved his ass, not to mention his Maserati. Besides, he would bury these drinks in the miscellaneous expenses for which he charged TMC.

Buzz-buzz. Sal reached for his cell phone and looked at the phone number of an incoming text message.

"Stewart's sent a note. Probably wants to congratulate me again. You were not easy to land." Sal winked at Harold. He started reading the message aloud.

"Need to contact Bohner. Deal is ... "

Sal lowered his voice, but Harold, blowing smoke rings in the direction of two young ladies at the bar, did not notice.

Sal read the rest of the message to himself: ... *off. Call me.* SN

Sal scanned the bar for a secluded spot. The best option in this highly popular establishment appeared to be the men's room. Sal motioned for the ladies at the bar to join them and asked the waiter to bring over a bottle of champagne, choosing from the least expensive on the menu—Harold might not be the savior he needed after all. He then excused himself.

"Nature's calling." Sal sauntered calmly toward the bathroom so as not to arouse suspicion.

Harold winked as Sal left, putting his arms around the ladies, who flanked him on the couch.

Sal banged on the door of the single bathroom in this prewar building on Manhattan's Lower East Side. The occupant cursed at the commotion. With one swift hip check to the old, rusting lock, Sal loosened the hinge.

"Out. Now." Sal spoke with such authority that the twentysomething sobered fast and exited the small water closet with shirttails and suspenders hanging.

Sal dialed Stewart's phone number.

"Stewart Narciss here."

"Stewart, what the frig is happenin' out there? I'm feeling like a yo-yo lately, dealing with you people."

"Did you give the package to Bohner?" Stewart sounded anxious.

"For Christ's sake, Stewart!" Sal was exasperated. "You told me to pick him up at the airport and make a big show of delivering the offer letter. I'm sitting at a very expensive establishment in New York City with him now."

"How expensive?"

"What the fuck?"

Sal forgot himself. He looked around the four narrow walls of the unisex bathroom for anything resembling a listening device. Old habits died hard.

Stewart's day had started very early, with loud pounding on his front door at two o'clock in the morning. The pounding was followed by extraordinarily crude expletives not often heard in his tony neighborhood, even when holiday lights were being strung from rooftops. Carol had been the pounder, reduced to physical contact when Stewart did not respond to her numerous e-mail, text, and cell phone messages. His wife had disconnected their home phone long ago.

Stewart explained to Sal that, not long after extending the offer to Harold, Carol had decided to rescind it. When asked why, Stewart suggested that Sal take a seat because it would not be a short story. Sal considered the seating possibilities and told Stewart, "Get to the punch line."

Desperate to close the deal, Carol had invited Harold and his wife to join her and her husband, Mark Foley, for dinner. Although terribly handsome and relatively wealthy, thanks to a trust fund and the early passing of his self-made parents, Carol's spouse was largely withdrawn. Mark's obsession with Internet surfing, cybercommunities, and virtual friends had not mitigated the deficiencies in his real-world social graces.

Her husband's physical charms hardly camouflaged his emotional challenges, so Carol took Mark out only when absolutely necessary to further her ambitions. When they did socialize, Carol ensured that they arrived fashionably late, left reasonably early, and that Mark always had something in his mouth.

Stewart reminded Sal that he had convinced Carol that closing Harold was going to require extra effort. Besides additional compensation and the weekend getaway, Sal had recommended dinner with the spouses.

So somehow this bullshit is my fault, Sal thought as he leaned against the door to prevent another patron from entering.

Stewart explained that Carol had put on the full-court press to get Harold to join TMC. The dinner had not been much of a party, but it was not a bomb, either, and Harold had been impressed with Mark, specifically their shared interest in cybercommunities. The gathering, along with a substantial sign-on bonus, was enough to push Harold over the top. He agreed to TMC's offer terms as dessert was being served.

After dinner, Carol sent Stewart a text message with the specifics of the financial offer that Harold had accepted. She instructed Stewart to get an offer package shipped out so that Harold would have the deal in writing as soon as possible. Since Harold was scheduled to leave town very early the next morning, Stewart did it one better. He arranged for Sal to meet Harold at JFK International Airport and personally deliver the offer letter.

Meanwhile, eager to investigate websites Harold had recommended, Carol's husband clicked onto ExecForce.net. Harold had constructed this site to promote his unique management-development philosophy. Exceedingly thin and acutely shy, Mark had suffered through humiliating bullying attacks as a young person. These events stunted his leadership capabilities, hampering many of his future business ventures. When not cybersurfing, Mark threw himself into strenuous workouts and daydreamed of taking on the insolent employees who pushed him around.

Harold, it turned out, had suffered a similar fate as a youth but decided to take quality-of-life matters into his own hands. In addition to bulking up physically and mentally as he moved up the career ladder, he launched ExecForce.net to support and showcase his hard knocks–influenced management values. Specifically, the website offered illustrations of boxing techniques, diagrams of time-tested intimidation tools, and photographs of masked, thinly clothed executives overpowering employees identified only as "Insubordinate Employee No. X." Harold's credo was: "Want to be a more effective manager? Let your employees know what's what."

In exchange for guaranteed results, Harold required complete adherence to the principles of the program, spawning a dedicated group of acolytes. Advertisements for personal fitness equipment, nontoxic body paints, and martial arts coaches subsidized the website.

Mark was particularly taken with the allegiance of Harold's followers. One God-fearing disciple of the management-development method had created a preying tiger across his chest hair using shower gel and a pair of cutting shears.

"I never would have figured that a little bit of dried soap and scissors could create something so intimidating," Mark sighed.

Delighted that TMC had gone progressive by hiring a daring visionary, Mark shared the website with his wife. The buzz around the Mr. Wishes episode had only just died down, and Carol was not nearly as enthused about Harold's modus operandi as her husband had been. Physical abuse, particularly down the chain of command, was usually discouraged at TMC.

"This is ridiculous!" Carol cried. "Grown men doing this to their employees! And what the hell does that say?" She pointed to a colorful tattoo, in a Gothic script, across Harold's belly. He was the only practitioner identified by name on the site.

"I'm not certain, but it looks like M-O-M." Mark traced his finger over the loops, made somewhat illegible thanks to a bariatric procedure that had shrunk the letters.

Carol rose from her desk chair and turned her head sideways to get a different view. The expensive dinner she had hosted for the Bohners had not yet digested, and Carol's stomach churned.

"Oh shit. An avatar in a virtual world wouldn't be good enough? No! Harold had to use actual pictures of himself to show off his techniques!"

Stewart also relayed to Sal the conversations he had been having all day with Carol, TMC's image consultants, and numerous free-speech attorneys. Stewart made it clear that, as senior vice president of human capital management, he fully supported Harold's personal life choices. However, coming on the heels of the Mr. Wishes mess, plus a dip in TMC brand recognition as reported by *Commercial Week*, everyone agreed that it was best to disengage from the highly spirited Harold Bohner.

"As an enlightened human resources leader, I'll be the first to admit that corporal punishment may well be an effective leadership development tool. I'll set up a commission to investigate it as an option for TMC. But, meantime, we need that offer letter back."

"You told me, and Harold said as much himself, that Carol pitched the offer directly to him already." Sal was angry.

"It isn't legally binding until it's in writing. I got so tied up orchestrating internal damage control on this, I forgot that I arranged for you to hand-deliver the contract. Can you tell him it has a typo?"

"A typo! For chrissake, Stewart. I thought you guys wanted 'transformational change.' If you ask me, TMC might benefit from Harold transforming some of your employees!"

Remembering his bathroom surroundings, Sal composed himself. He lowered his voice. "You let this guy go and it could take months to get someone in that job. Besides, what if he gets pissed off that you took back the offer? Sounds like a guy who doesn't take no for an answer." Sal did not want to lose this deal.

Anticipating as much, Stewart had arranged private security for him and Carol. He had a hunch that Sal could take care of himself.

During the past financial quarter, Carol had gone on an aggressive acquisition spree, spending a small fortune betting on the future revenue streams of other companies. Her theory was that this should keep the financial press, and her board, busy. Stewart recognized that this tactic also would provide cover for Sal to find another candidate.

"Sal, we are spending a lot of time and resources assimilating all the companies that Carol is buying. The added revenue from those acquisitions keeps Wall Street off our backs, so we have wiggle room to get the right person in the job."

Sal looked at the platinum Bull and Bear cuff links he recently had bought as a gift to himself for closing this executive search a second time.

"Why was Carol's husband looking at masked bullies pummeling subordinates on the Internet, Stewart?"

Sal never trusted that boy toy Carol married. He had introduced her to a half-deaf, half-dead, self-made multimillionaire with impressive business connections and no next of kin. But Carol had not wanted Ted to be intimidated by her choice of a spouse, so she chose inexperience, passivity, and substantial wealth over a sick husband and "sicker" wealth: "You have no idea what a megalomaniac Ted is. If he has any reason to believe my husband could be more powerful than he is, he'll find a reason to push me aside."

"Typical woman," Sal ruminated on the phone with Stewart.

"What?" Stewart asked.

"Fuggedaboudit. We've worked long and hard to get this deal closed, Stewart. My final invoice is being processed for payment, right?"

"Sal, those acquisitions are not cheap. TMC cash flow is tight. We are putting off paying unnecessary invoices until next quarter."

Sal heard whispering on the other side of the toilet door. He lowered his voice. "Unnecessary! I got obligations too, Stewart!"

Sal mulled over his years with Carol, from the chemical burns on the soles of his Gucci loafers and the sound of sirens pulling up to StreamLINE HQ to all the lying he had to do to get executive candidates to meet with Carol. Not that Sal had a moral issue with bending the truth, but Carol's negative reputation so preceded her in the talent marketplace that even his most outlandish fabrications often would not sway prospects.

What made me think that bitch was hot? So what that she's easy on the eyes! Those friggin' shoulder pads tell the whole story, Sal fumed.

Then Sal remembered the annuity on TMC's Turkmenistan business, the fees for all the executive searches that Carol initiated to hire executives she could push around, and the supplemental revenue streams he derived from access to the secure data of wealthy businesspeople. He had his epiphany.

It's her friggin' thirst for power that's the real turn-on. The money's not bad, either, he concluded.

"Sal, if we do finish this search quickly I'm sure I could loosen up some cash," Stewart interrupted his reverie.

"I closed this search twice already," Sal said. His pride made him want the last word, but he knew that the decision had been made. He reflected on the additional beating the Maserati salesman was going to have to get.

Poor bastard. Not his fault.

"Sal, the sooner you let Harold know he's dead to us, the sooner you can find new candidates. Every moment counts."

As he left the toilet, Sal marked a guy in the corner of the lounge. Black suit, white shirt, dark sunglasses. He was not there when Sal went into the john. Sal sneaked out the back door of the cigar bar. He would call Harold in the morning with the news. No reason to ruin his evening with the ladies. And no reason Sal needed to pick up this tab after all.

L X

That same afternoon, TMC's relocation team argued with Vera about the projected costs to move Harold's household goods to a new home by TMC headquarters.

"Vera, this guy has enough video equipment to produce his own TV show. What's his new job? To follow Carol around and film her every move?" the relocation consultant, familiar with Carol's reputation, asked snidely.

Vera's focus drifted as she quietly read an incoming text message on her cell phone.

Can U believe Harold is practically naked when he beats up his employees? This gives boxer shorts a whole new meaning. Call me!! Giana

"Guys, I got to go. Let's table this for now."

"OK, but we're going to go over budget on this move. Harold told us he had several hundred pounds of personal fitness equipment, too."

Vera called Giana but reached her voice mail. She looked at her instant message box. Giana had signed out. She ran down to Stewart's office, interrupting his work on a new logo for TMC.

"I received a very strange message about Harold Bohner," she said. "Is something going on?"

"Yes. We found out that Harold is the proprietor of an online, er, performance art business. Quite the cottage industry, as I understand."

"So? Isn't it a free country?"

"The country is free, yes, but TMC's brand isn't. We're still digging out of Mr. Wishes's "One Word: Trust" advertising debacle."

Stewart clicked his computer to Harold's website to show Vera their candidate's extracurricular activities and the reason they were pulling the plug on his candidacy. "TMC's code of conduct firewalls won't allow us to search the website, but you can get the general idea from these pictures of Bohner's headlock around that employee."

Vera collapsed in an armchair. The image of Harold, practically in his birthday suit, arms wrapped around a defenseless opponent was shocking and made her sick. She was also disheartened. Vera had worked diligently on this, her highest-profile executive search, and she knew TMC placed a huge bet on its successful outcome. Failure was not an option. Also, a successful hire this quarter would mean a nice, and necessary, bonus.

Given the poor state of TMC, with many of her colleagues walking or getting kicked out the door, Vera was worried about her livelihood. Her concern was complicated by the fact that the progression of her son's disease necessitated expensive medical treatment. TMC's health-care policy covered a bit of that expense, but the company's participation had dwindled as it continually sought profit-margin enhancements. Vera lived under the fear that her son might have to drop out of college and get a job to help make ends meet. She did not want that stress on him. An extra bonus at the end of the quarter could make all the difference.

"So what did Sal tell him, that we haven't found naked aggression to be an effective morale booster?"

Stewart flew off the handle at Vera. He reprimanded her, reminding his direct report that TMC was an equal-opportunity company and would not interfere with someone's inalienable right to milk a cow in his office, let alone post intimidating pictures online.

"I, for one, hope that Harold finds personal fulfillment," Stewart said in a huff.

"So Sal lied to him?"

"Of course he lied to him! We don't need Harold filming the next installment of his management philosophy on TMC's campus."

L X I

The press would not give Carol an inch. Various business news publications reported on troubles from her StreamLINE association. One read:

The Securities and Exchange Commission has launched an investigation into allegations of backdated options at StreamLINE Corporation. A shareholder fraud complaint cited former CEO Carol Himmler (currently running TMC Corporation) as well as the chairman of the StreamLINE board, Tomas Severe, and chairwoman of the compensation committee, Lulu Earl. According to preliminary reports, StreamLINE Corporation may have underreported the value of options awarded to Ms. Himmler when she served as CEO.

Reporter Clare Woodard piled on in *Economic Week*:

> Once a spirited competitor, today TMC is tormented by a paucity of bold
> leaders. Jaded CEO Carol Himmler told this reporter last month that she
> was close to hiring a superstar general manager for the distressed Solutions
> division, but that position remains unfilled. As a result, in addition to
> her day job, Ms. Himmler is now also leading TMC Solutions down a
> black hole. Maybe Ms. Himmler should take a novel approach to improve
> TMC's operating margins by gifting TMC the windfall gains she received
> for weighing StreamLINE down with underperforming acquisitions.

Carol called Stewart to tell him to stop screwing around and get the
Solutions general management job filled ASAP.

LXII

S al dumped his cold coffee in the fruit tree behind him, careful to avoid
a splash on his new suit. With a smile plastered across his face, he
feigned interest in a middle manager who had cornered him at the
technology conference. This manager was one of dozens who, in the course
of a three-day weekend, pitched Sal on the merits of their leadership experiences. According to Stewart, conferences were a good place to find executive
candidates, but given that Sal already had been turned down by virtually all
of the best people for TMC's general management role, he was slumming
his way through B-list prospects at this minor conference.

After lunch, he broke away from the hordes hawking their professional
wares to call his client.

"Stewart, this conference is a waste of time. I spent all this money on
a new wardrobe from the Banana Republic to build credibility with this
crowd. I haven't met one qualified candidate. And I hate these friggin'
clothes!"

Stewart found it hard to understand why Sal was having a difficult time attracting a good candidate to take this great job.

Sal must be doing something wrong, Stewart mulled.

"It must be your pitch, Sal. We're practically a Fortune 100 company! So we have a few problems," Stewart said, assuming he was being helpful.

Sal's phone beeped to indicate another call; he recognized his wife's number. On top of the lousy turn this search had taken, he had accidentally left the details of his itinerary, including his weekend getaway with his mistress, on his wife's voice mail. It had been a long month.

Sal found Stewart's naïveté aggravating. He reminded his client of all the executive candidates he had introduced to TMC, many of whom had been with direct competitors of the company. He jogged Stewart's memory for his own interactions with Carol.

"As you know, Carol's developed a reputation for disposing of her second-in-command once she needs a scapegoat," Sal said. "I'm running out of good material to hook people."

Averaging three depositions a quarter for lawsuits filed by employees who claimed unfair treatment, Stewart was well aware of his CEO's reputation. Secretly, he admired Carol's consummate ability to handcuff the board of directors and protect her flank. The middle-aged and older men on the board were putty in her capable, succulent hands as unrest and a declining stock price swirled around her.

"Of course, there's always brute force, but you had objections to Harold," Sal said, unable to resist the dig.

Desperate to get this search assignment put to rest and Carol and the Maserati franchise off his case, Sal had even tracked down his old partner Kenny Logan. Kenny was working at a pawnshop in New Mexico, where he had gone to lay low after a series of bad bets got him in deep with a Vegas bookie.

Kenny hacked up phlegm as Sal explained his predicament. In the background, another pawnbroker could be heard negotiating the value of a wedding band.

"Sounds like a tough search," Kenny replied. "I don't know this Carol chick, but from what you describe, she sounds like a real hard-ass. Going to be tough to get a big shot to work for her. Maybe you should consider someone who used to work at TMC. They will know the environment and might go back, if you make the compensation sing. Hang on. I read something recently about a guy who used to work there."

Sal heard the pawnbroker close the deal on the wedding ring as Kenny rifled through the papers on his counter.

"Yeah. Here it is. This guy, Dandy Liege, just sold a company. Maybe he's interested in doing something new. I remember him. He was a wunderkind in the supply chain years ago. Must have made a lot of coin when TMC stock went public, because this article says he's been buying and selling businesses the past few years. The company he recently sold manufactured a coating for horseshoes. This is incredible. Where is that quote? 'Mr. Liege's R & D team, currently on sabbatical on a Nepal mountaintop, claimed that the application of this antimicrobial substance to the interior sole of horseshoes mitigates bad karma. The company's clients found this product advantageous, particularly during a championship race.'"

"What the frig? What newspaper is that in?"

"It's last week's *Racing Sheet*."

Sal jotted down the particulars that Kenny remembered about Dandy. As a quid pro quo, Kenny asked his former partner to cover a bet on a horserace. Sal reminded him of the true cost of the last bet that Sal was asked to cover. Sal already had his hands full. Plus, he hedged that a bet on TMC would have much more cash-flow potential than one on Kenny would have. Kenny withdrew his request.

"Hey, I got to go," Kenny said. "It's bingo night on the reservation. There's already a line forming out the door. And you and I, we never talked, right?" Kenny bid Sal good-bye.

Sal pressed Stewart to consider outside-the-box candidates, including TMC alumni. He referenced the recent article about Dandy. Stewart knew there were one or two holdovers from TMC's early days who were still on the board and remembered Dandy fondly. Actually, it was more the money that Dandy's supply-chain activities indirectly made for them that they recalled fondly, but that was a mere nuance. His own relationship with Dandy was strong enough that he ought to be able to deliver him, like a savior, when and if circumstances dictated.

Dandy will need some good media exposure that I can take to the board. Not this horseshit that Sal reads, Stewart said to himself.

Stewart decided that this idea was a keeper, but one he should hold aside for a rainy day. If he needed to use it, he wanted the board to think Dandy was his idea. So he put Sal off the trail.

"Sal, we've discussed this before. We don't like also-rans. Who else do you have on your list?"

Sal was tired and he did not have much of a list, so he acquiesced to another of Stewart's recommendations: He would attend a diversity-focused summit.

"Participating in the InterGender Conference is a smart move, Sal," Stewart encouraged him. "This group sponsored an event in Dallas last quarter that was well attended by senior professionals from many industries. Although I found the participants a bit cliquish, your personal charm should cut through any crowd."

The InterGender Conference turned out to be quite productive and, despite Stewart's insular perspective, inclusive. While Sal was not interested in the seminars (e.g. "A Transgender Guide to Dressing for Success" and "Flexible Spending Accounts and Sex Reassignment Surgery), the food was great and the attendants were inviting. Sal's coolly menacing style played well with the participants. As he could not always accurately identify the sex of his dinner partner, Sal managed to keep the discussion, and his behavior, asexual. He picked up a few leads for new clients. He also managed to coax Pat Reilly, vice president of resolutions for XLNZ, to interview with Carol. When Pat asked how to dress for the interview, Sal suggested business casual, as Pat's sexual identity was not one of the more easily pegged.

LXIII

Abuzz with the prospect of winning a senior leader from a major competitor, TMC leaders also recognized that Pat could be a key diversity hire for the company.

"Can you believe it? We have a candidate who is so diverse, we don't even know if Pat's a man or a woman! This is outstanding!" Stewart squealed with delight as he considered the multiplier on his bonus that quarter. Vera presented Pat's interview schedule and recommendations for topics to cover with this candidate.

"By the way, Sal called," Stewart told Vera. "Pat's engaged. Sal recommended we send a gift to commemorate the engagement. What do you think we should send?"

"To Pat and the betrothed?" Vera wanted to be sure she knew what Stewart was asking.

"Exactly."

"Vase?" That would be innocuous enough, Vera reckoned.

Stewart contemplated this choice. "Maybe too feminine?"

"Hmmm. Bottle of booze?"

"Not feminine enough," said Stewart. "Just in case," he added quickly.

"Champagne?" Vera was running out of ideas.

"Too ambiguous. Might be insulting," he advised.

"Card? Naw. Not enough of a statement," Vera corrected herself.

"Flowers?" Stewart offered.

"How can you go wrong with flowers?" Vera liked Stewart's idea.

With that settled, Vera picked up and examined several pieces of bling that were strewn about Stewart's desk: earrings, cuff links, a money clip, and a pen.

"What's this?" she asked.

TMC was etched in the earrings, and the money clip spelled "TMC" in solid yellow gold. The monogram for the company was underscored by the tagline, "We're IT." The cuff links and pen carried the branding statement in white gold and platinum, respectively. Vera opened the money clip but could not get it to close around a piece of paper.

Stewart pulled it from her. "We are having issues with the hinge."

"Doesn't seem very useful for securing cash," Vera suggested.

Stewart had a fleeting recollection of advice he had received from his divorce attorney some time ago: "Give Mariellen the cash and hold on to the TMC stock options." Turned out, those options had not always been useful in securing cash. Particularly in the past few years, as he waited, watched, and prayed for TMC to recover some value in its stock price, many of his stock options had expired, worthless. Meanwhile, Mariellen was to be married to the former caretaker of the lake house she received in the divorce. His ex-wife's betrothed had taken great pleasure, aided by Mariellen's hefty bank account, in securing someone else to look after the property that he would now lord over.

"What's all this for? And why does it say 'we are information technology' under the TMC logo?" Vera's voice agitated Stewart back to his present issue.

"It doesn't say that. It says, 'We're IT.' It means TMC is the solution you have been looking for. Stop right here. You don't have to go any further to have your problems solved," Stewart explained.

Vera examined the logo thoroughly. "It says all that?"

Stewart had assumed that his days of being exasperated by Vera's uppity ways would be over when he replaced her as his assistant. He collected all the pieces and put them back in their respective boxes. They were destined for the members of the board as a prelude to the launch of TMC's new logo, Stewart's latest marketing initiative.

"Isn't our motto about trust? Here's an idea: Why not create a campaign around value?" Vera asked.

"The 'One Word: Trust' campaign lost credibility," Stewart explained. "Value went out the window when we passed along component price hikes to our customers. This logo is hip. It says TMC is *now*." Once again, he tried to fix the clasp on the money clip.

"*Now?*"

Little did Stewart suspect, nor did he desire, that Vera would have been so successful in the recruiting department that he would end up having to deal with her again on a regular basis. "This jewelry reinforces the upscale value of TMC," he said.

When Stewart leaned forward, something on the side of his face caught Vera's attention.

"What's that on your ear?" she asked.

Stewart felt his ear and smiled. He was wearing a gold post earring carrying the new TMC logo. "I believe all senior executives should demonstrate their commitment to the success of this company," he said.

"What's wrong with a pep rally?" Vera shot back. "How about if you sent a message to worldwide employees thanking them for their efforts during these challenging times? You couldn't hold a press conference describing the good that TMC has done for customers, the community, the workforce, Stewart? Instead you pierced your ears?"

"If you must know, I looked into getting a TMC tattoo, but it turns out that defiling the body is offensive to the indigenous tribes of Madagascar, where we plan to build four manufacturing facilities next year. They have no issues with earrings, however. Besides, Kristie likes it. The executive admins told her they think it's attractive."

At the mention of Kristie, Vera remembered the salary increase Stewart had asked her to process for his administrative assistant. She reflected on the negative state of her own savings account.

Vera's brooding prompted her also to recall a conversation she had had that morning with Charlie Watkins. Her former colleague's practice at CCA Executive Search had flourished. Clients so appreciated Charlie's efforts to recruit the best-qualified executives that they trusted him with more illustrious and lucrative assignments. Although it had not been a typical assignment for Charlie, Vera had been impressed, and very appreciative, when Charlie connected her son Christian to a promising entry-level job with his new client, the Kiddles Corporation. Vera's aggressive management of Christian's medical condition had paid off: Her son was now a thriving young adult. His personal story of overcoming adversity roused the interest of Kiddles's health and beauty aids general manager, helping the young man secure a good job with solid health-care benefits. The Kiddles offer included a scholarship to help Christian continue his education, which lifted a large piece of Vera's financial load.

In spite of his growing practice, Charlie made time to meet with his old colleague and encourage her fervor for equality in the workplace. They had discussed a specific opening with one of his clients, a nongovernmental organization. The NGO was recruiting a human resources consultant to build a program in support of employee benefits and workforce rights. Charlie felt the position offered Vera a chance to help workers across a wide range of industries. The compensation was good, not great, but with Christian well situated, Vera had a little financial flexibility. Charlie knew that this initiative would be something about which Vera could get passionate. Also, he advised that she would have more freedom, and greater opportunities for career growth, within a smaller organization.

Vera looked at Stewart as she thought about her conversation with Charlie.

"What?" Stewart mistook her intense focus as a desire to harangue him further.

Vera shrugged. "Nothing for you to worry about." She walked out of Stewart's office determined to accept Charlie's invitation to interview with his client.

LXIV

The area surrounding baggage carousel number three filled with passengers from the last arriving plane. As they picked up their luggage, the terminal quickly emptied of all but two baggage handlers, a broken baby stroller, a young man completing missing-luggage forms, and one Town Car driver, who called his dispatcher.

"I'm at the airport, and Pat Reilly is a no-show. Yes, I confirmed that with the airline. No, there aren't any more flights coming in this evening. Next flight arrives at 5:54 a.m. Want me to come back in the morning? OK. Call my cell when you decide. I'm going home."

GIANA NOTICED THE blinking message light on the office answering machine. Ever since a bar fight and an unanswered phone call earned Lenny Knuckles an extended stay in the witness protection program, Giana had made it a point to check the answering machine first thing each morning. By the time she had retrieved Lenny's SOS, it had been too late to mitigate exposure of Sal's enterprise. Lenny currently lived under an assumed name in a distant city, courtesy of the FBI. Sal lived under the constant worry that the other shoe would drop and had been regularly irritable ever since.

Despite the loss of his underling, Sal's firm commitment to change his stripes where negotiating techniques were concerned meant that Lenny's absence had not hurt Sal's recruiting operation. And, although Lenny's mother had expressed concern about his abrupt disappearance, his cousins in the Northeast-corridor trucking operation were happy with a fatter envelope each week, so they decided to leave well enough alone.

And, setting aside Sal's irritability, one unforeseen benefit of Lenny's limited mental capacity was that the district attorney had not been able to cobble together enough evidence to invite Sal to participate in a criminal lineup, never mind an actual interrogation by law enforcement. The one significant operational change was that Giana became responsible for bringing the morning doughnuts. She had a regular Saturday night thing going with the local baker, so the pastries had improved considerably.

Eager to get after the business at hand, Giana hit the message button and pulled out a pen and slip of paper. She did not recognize Pat's raspy voice until she had played the recording a few times. That's when the content of the message hit home.

"Sal, I don't think I'm going to be able to make it to the meetings at TMC. I'm sorry for the late notice, but something came up. Call me."

Giana dialed Sal's cell phone immediately and relayed the message.

"I'm over here friggin' wondering why I'm getting all these frantic messages from Stewart and Vera," Sal responded.

"Didn't you call them back?" Giana could not believe Sal would not have returned calls from his best client.

"Tell you the truth, Giana, those TMC guys have been driving me friggin' nuts lately. They whine about every candidate we introduce: 'We don't think this candidate has enough intellectual horsepower.' Or, 'I can't put my finger on it, but this candidate is not the right fit.' I just wanted one good night's sleep before they started complaining about Pat."

"What's that?" Giana said. "Are you at home? That didn't sound like your wife."

"Whateva. I've been entertaining another possible client." Sal lifted a pink silk negligee off the floor and placed it on a side chair.

"Sal, that's terrific. We need diversification around here!" Giana was overjoyed with the possibility of not having to jump at Carol's commands anymore. She left Sal to pick up the pieces with Pat.

SAL HAD LEARNED the hard way that it was best to assume a constructive tone in conversations with candidates. However, after the browbeating his wife had given him when her credit card was rejected at three high-end boutiques, he was really aggravated.

Man or no man, Pat deserved to be told off, Sal thought. Even if Sal took his Maserati payments out of the equation, it was bad form to cancel business interviews at the last moment. Sal dialed Pat's office number. He connected to a recorded message directing him to speak or type in the extension of the person he was trying to reach.

"Fuck. I don't know the extension!"

The recorded voice responded to Sal, "I didn't understand you. Please speak or type the extension number. Thank you."

Sal reluctantly punched zero and waited for an operator to join the line. After two or three minutes, the line was disconnected.

"For chrissake!" Sal dialed Pat's cell phone number. His internal voice cautioned him to hear Pat out. He swallowed hard and initiated the conversation with a friendly greeting. Pat immediately requested a few moments to return the call.

"I'll step outside and call you back on this line from a pay phone in the candy store on the corner," Pat said.

Sal hung up. "What a friggin' mess."

A few moments later, Sal's phone rang.

"Sal, I'm sorry about this cloak and dagger stuff, but one of my co-workers approached me yesterday," Pat said. "He told me point-blank that the XLNZ higher-ups knew I was meeting with TMC."

Sal remembered how thrilled Stewart had been to hear that Pat was a diversity candidate.

They were so hard up to close this search and generate good news, I bet Stewart or Carol leaked this to somebody, Sal thought.

"Now, wait a minute, Pat. Let's remember why you were interested in TMC in the first place. What is XLNZ doing for you? What about your financial future?"

"Sal, TMC's stock price is at a new fifty-two-week low."

Sal felt his qualified, diverse executive candidate slipping away.

"Pat, there are a lot of people on Wall Street who would tell you that this is the right time to join, to lock in a low strike price on your stock options."

Sal refocused the discussion around Carol's leadership. He referenced his personal experience, having seen her turn around the fortunes of several companies. He did not feel the need to elaborate on how those fortunes had turned.

"Sal, it's too late. XLNZ just asked me to run Europe. I've wanted an international assignment for a long time. TMC can't offer me anything like this. And they probably couldn't match the salary increase that XLNZ is giving me."

Pat's emotional state changed from fear and concern to annoyance and anger as the discussion moved to speculation about how XLNZ found out about the interviews.

"Sal, I don't know whom I can trust at TMC. And, to add insult to injury, they sent flowers to congratulate me and Chris on our engagement."

Sal, unaware of the floral gift but also not clear about why Pat would find flowers offensive, was confused.

"Flowers?"

"Yeah, Sal! What's that supposed to mean? They came from TMC's HR department, too! I would have hoped that that team would have been enlightened!"

Pat took a few deep breaths to calm down. After all, none of this was Sal's doing.

"Look, Sal. I am sorry about what this means for you, but it actually turned out pretty well for me. Good luck on the search, but please don't call me again."

Sal considered a few painful ways he could pay Pat back and was about to detail them for his candidate when a text message from his wife beeped in. He glanced at her text:

"I NO where U R. U slime-bucket. Too bad about the boat. Call meeeeeee!!!"

Sal capitulated on account of this more immediate and perilous situation, letting loose only a few relatively mild expletives. Then he hung up on his third candidate for the TMC Solutions general manager position.

A new text message came in, from Giana.

"Vera is looking for Pat. Interviews start in thirty minutes. What do I do???"

Sal wrote back that Pat Reilly was a late scratch.

"And tell TMC to eighty-six the flowers going forward."

L X V

"**S**tewart, why am I hearing from Jill that my top-notch, gender-ambiguous candidate from our major competitor missed his plane?" Carol grilled him.

Stewart remembered the days of management consulting, when he was paid for advice whether it was good or bad. Back then, he presupposed that the perks and power that accompanied a senior corporate job would be worth the personal sacrifices necessary to climb that career ladder. Today, as he fretted about answering his CEO, he longed for those early-career days of nonaccountability.

Stewart reminded his boss that the candidate "may have missed his or her plane. We can't be sure."

"Whatever! Why wasn't Pat Reilly on that plane?"

Stewart was running out of scapegoats. Charlie had left long ago for the financially more rewarding and less encumbered executive-search business. Harry Habet had assumed more-senior human resources leadership roles at a succession of different companies after departing TMC. As TMC's most senior executive recruiter, he needed Vera on his side to get through the agenda he had for this trying year, so he did not want to get her nose out of joint by getting Carol mad at her. What's more, Stewart blamed so many day-to-day things on Vera that he sensed it would not sit well with the CEO if he laid this one at Vera's feet, too.

"Carol, I know you are close to Sal," he said. "He's done good work for us in the past, but lately he seems to have lost his touch."

Carol found this line of reasoning compelling, especially given the irrational behavior of the past few candidates, all of whom Sal had recommended. Also, she was always keeping an ear to the ground for an opportunity to break Sal's hold on her. If Stewart were the heavy and took Sal to task because of the failures on this search, Sal could not hold Carol accountable. Even if he did get annoyed, Sal was smart enough to figure out that they could all be out of TMC if the Solutions general management job did not get filled soon.

"Someone's head is going to roll because of this, and it won't be mine, Stewart. I've been quoted as saying the Solutions leadership role is key to our business reversal. I may be forced to make changes."

Having been responsible for processing all the changes Carol had been making in the executive suite, Stewart knew exactly what it could mean for his future career, not to mention his current pocketbook. Sal was definitely the problem. That settled, Stewart put on his chief administrative officer hat. It was time to demonstrate achievement against his quarterly bonus goals. He suggested a stock buyback program.

"Companies start buyback programs when the stock is undervalued, at least that's what the public thinks," he said. "We might be able to create the impression that we are better off than we are."

Carol mulled it over. She needed to do something that would make the company appear desirable. Her recommendation of another public offering of TMC stock had not been met with enthusiasm. Wall Street was being selective about what it would support, and the board did not believe that TMC had the growth projections to garner the attention needed.

"A stock buyback might just work," she said. "Good thing we moved Emily over to treasury. Tell her to persuade Mercedes that it's a good idea."

LXVI

Lee Kemp, a retired but still highly sought-after software executive, was enjoying the sun, the pool, and the top-shelf margaritas on the inaugural Festival Line cruise to Bora Bora. He might have continued to enjoy this family outing, organized for his dad's seventy-fifth birthday, had it not been for the call Sal received from the president of the leasing company that held his note on the Maserati.

The salesman that Sal had been dealing with since he purchased the car was out on medical leave. His accounts had been reassigned to an efficient and ambitious bookkeeper at the leasing company. She was well aware that salespeople's ability to maneuver revenue reports was rivaled only by their manipulation of customers' critical thinking skills. She easily discovered that Sal was behind in payments on a $100,000 automobile and promptly reported it to her supervisor.

As a result of the call from the leasing company, and the prospect of wasting another weekend with underqualified and overstuffed shirts at a recruiting conference, Sal booked the Festival Line berth next door to Lee. He managed to bump Aunt Betty from the Captain's Table, joining the birthday celebration in time to toast the elder Mr. Kemp with Dom Pérignon. His father was duly impressed by the champagne, and the well-bred younger Lee agreed to a nightcap with Sal.

Kristie relayed Sal's ship-to-shore message the following morning.

"Stewart, Sal says to line up interviews for Lee Kemp. He can fly into town on the twenty-second of the month and meet the whole team."

Stewart acknowledged the message. And he hoped for the best. But he already had his backup strategy in the works, just in case Lee Kemp turned out to be a stiff suit.

LXVII

Tired of the midday work stoppages created by employees "innocently" spilling coffee on computer servers or by having to repair tires sliced by debris from late-night drag racing of the company's otherwise underutilized shuttle buses, several bitter co-workers reached out to Vera. Given her proximity to the leader of the human capital management function, they hoped that she might be able to influence their plight.

Countless corporate reorganizations saddled TMC's remaining workforce with heavier responsibilities and longer workdays. And there were indignities, too. A few employees were asked to interview for their own, newly outsourced jobs, and others were asked to train less-skilled, less-expensive replacements before they were shown the door. The lurking fear of being terminated infected the collective conscience of those who did not get the boot. It was not long before laptops began disappearing at alarming rates; direct deposits of executive payroll experienced higher-than-average glitches; and, soon after TMC's match on the company's savings plan was discontinued, a roasted pig was anonymously delivered to Carol's weekly staff meeting. All were palpable symptoms of employee dissatisfaction. Vera was persuaded to take action.

Although Stewart was irritated by the amount of disposable income he had to allocate to the removal of tomato stains from his clothing and car, he reminded Vera of Ted's mandate when Stewart first joined the company: "Make sure the executives get what they need when they want it. Make sure they have the right team to get the job done, and don't get in their way." Stewart left out the part about getting rid of people who screwed up because by now that was standard operating procedure.

"Vera, I fail to see how addressing employee rage is HR's responsibility," he concluded.

With her entreaties on behalf of co-workers falling on Stewart's deaf ears, Vera summoned her courage and set up an appointment with Carol.

"Carol, I figure you want to have a finger on the pulse of what's going on in this company," Vera said to open their meeting.

"Of course!" Carol replied. Jill had made sure Carol had not seen this meeting on her calendar until it was too late to cancel it. She knew what Vera was going to say, and she wanted her boss to hear it.

"You must have noticed that a lot of employees are fed up with all the demands and the extra time they must spend at the office just to get their work done," Vera said.

"Vera, if there are people who are not working efficiently, we need to get rid of them. Who are they?"

"Carol, that's not the point. These are loyal and hardworking people."

Vera explained that as each rightsizing seemingly brought TMC's financial situation into greater balance by lowering operating expense, the workload increased exponentially for those employees whose positions had not been resized. Although employees had been assured of enhanced team structures and streamlined work processes, the only clear difference each time had been more work.

"Vera, it's good for the soul to be challenged."

Taking a different approach, Vera offered compelling data. Overtime hours for nonexempt employees had tripled during the past two quarters, a period of time when workforce reductions, segment reorganizations, and team consolidations were commonplace. She argued that the downsizings might not make financial sense in the long run because overtime compensation amounted to 150 percent of regular earnings.

"Also, there are talented professionals who are talking about quitting," Vera said. "Some employees have taken to bad-mouthing TMC on the blogs. None of this is good for our company."

"Vera, I am on the cover of at least three national magazines a year," Carol said. "Think of the salaries these workers could command if they left TMC after having worked for me. In fact, HR should really think through how to ensure we are getting the most out of these employees now, because if they leave TMC, we won't get anything else out of them."

Vera took yet another crack at it. She reminded Carol that during the most recent round of layoffs, the so-called secure list of people to be axed got leaked to the local paper. Several vendors had rushed to take candy machines out of buildings before TMC employees knew that their plant would be closed.

"The employees are dispirited," Vera said.

Carol handed Vera the *Economic Week* article in which she was quoted as claiming that TMC's savior would emerge from the search for a new general manager to run the Solutions business.

"Vera, there is a lot of pressure on me to turn this company around," Carol said. "You really want to prevent your friends from getting fired? Then get this search over with ASAP!"

Recognizing that she was dealing with a much darker, more sinister, force than other TMC executives, for whom a carefully placed tack or a wink and a nod to the facilities team to loosen a few screws would register her dis-approval, Vera backed out of Carol's office and proceeded directly to church.

There's nothing left but prayer, she thought.

LXVIII

W hen TMC's stock price hit $20 per share, Wall Street demanded cost reductions, and investors called for significant change. Stewart led an HR investigation to find out who had commandeered Carol's e-mail address and sent termination notices to her direct reports. The guilty party cleverly covered his IT tracks, though, and Stewart, who had not received a recommendation to seek employment else-where, was held in contempt by his colleagues. The pretense of executive camaraderie that he had carefully nurtured year after year was shot to shit.

The financial press beat Carol up for taking too long to get TMC back on track. They had gotten wind of Lee Kemp's interest in the company and encouraged TMC to take the plunge with this well-regarded executive.

Even the board, though inured by the compensation increases Carol lulled them with each spring, had begun to tire of the regular lambasting that TMC and their association with the company took in the press. They got their respective heads out of the sand long enough to issue a stern warn-ing to Carol: She was not invited to their annual golf retreat.

"Close that deal with Lee Kemp, goddamn it! He can revitalize this company!" Carol roared at Stewart after complaining that this executive search had taken way too long. Now that they had a solid candidate who had credibility with Wall Street and was genuinely interested in turning the business around, Carol wanted him on board yesterday.

"And do something about improving operating expense in the meantime!"

When Stewart said he was perplexed regarding what he could do about operating expense because he was in lowly human capital management and

Carol was the senior executive officer, Carol offered him a few choices. He chose the least painful, for him.

STEWART LED A discussion with his team after they had completed another round of layoffs.

"I know that this comprehensive restructuring exercise was difficult, but, as hard as it is for you to inform an employee that his position is being eliminated, believe it or not, it is harder for an employee to hear that."

The HR Managers looked at each other in confusion.

Stewart counseled that Project Deliverance, the code name for this most recent company rightsizing, had been necessary to support a new approach to product development and customer interaction. He encouraged his team to consider the tremendous opportunities ahead for the company.

"These reductions in workforce are a distraction, but it's over for now, so get back to your work."

Nothing. Not a peep from the audience, and no one moved.

Time to inspire the team, Stewart decided.

"Don't allow these human capital actions to consume all your attention, or we might think we should have RIF'd you instead of your colleagues," he said.

Everyone in the room looked up.

Stewart smiled. *Finally. I reached them.*

LXIX

Normally unfettered, Sal was anxious throughout his call with Lee Kemp. Lee had great credentials, superior skills, and a bank account that would indicate he did not need to work for any company. He had made a big impression on the TMC board and aced the psychological tests required of all executive candidates. Sal could not fathom what might happen if Lee turned down TMC's offer. Aside from the obvious strain to the company's leadership and the further drag on the business, Sal's wife was on the rampage again. After her gynecologist determined that an unspecified sexually transmitted disease was the cause of severe abdominal cramping (which had started not long after Sal returned from the cruise), she hired an architect to design an extension on their home.

So obsessed with closing this deal, Sal did not get off on the right foot.

"Above everything else, Lee, Carol has so much credibility," he said.

"Are we talking about the same woman who regularly gets beat up in the financial press for mishandling rudimentary business issues?" Lee replied.

Sal defended his position.

"HEY! Those reporters are out for themselves. Some of them are even on the competitors' payrolls. I know how that works, because I used to be in that business."

"Journalism?"

"Extortion."

Lee was confused, and concerned.

"Whateva," Sal said. "You can't take a joke or something?"

Sal laughed loudly, but he knew his anxiety was getting the best of him. Quickly contemplating his options, he decided to cut out the small talk and present TMC's compensation proposal to Lee.

It turned out that the full-court press was not needed—Lee had done his homework. Bad press aside, TMC's long-term business fundamentals were sound, supported by Mercedes Rodriguez and her strong financial leadership team. Lee would not have to worry about a financial restatement. Also, the board of directors, while weak, was showing signs of weariness with Carol's leadership. That might open up a shot at the CEO role sooner than Sal or Carol figured. And Lee felt that TMC had decent footholds in the right services markets to succeed—with the appropriate executive inspiration, which Lee felt he could offer.

Sal leapt out of his chair when Lee stated that TMC was the type of challenge that got his juices going.

"Tell them I will join TMC, Sal, assuming my attorney agrees with the terms in the offer letter."

"You won't regret this, Lee."

The strain of this executive search had taken a toll on Sal's personal habits. His media room–turned–office wastebaskets overflowed with invitations to leadership events. Broken pencils and dried-out pens filled his desk drawers. Business magazine clippings covered his desktop. He rummaged around the paper-strewn desk for a functioning writing utensil and something to write on, finally scribbling Lee's name and the address and phone number of Lee's vacation home on a sticky note, which he stuck to his desk calendar.

"I'll let Stewart know you are at your cabin and get this contact info to him," Sal said. "He'll put the financial proposal into an offer letter for you right away."

Sal congratulated Lee once again and hung up to call Stewart with the good news. But before he could dial Stewart's number, Sal's cell phone rang. It was the big boss.

"Oh, hey boss … I'm always in a good mood, boss. Nope, we haven't finished that TMC search yet. Tell you the truth, those guys are screwing me on the money they owe me. Don't know if I'm ever going to see it. You know those corporate types. Always trying to put the muscle on the little guy."

Sal tidied up as he listened. Feeling his anxiety lift, he rearranged the objects on his desk and then rearranged them again. He stacked magazine articles in one pile, neatly arranging the corners so they lined up. He stuffed a paper cup with dirty napkins and crumpled bits of paper and winked at his cousin Ernie as the young hoodlum joined him. Quietly taking a seat beside Sal's desk, Ernie deduced from Sal's tone and word choice that he was talking to the big boss.

"Fuggedaboudit." Sal smirked at the information the boss shared. He picked up the sticky note with Lee's personal contact information and moved it around on his fingers as the boss described a business situation.

"No fuckin' way. What nerve!" Sal slammed his hand down on the table. As the conversation continued, Sal's hand gestures indicated further astonishment. He picked up his pen again and wrote information from the boss on another sticky note.

"I got it. Yeah, yeah. No worries," Sal signed off. Feeling uncomfortable, he looked at his desk and moved things back to their messy places.

"The boss wants us to do this job." Sal handed his cousin a sticky note with a name, phone number, and address.

"Got it," Ernie said as he put the sticky note in his pocket. "You look a little stressed, boss."

"Stressed? Me? No friggin' way. I'm relieved! I closed this big, pain-in-the-ass search today. And if ever a guy needed closing! Turns out, this guy is a great guy on top of it. I really like him. I'm going to talk to him about some business ideas I got after he gets a little time under his belt at TMC."

Sal smiled broadly and took a deep, relaxing breath. He stretched, put his feet up on the desk, and lit a cigar.

"D'you know I thought this executive search business was a breeze when we first earned this partnership? Couldn't believe people were making this kind of money without getting dirty. Then I started trying to close these executive candidates. These guys, and girls too, they been sitting high on the hog for so long, they're a bunch of pansy asses when it comes to making a change. Tell me, how hard is this to figure out: You're an executive. You got one job, pays you a six-figure salary, and at the end of the year you get a cash bonus."

"They gotta wait a year to get any extra incentive?" Ernie asked. "That seems a long time to me."

"In the meantime, they get stock in the company. Equity. A long-term investment. Imagine you didn't have to worry about who's going to take care of your ma with the Weimaraner Syndrome."

"Ma's got Alzheimer's."

"Whateva. Don't interrupt. So, you got a nice chunk of cash for the week, more cash at Christmastime, and, in between, your company's stock goes up and your future's looking bright. It's all good, right?"

"Sounds good if I don't have to worry about ma no more."

"Did I say or did I not say don't interrupt?"

"Sorry, Sal."

"Now along comes another company. They are going to increase your weekly take-home, give you more money at Christmastime, AND this company's growing or maybe it's in a turnaround situation."

"A what?"

"You know. It's like when things aren't going so good down at the docks and we've got to make it right."

"They use bats at big companies, too?"

"Am I ever going to get to finish this story?" Sal sneered at his lieutenant, and Ernie conceded the floor. Sal enlightened his cousin with a tutorial on why companies, be they in growth mode or turnaround situations, required additional executive talent. Furthermore, he explained that, to sufficiently motivate executives to leave one organization and join another, the acquiring company offered more money and more stock. Private jets, country clubs, and other forms of red-carpet treatment were also often rolled out to turn heads. "Some candidates even get fruit baskets," Sal said.

It annoyed him that so many executives were not grateful. "All this, and a lot of these people whine: 'I don't know if this job is the right career move for me.' Or they say, 'My son's team made all-state last season. I'd hate to make him move before his senior year.'" Sal mimicked a pathetic executive complaining.

"I wanna say, 'Are you friggin' crazy? Get off your ass, be a man, and tell your spoiled-brat son where he is going to school. Buy him a scholarship with the additional money you're going to get!'"

"Makes sense to me." Ernie bit his fingernails as he took note of his boss's problems.

"But I can't fuckin' say that. I did it once, and the candidate dropped out when we were going to make an offer! He told the HR manager that he felt intimidated by me. I told the HR manager that that guy was intimidated by the truth. Then I had to go out and find a different imbecile to court and pray he didn't do anything stupid like turn down the job. That was an expensive lesson to learn. I won't do that again."

One of Ernie's attributes was that he knew when he was out of his league. He was getting a headache trying to figure out Sal's recruiting business, so he decided to focus on the job he knew.

Ernie checked the address on the sticky note. Out of the area. "When's this job need doin'?"

Sal gave Ernie a steely-eyed look.

"Yeah. OK." Ernie put his jacket on. "See ya around."

The next morning, after several attempts, Sal finally reached Carol at her desk. He wanted to boast about how his negotiating prowess closed Lee. She did not care what Sal did to convince Lee. But she was elated that this job was filled.

"That's great news, Sal. We really need Lee. By the way, we don't want him changing his mind, so we should stay close. I'll call to congratulate him."

"Don't worry. I made sure nobody could shoot holes in this deal," Sal assured his client.

In the midafternoon, Carol called Sal back.

"Sal, I haven't reached Lee yet. Hope he isn't changing his mind! Can you try him?"

Sal's antenna went up. *Not again. Shit. I should have known this was too good to be true.*

Sal called Lee's cell phone, then his vacation home. His wife had not heard from him all day. It was unusual behavior, and she was worried. Sal asked if she was excited about the move. Yeah, sure, she said. She agreed that a house with a pool and wine cellar would be good for resale value.

"Well, let him know I was thinking of him," Sal closed. "Just calling to say hello."

Sal was disgusted with himself. *Do people really talk like that?* All the same, Sal had been glad to hear that Lee's wife was positive about relocating.

He's not going to back out of this deal now. He felt relieved again.

Later that afternoon, well past the time to start the gravy for supper, Ernie hurried in. Sal much preferred his cousin's sauce to his wife's, so Ernie had been deputized in the kitchen as well as in other aspects of Sal's affairs. Somewhat disheveled, Ernie exchanged his jacket for an apron and inspected several tomatoes Giana had left sitting on the bar.

"Where the hell you been, and why you look such a mess?" Sal asked.

"I did the thing. It was a long drive, so I stayed overnight in the area," Ernie laughed. "Plus, the other side was slow to the negotiating table. In fact, I would say that he didn't want to do the deal at all."

Extracting a plastic cutting board from the cupboard above the bar, Ernie quickly diced the tomatoes. He looked around for a bowl. Finding a clean container for the tomatoes amid the used espresso cups, empty San Pellegrino water bottles, and old newspapers proved difficult. Ernie, too, would be glad when the TMC search was over and Sal returned to his meticulous self. Without Sal's constant nitpicking, Ernie's natural slovenliness and Giana's indifference took root.

"But you helped him see the light," Sal smiled at Ernie.

"Yeah, if you consider heaven a form of light." Ernie chuckled again.

"You're wearing your lunch on your shirt."

"That's not lunch. It's the job." Ernie wiped his silk shirt with a cloth. He threw the cloth into the wastebasket. Sal retrieved the stained cloth, placed his lighter to one end, and put it in an ashtray to burn.

"Whateva," Ernie said. "Consider it done. Closed, like you said." Ernie scraped the tomatoes into the only clean espresso cup he could find.

"Yeah." Sal flipped through a newspaper on top of the bar. His eye fixed on an advertisement for imported leather jackets.

It would be nice to have a new jacket when the boat gets out of the body shop, he thought. *That oughta teach me to leave baseball bats onboard. Who knew my wife had such a swing?* Sal shook his head at the thought of his wife smashing a hole in the side of his boat.

He looked up suddenly.

"Closed?" he asked.

"Yeah. Closed. Like you said yesterday, 'We gotta close this guy.' I closed him."

"What guy? What guy are you talking about?" Sal was anxious.

"The guy you and the boss was discussing yesterday. You know. The THING. Here. Where the hell is that paper?" Ernie checked his pockets. "Oh, here it is. It stuck to my wallet." Ernie handed Sal the sticky note with Lee's name and address scribbled on it.

"Lee Kemp! You whacked Lee Kemp! He's my candidate for the TMC job!!"

"Why'd you want to whack your candidate?"

"I didn't want to whack him. I wanted to whack . . ." Sal looked on his desk for the sticky note with the contact information of the actual intended victim. "Here! Here is the guy that needs whacking. This job is still not done."

"The boss is gonna be pissed." Ernie was worried.

"The BOSS is gonna be pissed? What about Carol, when she realizes her new employee is dead!" Sal paused. "He is dead, isn't he?"

"What? Do I look like an amateur?" Now Ernie was insulted.

"What did you use?"

"The new blade I got last year. It was perfection. I got traction with it during the hunting season."

"Maybe he's not dead! Remember the guy down on the shore with the thing?" Sal needed to be hopeful.

"That was years ago. I was very young. I don't make those mistakes no more."

"Hey, do you know how hard this search has been? I don't have any other breathing candidates lying around!" Sal was emotionally spent. Besides the injury to his sense of style and decorum, managing divergent business models was taking a psychological toll.

Tired from the job earlier in the day and feeling wrongfully accused, Ernie went on the offensive.

"This isn't my fault! Look at all the shit in this place. Every time I want to watch a game, I gotta search for the TV remote control buried under a bunch of clothes you normally wouldn't be caught dead in. Never mind I can't find a decent place to sit and read the newspaper because there's resumes covering the couch. No wonder the papers got messed up. Your client lady will understand. She's the CEO of a company. She must know how stress can affect the workplace."

Sal bit his tongue. He needed a plan.

"Maybe we should call an ambulance. Where is he?" Sal asked.

"Where's who?"

"Where's the job?"

"Which one? The job that got done by mistake or the one that still needs to get done?" Ernie truly did not understand.

Sal hissed at his cousin.

"In a Dumpster behind a convenience store," Ernie said.

"We'll call 9-1-1 and give them an anonymous tip. Maybe if they can get an IV in him in time—when did this happen?" Sal started dialing.

"A while ago. You might want to tell the ambulance to bring blood, too. A lot of blood," Ernie suggested.

Sal gave Ernie a stern look.

"What? I thought he WAS the job. What the fuck! Where's that other paper? I gotta go do that thing now before the boss calls again."

LXX

Stewart could not believe his bad luck when Lee Kemp turned up dead. He was in Washington DC to accept an award from the Democratic Association for Rewarding Executives (DARE), an organization dedicated to championing compensation ambiguity within the executive suite. The previous autumn, Stewart had thrown his body down in front of the chauffeur-driven sedans taking members of Congress to vote on a bill requiring transparency in executive compensation. As a result of his action and the heavy foot of one of the chauffeurs, the limelight shifted to an ambulance whisking Stewart to the hospital. Several congressmen, hastily chasing the TV news trucks, missed the vote, requiring the legislation to be tabled. Subsequently it was decided that further review of the issue was warranted, which dimmed the transparency of executive compensation for the foreseeable future.

Stewart was presented with the organization's greatest honor, a bronze-plated treasure chest filled with coins and semiprecious jewels, in recognition of his no-holds-barred defense of DARE's raison d'être. As photographers snapped pictures of him shaking hands with the CEOs of several multinational companies, he imagined his own CEO on the warpath after having lost another highly publicized candidate. Stewart knew what the buzz would be at TMC. He knew his seat at the movers-and-shakers table was under siege. He wanted to enjoy a little peace and attention before he was sucked back into the fray.

After the DARE event, Stewart ratcheted up his battle plan. The first step was to set up the players. He called Clare and complimented her excellent reportage on Dandy's productive life after TMC. Her article was even better than Stewart had imagined it could be when he suggested the angle to the journalist.

Clare had been fishing for a positive human-interest plot in the aftermath of a conversation with her editor about a downward trend in *Economic Week*'s circulation and the editor's alarm upon discovering a bull's-eye sketched around a photo of Carol that was taped to Clare's computer. Stewart was fishing, too: His desire to get Dandy exposure that would make him seem relatively normal, if not downright extraordinary, was the bait for Clare. The human resources executive offered to introduce his reclusive friend to the reporter desperate for a hook. In her article, Clare portrayed the former operations executive as having reinvented himself as an all-around general manager. Her feature on Dandy was to be the first in a series, "Gray Is the New Green: Reduce, Reuse, and Recycle Retired Business Executives."

Clare also felt obliged to offer congratulations to Stewart on the publication of a recent TMC employee survey. Many HR consultants had cited the study as an example of the superior work one could expect from a leading-edge human capital management team. However, uncertain about the survey's significance and confused about its findings, *Economic Week* had declined to include the results in its series on workforce planning.

Hurt that Clare's magazine had decided against publishing or even referencing his groundbreaking work on employee motivation, Stewart crowed that the assessment reinforced TMC's strengths as an employer of choice.

"We are fortunate to have a workforce we can learn from," Stewart told her. "Fifty-seven percent of those who responded believe that 99 percent of employees didn't know why this survey was important. Forty percent believe that half the workforce judges the survey to be useless. Another 3 percent didn't understand the question. With the right focus on this issue, I think we can eliminate that last category."

Assuming that Clare felt guilty about discounting his survey, Stewart took advantage of his time with the journalist. He knew she liked to keep the heat on Carol, and this often bolstered Stewart's value to the CEO, so he tried to season her perspective with his opinions about the Solutions general manager search as deep background for another article she was working on.

Stewart's next move was to shuffle the balance of power. He called Bill Zilch, TMC's general counsel.

L X X I

S al fully expected to be called on Carol's carpet to explain the latest debacle, but he considered it heavy-handed, and incredibly ignorant, of Stewart to set up a meeting with the general counsel.

That SOB. To think I was puffing him up and teaching him how to work the board. Sal was irked.

Bill Zilch was one of the few senior TMC executives in whose hiring Sal had not had a hand. He had been an entry-level attorney on Chemix's legal team when Carol first worked with him. His father's standing with the homeowners association of a community surrounding a Chemix plant helped the company negotiate a reasonable damage settlement when containers leaked chemicals into the area's soil. Carol had vouched for Bill's efficacy, if not his ethics, which helped the attorney secure TMC's top legal job many years later. Thus, Bill, seventieth out of seventy-two graduates of the 1998 class of eLegal University, was TMC's general counsel.

Lori Valle, a human capital generalist whom Stewart had assigned to take notes throughout the meeting, sat at one end of the conference table as Sal took a seat at the opposite end. Bill joined Lori at her end, hoping to intimidate Sal by creating distance between the TMC team and the executive search consultant. To the contrary, it provoked Sal.

Lori, hoping for a promotion and thus eager to demonstrate how tough she could be, opened up on Sal.

"Mr. Scruci, TMC is paying very good money to your firm to find qualified candidates for critical executive positions. Lately, we've experienced one mishap after another. As a result, we are up in search-firm fees but in the red relative to important headcount. I'm talking real money, not blood pints, Mr. Scruci."

Except for a slight flare in his nostrils, Sal sat completely still.

Lori continued. "We are a growing company. I'm certain there are other executive-search firms who would like our business."

Bill, who wisely figured that outright threatening would get them nowhere, interrupted.

"Uh, we all know why we're here. We've got an opening for an imperative executive role, and we are losing candidates. I know there might be a logical reason why this is happening, Sal, but TMC is concerned about the damage to our image."

Bill paused, waiting for Sal to say something defensive, but Sal said nothing. He placed his hands on the conference table, his increasingly active nostrils drawing breaths deep into his lungs to control his temper.

Bill returned to his script somewhat nervously, sensing Sal's anger. He might not have graduated at the top of his legal class, but, having spent his youth in south Boston, Bill was not blind to the machinations of the street. "Sal, we feel that TMC could have been put in a compromising situation because of . . ."

"What are you insinuating?" Sal finally spoke.

Bill felt Sal's unblinking eyes pierce him. He wondered if the executive recruiter could see through his clothes. He pulled out a handkerchief and wiped the sweat from his brow.

"Well, one of the candidates is . . . er . . . no longer—"

"No longer what?"

Although he had not moved a muscle, somehow Sal now appeared much larger to Bill.

"Well, he's certainly no longer a candidate."

"How is that my fault?" Sal pushed Bill.

Beads of sweat rolled down the general counsel's forehead, interfering with his ability to read from his notes.

"Yes?" Sal remained extremely calm and focused.

Bill cleared his throat loudly and choked on his phlegm. The right look from Sal often invoked this involuntary response in people. Bill wracked his brain for a safe way out.

"Sal, it appears we haven't interviewed enough women for this general manager role. Your recruiting efforts and the lack of female candidates might have put TMC in a compromising situation."

Sal pushed back. "Did it?"

"No, but it could have. You must know that TMC is an equal-opportunity employer, and we require that all of our suppliers be supportive of our goals. Have you had diversity training?"

Sal watched as Lori meticulously captured this repartee with pen and paper. "Lori, make sure you get all this down," he said.

Bill's hands shook as he reached for a can of diet soda. He knocked it over, spilling the contents on Lori, who jumped up.

"Oh, fuck. I'm sorry." Bill said.

Sal made a strategic move. "Bill, if you don't mind, I find that language inappropriate in this setting."

Bill became more nervous and embarrassed. He apologized. "I know. I've got to watch my language. I'm not in Boston anymore." He attempted a weak smile.

"Look, it's not like I'm unaccustomed to the bawdy language of truck drivers, but you would never hear me use that language in a business setting, especially when there's a lady present."

Lori appreciated Sal's sensitivity, particularly since Bill had stolen her thunder with his weak-kneed interrogation. She nodded politely in Sal's direction, then turned to Bill and announced tartly: "I'll be going to the ladies' room now to try to salvage this couture skirt."

Extracting a promise from Sal to find more female candidates, the emasculated and psychologically eviscerated general counsel ended the meeting. The entire episode accomplished little other than to rub Sal the wrong way.

I'll fix that Moondoggie knockoff, Sal vowed.

LXXII

A few nights later, Sal dreamed of revving the foot pedal of a humming silver sports car, the wind lifting his hair as he sped down the coastline. When he came to a light at the intersection of Life's Breezeway and Equity Lane, a buxom twentysomething blonde asked for a ride. As he reached across to open the passenger door, his hand fell on the handle of a midsize sedan. He watched as the entire Maserati was converted into a sputtering, lime-green Saturn, and his kittenish companion ran away. He checked his location again. The street signs now read TMC Alley and Narciss Drive. A police car pulled up behind him.

"Sal! Sal! Sal, wake up. There are cops outside."

Sal's wife shook him awake. Headlights of two police vehicles crisscrossed his bedroom ceiling. Muffled voices called out orders in the yard below them.

Sal told his wife to call his lawyer. He took a pistol and a chunk of cash from under his side of the mattress and dropped them in the hamper.

He walked carefully down the staircase, straining to listen to the voices outside. His mind raced for an idea of what might have tipped off the police.

Friggin' Lenny must have remembered something good.

As Sal got closer, he peered through a side window and saw an ambulance pull up. Paramedics rushed into his neighbor's house. Six or seven cops milled about, appearing relaxed. The activity was evidently focused on the accountant who lived next door.

Curiosity got the best of Sal. Maybe the accountant had cooked the books of some big company. If that were the case, the company would need a new accountant. He stuck a few business cards in his pocket and told his wife not to call his attorney after all.

Sal walked outside in his bare feet. He cut across the side yard to his neighbor's house.

"Aw, shit." He had stepped in something soft and smelly.

"That's about right, sir." A police officer approached from the back of the house. "Bear shit, probably."

Sal examined the bottom of his foot and wiped it off on the grass.

"Bear shit?"

"Yep, we've had a few sightings these past few weeks. They are coming down from the hills looking for food. But this is our first mauling." The officer held his nose as he handed tissues to Sal.

"Mauling?"

"Your neighbor came home late, saw the garbage hadn't been put out yet, and wanted to get a jump on it before the morning. Regrettable for him, there was a full-grown male bear also trying to get a jump on the garbage."

"What happened?"

"When a wild animal is confronted, it will do one of two things. It will either run away to fight another day or it will attack. This animal was mighty hungry and aggressive. Fortunately, the bear underestimated its foe. Your neighbor's pretty banged up, but he'll live. Our guys got the bear, too, so he won't be bothering your neighborhood anymore."

Sal refrained from shaking hands, given the state of his, but he thanked the officer for protecting his family. He shook his head as the paramedics carried his neighbor out on a stretcher.

"Poor bastard." Sal wished the officer a good night and returned to bed.

LXXIII

B ecause the misfortune surrounding the Solutions general manager position continued, employees joked that Carol could not hire an executive worth his (or her) weight in newspaper tombstones. And, while it had the makings of Sal's handiwork, the whacking of Lee Kemp just did not add up for Carol.

Sal won't get paid unless this job is filled. He was as anxious as anybody to get Lee on board. Nope. This was just a random violent attack. Why am I plagued with so much bad luck?

Embarrassed by the public loss of the purported savior for this business segment, not to mention its uncanny resemblance to an earlier, also gruesome, chapter in her career, the CEO turned her sights, and vengeance, internally to find a way to dig her career out of the ditch. She surrounded herself with people such as Emily Harris, who would do her bidding, and filled in any gaps with Stewart.

"What about a government bailout?" Stewart asked. He believed he had finally hit upon the right idea to pull TMC out of its negative current state of affairs and Carol out of her months-old ornery mood. The stock buyback, the purpose of which had been to boost confidence in the company, had been overshadowed by the discovery of Lee's remains.

"Subprime mortgage loans drove the entire world to the brink of recession, and the government gave sweetheart deals to the financial services companies who issued them," Stewart went on. He considered his hefty-sounding title and fantasized about all he could have done if he had been chief administrative officer during the early days of TMC.

"Stewart, we're not a financial conglomerate," Carol said. "Hell, we don't even make parts for the automobile industry anymore. What would motivate the government to bail us out?"

"Why wouldn't Washington help us? We haven't done anything illegal recently. The worst we can be accused of is being bad businesspeople."

Lee's murder also had hit customer confidence hard, dragging down TMC product sales.

Carol thought of the well-worn green leather suitcase and pictured that treasury manager, hands tied behind his back, pleading with her and Emily to work a deal with the government of Turkmenistan.

"I'm surrounded by incompetents."

"Carol?"

This bailout idea might have some merit, she thought.

"I know that guy on the Senate banking committee," Carol offered.

"Which guy?" Stewart was tired, too.

"Marv Bertson, the head of the whole thing."

Stewart had worked with Carol for several years, and this had never come up before. Bertson had been chairman of this committee for a long time.

"Did your last company do business in financial services?" Stewart asked.

"No. I dated him a little."

"Carol, he must be forty—no, fifty years older than you!"

"It was Sal's idea! And I thought it could be good for business. Who knows, maybe it still will be."

Stewart stood, speechless, in the middle of Carol's office.

"I didn't know him that well!" Carol shouted.

Still, Stewart was not sure how far Carol might go. "So, how do we curry favor with a champion of government oversight?"

"Sometimes I wonder what's wrong with you, Stewart."

Stewart was embarrassed. *Of course Carol would not entertain anything unethical. We've already maxed out on scandals this quarter.*

"I'd dance with the devil to get out of this mess," Carol continued. "No, wait. I already have Sal on our side. So, I guess I'm going to have to sleep with the ninety-one-year-old leader of banking reform. By the way, I don't think you do enough to highlight what I do for this company, Stewart. If you did, maybe I wouldn't find any more stuffed pigs at my staff meetings."

Stewart asked for clarity about next steps.

"How should I know? Talk to Emily. She's the expert at rigging financial transactions! I'll find a reason to be in Washington next week. Hmm . . . I'm going to need some new clothes."

Carol's attention turned to her contact file on her computer. She found the number she needed.

"I hope my stylist is working out of his Beltway salon next week."

As she made the call to her personal groomer, Carol rattled off suggestions she had for cost-savings initiatives. Unfortunately, Stewart nixed one after the other.

"Cancel employer match on savings plan," Carol said.

"We did that last quarter."

"Cancel all international work assignments immediately and tell employees to find their own way home."

"TMC practice for several years already," Stewart countered.

"Reorganize to a centralized approach to better leverage workforce and resources."

"We completed that last quarter."

"Let's reorganize to a decentralized structure to better utilize resources and workforce."

"That's in the process of completion," Stewart said.

"Have we tried to spin off underperforming assets?"

"Well, Carol, given the state of things, that could mean an outright sale of the entire company." Carol decided against this one.

"At least there are no worries that the books are cooked," Stewart said. "Mercedes is as honest as they come. And good, too. How about that board call last week? She picked up on that revenue recognition item that everyone else missed. Good thing we didn't go down that road or we'd have REAL problems."

"Shut up, Stewart. CFOs are a dime a dozen," Carol said.

"*Economic Week* doesn't think so. Their editor called me this morning to tell me that Mercedes has been nominated as Femme Fatale of the Year, the magazine's highest honor!"

Carol was already irritated with Stewart for fumbling the chance to get her out from under Sal, the meeting with Bill having served no purpose—though it did take her general counsel out of commission. Bill had relapsed several steps on his rehab program. Now, when she really needed good press, her leadership development expert gave Carol's best shot at positive recognition to Mercedes, a regular thorn in the CEO's administrative side.

"Ow!" Stewart yelped.

The heft of Carol's coffee mug left a bluish indentation on Stewart's forehead before smashing against the hardwood of her office floor.

"You were supposed to make sure I got that nomination, Stewart!"

With myriad business challenges, some real, some imagined, Stewart had dropped that ball.

Stewart closed his eyes hard to will away the stars circling his temple and the nausea bubbling up from his gut. Grimacing, he suggested that they ask Colreavy Consulting to conduct another spans-and-layers exercise. The presumption was that this evaluation of scope and heft of responsibilities would lead to greater efficiency throughout TMC by eliminating a layer or two of middle management and, therefore, operating expense.

Carol offered a pointed barb at human resources' culpability in TMC's current situation: "I thought that seeking efficiencies with human capital is what my HR team was supposed to do."

LXXIV

S al flipped through the latest issue of *Economic Week*. Though Clare had convinced herself of her objectivity, she was increasingly outspoken about Carol's management of TMC.

Bodies Turn Up and Turn Down TMC

One look from Carol Himmler can turn anything to stone, be it an otherwise thriving business or an accomplished business leader. With superstar

Lee Kemp the latest casualty (condolences to the Kemp family), anonymous sources wonder how the communications technology conglomerate will entice the warm bodies necessary to breathe new life into the operation. Isn't it time the board eliminated the dead wood in its existing executive suite? On a related note, the Securities and Exchange Commission has completed its investigation into Ms. Himmler's compensation package at StreamLINE Corporation. Given compelling evidence that Ms. Himmler's stock-option value was not accurately reported, StreamLINE's board of directors agreed to restate earnings for the period during which Ms. Himmler led the logistics company and to pay fines totaling $75 million. After testifying that she was unaware of accounting improprieties, Ms. Himmler was not implicated in any explicit wrongdoing. However, the SEC imposed a monetary penalty. Specifically, she is required to relinquish profits stemming from backdated options. Given the soaring growth of StreamLINE under its current management team, led by industry veteran Don Freeman, the ill-gotten gains amount to roughly $20 million.

"Ouch," Sal mumbled to himself. "Carol's gonna be pissed."

The magazine also carried an article on technology infrastructure investment in northern China. Something about it attracted Sal's attention. It may have been the pictures of Suzy Ng, the attractive vice president of MAO-KaCHING, the financial powerhouse backing the initiative.

Born and educated in the U.S., Suzy was the youngest of twelve children whose parents escaped Stalin's stranglehold on their Buddhist enclave in Mongolia. Her much older parents promoted the nourishment of a disciplined mind as well as avoidance of behaviors that might lead to regret. Having grown up in the shadow of eleven decidedly self-examined, altruistic siblings, Suzy channeled her well-honed cerebral muscles with laserlike efficiency on material success and professional recognition.

Suzy was an Ivy League graduate with degrees in biology, economics, and information technology. However, her native inclinations and raw talent directed her toward a career in general management. Having already tackled large leadership roles within Internet and consumer packaged-goods companies, Suzy leapt at the opportunity to bring the weight of her experiences to the technology frontier in Asia, which was also her ancestral homeland. She was the pioneering architect behind the infrastructure initiative in a region of China better known for yaks and the ancient silk trade than computer speeds and feeds.

Sal read of Suzy's successful transactions for MAO-KaCHING, Beijing's closest equivalent to a private-equity company, with interest. Suzy took a personal interest in her projects and often assumed leadership roles within the companies she purchased, broadening her portfolio of skills.

There was brief mention of a husband, Tony Ng, who was a restaurateur ("Parasite," huffed Sal), and two small, preschool-age children.

"What do I have to lose?" Sal thought as he looked up MAO-KaCHING's website. It would be midmorning the next day in China.

"Maybe I'll get lucky." He dialed Suzy's office number.

L X X V

Carol tore her copy of *Economic Week* in half and tossed it in the trash. Her invitation to Tomas Severe's fifth wedding, on Sardinia, had been rescinded. Also, she had been asked to resign her position as chair of the Autumnal Ball, a fundraiser for Indigenous Tribes of the Tundra, a main beneficiary of Lulu Earl's unrestricted trust fund.

"How am I going to come up with $20 million?" Carol said to Stewart. "The TMC board doesn't want me preoccupied with raising money. They need me to focus on turning this company around." Although Carol had certainly prospered from her CEO stints, she was not about to give up her own money to pay this penalty. Not that she needed the $20 million to run the estate on Martha's Vineyard or the penthouse on Manhattan's Upper East Side. It was the principle of the thing: Her principle, her objective, was to hold on to her money.

Stewart looked at her with uncertainty.

"The human resources department of StreamLINE should have known better than to issue those backdated stock options," Carol went on. "You would never let anything like that happen here, Stewart. Thank God I have you to rely on."

Stewart, impressed with and thankful for this rare acknowledgement of his work, blushed. Unconsciously, he rubbed his fingertips over the now yellow bruise left by Carol's wayward coffee mug.

Carol despised blushing. Her grip around the water glass in her hands tightened so much that it broke, cutting her fingers. Stewart jumped up, offering his handkerchief. Carol called Jill to sweep up the glass.

"You can see the pressure I am under," Carol smiled meekly at Stewart. She sighed and shook her head as she looked at the broken glass surrounding her feet.

"You will make this go away for me, won't you, Stewart?"

Stewart bent down to pick up the glass.

"Sure, but isn't Jill coming in with a broom?"

Carol pulled her HR executive up by his shirt collar. She looked at him eye-to-eye.

"I mean the $20 million, Stewart."

LXXVI

Stewart looked at the interview process as a chance to lay the groundwork necessary to influence an executive in the future. It was an opportunity for a good forty-five minutes or more of uninterrupted, self-indulgent conversation. It baffled him why some TMC executives did not seize the possibilities inherent in this part of the candidate-selection process.

On the morning of Suzy Ng's interviews, Sal bought breakfast. Stewart complained about the state of the company.

"Things have gotten so bad, even our executives have lost heart. I actually needed to remind several of them to look happy when they meet Suzy. After all, it's a leader's job to convey hope, even if it means skirting over some issues."

Sal had found the entire episode with Bill Zilch and Stewart's HR emissary insulting. But the injury to his cash flow was a more critical concern—TMC was unlikely to release the purse strings until this Solutions search closed. Sal was biding his time to show Stewart just how much he had appreciated the introduction to TMC's general counsel and the prolonged blow to his revenue stream. He spoke next.

"I have to tell my guys, 'People got expectations of who you are. You want respect? You have to show a little strength.' Know what I mean?" Sal looked to see if Stewart really did know what he meant.

Stewart looked empty.

"This guy's thick," Sal half-whispered.

"How's that?"

"I said this coffee is doing the trick." Sal finished his cup and declined a second. He left Stewart to review Suzy's resume before his interview. As the diner door closed behind Sal, Stewart took good measure of his search partner. He felt that their interaction that morning had been a little chilly. Sal had not pumped him for information from the board, as he often did. Plus, it unnerved Stewart that the search consultant had never commented on his meeting with the general counsel.

I expected Sal to give me a hard time about that, but he said zilch about Bill.

Because Stewart's plan to leverage the legal team had backfired mightily, benching a key player in Carol's "Cover-Your-Ass" leadership strategy, she increased the pressure on him. Reflecting on his workday realities, Stewart considered a tagline for an advertisement to recruit a new general counsel: "Attorneys With Spine Need Not Apply."

Later that morning, Stewart met Suzy in front of TMC headquarters. He greeted the driver of her Town Car and confirmed Suzy's itinerary for the day before letting the driver go.

"Can't leave a stone unturned." Stewart winked at Suzy as he held the door for her to enter the building.

A big believer in small talk, Stewart decided to break the ice with what he thought was a little humor: "So, Suzy, I have to tell you. Sal has presented so many candidates to us these last few months that it is hard to keep them all straight. Are you the candidate with the pet pig, or are you the candidate who is very enthusiastic?"

Suzy sat still, gauging the situation. *Is this some new human resources process for assessing candidates?* she wondered.

"I must be the enthusiastic candidate, Stewart, because there is no room in my Singapore apartment for a pig."

Off to what he supposed was a good start, Stewart described the global opportunities that lay before TMC Solutions. He offered his opinion of what that division could achieve under the direction of a capable leader and emphasized the level of commitment that TMC required. Stewart had a good vibe about Suzy. He decided to amaze her with his sensitivity to the nuances that her candidacy offered. He had read that she could be a tough-as-nails negotiator, and Sal said she had a take-no-prisoners approach to competition. Stewart wanted to be sure to impress upon her that TMC was her kind of place.

Unfortunately, without Charlie around to keep him in line, Stewart's inclination for speaking without thinking, coupled with an overpowering need to impress, was often a recipe for trouble.

"Don't take this the wrong way, Suzy. You're here because Asians have a well-deserved reputation for being diligent workers. But my responsibility, when TMC is choosing leadership talent, is to assess a candidate's allegiance. Take this job, for example. It isn't for somebody on the mommy track. We need someone who is ready to make TMC Solutions the single most important focus of their life. A tigress willing to eat her own cubs, if you will."

Confidently, Stewart relaxed back in his chair, his cowboy boots on top of the conference table—which served to reinforce his discriminatory statements.

The first female vice president of MAO-KaCHING struggled to decipher this message. To her understanding, Stewart was the most senior individual tasked with maximizing TMC's human capital. Among other things, she assumed this meant creating an environment that encouraged the best in all employees, ensured fair treatment, and placed a high value on advancing diversity within the organization. Suzy wondered what it said about TMC that its senior vice president of human capital management was an obtuse buffoon.

"Stewart, where is this conversation going?" she asked.

"Uh, uh." Stewart removed his boots from the table and sat up straight. He was a bit surprised, even put off, by Suzy's directness, even though he regularly instructed his team that straightforward communication was a hallmark of TMC's culture. He made another attempt to lay things out for Suzy.

"Hey, I believe in transparency, in setting the right expectations upfront. We are one of the last bastions of the old boys' network, after all. That's a franchise we intend to protect."

"Stewart, if I wanted to debate my success as a businesswoman, I'd call one of my aunts in Mongolia. Of course, we'd be communicating by smoke signals and pouch-carrying yaks, but it might be more compelling than this conversation is shaping up to be."

Stewart was taken aback. He had no idea how Suzy had misunderstood him, but he was determined to set the record straight.

"Hey, I have nothing against women. I like women. In fact, several of my leadership awards were in recognition of my initiatives to eliminate workplace barriers for women. Nothing involving yaks, of course, but we are always interested in new ideas."

Suzy was standing now, collecting her things. "I left my children, my husband, and took several days of vacation to come to the U.S. for these meetings. Are you telling me I wasted my time?"

"Wait. You must meet Carol Himmler. I can see you have a lot in common." Stewart called Carol and arranged for the CEO to interview Suzy immediately. Although he did not understand why her feathers were so ruffled, he could not let this candidate—TMC's only one at the moment—fly away.

Suzy composed herself. She had traveled twenty-two hours largely to meet Carol. Despite the business challenges, and Stewart's insults, she assumed that not all TMC leaders would be clueless idiots.

After all, TMC is a large, global brand. They have gotten some things right, Suzy said to herself.

Her motivation to interview was driven by Sal's description of this general management position as the stepping-stone to the CEO role at TMC.

"Suzy, there is no heir apparent to Carol," Sal had said. "The board has charged me with finding a candidate who can assume responsibility for the Solutions division and also be a clear contender for the chief executive job when Carol retires." Sal reminded Suzy of this aspect of the search each time they spoke.

"When is Carol retiring?" Suzy had asked Sal.

While the board had suggested that it would be good to find a general manager candidate who could possibly succeed Carol, board members would make no promises about that next role or a time frame for it.

"Eighteen months, tops," Sal had responded.

Now, Suzy put her briefcase back down and waited for Carol to arrive.

Carol sensed from Stewart's comment about Suzy's candidacy ("Code Blue!") that a major resuscitation effort would be necessary. Carol put on the charm she normally reserved for the board, institutional investors, and reporters. She described her own career, including her ascendancy at StreamLINE and later TMC. Suzy talked of her family and their hardships as evidence of her training, focus, and ambition. Carol pretended to find it gripping. She was overjoyed that Suzy was a qualified, well-adjusted, gender-defined, and breathing executive who wanted the job. She decided that Suzy would not leave TMC without an offer letter in hand.

Suzy felt comfortable enough with Carol to reveal how her meeting with Stewart had disappointed her.

"Suzy, I understand. Stewart was a great asset to this company at earlier stages of our evolution, but sometimes the company moves beyond the individual. It's not anything negative."

"Oh, no. Of course not."

It had been a long, hard year. Stewart's bumbling on the marketing campaign, this search, and that missed opportunity to dump Sal with Bill filled Carol's thoughts. The CEO was just plain tired of Stewart.

It would be nice to have a clean slate when this business finally gets turned around. Stewart simply knows too much, Carol decided.

"Stewart's time has come and gone here at TMC," she said aloud. "This is confidential, but I feel I can trust you—we have so much in common. We'll be initiating an executive search for a new SVP of human capital management. Wouldn't it be great if we found a woman for the role?"

Carol could not care less if a man or a woman assumed the top human resources job, but she sensed that it might matter to Suzy. She laid it on thick.

"It would be great to have a like-minded woman on the executive team to help me define the scope of the HR function and help TMC identify the right leader for that mission. I would love to have your insights as we go through that process, Suzy."

Suzy sensed that negotiations had begun, so she wanted to confirm one thing before she got back on a plane.

"Sal indicated that he was looking for a future backfill to your role," she said. "How do you feel about that?"

Carol had no intention of leaving TMC until she had secured her next, more impressive gig, so Suzy's question was something of a surprise. However, she did not hold anything against Sal for using it to get Suzy interested. Whatever sealed this deal was on the table, as far as Carol was concerned. So, since no other company would even consider Carol for more powerful roles until TMC was turned around, and since she already had set up that she could peg the success or failure of this turnaround on the leader of the Solutions division, she knew what the answer had to be.

"Suzy, I feel that is the best plan for the future of TMC, a company to which I am wholly dedicated."

UNABLE TO REACH Sal, who was back on a New Jersey–bound plane, Carol called Giana with a message for her boss.

"Tell Sal that we are going to offer the Solutions general management job to Suzy. And have him call me right away about initiating a search for a senior vice president of human resources."

I'll be damned if I let Stewart screw up my plans, Carol fumed.

Carol was eager to sweep a few things up into the conclusion of the Solutions search, particularly because Clare was snooping around again. The journalist had called Lars Frankel about $10 million in stock incentive awards that TMC recently had awarded Carol. She could count on attorney-client privilege with Lars, especially since an introduction to Sal's Turkmen associates resulted in lucrative business for the attorney. But Stewart's increasingly nervous demeanor—the Valium was not working as well as Carol had hoped—plus the additional stock payments scheduled to hit Carol's investment account the next quarter made the whole scenario a little too high risk.

Two things happened next that would profoundly influence the course of events. The first was that Stewart received a call from his father's attorney of fifty-five years. The old family friend communicated that the elder Narciss had passed away about an hour earlier. The cause of death appeared to be a bad heart.

"I'm sure I don't have to tell you, he was never the same after he lost Precious," the attorney said.

Precious's tail, which was her primary means of feline expression, had been badly damaged in that Egyptian bathtub. Thereafter, Stewart's father's companion was gradually overtaken by an inability to convey even the simplest of emotions. The situation was aggravated by her sharpened senses, particularly around water, so a heart-wrenching scene ensued any time a faucet or lawn sprinkler operated within earshot of the cat. Her agitation was so acute that Stewart's dad had his Olympic-sized swimming pool filled with kitty litter. Even the top animal psychologists were unable to exorcise Precious's demons.

Finally, perhaps assuming that surviving cancer had left her with lives to spare, Precious tucked her tail between her hind legs and, with one final eardrum-splitting hiss, leaped off the catwalk surrounding her estate quarters and into the rottweiler pit below.

Stewart's father spent his remaining days sequestered in his study, the odd "squeak-squeak" from Precious's favorite toy the singular infringement upon the sanctity of their once shared parlor. His manservant discovered him slumped in his library chair, arms draped over Precious's scratching post. The corporate titan had been reduced to a broken man whose personal expectations had expired with his cat.

The attorney communicated that Stewart's father wanted him to serve as executor of his estate. The contents of the will dictated a liquidation of his father's assets, with proceeds going to a charity commemorating his long-time cohort: the Precious Narciss Foundation for Cats Without Hair to Live Without Fear.

The second decisive incident occurred as a result of an incentive program Sal put in place for his own team. Giana was rewarded with small bonuses for proactive, positive customer experience. Basically, Sal wanted to keep the skids greased at all times. Sufficiently motivated, Giana addressed even the smallest items. Therefore, before she did anything else that day, Giana called Stewart to thank him for giving them the new search for a human resources leader.

LXXVII

The connection on Sal's cell phone was not clear. It did not help that he was sleepy, but he wanted to get this deal closed ASAP. He reached Suzy as she landed in Singapore.

"Sal, I haven't even collected my luggage yet. It would be better for me to call you after I settle down at home. Besides, it's really late where you are."

"We can do that, but let me ask for your reaction to the offer." Sal suppressed a yawn.

"To tell you the truth, Sal . . ."

As far as Sal was concerned, good news never started with that expression.

" . . . I had ups and downs in the interviews."

Take control of this conversation, Sal told himself.

"I understand Stewart's been a bit of a disappointment lately," Sal replied. Carol had filled him in.

"Carol told me he brought a lot of value to the company in the early days."

"Yeah, yeah. Good guy all around, just not what is needed at this juncture. I've got the search assignment to replace him. In fact, I'd like to get your recommendations for the role. Someone you would be comfortable working with." Sal's plan was to draw Suzy in further so she felt like part of the TMC leadership team as soon as possible. The more emotional hooks he could get into her, the better the chance she would accept the offer.

"Well, my meeting with Carol largely got me over the bad taste I had from Stewart, but then I read this offer letter when I got on the plane. I can see why she's replacing him!"

Sal was unaware of any issues with the offer letter. *What the hell now?*

"Yeah, that offer letter is a relic. They should send the details electronically, is my take on it." He fished for something that would put this issue, whatever it was, to rest.

Suzy explained that the offer letter was full of mistakes, from the reporting structure to the salary. Even the Social Security number was wrong.

"In fact, TMC could have put someone else's identity in jeopardy, though I would never use this information underhandedly. What's that, Sal? I couldn't make out what you said."

"I said shucks."

"Of course, it makes me wonder what they've done with my personal information."

Sal's sinuses were beginning to ache. He popped two aspirin.

"This is serious, Sal. Why would I want to join a company that is reckless with something as important as an offer letter? No wonder TMC is in the trouble it's in."

Sal wondered how much this mistake was going to cost.

"It appears they really need someone like me to set things straight," Suzy continued. "Hold on, Sal. There's one of my bags."

Sal could hear Suzy asking another passenger to allow her access to the baggage carousel. He recalled Carol's admonishment not to lose this candidate. His guess was that the offer would need to go up by $200,000.

Sal waited while Suzy retrieved the luggage and went to her car. He heard her give the driver her home address. Then she got right back on track.

"I'm in the car now, so there is more privacy. As I was saying, all this made me wonder how serious TMC is about solving their problems. I mean, what are they truly willing to do to change, Sal?"

I wonder if $300,000 will do it, Sal wondered.

"And don't you think it's odd that I didn't meet anyone from the board, if this position is a future backfill to the CEO?" Suzy inquired.

She's going to write her own ticket, Sal realized.

Sal recalculated the offer in his head and added a $500,000 sign-on bonus. It occurred to him that that kind of money could buy a stake in the local casino an Indian tribe was building.

This is so screwed up, he thought. *In my business, five hundred grand is payment for a very dirty job. This broad's going to get all this cash up front before selling one piece of equipment*. Sal buried his jealousy under a heavy sigh.

Then he realized that the longer he stayed on the phone, the more it was going to cost TMC. Since his recruiting fee was a percentage of the executive's compensation and would increase as that compensation increased, he considered his car, his house remodeling, and the consolation jewelry he had bought his wife when a second opinion confirmed her diagnosis of a sexually transmitted disease.

Sal placed his feet up on his desk, settling into a comfortable position.

"Suzy, I am here for you. I am your advocate. I am not satisfied with my work if you are not pleased. Tell me what's on your mind. Don't worry about the time. For you, I have all the time in the world."

Before he fell asleep, Sal left Carol a voice-mail message with his recommendation about what it would take financially to close this deal with Suzy.

GIANA MADE EXCUSES for Sal when Carol called late the next morning, but after the third exchange, she figured she'd better find him. Carol's message involved a request to "get his ass on a plane ASAP." Giana reached him at home, nursing a sinus headache.

"I had a late call with an extremely irritated candidate," Sal said by way of explaining his physical state and Carol's emotional one. "Suzy wants a whole lot more to join TMC than Carol budgeted for, largely because that goofball pissed her off." Sal held an ice pack to his temple.

"Which goofball?" Giana asked.

"Good point. Whateva. I got to go out there now and help them write up a new offer." Sal glanced at the rumpled suits in his disorganized closet. "This traveling is getting old."

He poured himself a glass of orange juice, added a little champagne for kicks, and started repacking.

LXXVIII

As Sal was getting organized to return to TMC, Vera was summoned to Stewart's office. Stewart discovered the mistakes in the offer letter that his administrative assistant had prepared for Suzy only after it had been dispatched. Kristie blamed Carol for the errors because the CEO waited until the last possible minute to let Kristie know she needed the letter. And Stewart was nowhere to be found when Kristie wanted him to review the material before she handed it to Suzy.

Vera registered the dour expression on Jill's face as she passed by Jill's desk. In the past several quarters, Carol's assistant had gone from regularly cheerful and helpful to habitually cross and contrary. Jill barked a question at Vera as she passed. Vera confirmed politely that she and Stewart were going to discuss the offer for Suzy Ng.

"Ah, yes. Stewart's got good experience enlisting lambs to the slaughter," Jill smirked. Vera paused, not understanding the reference.

"Stewart recruited me to TMC," Jill explained. "He was the first person here to lie to me."

Vera declined Jill's offer of hot tea, uncertain about Jill's emotional stability and the proximity of cleaning products to the sugar packets. She continued to Stewart's office, berating herself for procrastinating on the offer to join Charlie's client. She found Kristie wiping her red, puffy eyes while Stewart nursed a powerful headache.

"What's wrong with the offer letter?" Vera asked, knowing that it would fall to her to fix the problem. Kristie withdrew to her desk so she would not have to suffer through another lecture from Stewart.

"It has so many mistakes that it is at best confusing and, more likely, worthless. It states that Suzy will report to Iago Thomason, our long-gone CFO, which is embarrassing. The base salary stated in the letter is $50,000 less than she is currently making, and far less than we offered her, which she may find insulting. On top of that, the letter was addressed to Suzy Ng, but the material we sent her to get set up in TMC payroll contained the Social Security number of a different person."

Vera picked up the folder containing Suzy's personal data and a copy of the slipshod offer letter. She considered the potential exposure TMC faced as a result of these mistakes and made a mental note to engage the legal team before she issued a revised employment contract.

"Carol can't be too happy about this," she said. A shiver ran up Vera's spine as she recalled her frosty conversation with Carol about employee engagement. It had taken a very long, very hot shower and three-quarters of a bottle of gin to warm up after that meeting.

Stewart held his own copy of the offer letter and looked at the phone. He chased four more aspirin with a large glass of cold water as he considered his response.

After hearing from the lawyer about his dad's final insult and learning from Giana of Carol's betrayal, Stewart spent the evening on the floor of his wine cellar, drowning his pain with large doses of Canadian ice wine. Unfortunately for his newly tiled floor, a rise in blood sugar hit his stomach before the alcohol numbed his senses and he vomited $600 worth of a rare dessert wine across his male sanctuary. The expensive regurgitation woke him up in more ways than one. Upsetting images crossed his mind: patching broken dishes Mariellen had hurled when holiday dinners cooled as the two awaited Stewart's father's arrival; scrubbing porcelain litter boxes during Precious's chemo treatments; and, as an adolescent, watching his father empty more than one trust fund into the eager hands of local law enforcement to keep his mother's good name out of the police blotter.

Stewart had reflected on the rewards and accolades he had chased in order to validate his self-worth and gain the attention and respect of his father. He had wrenched from the wall above the fireplace the one item his father had bequeathed him: a portrait of the elder Narciss caressing Precious as the sphynx cat slept in his lap. The final irony was that the man responsible for corporate leadership succession had been backfilled by a bald cat in his father's heart. Replaying these memories reminded Stewart of another assault, this one on his rightful place in the corner office. He shivered between dry heaves as he imagined Carol courting human resources executives to take his place. Lying face down on the cool, subterranean floor, Stewart had an epiphany.

Carol had been a ruthlessly ambitious general manager when we first met. I should have realized that the logical progression was to backstabbing CEO.

"She used me," he cried.

In relatively few years, Stewart had watched Carol monkey around with the careers of honest, hardworking people, screw up and then cover up imprudent business deals, exploit colleagues to promote her own schemes, bribe the government of a foreign country, and, most recently, throw herself at a ranking committee member in the U.S. Senate.

It has never been established who killed StreamLINE's Chuck Goodfellow. Nor has it been confirmed who did not, Stewart reflected.

And what of his contributions to TMC? The press accolades Stewart arranged for executives, especially Carol; the awards for human capital leadership and innovation, for which he lobbied unceasingly; the step-function changes he introduced to the organization, such as Managing OPEX through Forced Attrition (MOFA). How about the $20 million in stock awards he coaxed and cajoled the board's compensation committee to provide Carol? He convinced them it was a necessary retention device, despite Carol's dismal performance as CEO.

It was a stroke of genius to remind the board that Carol had emerged as the most apparent among a very dynamic group of executives seeking to be Ted Barone's heir, Stewart considered.

Stewart had saved the list of prospective succession candidates from that project, the one Harry had screwed up. He had presented that roster, with all of the names crossed out except Carol's, and a dossier of media coverage to build a case with the board that Carol would be hard to replace. The fact that a more recent rash of executive candidates had gone AWOL, for one reason or another, underscored his point.

She never would have gotten that money without my help.

Also, Stewart had directed the compensation team to prepare a financial analysis of the price tag for backfilling Carol, in case the board was of a mind to give her the axe after all. The costs were prohibitive, exacerbated by the fact that a CEO's sacking would involve a very public search for her successor. This data convinced board chair Rick Robertson, who was anxious to bury the issue and refocus energy on getting the business back on track. He encouraged his fellow board members to approve the $20 million in stock grants.

How dare she take away my position of influence?

Stewart sighed as he retrieved a well-worn legal-size envelope from beneath his favorite bottle of aged cognac in the cellar. He opened the envelope and spilled articles about Jim Collins onto his lap. One after another, in ink that had smudged from Stewart's handling over time, the stories praised Jim's career accomplishments. Several cited his keen leadership strengths, referencing the successful careers of other executives whom Jim had mentored and inspired. All of those executives were now in positions of increased responsibility.

If only . . . Stewart pined.

But Jim long ago crossed anyone associated with TMC off his list. Even board members could not entice him to join them in other ventures.

After wallowing in what might have been, Stewart slept for a few hours.

Then he consumed two pots of black coffee, took a hot shower, and returned to his office. As he sat at his desk reflecting on the previous evening, he had a second epiphany.

Sal was right. I need to be my own man. I need to take a stand with the board. They'll see what a courageous leader I can be.

"Maybe Rick would make me the next CEO," Stewart said aloud.

"What?" Vera had been sitting silently, watching Stewart's unusual facial expressions as he relived the prior evening in his mind.

If that doesn't fly, Rick might be interested in Dandy. And Dandy likes me. I could be his consigliere, Stewart reasoned.

Stewart snapped out of his reverie and turned to Vera.

"Why does Carol have to know?" He answered Vera's original question with a question of his own.

Vera moved closer to Stewart. This was shaping up to be a very interesting conversation. She nudged him to continue.

"Suzy didn't do as well with the rest of the interview team as she did with Carol," Stewart said. "Some of us don't feel her experience is heavy enough to be successful in the GM job. These mistakes in the offer letter might end up being helpful if we decide to rescind the offer," Stewart explained.

"RESCIND the offer?"

"Calm down, Vera. I don't know if that's the action. I have to discuss it with the board."

"Does Carol know you are going to talk to the board?"

"Carol and I don't see eye to eye on this, but I feel it's my duty as the senior human capital leader to take a stand on this issue."

"You're taking a stand on an issue?" This last revelation was too much for Vera. She jumped up so forcefully that she knocked Stewart's glass of water from his desk and clear across the room.

Stewart surveyed the water-soaked carpet and retrieved his unbroken glass. Shaking his head at the nuisance of his now-wet rug, he escorted Vera to the door of his office.

"Maybe," he said.

Stewart instructed Vera to await a call about next steps.

LXXIX

"What do you say, Vera? Finally tired of TMC battle scars?" Charlie hoped his former colleague would accept his client's offer of employment. The Universal Employee Advocacy Project wanted someone with the intelligence and drive to fight for workforce equality in areas such as compensation and benefits, representation, and career development. Additionally, this person would have to build bridges between the organization and companies around the country in order for initiatives to be successful. His client chose Vera. Charlie knew she had the right experience and the passion. He also wanted to get her out of TMC before she lost heart or her practical jokes got her fired.

"This sounds like such a great job, Charlie. Makes me wonder if I could have done more for TMC."

"You can only do so much with the leadership cards stacked against you."

Hesitant to take the plunge, Vera manufactured reasons to stay.

"I have so many friends here. Well, I used to, anyways, before they started getting bumped off. And I know how this place works. What if I'm not successful re-creating my career in another company?" she worried.

"Vera, way back when, TMC was doing something unique. And, no matter what we faced, the leadership seemed to get us back on track. Now, from the outside in, it looks like the company is in a death spiral."

Charlie's view, that TMC might no longer be the place to build a healthy career, was compelling. Vera acknowledged that internal vultures had begun picking over their colleagues' career carcasses.

"And dressing up the corporation to make it look like a better value to investors is still just lipstick. It might be expensive lipstick, too, if the news accounts are accurate about what TMC has been paying for acquisitions," Charlie said.

Charlie was certainly selling, but he was also concerned. He knew Stewart was weak and Carol was callous. Throwing Sal into that mix made the situation ominous. He also realized that the immaturity and hubris of the TMC executive staff had eventually infected the entire organization, contributing to the current state of the business. But Stewart's sins of omission were particularly vexing: delaying the opportunity to turn around TMC's early misfortunes with a more seasoned leadership team; hiring a talentless suit to build TMC's talent management plan—and later disposing of the emperor when he was discovered to have no clothes; and turning a blind eye to Carol's boundless ambition.

Her blood beginning to boil, Vera thought about what Stewart took for granted, particularly the honest efforts of employees loyal to TMC's mission. Putting the finest point on it, she asked, "How has Stewart survived these blunders?"

Charlie had an answer.

"Vera, unfortunately, bad executives don't go away. They simply reinvent themselves. Unless, that is, someone is bold enough to get rid of them."

Vera filled the air with a heavy sigh, the reality of her situation setting in.

Charlie understood Vera's angst, as well as her hesitation. He had experienced similar mixed feelings leading up to his departure from TMC. However, he counseled her that as long as TMC leaders were blinded by their own reflections, it was dangerous to remain. "Narcissists are incredibly, and largely incurably, naïve," he said.

"How could that be?"

"They're so consumed with their own agenda that it crowds out anything else, even things that are good for them. Stewart's blind spot is so large that anyone who knows where it is can drive a truckful of awards through it. Carol has wrapped herself so tightly in power of her own taking that she might underestimate the strength of a rival's move.

"Those corporate vultures you mentioned, Vera, won't be dazzled by fancy clothes, big awards, or impressive titles. In fact, your self-absorbed leaders, and anyone around them, risk being done in by the trappings of their own agendas."

L X X X

S al never knew Carol to beat around the bush, and he suspected that this was not the time she would start. He also was not in the mood for games. He had hooked the president of the leasing company up with his best girl and a line at the track, but that bought him only a little time before the pressure to make Maserati payments started up again.

"We have two problems, Sal," Carol said. "Do you know what they are?"

He shrugged his shoulders.

"So, we know that Suzy wants a better title, a bigger job, and what amounts to a down payment on a new, extraordinarily large house, right?" Carol wanted to confirm the details.

"Right."

"Let's solve that problem. Tell Suzy we'll give her everything she wants, provided TMC can announce her new role with us before the market closes tomorrow. Capisce?"

Sal did not underestimate Carol. He knew she hated to lose even more than she liked to win.

"Got it. Problem number two?" he asked.

"Stewart got wind of the search for his replacement."

"How do you know this?"

"I didn't get where I am without a lot of eyes around the company, Sal. Anyway, that's his motivation, but it's not our problem."

"Motivation for what?"

"For doing us in. I got a call from the chairman of TMC's board, who was energized about Stewart's suggestion that we bring back Dandy Liege, a retired TMC vice president, to run the Solutions business. He also said that Stewart recommended Dandy as a future backfill for me."

That SOB, Sal fumed. *That was my idea. I bet he would have tried to get out of paying a fee on that.*

"Sal, are you listening to me?"

"Yeah, but I'm confused. Are we going to offer the job to Suzy, or Dandy?"

"Sal, do I look like a masochist? Dandy is revered around here. The chairman called me from a private island off the Florida coast that he purchased with gains from TMC's IPO. He credits Dandy's supply-chain advances with driving the stock to its height. Why would I want someone as strong as Dandy Liege as my number two?"

Sal was tired from the long flight and the longer search.

"OK, I get it. What do we do about Dandy?"

"I convinced the chairman that Dandy has been a retired mountain man too long to jump into a leadership role at a large, public company. I suggested that he focus Dandy's brainpower, and the chairman's family trust fund, on some nanotechnology project to support the environment. But, there's still Stewart. Six months ago, he wouldn't have had the nerve to go behind my back to the board. Today, betrayal is all around me. You read the papers, Sal."

Whispers of a proxy fight had breached the boardroom walls and landed in the business section of major newspapers, threatening Carol's chances of assuming the additional mantle of chairwoman of the board when Rick Robertson stepped down, not to mention endangering her current job. Given the prospect of stockholder opposition to her leadership, as well as an aggrieved board anxious about their role in paying off Carol's financial obligation, she could not allow Stewart to talk to the board again. It might not take much for the board to go from put out to putting her out. She reminded Sal that Wall Street demanded that the redeemer for all of TMC rise from the Solutions business.

"All due respect, Carol, you fed them that line."

"It is what it is, Sal. If I'm out, who's your next-largest client? Stewart is none too happy with either of us for plotting to replace him. You think he'll trust you with more search work if I'm not around?"

Although she could be a supreme pain in the ass, Carol's position as CEO of this Fortune 100 company had generated a good income stream for Sal. If she lost this job because TMC failed, she would not likely land another big job, at least not for a while. That would be negative to his cash flow, especially now that Stewart had shown his true turncoat colors. It seemed to Sal that two issues remained on the table and one had to do with helping Carol save the business and their partnership.

"How about your meeting with Marv Bertson?" Sal asked. "He was so taken with you way back when. Talk about a sweetheart deal. I can't believe you dumped him when he was on the way up. He's a senior senator now."

Carol had found Marv, her former beau, to be as gracious and hospitable as ever when she visited him in the nation's capital. She also found him to be happily married.

"Sal, he actually said he doesn't want to be unfaithful to his wife!"

"Huh?" Sal regrouped. "What about the patriotic approach? Didn't he want to help the company, an American icon?"

"Did you hear me? He rejected me!"

Sal got the message. Case closed.

"OK, I'll bite," he said. "So, how do we persuade Stewart to drop his vendetta so we can get Suzy on board and everyone else off your back?"

Before summoning Sal, Carol had carefully considered her prospects. Relieving Stewart of his command was one option, but since TMC alumni who had been part of her earlier reassignment initiatives had gone sour on Carol to the Kiddles board, there was no telling what Stewart's knowledge of her history might mean to her future. On top of that, although Carol had confiscated all the blood pressure tools in Stewart's office, his obsession with his health kept him constantly on edge. Plus, his association with Dandy's yogi encouraged a "oneness with the universe" that lately had led to gut-spilling exercises in the midst of her staff meetings. That Stewart had gone to the board behind her back convinced Carol that her lieutenant's allegiance was rocky at best.

Thus, given Stewart's medical issues, loose lips, and, as Carol viewed it, limited career alternatives, she rationalized that Sal would be doing Stewart a favor by putting him out of his (and her) misery.

"We've seen this type of no-win problem before, Sal."

Sal rubbed his chin. He had had a long week, including multiple trips between New Jersey and TMC headquarters in the past few days. He took time to make sure he got things straight. He was sitting in the office of the chief executive of a large, publicly traded company. She had approved increasing the offer for his top candidate and told him to close her today. Then they talked about resolving another predicament.

He stared into Carol's eyes. She did not blink.

Sal was angry with Stewart but not enough to seek a permanent solution. Besides the fact that Stewart had kind of grown on him, albeit in an itch-you-can't-reach kind of way, Sal considered the TMC setup to be a pretty good one. Carol hired him to do the executive recruiting, and Stewart made sure he got paid. Sal was not one to bite the hand that fed him.

On the other hand, if Carol decided she wanted someone else to do Stewart's job, that was her prerogative.

She is the boss, Sal thought.

He also considered that if he did not help Carol relieve her organization of Stewart, the next senior vice president of human capital management might find reasons to cut him out of future executive-recruiting work.

"Sal, it's just business," Carol interrupted his thinking.

Nothing personal, Sal thought to himself.

"I don't know how the rest of your business interests are going, but you must want to get paid for this search. Haven't I seen you in that suit before, Sal?"

Sal winced. Carol knew her audience.

"So, these loose ends. They get tied up and then the thing can get done?" Sal asked.

"Then the thing can get done and our business association can continue. Unchecked," Carol added.

CAROL ARRANGED FOR Stewart to fly east with Sal later that afternoon.

"I'd really like you and Sal to work out the final details of the offer for Suzy without any interruptions," she said.

Stewart was not eager to leave town. He had a meeting with Rick the following day, but he did not want to let on that he was scheduled to speak with the chairman of the board.

"Why can't we knock this offer out in my office?"

"I told you, Stewart. The Alliance of Corporate Relationships has nominated TMC and our human capital management department for a lifetime achievement award. There are three companies up for this honor, so they want to interview each of the HR leaders in person before choosing the winner."

"I don't understand why I wasn't notified about this earlier."

According to Carol, the New York–based alliance kept the award process secret so there would not be undue influence from corporate chiefs plugging their HR leaders.

"Of course, I don't have to plug. Your accomplishments precede you, Stewart." She passed along the compliments of the board on the new logo design as she handed the HR leader his airline tickets.

"They were grateful for the gifts," she said. "Very clever use of the TMC logo on those pieces."

Stewart was pleased that the board was pleased. Although it would not be ideal, he reasoned that the meeting with Rick could take place by phone. The interview with the alliance could not.

"I notice you've taken this new marketing push seriously." Carol's finger traced the TMC earring that Stewart wore.

Stewart's body temperature dropped when Carol touched him. He likened it to the kiss of a black widow spider. Stewart assumed the moral upper hand was his, and his rejoinder was not muted.

"I'm loyal, Carol."

"Stewart, I know just how loyal you are. I will remain as faithful to you."

Stewart trembled.

LXXXI

E rnie picked Sal and Stewart up outside the baggage claim area of the
Newark airport. Sal left his luggage on the curb and motioned for
Stewart to do the same as he opened the passenger-side door and
entered the car. Ernie dutifully loaded the luggage into the back of the SUV.

"That's an interesting earring, Stewart. What's it mean?" Ernie looked
in the rearview mirror to talk to his guest in the backseat.

Stewart felt his ear and answered.

"Thank you. I had earrings made with the TMC logo. I'll get you one or
a pair, if you like." Stewart leaned forward to see if Ernie's ears were pierced.

"Uh, no thanks, man. My ears aren't pierced. You ask me, it's pretty
ballsy for a straight guy to wear earrings."

Sal hit Ernie on the side of the head.

"OW! What? What'd I say?" Ernie massaged his ear, which had taken
the brunt of Sal's blow.

Sal turned around to face his client.

"You do what you can to train them, Stewart, but sometimes you can't
take the brute out of the thug."

Sal turned back to Ernie.

"I was going to invite you to join us for dinner. Now you've gone and
insulted our client."

Ernie continued to rub his ear and then looked again in the rearview
mirror.

"Sorry, Stewart. I didn't mean nothing by it except that it's pretty macho
of you." Ernie smiled.

"No offense taken, Ernie. In this day and age of diversity, my take is that
we're all exploring our shades of gay. Don't you agree?"

"Not friggin' me," Sal and Ernie said simultaneously.

Stewart offered his itinerary for the next day as an excuse for begging off
dinner. Since the subject of a search to replace him had not been broached
during the flight to New Jersey, he could only assume, without being certain,
that Sal was complicit in Carol's plan to send him packing.

Probably getting even with me for setting Bill Zilch on him, Stewart thought.

Leveraging his relationships with Rick and Dandy, Stewart intended to turn the tables on the entire affair. In the meantime, a last supper with Sal held little appeal.

However, Sal insisted that they break bread together.

"Would you insult me in my own town, Stewart?"

Feeling obliged, and hungry, Stewart agreed to a light dinner.

Sal recommended Antonio's, a small place close to the airport where they could grab a quick bite. When they arrived at the restaurant and Stewart adjourned to the men's room, Sal informed Ernie that he had a job for him.

"Did the boss call?" Ernie said. "I took care of that other thing after the first misunderstanding. I hope he knows that."

"He knows, he knows. Another boss, so to speak, called. It's a different kind of job, but not really. It's the same job, but it's like it's for another client."

"We working for a new crew? You fuckin' crazy? You talkin' treason, Sal. What are we doin' here?"

Ernie's outburst called attention to their table. Sal reached an arm across the table and grabbed his cousin's shoulder.

"Would you settle down? It's not like that. I only got a minute to fill you in." Sal looked in the direction of the men's room. No Stewart yet. The waiter filled water glasses and placed a cold antipasto on the table.

"I kind of hate to do this," Sal said. "Stewart and I have been through a lot."

He grew quiet thinking about all he had shared with Stewart as they tried to persuade people to work for Carol.

"But, then again, he pulled that bullshit with the general counsel a few weeks ago. That really pissed me off."

"He had you do a general? What kinda clout does this company have, for chrissake?"

Sal looked at his cousin and figured that here was a case where less was definitely not more. He kept talking, largely to himself.

"Business is business, and I gotta get this friggin' search filled. Besides, Stewart even stole the idea I got from Kenny Logan. Remember Kenny? No, you wouldn't. Now that I think of it, the other guy knew him. Rat bastard." Sal mumbled under his breath as he recalled Lenny Knuckles, another former friend. Stewart bounced around the corner, excusing himself as he bumped into the maître d'.

Ernie glanced up and remarked, "Stewart kinda looks like the actor from that old movie about surfers. What was the name of that movie?"

Sal noticed a waiter gently jab a busboy and, pointing at Stewart, make a "get-a-look-at-this-one" face. The busboy raised his eyebrows in the direction of Sal's table to clue in the waiter.

"That's right!" Sal exclaimed. "That Moondoggie thing! That really friggin' annoys me." Sal recalled his exasperation with Stewart's wardrobe choices, haircuts, and ever-evolving appearance. Stewart's style preferences chafed at and humiliated Sal, especially tonight in this, one of his usual, haunts. Somehow, Sal felt relieved. He gave Ernie a familiar look and then glanced at Stewart, who had just approached the table.

"As I was saying, it's coming up on summer and my pool needs work," Sal said. "Those pool guys. What a racket they got. Opening pools, closing pools. Charge me an arm and a leg to do that and then they sit on the beach for the rest of the year. Geez."

Stewart rejoined them.

"Stewart, we're talking about the work that Sal's gonna have done around his pool. Beautiful spot he's got, right on the edge of the woods. Ever been there?" Ernie asked, knowing full well that Stewart had never been to Sal's house. Stewart congratulated Sal on his beautiful home. Ernie took the lead.

"Why you keepin' Stewart away, boss? He's your top client, for chrissake. Your place is not too far from here. Why don't we stop for a drink after dinner?"

"Great idea," Sal said. "It's a short ride. By the way, Stewart, can I borrow your pen?"

LXXXII

S al finished up his call with Suzy and shouted, "Hallelujah!"

Ernie and Giana looked at him.

"Suzy accepted TMC's offer and resigned from her current company. She's going to call Carol so that TMC can announce her new role before the stock market closes."

"Woo-hoo!" Giana exclaimed. She took out a calculator to determine her bonus on this assignment. Ernie did not usually work on this side of Sal's business—last night was an exception—so he simply offered his congratulations and got back to the Racing Sheet.

"Don't you all want to know how I did it? How I closed her?"

"Oh, of course, boss," Ernie said as he and Giana redirected their attention to Sal.

"Well, to start off, she was a real pain in the derriere. And then the TMC guys screwed a few things up, so that gave her more negotiating power. That was the easy part. You either have money or you don't. Luckily, TMC had the money. But this other stuff she wanted! Asking me does TMC have a vision statement. A vision statement! You believe this? How stupid could she be? If they had that, they certainly weren't reading it this year, so what the fuck good is it?"

"Good point," Ernie said.

"Whateva. Then she asks me, 'Does TMC have a robust sustainability program?'" Pointing to a specific part of his anatomy, Sal said, "I wanted to tell her: 'Why don't you sustain this robustness, sweetheart?'"

"TMC is going to give her more money than she ever dreamed of. They are going to double her equity. They will even pay for her good-for-nothing husband to finish his PhD program. What part of this math problem is hard to understand? These people think they are so smart. They kill me," Sal added.

"What DID you tell her?" Giana was interested.

"I told her they loved her so much that if she's not CEO in a year, the board will buy her another company to run."

"That's great that could happen for a woman," Giana said, impressed.

"What the fuck. I made that up. But c'mon, what's she going to do by the time she finds that out, quit? As a show of confidence, I made her pack her shoes and put them on a ship leaving Singapore for the U.S. tonight. You know how many pairs of shoes she's got? We had to rent an extra container just for the boots. She ain't gonna quit."

LXXXIII

The following month, Carol graced the cover of three national business publications. Despite harboring a grudge because Carol had lied to her about giving her that first exclusive many years ago, even Clare had to admit it looked like Carol had turned things around. She could not have known that, before he disappeared, Stewart had teed up the coverage in response to Carol's demands to generate positive publicity for her. When Suzy Ng was hired and, luckily, TMC reported positive results for the quarter, the media outlets rushed to publish some good news.

Under pressure to mitigate further damage to *Economic Week*'s subscription rates—chiefly the loss of readers to Delilah Fabrikant's popular blog, which featured transformational leaders—a born-again Clare penned a story showcasing Carol as a talented executive who could assemble the right team, turn around an organization, and inspire investor confidence:

With her pit crew in place, Carol Himmler has set her sites on driving TMC's recovery across the finish line.

Ms. Himmler, president and chief executive officer of the global communications technology and solutions company, had been wearing multiple hats during a difficult period. Recently, Suzy Ng was chosen to succeed her as worldwide president of the critical TMC Solutions business segment. Having steered the services division of MAO-KaCHING to profitability during the Asian economic crisis, Ms. Ng offers battle-tested leadership credentials to TMC Solutions' war-weary workforce. Ms. Ng was also named an officer of the company.

Ms. Himmler is now expected to focus, laserlike, on supply-chain strategy as well as customer relations. Staking her legacy on these core principles that drove TMC to early and sustained achievements, Ms. Himmler leaves the experienced Ng to revitalize TMC Solutions.

"Thank goodness I can lay this at her feet," Ms. Himmler said.

Despite shareholder concerns about operating margins, Rick Robertson, chairman of TMC's board and a director since TMC's early days, has Ms. Himmler's back. He forcefully defends her tweaks to product quality as well as expansion of the company's global footprint, particularly the expansions of the Middle Market and Solutions segments.

"Most notably, Carol provided the insight and leadership necessary for strategic initiatives, including trusted relationships with Central Asian partners, which increased sales significantly," Mr. Robertson said. "You might also say that she shattered her own glass ceiling when she chose a woman to succeed her as chief of the essential Solutions business. This action is yet another example of Carol's determination to conquer impediments to advancement."

Although the grapevine has been buzzing about Mr. Robertson's possible resignation from the board in the wake of a proxy fight, no mention was made of nominating Ms. Himmler to the additional post of chairwoman of the board for this game-changing company . . .

Still nursing lingering suspicions of Carol, Clare insisted that she also cover Mercedes Rodriguez, TMC's outgoing CFO and the magazine's choice for its annual Femme Fatale of the Year award, in the same issue. The article about the recipient of this important business award detailed Mercedes's stewardship of the finance function during tumultuous times for TMC. The story credited her hard line on complicated international transactions with creating the credibility needed to encourage institutional investors to retake large financial positions in TMC. With confidence in the company restored and Wall Street analysts raving about Mercedes's integrity and leadership, TMC's stock jumped out of the doldrums.

The accolades showered upon the CFO led to offers for her to join other significant corporations. Mercedes settled on the CEO role at the $30 billion consumer-products company Kiddles Corporation. Among the people she was quoted as thanking was Charlie Watkins, senior partner of the CCA Executive Search firm.

"Charlie has been an integral player at key moments in my career, from my first job at TMC to recruiting me to this wonderful opportunity at Kiddles," Mercedes said.

Asked for a comment on the contributions of her outgoing CFO, Carol offered through a pinched smile: "Under the right leadership, anyone, er, everyone can be successful."

A sidebar photo portrayed Mercedes accepting an Austrian blue crystal trophy depicting a woman riding sidesaddle, wearing a pin-striped business suit and stiletto heels. The picture also captured Carol's icy smile as she deigned to support her CFO's accomplishment.

Charlie, who was among the attendees at an award luncheon honoring Mercedes, spied Carol cautiously for any unusual conduct. Before she left TMC, Vera confided in Charlie that Stewart had finally found the backbone to go over Carol's head to the board. Curious about Stewart's mysterious disappearance, Charlie wondered if Stewart's first stand had also been his last. Yet the only odd behavior Charlie noted was Carol's discomfort when the limelight shifted to Mercedes. Then again, envy was hardly unusual for Carol. As much pleasure as he derived from the bananas foster,

Charlie's just dessert came as he observed a squirming, silent Carol on the dais as Mercedes received this singular honor.

To her detriment, Carol also had underestimated Rick's motivation to get Dandy back into the TMC leadership fold. Before the end of the quarter—rumored to be Rick's retirement date—he made a herculean effort to save his family's substantial investment in TMC. He persuaded his fellow directors, as well as a majority of common-stock shareholders, to avoid a proxy fight by nominating Dandy to succeed him as chairman. He argued that Dandy had the gravitas and credibility necessary to influence investors and employees alike. Dandy also brought a fresh perspective to the corporation, balanced with an insider's knowledge of the original culture that propelled TMC's early success.

Behind closed doors, Rick reasoned that Dandy would be the board's inside eyes on, and a strong counterpoint to, Carol. He persuaded his colleagues that if anyone could recoup the over-the-top $20 million outlay for Carol, it was Dandy. Finally, by placing Dandy in the chairman's seat, thereby suppressing Carol's total control over TMC, the chairman felt he could secure his investment for his heirs.

When he had discussed Dandy with Carol, Rick acknowledged the CEO's concern that Dandy had been out of the corporate sphere for too long to step into a large managerial role. However, Rick asserted that Dandy had the innate leadership traits, coupled with technological intuition, to assume the mantle of the board. He referenced a recent story by Clare about Dandy's achievements with leading-edge technology companies—a compelling example of how the new chairman had reinvented himself, Rick said.

Carol's buy-in on Dandy was important: In order to persuade him to take the leadership reigns of the board, Rick agreed to have TMC buy out Dandy's investment in a company that manufactured environmentally sensitive chips for use in communications equipment. Rick persuaded Carol that this acquisition would make others see her as a "green" visionary. He went so far as to hint that TMC might fund an environmental studies leadership chair in her name at MIT. Assuaging the dents to Carol's ego, Rick also promised to go out of his way to praise her leadership when reporters came calling.

Having been politically weakened by bad press and ongoing issues, and therefore eager to dodge a proxy fight for her own reasons, Carol complied with the desires of the outgoing chairman, going so far as to suggest that she would like to invest in one of Dandy's nanotechnology funds.

Carol played this hand coolly. All smiles in the boardroom, she marched directly to her office after being handed this comeuppance regarding her leadership.

Dandy Liege! I'll fix that scavenger trying to pick at my corporate bones, she fumed.

She reached out again to the savior of her staffing conundrums. If anyone could make Dandy go away for good, it was Sal.

Sal, however, had ideas of his own. He had firsthand knowledge of just how loyal Carol could be. He introduced himself directly to Dandy as not only a long-standing TMC vendor but also a good and perplexed friend of Stewart. Sal suggested that together they initiate a search to locate their mutual friend. Not that Sal was taking sides; he simply thought it prudent to hedge his bet. Maybe Dandy would not be the true partner his relationship with TMC warranted. But, then again, maybe it would be Carol who would have to go away.

Without a viable alternative, Carol demonstrated her appreciation of Rick's arrangement by placing a large short position on TMC shares through an untraceable account she held in a Swiss financial institution. Then she called Scott Landing to inform him, confidentially, that she was on the job market.

A new director was also elected to the TMC board. Thanks to an early career in human resources, former U.S. Senator Piers Heartles was well qualified to assume responsibility for the board's search committee to recruit a new senior vice president of human capital management. Filling Stewart's position became critical when the HR team was not able to track him down to sign off on the quarterly management-by-objective awards.

There had been no phone call between Stewart and Rick, no interview with reporters commending his role in Mercedes's development or Suzy's successful onboarding, not even a text message inquiring about his applications for various HR awards. A hastily prepared trip east suggested that something might have gone awry, though Carol attributed the unusual circumstances of Stewart's departure to the stress of not scaling with his job.

Rumors circulated that Stewart had taken an equity stake in Iago Thomason's string of escort services in southern Europe. Dandy had been disturbed by the desertion of his good friend, particularly when he learned how much a new leader of human resources was likely to cost the company. Piers offered as consolation the credentials of several progressive HR executives, any one of whom, if selected, would insist on incorporating on-site daycare into the menu of TMC employee benefits.

"Think of the positive impact to productivity," Suzy told Dandy. "Also, by leveraging resources, childcare expenses for the workforce could be alleviated considerably." Suzy pointed out what was sure to be attractive to the fierce proponent of continuous improvement and the parent of infant twins. Dandy was duly motivated to find merit in the theory that Stewart's real estate speculation had taken on a Mediterranean hue.

To welcome Piers to the board, Carol prepared a care package, including trinkets Stewart had commissioned in recognition of TMC's success: a monogrammed pen, cuff links, and a money clip. With regard to this last item, the CEO explained that, although Stewart had had some trouble with the original design, she'd had his clasp adjusted to ensure that nothing slipped out again.

Vera read about the intrigue and leadership changes at TMC from a distance, and safety, of her new office on the other side of town. Having slept with the lights on ever since her unsuccessful meeting with Carol, she had her suspicions about Stewart's disappearance. Although she had awaited his instructions about the Suzy Ng offer, Stewart never called her after speaking with the board. In fact, the last time anyone had seen Stewart was the day before Suzy was announced as the new Solutions worldwide president.

What if Carol had found out that Stewart went to the board? Vera worried.

Vera's current boss was so impressed with the media coverage highlighting TMC leadership achievements (with headlines such as "Carol Himmler Gets It!") that he asked Vera if she might persuade Carol to speak at one of their management conferences. Vera suggested that approaching Carol later in the year, when TMC's challenges might have fully dissipated, would make it more likely they could get her attention. She then quickly redirected the conversation to an initiative she advocated. Giddy with the prospect of a senior leader such as Carol participating in one of their symposiums, her boss readily agreed to launch Vera's series: "Do the Right Thing: Positive Compensation and Advancement Practices in the Workplace."

After setting her new seminar in motion, Vera opened the day's newspaper to the want ads. Like the indelible mark left by a laundry pen even after innumerable washings, Vera's scars from mixing it up with the narcissists at TMC were deep and permanent. She began looking for a job that would not require interaction with other people.

Other than that vow-of-silence thing, the monastic life sounds pretty appealing, she thought.

EPILOGUE

Later that spring, Sal hired a local company to ready his pool for a Memorial Day opening. He sat in the kitchen fielding calls from executives interested in meeting this "fresh face in executive recruiting" (a quote from Clare Woodard's newly released book, *Deadly Decisions, Disasters, and Discoveries: The Executive Front in the War for Talent*). He also read the latest issue of *Economic Week* magazine, which contained an article on Dandy's triumphant return to TMC.

How friggin' ironic. The new gay chairman of the board is generating great press for the company. TMC's integrity was rescued by a competent female CFO who was rewarded with a bigger job in a larger organization. And, of course, Carol is still the only executive with stugots in the entire operation. If I didn't know better, I'd expect Mr. Equal Opportunity himself to turn up, bragging about some new award he received for creating the most diverse leadership team.

Three guys from Brazil scrubbed Sal's deck, backwashed the pool water, and wiped stains from the previous summer off the cushions of the chaise lounge. Suddenly, one of the workers ran frantically around the backyard, waving something small and red in the air while shouting in Portuguese. To calm him down, his manager threw the worker into the pool, which caused him to loosen his grip on the item. The worker settled down and identified a human ear, now floating in the pool. The manager scooped up the organ with a net, examined it carefully, and confirmed that it certainly did look like an ear. Noting an earring affixed to the displaced body part, he announced that the ear must have belonged to a woman. Suddenly feeling ill, he dropped the ear and ran behind a shed to vomit.

The frightened manager waved to Sal, who had been standing in the doorway of his kitchen watching the antics.

"My guy ... he told me he found an ear. A person's ear. I thought it must be mistake," the manager explained in broken English.

"Let me see it," Sal responded coolly.

The manager pointed to the grassy area outside the pool shed. Sal walked toward the shed and spotted something small on the ground. He picked it up and immediately noticed the TMC logo on the earring. He put it in his pocket.

"Big problem with bears in this neighborhood," Sal said. "My neighbor got mauled. Haven't you been watching the news?"

Trying to be helpful, the manager suggested that the letters on the earring might point to its rightful owner.

Sal held the ear up but out of view of the others.

"These aren't normal letters," he said. "You were holding it wrong. This is what they call hieroglyphics. It's an ancient language. Yes, some poor Asian woman is missing an ear. Come to think of it, there was a Japanese tour bus in this area last week. Some ambitious, clueless visitor must have had an up close and personal face-off with an American black bear. Friggin' tourists. That poor bear probably felt cornered."

The pool boy ranted in a mix of Portuguese and a local Brazilian dialect that he did not want to finish this job if there were bears around. Sal was anxious to have the work finished quickly and, as if it were possible, normally. He tucked the ear back into his pocket.

"Fuggedaboudit. Bears are what you call nocturnal. That means they only come out at night. Besides, nothing for you to be concerned with. Not enough meat on you to feed a raccoon. That shed is a mess. Clean it up good, would ya?"

THE END

ABOUT THE AUTHOR

BORN AND RAISED in Brooklyn, New York, Catherine McGuinness graduated with a BA in English Literature from Fordham College. Building a career in executive recruiting from London to New York City to Austin, Texas, she has worked for global executive search firm Heidrick & Struggles and Fortune 50 company Dell Inc. Catherine's New York City roots coupled with her corporate human resources background offer a unique perspective through which to view the decisions that drive executive hires and fires, captured in this satirical novel where *The Office* meets *The Sopranos*. Catherine currently resides in Austin with her husband, daughter, and two dogs. She remains active in recruiting through her partnership with Preod Corporation, a boutique executive search firm.

catherine@catherinemcguinness.com

www.CatherineMcGuinness.com